Their passionate hunger was equaled only by their fiery hatred!

In the eerie candlelight of the underground tunnel, Katerina was suddenly imprisoned by hard, muscular arms. The relentless arms of the Mongol prince she hated—and couldn't resist! Everything was forgotten as his demanding lips closed on hers and sent her senses reeling. Nothing mattered now, as the white fires of passion consumed her.

"Later," he whispered, "later I'll come to your room. Later we'll be as one," he said, tearing his mouth from hers. Shaking, she straightened herself and drew the ermine cape around her slim, luscious body. She wanted him, needed him, desired him. But she knew when he came to her room, she wouldn't open the door. Not to this Mongol! Never this Mongol!

THEIR LOVE WAS CONCEIVED IN BARBARIC VIOLENCE AND CONSUMMATED IN THE FLAMES OF UNDYING PASSION!

WHITEFIRE

❋ ❋ ❋

IRIS SUMMERS

BALLANTINE BOOKS • NEW YORK

Library of Congress Catalog Card Number: 78-61545

ISBN 0-345-27712-0

Manufactured in the United States of America

First Edition: December 1978

Chapter One

✿ ✿ ✿

KATERINA VASCHENKO led the last of the horses from the underground paddock and secured them for the night in their roomy stalls. She walked among the animals, counting silently as she patted and stroked the horses' flanks. "Mikhailo!" she shouted. "Where is Wildflower?"

Mikhailo Kornilo lumbered into the stable and eyed the young Cossack girl with fear in his eyes. "I thought she was with the other mares."

"Wildflower has been skittish these past days, so I allowed Stepan to work with her alone. He wouldn't be foolish enough to take her outside for air, would he?" she asked the wizened old man anxiously.

Mikhailo ran gnarled old hands through his sparse white hair and made his own quick count of the noble animals. "Stepan may be foolish, but not that foolish. He knows the mares are not to be taken outdoors until the last of the snows are gone and the temperature rises. No doubt he's walking her around the arena for exercise. The Kat will be happy with the price this particular foal will bring," he said confidently.

"Mikhailo, I checked the arena on my way here and it was empty. Fetch my father and have the others make a search. The mare has to be found."

Her face a mask of concern, Katerina drew the sable cape closer about her slim shoulders and fastened the hood over her coppery hair. Stroking the muzzle of the closest mare, she crooned soft words to the quiet animal.

The sweet, pungent smell of the horses stayed with

1

her as she made her way down the damp corridor to the stone stairway.

Quickly, before she could change her mind, she thrust open the heavy pine doors and ran outside. Biting snow lashed against her as she fought her way to the outdoor stables, instinctively skirting a deformed clump of brush.

The wind drove the breath from her body as Katerina flung herself against the stable doors. "Stepan, are you in there?" she shouted breathlessly. "Is Wildflower with you? Stepan, answer me!" she screamed as she shut the weighty panels behind her. Her only reply was a skittering noise to the left of her foot. One of the cats. In her heart she had known Wildflower and Stepan were not there even before she had come inside. God, what had the boy done with the horse?

Shivering, not with cold, but with a fear so deep her blood seemed to freeze in her veins, Katerina whimpered silently as she pushed open the door and trudged back to the House of the Kat. Of all the horses to be gone, why did it have to be Wildflower?

The moment she entered the house, harsh curses from the men met her ears. She had been right—her father was livid.

"I don't know how it happened, Father. Stepan was exercising the mare because she was skittish," she said to the man advancing on her, his dark eyes spewing fire. "I just came from the outdoor stable and the boy's not there."

"We have searched every inch of this house and Stepan and the mare are gone. If the mare managed to find her way outdoors, it will be the end of her and the foal she carries. How could you have been so lax, Katerina, you know the mares are your responsibility."

"Father," she said, laying her hand gently on his shoulder, "don't be angry with me. I'll search them out and bring both of them home. As you said, the mares are my responsibility."

"The boy is not capable of making a decision concerning Wildflower, he has the mind of a ten-year-old child!" her father shouted furiously, his black eyes snapping.

"I only have one set of eyes, and there has never been cause to worry over Stepan's care of the mares before. There must be an explanation."

"I only agreed to allow the boy to help you because you said he could be trusted. I see now that I was wrong."

Katerina listened to her father's harsh tones and felt bewildered. He had never spoken to her in such a manner. Eyes downcast, she knew she had failed him. Her large amber eyes widened in shock and her body felt numb with the realization. "I'll bring them back."

"There's nothing you can do now. Don't act as foolish as the boy. Where will you go? Where will you look for them? You just returned from the outdoor stables, didn't you feel the wind and snow? Women!" He spat venomously.

Katerina stared into her father's eyes, her back stiffening at what she read. "And while you're blaming me, ask yourself where Mikhailo was," she defended herself. "Women are only as foolish as men allow them to be." The large eyes were pinpoints of flame, threatening to burst into a raging bonfire. Her cheeks were flushed with anger as she retied the hood of her cape securely. "Since the mares are my responsibility," she said coldly, "I'll find the boy and the horse and bring them both back."

"Fool! How long do you think you can survive in that blizzard? I tell you, it's too late!" he shouted, his broad chest constricting in fury.

"It's only too late when I see their dead bodies or . . . when you see mine. And I have no intention of allowing that to happen."

"I forbid you to go out in the storm, Katerina. What horse did you plan on riding? Ah, I see by your expression that Bluefire is your choice. Another foolish mistake. You would endanger still another horse, is that it? Women!" He spat again.

"So I'm a foolish woman. At least I'll try, which is more than I can say for you and the other men. How do you know it's too late? How can you say the boy isn't secluded in some cave, safe, along with the mare?"

Katlof Vaschenko looked at the amber eyes and at the grim, angry set of her narrow jaw. He knew he couldn't stop his daughter, and he had no wish to see her lash out at him for trying. An unfamiliar feeling settled between his shoulders as he watched Katerina pull on heavy woolen gloves. His shoulders slumping, he made his way to the warm kitchen, where his ailing father waited. "I'll pray for your safety, little one," he whispered silently.

Katerina placed a heavy blanket over the gelding, Bluefire, and she was ready to go. Was the snow falling faster or was she so petrified she couldn't see straight? All that brave talk in front of her father was just that —brave talk. How could she live with the others and have them think she was unfit for her duties? She was her father's daughter, and so she had to prove herself time and time again. No Cossack was shown favoritism. Each stood on his merits. Each was proud of his heritage and would die to protect it. She was no different. She would find the mare or die trying.

Within moments Katerina was smothered by the stinging, rice-sized pellets and could not see the reins she held.

She worked the sable hood down over her forehead till it resembled a shroud. The grisly thought made her clench her teeth in frustration at her position.

I'll freeze, she thought as her hands sought for and found the horse's thick mane. Already the reins were crusted with ice and slipping out of her grasp. If only she weren't riding into the storm with the full force of the wind in her face, she might have a chance.

Hunching her shoulders, she rode with her face pressed into the horse's warm neck. From time to time, Katerina feebly called out for Stepan.

The slim figure astride the white gelding battled the elements for over an hour. She raised her head when she felt the snow and the wind slacken off. "Good boy," she said, thumping Bluefire on his side. "I knew you would get me into the forest. Easy, boy, slow and easy," Katerina said softly as she rubbed her snow-crusted hands over the horse's neck. "Just get us down the mountain and out to the steppe. That's where we'll find Stepan and Wildflower. You can do it," she continued to croon to the magnificent animal. Stepan just wanted to take the mare back to Volin to be with his family. He meant no harm, she reasoned.

Bluefire trod lightly, aware of the girl on his back, sensing her fear and agitation as he picked his way through the quickly building drifts.

It was so cold, so very cold. If she could just sleep. The thick, sooty lashes lowered, and she dozed, unaware of the huge overhanging fir branches that seemed to move with a will of their own as the horse made his way carefully down the mountain.

An inner voice needled Katerina's subconscious: you can't sleep, you have to stay awake. Suddenly, she was jolted in her saddle. She forced her eyes open and looked around. The snow was too deep for the horse to carry her. She would have to walk.

She slid from Bluefire's back, grasped the reins in her hands, and trudged alongside the gelding. She lurched to the right and then to the left. Forcing her mind to concentrate on walking, she counted—one, two, three, four. Over and over Katerina repeated the words till her throat was dry and harsh. Her legs were getting heavier and harder to move. Bluefire was having as much difficulty as she was; she could tell from the tightening of the reins that the gelding was tired. She had to stop or they would both die. No, they had to keep moving. If she stopped, she would sleep and never wake up.

Think about the men back at the House of the Kat, sitting in the warm kitchen, drinking vodka. Think about that, she told herself. Through clenched teeth, she muttered, "Do they care if I freeze to death? Do they care if Bluefire freezes too? All any of them cares about is Wildflower and the foal she carries. Horses! That is all they care about. Men are bastards, all men are bastards!" she seethed.

The anger that raced through her like raging fire was all the impetus Katerina needed to make her pick up her feet and plod through the deep snow. Her mind and body gained a new will, a searing urgency to win, to prove she could do what the men did. She would find Stepan and Wildflower and bring them, safe and sound, to the House of the Kat. Just pray, she told herself, that Stepan left before the snow began and is safe in Volin. He is safe! She could feel it in her bones.

The gelding reared back on his hind legs, whinnying softly. Katerina raised her head and looked about, the low-limbed fir trees with their coverlets of sparkling crystals blinding her momentarily.

The steppe.

Bluefire waited placidly while Katerina made up her mind. The snow wasn't as heavy here as at home, and the falling flakes seemed to be abating. Sighing deeply, she rubbed her eyes, forcing them to stay open. She had to go on. The gelding would find his way across the steppe without any help from her.

One more day and she would be at the Cossack camp. It was twilight now, her favorite time of day. She would be in Volin tomorrow, and then she would see for herself that Stepan and Wildflower were safe.

Her spirits lifted at the thought, and Bluefire sensed her mood. His legs lifted a little higher and he snorted, mist billowing out of his mouth in the cold, bracing air.

"Good boy," Katerina purred into the horse's ear. "I knew you could do it," she said, remounting her horse.

She rode steadily, the blinding whiteness all around her. So vast, so endless—like time. No sound permeated the air save the horse's breaths as he carried the beautiful young woman forward.

Katerina shook her head to free it of the warm sable hood and reined in. "Stepan is right, this is where we belong. This great, endless plain is ours, our heritage.

Not that godforsaken stone fortress in the Carpathians. This is home. This is where we belong. It belongs to every Cossack who lives and breathes. Stepan knew this, and that's why he brought Wildflower here."

The gelding whinnied softly and pawed the snow, a sign that he was anxious to be traveling again. Intent on her thoughts, Katerina failed to see a small spiral of bluish smoke to her left.

Katerina dug her heels into Bluefire's flanks, and the horse reared again and danced his way through the great whiteness toward Volin.

The small campfire blazed brightly as one of the men threw on some extra brush. Another added some grease from his saddlebag, and the fire hissed and spurted. The men laughed uproariously as still another of the men raised a jug of vodka to his lips and passed it around to the others. One man, however, stood aloof, observing the merrymaking men that rode with him. They were good soldiers, dedicated to their cause and what they believed in. They served him well, and he had no complaints. Someday soon, with the proper training, they would all take their place in the Khan's army and do whatever was expected of them. For days they had ridden into the vicious storm with no respite from the elements, their only food dry bread and moldy cheese. They deserved their carousing and the three freshly killed rabbits that turned on the spit.

Banyen Amur stared into the openness around him, his indigo eyes narrowed to ward off the harsh glare. He hated this plain, and he hated the Cossacks that could and did live on it.

He was cold and hungry, and he needed a woman. If he had his choice, he would take the woman first, for she would warm his blood and be food for his soul. His belly could wait for another time and another place.

He was tall and muscular, with a broad chest and a loose-limbed stride. His hair was the color of a raven's wing in bright sunlight, and while his forehead was broad, his nose was chiseled and sharp, adding character to his strong, square chin.

His men called him an arrogant son of a bitch, but admitted he was a fair and just man to serve under. Women jostled each other and swooned when he favored them with one of his rare smiles. One look out of the agate eyes and a woman turned to what he called mush, and brought a smile to his sensual mouth. He chose his women with cool, calculating deliberation, the dark eyes measuring the curve of their breasts and the length of their thighs. If the return look was coy or vapid, he would go to the next woman, until he found a match for his own measured look. He liked fire in his bed, not warmed-over mush. One day he would find a woman that suited him, and he would give her the supreme pleasure of bearing him a son. He would rebuild his estates and get married and keep his wife pregnant nine months out of every year. He would have a mistress in his house, and one in town for the awkward months. Women belonged in bedrooms and kitchens. What else could they do . . . He smiled to himself. Thoughts of love never entered his mind. Love was for fools and old men who didn't know what to do with their loins in their advancing years. He would never be caught in that trap. Women had their place so far as he was concerned, and he planned to keep it that way.

Men made fools of themselves over women. Men fought and died for women. Men lost empires because of women. The only thing he would give a woman was the honor of bearing his child and his name.

Banyen patted the black Arabian stallion fondly and slouched nonchalantly against the animal's hard belly. He straightened his shoulders and shrugged the sable burnoose he wore to a more comfortable position. The soft leather boots that caressed his sinewy legs were due to be changed to fur and warm socks for his feet. He might as well do it now so he could eat his portion of rabbit in comfort.

A small sound suddenly caught his ear, and immediately his hand went to his saber. A horse out here in this godforsaken emptiness! Who? What?

He looked at his men and motioned for silence. Weapons were drawn and the roasting rabbits forgotten as tired eyes became keen and alert. Banyen raised one finger to show that it was a lone rider who approached. "Where there is one, there could be more," he said softly to his men.

Katerina stared intently in the last rays of the evening light. A camp with a fire. Food! Which Cossack tribe was it camped in the middle of the plain, and why? An uneasy feeling settled over her as the horse trotted closer and closer. Her eyes widened at the garb on the tall figure standing near a horse and the campfire, surrounded by men. Mongols! What would they do? Would they let her pass? Would they believe her when she told them she had Mongol blood in her veins? Not likely. She looked like a Cossack. Her shoulders straightened imperceptibly as she advanced to the camp. Deftly she reined in Bluefire and watched the man who appeared to be the group's leader admiring her gelding.

Neither spoke. Katerina waited. Banyen waited. The men waited. A worm of fear found its way into Katerina's stomach and worked its way up to her chest. She swallowed and looked at the tall man, who was staring at her with bold, arrogant, lustful eyes.

White teeth glistened in the dimness of twilight as Banyen smiled. "Prince Banyen at your service," he said, bowing low with a flourish. His tone was cool, mocking, as he walked over to her placid horse. Katerina dug her heels into Bluefire's flanks, and the gelding slowly backed away from the advancing Mongol.

Katerina nodded. "What are you doing here? This is Don Cossack land."

At the sound of the soft, melodious voice Banyen's face registered shock. A woman! "This is Cossack land?" Banyen mocked her words, straining to get a glimpse of her face. "As long as I'm standing on this land, it belongs to me—unless, of course, you would like to fight me for it. I see no Cossacks protecting it. You're a Cossack, aren't you? No one save a Cossack rides pure whites, especially a horse such as yours. Well," he said harshly, "will you challenge me for this ground I stand on?"

"You can stand here till you take root for all I care," Katerina snapped. "And, no, I have no wish to challenge you or your men. Others like the vicious Tereks will challenge you."

Banyen laughed, his head thrown back in merriment. "What others? There is no one on this godforsaken steppe except you, me, and my men," he said, bowing again. "Come here, let me see what you look like," he said, advancing. Nimbly, Bluefire again backed off a pace and then two more. "Please," Banyen said, holding up his hand, "allow me to extend an invitation to dinner—roast rabbit, newly caught. I insist," he said, lunging toward her. "Don't make the mistake of refusing my generous offer."

"I'm not hungry. Thank you for the invitation, but I must ride on."

"Perhaps the cold has affected your hearing. I said don't refuse my offer!"

The clear amber eyes narrowed. "And I told you I'm not hungry!" Katerina's foot came up and knocked his hand from her arm. Filled with panic, she lowered her head and grasped the gelding's mane as her heels dug into the horse, spurring it on.

A roar of outrage reached her ears as Bluefire raced through the snow. She knew in her heart she would be caught. The gelding was as tired as she was, but the Mongol prince and his stallion looked rested. Oh, God, what was she going to do? You were right, Father, you may yet find my frozen body, but it won't be because of Stepan and Wildflower. Damn him to hell! Who did he think he was, ordering her to share his dinner? Cossack rabbits that were needed for her own people. As she urged the horse to do his best, she turned her head, and momentarily the noble animal was thrown off stride. The stallion was gaining on her. "O God, I don't want to die!" she cried quietly to the shimmering stars.

As she dug her heels into Bluefire's flanks, she apologized to the galloping horse for the pain she was inflicting on him, then begged, "Please, please!"

Out of the corner of her eye she watched the stallion advance, the man's arm outflung to pull her from her seat. Katerina leaned precariously to the right and all but slipped from the animal beneath her. When she righted herself, she was pulled from Bluefire's back and literally flung through the air. She came to rest against the side of the skittery horse, as it was trying to stop.

"Let me go! Take your hands off me!" Katerina screeched.

"And if I do that, what will you do?" Banyen laughed, delighted with this unexpected challenge.

"Kill you, that's what I'll do! I'll scratch your face till it's nothing but a bloody pulp!"

The stallion stood quietly as master and girl spat epithets at each other. "And what do you think I'll be doing while you're scratching my face to a bloody pulp?" Banyen laughed.

"Bleeding!" Katerina snarled.

"A she cat."

Katerina tried to free herself from her awkward position, one arm pinned against the horse and the other flailing in the air. Each time the man jerked her closer to the horse, her feet left the ground and her arm twisted painfully in his viselike grip. She bit into her full bottom lip and felt the salty taste of her own blood. Her mind raced as she tried to figure how she could get away from him. Suddenly she relaxed, her muscles loose and flexible. Banyen leaned over to grasp her other arm and draw her atop his horse. Her small fist shot out and made direct contact with his eye. Stunned, he relaxed his hold. Seizing her opportunity to escape, Katerina was off and running instantly, the snow spurting up from her heels. On and on she ran, with no sense of direction. Her breathing

was harsh and ragged as the cold, bracing air was
forced into her lungs. With her long legs, Katerina
could usually outrun most of the youths in the village,
but the heavy accumulation of snow was hampering
her now and she wondered how much longer she could
last. She was so tired. A razor-sharp pain ripped across
her chest and Katerina doubled over, falling to her
knees. Before she could get to her feet, she found herself pinned to the ground, a lean hard body above her.

Banyen fought to control his own labored breathing
as he felt the hot softness of the girl beneath him. The
anger he had felt moments before left him and was replaced with a ripe, full-blown passion. Straddling her,
Banyen pinned Katerina's arms above her head, then
leaned over and brought his mouth down on hers. His
head jerked upright as if a snake had bitten him. He
felt blood trickle down his chin as he brought his hand
up to his mouth. "Bitch!"

"Bastard!"

Banyen reached out a long arm and grasped her ankle as she tried to get away. He flung her back so hard
that she felt her head snap. "Stupid Cossack woman,
with your thick stockings and a man's boots," he said
harshly as he again forced her to the ground.

"Smelly Mongol pig!" Katerina hissed.

"You belong with a farmer at the plow," Banyen
said raggedly. "What kind of clothes are these?" he demanded, releasing one of her arms so he could finger
the thick material of her dress. "Even peasants wear
better than this."

Katerina brought up her knee, and Banyen was
thrust backward by the force of her blow. Madly, she
scrambled out of his way as he bent over, his muscular
hands clutching his groin.

"I hope I kill you!" Katerina screamed as she got
to her feet. "When they bury you, I'll sing a dirge
about the way you died."

"Bitch!" Banyen said through the mist that threatened to choke off his vision.

"Bastard! Dirty, sneaky Mongol pig!" Katerina

screamed as she plunged recklessly forward. Rough hands seized her and dragged her backward. The men from the campfire!

"Here she is, Banyen! Do you still want her after what she did to you," one of the leering men asked, "or will you be generous and allow the rest of us to have some sport with her?"

"Bring her here!"

The icy words sent a wave of fear down Katerina's spine. She was flung to the ground and pulled by her long cascading hair to his side.

"One more move out of you and you'll be the first bald-headed Cossack woman on these plains." He nodded curtly to his men, and they withdrew to the campfire.

"I should kill you for what you just did to me," Banyen said harshly.

"I won't make it easy for you, so be prepared. How many times can you survive what I just did to you? I'll do it again and again, every chance I get. Let me go, you foul Mongol! I've been in stables that smelled better than you do!"

"And I've smelled and seen better whores than you!" Banyen retaliated.

"Then go find one and leave me alone! I'm warning you, I'll do what I said. Let me go!"

"Not till I see what you look like underneath all those blankets you wear. I'll say one thing for you, you wear enough clothes to cover an army. I'm going to have you one way or another, so why don't you save yourself all this anguish."

"Men are all alike," Katerina said hoarsely as she felt his strong hands tear at her clothing. "Why do you have to take a woman physically and degrade her? I'll kill you for this, my word as a Cossack!"

Mist escaped both their mouths as they struggled on his lush sable cape, which lay like a blanket on the hard-packed snow. The silvery moon, hidden behind dark clouds, made it impossible for Banyen to see the face of the young woman beneath him.

"I'm not a cruel man—hard and demanding, perhaps, but women need to know they lie with a man. I'm not one to inflict pain," he grunted as he tore apart the top of her coarse woolen shirt.

His searching hands on her exposed flesh drove Katerina to near frenzy. By all rights, she should have been freezing to death from the biting pellets of snow that covered her tender skin, but his frantic movements atop her made her oblivious of them. When his scorching lips touched hers, Katerina relaxed every muscle in her body and allowed her lips to respond against his. She moved slightly and opened her mouth invitingly, her tongue seeking his. The moment he tilted his dark head and moved his arm slightly, to position himself better, she sank her teeth into his cheek, and felt the flesh tear when he tried to pull away from her. With one mighty shove, she sent him sprawling backward and was quickly on her hands and knees, crawling away, her clothing hanging in tatters. However, she couldn't resist a parting comment as she scrambled to her feet. "You can mark that down to hearty peasant stock. I told you I wouldn't make it easy for you, and I hope your blood floods this plain!"

A bellow of anger ripped through the night. In two long-legged strides, Banyen had her imprisoned in his arms. Once again she felt her feet leave the ground as she was thrown onto the sable blanket. She resisted the raging Mongol with all the strength left in her, knowing all the while she was no match for him. She felt a reeling blow to the side of her head, and then Katerina knew no more.

Banyen took her brutally, savagely, again and again.

Spent, he staggered to his feet and stood looking down at the naked body of the young girl. A pity he couldn't see what she really looked like in the ebony night. His own words rang in his ears: "I'm not a cruel man . . . I'm not one to inflict pain." He shrugged. Every man was forced at one time or another to tell a lie. Why should he be any different?

He leaned over the unconscious form and drew his burnoose over his head. Carelessly he tossed it over her bare flesh and walked away, his hand to his cheek, the cut stinging sharply against the palm of his hand. He stopped, the temptation to pick up the burnoose which covered the nude girl was so strong that he had to clench his hands and force himself to walk back to the campsite without it. She needed it more than he did.

Katerina woke as Bluefire nuzzled her cheek. Her vision was blurred. Moaning softly, she rose to her feet uncertainly and looked around, the inky night cloaking her bruised and battered body as a mother shields her child from harm. There was no sound in the velvety darkness except Bluefire's soft whickers.

Her hands found the burnoose. Shock coursing through her, she dropped it to the snow the moment she realized what it was. Then, painfully, she bent to pick up the rich fur cape and wrapped it around her cold, numb flesh. Bile rose in her throat, and she gagged. She leaned weakly against the horse's side and let the tears flow. To be taken like an animal was more than she could bear.

Who would want her now? She had disgraced her father and her grandfather. She was no longer a virgin.

The amber eyes lightened till they were the color of a ripe apricot. She was alive and that was all that mattered. It would be her secret, hers and the Mongol's. Somewhere, somehow, she would meet him again and she would have the advantage. He would pay dearly. At least she knew what he looked like. He couldn't say the same. At the campfire, she had been far enough away from the flames, and the hood had cast her face into shadow. No one would know. It would be her secret, and she would die by her own hand before she let another Cossack know she had ever come out second best.

A violent fit of retching overtook her. When Katerina was finished, she grasped Bluefire's mane and climbed onto his back. Trembling, she urged the horse forward, her neck buried in his soft hair. Bluefire picked his way gently over the snow as the girl sobbed heartbrokenly. Then she slept.

It was the mute boy, Stepan, who first saw her and hurried to the road to lead the gelding to the summer stables. Shyly, his eyes full of love and trust, he helped Katerina dismount and led her shaking body to a stall at the end of the stable. He pointed to the alabaster mare, who was contentedly nibbling at some hay. His round head bobbed up and down happily as he kept pointing and grinning at the horse.

"She's safe, is that what you're trying to tell me?"

Stepan nodded, a smile on his face. The boy opened the stall and pointed to the horse's broad belly and then to her hooves. He rubbed the horse's snout fondly, and the mare rewarded him with a soft whinny of delight.

Katerina would chastise him later, for all the good it would do. For now, all she wanted was a hot bath and some clean clothing. God, would she ever feel warm again? Would she ever be the same again?

"Stepan, would you please build a fire in my father's house and boil some water for me?" The youth grinned and waved his hands in the air. "You already did that when you saw me riding across the steppe. Thank you. Stepan," she said wearily.

Tenderly, she patted the boy on his arm, her eyes full of tears. "Stay with Wildflower and give her some hay and a few oats and then bed her down for the night. Do the same for Bluefire." The boy smiled and entered the stall, careful to latch it behind him.

Other women had been raped and had survived, and so would she. She would find her own way to live with it, and she would manage as the others had. She was alive, and that was all that mattered. Someday she would find a man who would love her despite her secret. She would watch his eyes when she told him. Eyes could tell a person more than words. She would not explain, and she would not apologize. Somewhere there was a lover who would understand. Until the time when they met, no one would know of the hateful truth.

Katerina would have a week of living by herself, until the others came down from the Carpathians. In seven days one could school oneself to many things. Aside from the one change, she was well, and Wildflower was safe. That was all that mattered.

Chapter Two

THE FIRST SCENT of spring wafted in the air as the tenacious grip of winter held fast the last remnants of snow to the onion-domed towers of the Kremlin. As the snow began to ebb, the glory and magnificence of St. Basil's Cathedral, just outside the Kremlin, slowly emerged to the wonderment of all. The nine soaring, bulbous domes, each different in color and design, struck a note of exquisite beauty for all of Russia to behold. Czar Ivan Vasilovich was justly proud of his creation.

The Terem Palace, official residence of Czar Ivan IV, which stood within the walls of the Kremlin, stood with equal majesty. The Czar, like others before him, surrounded himself with the indigenous art of the Russian people. Everywhere the eye could see, the ornate frescoes, paintings, and motifs were embellished with gold overlay or blazoned with precious stones.

Princess Halya Zhuk's bearing was regal as she crossed the main floors of the palace, confident that her flaxen hair was arranged with care and precision to show off her delicate features to every advantage. As she began her ascent up the stone stairway to the

Czar's living quarters, she smoothed the sea-green gown, which reflected the emerald depths of her eyes. In these quiet moments when she was alone, she never ceased drinking in the splendor of the decorative walls and ceilings. A sensitivity that lay deep within her, a sensitivity that she kept completely hidden, stirred in her breast as she weakened and completely enjoyed her surroundings.

Steps that once were filled with joy now became steps of anguish. Each encounter with Ivan was totally unpredictable. One minute he would be loving and forgiving, and a moment later, as though possessed, he would perform cruel and sadistic acts, terrorizing everyone in sight. She wondered fearfully what he would have in store for her today.

Halya stood a moment before the carved door to Ivan's receiving chamber, forcing herself to reach for the golden knob. She withdrew her hand and paused a second longer, finally deciding to knock.

A voice boomed imperiously, "Whoever it is may enter my chambers."

Composing herself, Halya answered, "It is Halya, Ivan. I came as quickly as I could when I received your summons."

"I need the gentleness of your touch and the softness of your lips to quell my surging blood. As usual, my day has been nothing but problems, problems, and more problems. If I don't do everything myself, nothing gets done," he said petulantly. "I summoned you for another reason, Halya, not to listen to me complain. Come into my chamber, where we can speak privately."

Halya's mind reeled with thoughts of what was to come. Months before, it had been a pleasure to be bedded by Ivan, for his body was hard and muscular, and his lovemaking was the same way, hard and demanding. In recent months, however, Ivan had neglected himself, so thoroughly he was now flabby. When he stood before her unclothed, the bulged and flabbiness were offensively apparent. She felt repulsed when her eyes noted the limp flesh that extended to his manhood. Her heart pounded with fright as she wondered what obscene acts he would ask her to perform to arouse him sexually.

"Halya, many times you have expressed the desire to become my fifth wife, or is it my sixth? If that is still your wish, then you must continue to please me. As you know, my true and first love is being Czar of Russia; second is my devotion to the church. Third is deciding how I shall put to death a traitor. My last love, Halya, is a wild, uninhibited woman in my bed. That is the reason I have decided that one day soon you will be my wife. You are an excellent whore, and the thought of marrying you delights me. I'll notify you when I decide to make it official," he said, leering at her, his eyes glazed with lust.

Anger rose in Halya at his words, but she said nothing. In her heart she knew her true test was about to begin. Could she play at passion and desire and arouse his sagging member? Her mind raced: she would pretend, she would entice, she would seduce a young soldier; and then, as suddenly as she had thought it, she negated the idea. No, her imaginary lover must be a king, an emperor, or someone else of great stature. She would perform for a Khan and be a captured woman who was brought before him to delight and heighten his desire. Failing, she would die. Ivan's voice broke through her thoughts, making her aware of what she had to do.

"It's time to begin, Halya. I'll set the stage for you, and you will do exactly as I say. When you are performing well, and my blood begins to pound, you will not hear my voice. When that happens you will know I am pleased and your lustful acts are engulfing me. I am now ready," he said, lying back against a mound of pillows.

Halya fought a welling retch as she watched him lick at the saliva that drooled from the corners of his mouth.

"You will of course undress; however, as you dance

around the room I want you to drop your clothing, piece by piece, on top of me, as I lie here in bed. For every garment you drop you will remove an article of clothing from me. Before you start to perform I think we should have an audience. I will summon two passionate men from my private guard and watch them squirm in ecstasy as they watch you. A magnificent idea, why didn't I think of it sooner?" Ivan cried happily as he rang for his boyar.

"Fetch me two virile men from the Oprichnina. Bring me the two who boast and fornicate the most. You will have no trouble finding them, word travels fast among men of their conquests," he ordered the boyar, who stood at attention, a stunned look on his face.

The boyar scurried from the room to do Ivan's bidding. He could barely contain himself at the thought that soon he would have another lunatic escapade of the Czar's to recount to the other boyars.

"Halya, my love, have you given any thought to your dance of seduction?" Not waiting for a reply, he continued, "My blood boils at the thought of how the young bucks will react to my mistress swaying naked before them. You *will* be naked, won't you, Halya?" he asked hesitantly.

Halya nodded. Oh God, oh God, Ivan was insane and she was crazy to do as he asked. Everything would have been different with Kostya.

"Your men, as you requested," the boyar said quietly as he thrust open the door, admitting two handsome soldiers from the Oprichnina.

The Czar lolled on the bed, spittle dribbling from his mouth as he addressed the two men. "Princess Halya is going to dance, and I wished a small audience to join me so her talents can be fully appreciated. You are to stand near the door in a stance so: your feet slightly apart, body erect, and hands clasped behind your backs. You are not to utter a sound."

The soldiers nodded, puzzled looks on their faces.

"Begin, Halya," Ivan said, reclining again against the overstuffed cushions.

Her body trembling, Halya moved to the center of the floor, trying to sort out her thoughts. She felt humiliated and embarrassed at the way the men stared at her. Still, she supposed it was better than being put to death by Ivan for refusing to do his bidding. She risked a second glance in their direction and found herself wondering how they would look without their handsome uniforms. Their imagined nudity made her remember Ivan as he was when she first saw him. Now, beside the flabbiness, his aquiline nose seemed more obnoxious. His black hair, which had once blended into a comely mustache and beard, had turned into wisps of straggly, unkempt hair. The clear bright eyes were glazed, and his sensual mouth was slack and unappealing. But she was also reminded of another person, whom she had loved with all her heart and soul . . . Quickly she forced the memory from her mind to concentrate on her job—surely he was dead.

Halya turned to Ivan and pouted coyly. "My Czar, would it be possible to summon a balalaika player to sit outside the door and play for me?"

"Very well, but no more delays, Halya," he grumbled, the spittle from his mouth dribbling down his chin and onto his neck.

With the first sounds of the melodious notes Halya began to dance, her movements slow and sensual as she responded to the music. Her slim body lent itself to wantonness as she brought into play the proud high-tipped breasts and rounded haunches. As she swirled and swayed to the rhythm, her tiny feet barely touching the floor, her hands caressed her body, lingering in a display of blatant sexuality.

Perspiration beaded the faces of the soldiers as their eyes filled with unabashed desire. Sensing their craving, Halya threw herself into a frenzy of immoral gestures and moves that she knew would delight Ivan.

Her fingers tore at the buttons of her gown as abandon rose like a tidal wave throughout her body.

Dropping her dress at her feet, she cupped her breasts, still hidden beneath her camisole. Slowly, inch by inch, she removed Ivan's gold caftan, delighting in his moans of mounting passion as her hands touched his naked flesh. His eyes were wild; his tongue dangled from his gaping mouth.

She whirled away from the Czar, working with slow deliberation at the ribbons of her camisole. She knew both Ivan and the soldiers were waiting for her to divest herself of the garment, waiting in pain for the first glimpse of her bare skin. She glided out of reach, her tight haunches moving to the rhythm of the balalaika as her body began to undulate provocatively. Sensuously she moved her fingers to the tiny ribbons, undoing each one with a wicked smile on her face.

The Czar rolled over on the bed, his eyes glazed as he stared first at Halya and then at the two soldiers. He cackled gleefully at the sight of the well-fitted black trousers bulging with the swollen manhood trapped within. As he watched, the swelling pushed forward, fighting to escape to freedom. He jumped up and down on the bed, pointing a sticklike finger at the two men, his laughter insane and shrill.

Halya continued dancing, her fingers untying the last bow. As she leaned toward Ivan, her breasts spilled from the dainty embroidered camisole. A knowing smile played about her mouth as she heard low groans coming from the direction of the doorway. She, too, now noticed the growing, aroused manhood bursting at the confines of their trousers.

She ripped away the undergarment with a flourish, freeing her taut, full breasts for all to see. Cupping them, their rosy crests pointed and erect, she swayed ever closer until she was directly in front of the soldiers. Her movements taunting, she flaunted her body without restraint. Moan after moan followed her as she danced back to Ivan. Slowly she extended a long, shapely leg from between the open front of her lace petticoat. Languidly she thrust it out and withdrew the stocking from thigh to toe. Twirling it in the air, Halya swept past the soldiers, her naked breasts heaving as she allowed the stocking to brush across their agonized faces. At Ivan's bedside, she dropped the silk and reached down to remove his slippers.

The soldiers continued to watch, their faces full of incredulous shock. Before them lay the Czar, completely stripped of clothes. The princess was still dressed in her petticoat and one sheer stocking. How much more were they to endure?

Moving over to a chair closer to where the soldiers stood, Halya lifted her leg, reached to the top of the limb, and, again slowly, removed the remaining stocking. She caressed her body, her fingers sliding over her breasts and arms, down to her flat stomach, and finally once again cupping her breasts.

Her eyes were fixed on the soldiers as she worked at her petticoat, dropping it from her satiny waist. Halya turned at the sound of a deep groan, knowing she had driven the men beyond human control.

Ivan, in a state of tightly checked arousal and anticipation of what was to come, made no comment when the soldiers ran from the room, their trousers wet and stained.

Halya danced as if passion had become the driver and ruler of her undulating body. Gliding gracefully to the bedside once more, her pear-shaped orbs hard and firm, she motioned for Ivan to touch her. Salivating, he clutched at her breasts, her thighs and legs, as low animal-like noises escaped his mouth.

Perspiration dripping from his face, Ivan felt blood soar through his veins as the pain in his loins became unbearable. He reached for Halya, clutching at her golden hair, moaning wildly as he brought his mouth crashing down upon hers.

"Ivan, take me! Please! Take me!"

Ivan mounted her, hoping against hope that all his soaring blood would erect his manhood. When it failed to do so, he rolled from her body, tears streaming down his sunken cheeks.

Exhausted, Halya lay next to Ivan, who, unfulfilled,

nibbled at her still-erect nipples. Halya lay quietly, indifferent to his touch, wishing she were with the one man who could have fulfilled her.

Determined to overcome his impotence, Ivan continued to nibble at Halya's swollen breasts. His hands traveled down her body, searching out the coveted moist, warm place between her slim thighs.

Halya's body became alive, responding once again to his tender caresses.

"Try, Ivan," Halya pleaded as she parted her legs, welcoming him to her. Silently she reprimanded herself for the charade she was acting. Halya tried desperately to convince herself she might one day love Ivan and forget Kostya.

In desperation, Ivan strained every part of his being to produce the taut muscles necessary to satisfy her. At Halya's scream of despair, Ivan fell back in resignation, ignoring the princess, totally absorbed in his own despair.

Halya lay back on the bed, her eyes closed to prevent the threatened tears from spilling down her cheeks. Was this going to be her life from now on? God, help me, she prayed silently.

Though it was early when Halya woke, her eyes searched every corner of the room for Ivan. When she was satisfied that he was not there, she slid from the bed and quickly dressed to return to her own quarters. She needed a warm bath to help her forget the previous hours.

Halya placed her hand on the doorknob, but was unexpectedly thrown off balance with the Czar's entrance into the room.

"I want to commend you on your . . . your performance last evening. You were exquisite! I do try to please you, Halya, I think you know that," he said, his voice a soothing melody.

"Yes, Ivan, I know you try, and I understand you have many tragedies in your life," she said quietly. As soon as the words left her mouth, she realized her mistake. "Ivan, I . . . I'm sorry—"

Obscene expletives flew from the Czar's mouth. His aging, aristocratic face turned purple with rage. "You were told never to refer to my past!" he screamed at the top of his lungs. "You are here for one purpose and one purpose only—to brighten my life and make me happy. Get down on your knees and beg me to forgive you!"

Halya did as ordered, tears streaming down her cheeks. "Please, I beg of you, forgive me," she pleaded.

"Very well, I forgive you, this time," he said, his rage forgotten. "Come near me, let me hold you for a moment." Halya nestled nervously in his arms. "Let me kiss the lips that drove me to the heights of desire last evening."

Suddenly he thrust her from his arms and looked directly into her green eyes. "I have something to tell you, something that will make you happy."

Moving to the edge of the bed, Ivan motioned Halya to sit beside him. The stale scent of the past hours lingered in the air as he clasped her soft hands in his tight grip. "I am so pleased with you that I have decided to make you my next wife. You soothe me and at the same time you excite me." Gently he cupped her chin in his hand and stared deeply into her eyes. "Does my offer make you happy, Halya?"

Her stomach lurched at his words. Forcing a smile, the princess spoke enthusiastically for his benefit. "Yes, Ivan, it makes me most happy." Halya knew she would do anything that would enable her to sit beside him on the throne of Russia, even if it meant acting out the sexual fantasies he demanded. Her eyes closed momentarily when she realized that, as Ivan's Czarina, her name would become as famous as his, and perhaps her one true love from childhood would seek her out when her whereabouts became known—unless he was dead, as she feared.

"Now I must tell you of my other plans," he said

coolly, his mood changing once again. "I have a mission to be filled and I need a man with knowledge of horses, an equerry. Soon the Don Cossacks will be bringing their herds to the steppe and readying them for sale. Each year in the spring I send an emissary to pick the best of the Cosars for my Oprichniks. This year I have decided my equerry will be your brother, Yuri. Even now he is beginning his preparations for the journey, and tomorrow he will leave for Volin."

"Volin! My brother! What are you telling me?" Halya asked fearfully. "Ivan, my brother is too young to be sent on a mission. He just passed his eighteenth birthday and only trained in the Kadets for a year. Just this past month, he entered the Zemsky Sobor, and you know he has another year to complete his apprenticeship for the assembly," she said tearfully, her eyes wide and full of apprehension.

"I am aware of his apprenticeship, and I considered it carefully before I reached my final decision."

"But, Ivan, he's just a boy," Halya continued to plead.

"Enough! I will say the following to you and then the discussion is closed. When I was three, I was crowned Czar; when I was sixteen, I was married; and at twenty I led my armies in two battles. Don't speak to me of an eighteen-year-old being a boy. He's a man, and if he isn't one now he will be when he returns. I chose him because of his knowledge of horses, the same knowledge you yourself possess. You were the one who informed me of your family's equestrian background. You told me once that you and your brother could ride a horse before you could walk a straight line. So you see, Halya, he is the man for my mission. The matter is ended."

Her anger in check, Halya rose from the bed and quickly strode toward the door. As she walked on lagging feet back to her bedchamber, her mind raced. Why was the Czar sending Yuri to Volin? Certainly not for the reason he stated.

Once inside her room with her bath prepared, Halya

slid into the warm wetness and allowed the water to calm her shattered nerves. How unfair it is, she thought sadly. Yuri is still a boy, and when he's gone I'll have no one except Ivan. Her full lower lip trembled and tears gathered in her moss-green eyes at what she considered her unjust life. Was it only three years ago that she had been brought to the palace to become Ivan's fourth wife? It seemed like an eternity ago that the missive reached her parents in Moldavia informing them that Czar Ivan wished the Princess Halya to be presented to him with the intention of making her his wife. "God help me," she moaned softly as her mind reeled back in time.

Within days after the message was received, her trunks and Yuri's were packed and they were sent by coach to Moscow, she to become Ivan's wife and Yuri to become a Kadet.

The driver of the three-horse sleigh had carefully reined in the animals as he maneuvered the sleigh through the maze of streets lined with log houses that encompassed the Wooden City, so named because of its principal building material.

"Has anyone told you of Kitai Gorod?" the driver asked, amused at the pair as they stared in awe at their surroundings.

"We're new to Moscow," Halya had said hesitantly. "What is Kitai Gorod?"

"It is the third city within Moscow and so called because the people who live here fill their kitas with earth, piling the one on top of the other against the walls to stave off attacks from invaders."

"I want to see the palaces where the nobles and the Czar live!" Yuri had cried out in boyish excitement.

"First we have to travel through Red Square. Once we travel through Spassky Gate we will be in the Kremlin. To your left is Czar Ivan's home, the Terem Palace. To your right are the chasovnyas, the private chapels of the influential citizens of Moscow. The structure you see being worked on is St. Basil's, the Czar ordered it built to commemorate his victory over the Tatars. Your tour is over. Wait on the stairwell and servants will take you to the Czar."

Was it only three years ago when she and Yuri stood on the stairwell waiting for Ivan's servants?

Yuri had succeeded in becoming a soldier. But instead of becoming the Czar's wife, she had become his mistress.

Aware once more of her surroundings, Halya stepped from her bath into the robe her maid held out for her.

"Fetch my clothes and dress my hair, quickly now, for I have little patience this day. I want to spend as much time with my brother as possible," she explained to the fearful servant.

The girl, near tears, worked in quiet desperation, knowing the princess would show no mercy when it came to anyone save the Czar and her brother.

The maid stood back respectfully, hoping for a quiet word of approval.

"It took you long enough," Halya said furiously. "If you're finished, why do you stand there? Leave me!"

When the door had closed behind the trembling girl, Halya examined herself in the mirror, pleased with her appearance except for the hateful expression on her face. Studying herself, she realized her callous behavior toward the maid was meant for Ivan. God, how she detested him for what he was doing to her brother. Forcing a smile to her lips, however, she flounced from the room to console Yuri and wish him a safe and speedy return.

Halya walked through the halls and archways and down the stairways that led from the Terem Palace to the building where men of the Zemsky Sobor were quartered.

Thrusting open the door of Yuri's room, she threw herself into his arms. "Yuri, tell me it isn't true, tell me you aren't going to Volin. Did you do something? Is the Czar banishing you? If you did something wrong, perhaps I can help you," she pleaded desperately.

"Halya, calm yourself. It is not a punishment. The

trip to Volin could well be the greatest opportunity of my career. Don't you understand, Halya, the Czar chose me to represent him, his own emissary, to the Cossacks. I'm to have the privilege of handpicking the horses from the Cosars! It's an honor, Halya, and one I am proud of," he said excitedly, his handsome face beaming. "Be proud of me. Of all the men he could have chosen, he selected me." Enthusiasm burst from his whole being, culminating in his handsome face, his grin emphasizing the deep cleft in his chin.

Halya was shocked at his words. Indebted to the Czar for sending him on a mission that could be extremely dangerous! She must get through to him and make him understand how dangerous and unpredictable the Cossacks were.

"If I do all that is asked, this could be the beginning of a great career for me. Both of us should be pleased that the Czar chose me. Halya, do you see . . . ?"

"Yuri, stop it. He's using you. Ivan never does anything without some insane reason behind it. Why can't I make you see? There are older, more responsible men than you, and far more capable of handling this mission, and that is what concerns me. Why is he sending a boy to do a man's mission?"

"Are you saying you have no faith in me?" Yuri asked angrily.

"It's Ivan I have no faith in. I know you will do well and I wish you well. It's just that I feel so protective toward you and I want nothing to go wrong. You're all I have and I don't want to lose you," she cried tearfully.

"You won't lose me, Halya. When my mission is completed I think we should ask permission to travel to Moldavia to see our parents. Would you like that?" he asked, hoping to divert her from her unhappy thoughts.

"Of course I would, and I'll look forward to it. Godspeed, Yuri."

"I leave at dawn, Halya, so let this be our temporary farewell. I want you to spend your time thinking about how happy our parents will be to see us. Promise me, Halya, that you will not worry about me, for if you do, then I will not be able to function with a clear head."

"You have my promise," his sister said, throwing her arms around Yuri and smothering him with wet kisses.

As she ran to her room she cried over and over, "If it's the last thing I do, if it takes my last breath, you'll pay dearly, Ivan, for what you're doing to my brother. Yuri is all I have and you're taking him away from me, just as I was taken from my one true love to be brought here to be your mistress."

Inside her room, with the door bolted, she threw herself on the bed and cried brokenheartedly. Later, when she dried her tears, her face was cool and composed. Looking in the mirror, Halya spoke slowly and distinctly. "If anything happens to Yuri, I will kill you without a second thought!"

Chapter Three

❧ ❧ ❧

KATERINA LAY in the middle of the fluffy pedina and delighted in the warmth the goose-down quilt exuded. Warmth, precious warmth. "God, I thought I would never be warm again," she sighed. For now, she had the comfort of the soft quilt, her home, and the fire burning in the oven. She felt safe and protected with the devoted Prokopoviches, Stepan's parents. This was what she wanted, and what she needed, this secure feeling. Here in her own bed, the Mongol couldn't reach her. All he could do was invade her mind. In her bed, in her house, he couldn't reach out his long arms and touch her, nor ravage her as he had on the steppe.

Here, in her room, she was Katerina Vaschenko; on the steppe, she had been an animal taken by another animal, a wild, ferocious animal. "It's over, I'm alive and it's over," she whimpered as she buried her head in the pedina. "On the outside I'm no different than I was when I rode from the mountains. No one will ever know what happened to me unless I tell them. I'm still the same. Then why do I have trouble looking in the mirror? Why can't I look at myself? Why do I feel that somewhere, somehow, the Mongol will find me again? Will he be the hunter and I the hunted? Will he be the fox and I his prey? If he catches me, will he devour me as he did on the steppe? God, help me," she sobbed again. "Make me forget, make me the same as I was before. Help me!"

She was fully awake, but she stayed beneath the pedina, unable to leave its warmth, as she remembered the last two days and that cold, vicious night. Katerina let her arms creep above the cover, and at the first touch of the chill air against her bare flesh, she quickly snuggled down into the depths of the soft comforter.

Her hazel eyes focused on a closed shutter where light was seeping through a crack. Her thoughts began to drift, and the Mongol again began to take them over. Katerina fought him, pushed him away as she had in the snow. "I won't allow you to . . . I won't let this happen. I'll think of other things, things that please me and make me happy. I'll think of the steppe when I was a little girl, and my father. My father and me . . ." It was working. For now, she was a five-year-old running through the high grass of the plain. She saw herself playing in the fields of flowers that grew there: pale blue, indigo, and lilac cornflowers, the yellow broom and the white meadowsweet. Millions of blossoms that turned the vast expanse into a shimmering, waving ocean of breathtaking color. In her mind, she became a bird taking wing, soaring to the heavens and looking down from the sky, reveling in what God had created.

Not until she was full grown and seated upon her

horse was she able to see the great distances the grasslands covered. Every Cossack on the steppe knew the
flower stalks grew taller than any child and the high
grasses could swallow up a man on his horse so he became invisible to the naked eye.

As a child, Katerina loved playing in the fields.
Vague images of her mother looking for her as she hid
came floating back. Hard as she tried, she could not
see her mother's face. If only she were alive. But she
had been killed by invading Poles soon after Katerina's
fifth birthday. They had cut down her mother and
older brother as if they were sheaves of wheat. If they
were alive, they would be with her in the mountains
and she would be . . . safe. Just the thought of that
word, and the Mongol wove his way vividly into her
mind. Katerina shook her head fitfully to clear his
hateful face from her tortured mind. Her eyes drifted
to the wooden icon hanging on the rough plank wall.
She prayed silently, the familiar words giving her some
small measure of comfort.

You must get up, an inner voice whispered. You've
got to keep busy. You must work so there is no time
to think. And when your body cries out for rest, then
you will sleep. In sleep, you'll be able to forget.

Quickly, before she could change her mind, Katerina
slipped from the cozy bed and dressed hurriedly. She
splashed water on her face from the wooden bowl that
Stepan had placed near the hearth and felt ready to
confront whatever the day would bring. Woolen underclothing, a wide-sleeved Cossack blouse, snug-fitting
trousers, and fleece-lined boots would keep her warm,
yet would not hamper her while she worked. Satisfied
with her appearance, Katerina left the crackling fire
and started the short walk to the Prokopoviches' house.

Stepan waited impatiently, his round blue eyes full
of concern. Katerina was late. Breakfast, always served
at the first sign of dawn, had been over two hours ago.
His round, childish face puckered up in thought.
Should he go after her and make sure she was all right?

He turned to his mother, who was standing near the oven, and waved his arms in agitation.

Olga Prokopovich placed the ladle she held in a heavy wooden bowl and looked fondly at her son. She shook her head, jostling a strand of dark hair loose from under her kokoshnik. "She's tired, Stepan. She's probably still sleeping." Olga laid her head in the crook of her arm and closed her eyes, demonstrating, so the boy would understand. She laid a plump hand on his muscular arm and looked up at Stepan with twinkling blue eyes. "Put the bowl and the cup on the table for Katerina," she said, hoping to take his mind off the time. Stepan nodded happily. Olga's glance met her husband's, and they smiled. How they loved this man-child. In their opinion he was as strong as any Cossack fighter. He was their son and they loved him unashamedly.

A cold draft of air swirled and eddied about as Katerina entered the room, stamping the snow from her boots. "I know I'm late, but Stepan's fire was so warm I couldn't bear to leave my bed," she said as she tousled the boy's fair hair. She turned to Olga. "Today was my one day of luxury. From now on I'll be here on time for breakfast."

The older woman nodded and smiled as she looked into the girl's amber eyes. Where was the sparkle, where was the merriment that was always there? Out of the corner of her eye, she looked at Ostap to see if he, too, noticed. Her husband was lighting his short Cossack pipe, the fragrant cloud of blue-gray smoke swirling around him. Only to Olga was his sharp gaze apparent.

His pipe going to his satisfaction, Ostap pulled on his sheepskin coat and buttoned it to the neck. "I'll leave you women to your talk"—he grinned—"and see to my other women. The ones that don't answer back and complain when there's no fresh-cut firewood."

Olga clasped his round, ruddy face in her plump hands and kissed him resoundingly. "Go then to your horses and see if they can keep you warm, and before dinnertime you'll be back and in our bed, looking for me to cuddle you." She laughed, her body shaking in delight.

Ostap grinned and winked at Katerina. His expression clearly stated, Women!

Olga ran her hands over her slate-gray kirtle and offered Katerina a cup of tea. Stepan set a bowl of steaming porridge in front of her and made a motion for his friend to eat.

She laughed. "After two days of nothing but black bread, this is going to taste like caviar."

"Each morning until your father and the others return you will breakfast with us," the old woman said matter-of-factly.

Katerina smiled. "I was hoping you would ask me."

When the simple meal was over, Katerina motioned for Stepan to sit next to her. "There is much that has to be done, and we're going to work long and hard to prepare for my father's return. We will both be so tired at the end of the day your mother will have to feed us with a spoon."

Stepan uttered a gurgling sound of approval as he held up Katerina's spoon for his mother to see. She nodded at Stepan, a wide smile on her pleasant face.

Katerina clasped the rosy-cheeked woman to her, to Stepan's delight. "Your cooking is delicious, and thoughts of your wonderful dinner will keep both of us hurrying throughout the day."

"Hot beet soup, roast lamb with dumplings, and a spiced honey cake baked especially for you."

Both women laughed as Stepan rolled his eyes and rubbed his stomach.

Without waiting any longer, the two young people headed for the barn, Stepan running slightly ahead. He turned once, motioning for Katerina to hurry, anxious for her to see the care and attention he had given Wildflower.

Inside the moist, sweet-smelling stable, Stepan placed Katerina's hand on the mare's belly and grinned.

Katerina laughed. "What do you think, Ostap, is the mare well?"

Ostap shrugged. "There are no signs of complications, and the mare is hale and hearty, thanks to my son's care."

Katerina nodded as she pulled a woolen cap over her hair. "We are going to walk around the village and see what has to be done in preparation for Father's return."

Ostap puffed on his pipe and motioned to them to hurry and close the door before the mare felt a draft.

Katerina spied her father's summer home, the largest in the village, as was proper for the hetman, and felt fear settle over her. Her large eyes raked the quietness around her. The village was no different from any other Cossack settlement, the huts, constructed of logs were insulated with moss to conserve heat in the cold months, each boasting an oven made of baked clay, laid out in a circle surrounding the camp to prevent attack from wild marauders. Wearily she rubbed at her temples.

Inside one of the huts, Katerina forced her mind to the task at hand. She had to pay attention to Stepan and the work she had to do.

On the rough plank wall hung the only adornment, the treasured icon that held a place of honor on a wall in every home. The Blessed Mother with Christ Child, painted on a smooth wooden plaque and trimmed in gilt, pleased Katerina as she gazed at it. She, like all the people of the Ukraine, had been taught at a very early age two values: love and protection of the steppe and reverence and preservation of their Eastern Orthodox religion. These were dearer than life itself.

Together, Katerina and Stepan cleaned the hut, sweeping and dusting with zeal. The spring move down from the mountains was almost at hand, and she wanted the home to be neat and refreshed for the Kat's arrival.

Their task finished, Katerina spoke. "I know your father has kept the fences in good order, but let's check

them to be sure none of the posts have worked loose."
They walked in companionable silence to the southeast
corner of the village, where the animal compound
stood empty, waiting to open its gates to the horses.
Katerina's eyes darted about, looking for a fallen post
or split rails. All appeared to be in good order, with the
exception of a protruding nail here and there inviting
the blows of a hammer.

They continued their inspection until reaching the
massive barn. "In the next few weeks this area will be
filled with wonderment. Mares will birth their foals,
the foals will test their new legs, and, once tried, their
wobbly legs will carry them eagerly to their mother's
milk. There they will suckle until their bellies are full.
All will be quiet again, until the mares and the foals,
nestled in an atmosphere of love, talk to each other.
The sound will be heard throughout the village. Then,
in three years, the fillies and colts will be ready for
market. In seven years those blotchy gray-white foals
will be pure white Cosars," she whispered to Stepan,
who nodded his head in agreement.

Katerina sought the compartments containing mountains of hay, wheat, and oats. The storage bins were
filled to capacity. "We'll begin by laying straw on the
floors of the stalls and fill all the feed and water
troughs. When we finish here, we'll check the storehouse to see if we have enough smoked meats, and the
root cellar to see how well the vegetables fared through
the winter. The men will bring back the sheep and
goats, and fresh meat will be in abundance, except for
game and rabbit. If we complete our chores ahead of
time, we'll go hunting. Would you like that, Stepan?"

The boy waved his arms wildly, a grin splitting his
face.

"Roast goose for the first night back." Katerina
laughed. "I have an idea, Stepan. With your mother
and father's help we can carry all the tables and
benches from the huts to the barn and prepare a feast
for the men's return. A feast for all to enjoy before the

hard work of spring begins. Start with the straw, Stepan, and I'll get the water."

The sun was high in the west and the shadows grew longer as they entered the storehouse. "We'll have to do this fast, Stepan, the light is fading." Quickly they checked the shelves and hooks in the storehouse. Seeing that the smoked meat was plentiful, they turned to the fragrant root cellar, which they found to be pregnant with foodstuffs. "No problem, Stepan, there's plenty of food until the next harvest. If you aren't too tired, we can check the toolshed now and get an early start in the morning."

Stepan nodded and pulled on her arm to show that he was willing to go with her.

Inside the shed the lantern cast eerie spectral shadows upon the rough walls as Katerina inspected the tools. "Your father has a system all his own," she said, laughing. "You see how all the tools on these three walls have been finished, sharpened to perfection. These," she said, pointing to the fourth wall, "are still to be done."

Katerina leaned against the wall as Stepan removed one tool and then another to test its sharpness. Wearily she let her thick lashes drop; she was tired, but not exhausted enough to sleep. She opened her eyes again as Stepan bent down to pick up a tool near her. Katerina's breath caught in her throat for a second. If only she had had a weapon with . . . would she have used it? Could she stick a knife in a man's ribs or heart? Could she bludgeon to save herself? The Mongol's face with his midnight-dark eyes swam before her. Could she have killed him? A shudder ripped through her slender body as Stepan reached up to take the lantern from where it hung above her, a puzzled look on his face. "It's all right. I'm just tired," she said, trying to reassure him. "I'll race you back to the house. The first one there gets all of the spiced honey cake." Stepan's eyes lit up as Katerina tore ahead of him. He loped along behind, the lantern bobbing freely in the air, the yellow light twinkling and winking in the darkness.

The following days were grueling. Katerina worked with Stepan at her side from dawn till dusk. She ate her dinner quickly, took a hot bath, and fell into bed. When she slept, her dreams were invaded by a dark-eyed man with hair the color of night. He stalked her slowly, insidiously, through the thick trees. She always woke just as she was about to be captured, a hammer raised in her hand, her coppery hair wet and matted, and a sheen of perspiration on her face. Could she slay him when the time came? Finding no answer, she would crawl from her bed and work non-stop throughout the day, only to fall into bed and dream of the same terror.

"Volin," she said to Stepan one morning, "will shine like a kopeck when we are finished. My father will be proud of me." She still hadn't forgiven him for berating her the way he had, but she knew she would the moment she saw him. At that moment she would forgive him anything, because beneath their arguments they deeply loved each other. Their quarrels were usually caused by their similar temperament.

By the end of the week Katerina noticed the dried, yellow grass poking through the snow and pointed it out to Stepan with the toe of her boot. He waved his arms and uttered a sound much like that of a new baby. It was the first sign that winter was slipping away and spring would soon cause the earth to give birth to its greenery. Once again the steppe would be covered with a rainbow of color, as animals and birds returned to sing the sounds of life.

"We have a few good hours of daylight left, Stepan. Come, we're going hunting." An hour after sunset, they returned with nine geese and seven rabbits. "Hardly a feast, but each will get a portion."

Stepan waved his arms and hands to show he agreed as they thrust out their bounty for Olga and Ostap to see.

That night as Katerina soaked in her bath, the

steamy wetness relaxing her, she thought of the coming weeks. Soon the farming would begin and the fields would be seeded. Once the sowing was done, the buyers would begin to arrive and the bartering for the Cosars would start. It was exciting to watch the outsiders and her father trying to outsmart each other. She slid farther down into the tub and tried to remember what it was she had to do the following day. She wanted everything in order for her father's arrival. How could she have forgotten? She had to stack the wood, light the ovens, and lay the oblong lace cloth on each bread table, in a north-to-south direction, and place an unlit candle, a loaf of black bread, and a tiny dish of salt upon it. This was the Cossack custom for good health and good luck in the new year. When she finished she would walk to the end of the road and watch for her father. She missed him, Mikhailo, the horses, and the old man who sat by the fire waiting to die.

The bath water was cooling; it was time to get out and snuggle into the warm bed. Lord, she was tired to the very bone. If only she could have one good night's sleep, one without the Mongol invading her dreams.

It was not to be. As soon as the dark lashes were stilled and her breathing was regular, a dark-eyed man on horseback raced after her as she spurred Bluefire onward. She thrashed about in the big bed, the quilt sliding onto the floor from her frantic movements. He was gaining; closer and closer he came, until he was abreast of her. His dark eyes were laughing and his white teeth gleamed in the early night. He wore a brown sable cape, which he threw to the ground as he reached out a long arm and dragged her from Bluefire's broad back. She fell to the ground, and from somewhere she felt her fingers touch a heavy wooden mallet. He stood over her, laughing, his stance arrogant, his face amused and mocking. She struggled to her knees, the mallet raised, ready to strike. A blood-curdling scream ripped from her mouth as she tumbled from the high bed onto the softness of the quilt.

She rubbed the back of her hand across her forehead, and was not surprised to see it come away wet.

Her heart beating madly, she gathered the covering around her and walked to the huge oven. Katerina secured the quilt around her and lay down on the felt-covered floor, her eyes wide and staring.

The following morning Katerina and Stepan worked diligently to finish their tasks, scurrying from hut to hut performing their specific duties.

Laughing and teasing each other, they walked to the end of the road. Suddenly Katerina commanded, "Sh-h-h, listen. Do you hear them?"

The boy tilted his head toward the open steppe. He motioned that he heard nothing.

"Listen again," she urged, "the hoofbeats are louder now, you should hear them." Again he turned his head, intent on listening, his face brightening and a broad grin emerging, acknowledging that he, too, heard.

As the horses thundered closer, Katerina stood directly in the middle of the road, her hands on her hips, her legs astride, waiting for her father. Moments later, Katlof came thundering down the road, majestic atop Snowfire, almost running her down. She didn't move a muscle. Her father brought the horse to an abrupt stop.

"So, you're alive after all!" he shouted, looking down at her fiercely.

"Yes, I'm alive, and so are Wildflower and Bluefire!"

Katlof dismounted and stood at the side of his horse, a stern look on his face. "Then come here, baryshna, and give your father a proper welcome home."

As Katerina ran toward him, the stern look dissolved, a broad smile crossing his face. As they embraced each other, her father said, "In my heart I knew you were alive. Why didn't you send word? Why didn't you return?"

"Because, Father, I haven't forgotten your scolding, and I hadn't forgiven you until this moment. I was angry with you so I thought I would let you spend a week agonizing and praying for me," she said coolly. "I thought it would do you good."

"Ha!" roared Katlof. "Spoken like a true Cossack," he said as he gave her a hearty slap on her back. "A true Cossack, that's my Katerina!" he chuckled.

A Cossack rode up and led Snowfire away as Katlof and Katerina walked toward their summer dwelling together. "So, daughter, tell your father what you have been doing this past week."

"You'll see." She laughed as she led him through the town toward their hut.

Before they entered, Katerina looked out across the endless plain and thought, The steppe and I have something in common—it goes on endlessly, as does my nightmare. She knew then she would never be free of the Mongol. A feeling of panic began to engulf her. She silently pleaded, God, dear God, help me! "Please!" she whispered as she closed the door behind her.

Again they embraced fondly. Katlof stepped back, staring down into her eyes. "I'm sorry for my tirade back in the fortress," he said gruffly. "How like your mother you are. You have the same fiery Mongol temper and the same gentle persuasiveness."

"Was she beautiful, Father?"

"You have only to look in the mirror to see the beauty of your mother. Because of you, your mother is always with me," he said tenderly.

Katerina threw herself into his arms, burrowing her head into his broad chest.

His words, softly spoken, were barely audible. "How I love you, child, you're my life, my reason for being. Without you I would have nothing."

Tears welled in the amber eyes. "I'll never fail you again, Father."

Spring was everywhere. Most evident was the farmland, where the ground, now softened by the thaw, left the earth ready for the plow. Cossacks could be seen with plow straps draped around their shoulders as the Cosars that were fit only for farming pulled the primitive plows forward.

The village bustled with activity as each Cossack performed his tasks. There were farmers, hunters of game, lumberjacks, and the women who worked in the homes and helped in the field. The remaining Cossacks tended the famed Cosars.

Katerina and Katlof spent their days in the barn with the mares, watching the miracle of birth. The birthing made her feel clean and near to God as she watched the foals leave the shelter of their mothers' wombs, bringing a closeness between her and her father that was renewed every year at this time. As they watched, the attachment expressed between mother and foal engulfed them also. Katrina looked at her father with love-filled amber eyes as he enfolded her in the crook of his arm. She felt safe and secure, out of harm's way. Safe from the Mongol for the moment.

As the weeks passed, the steppe was again a playground for wild game and birds. The young fillies and colts frolicked and ran along with the wild inhabitants through the short grass and budding flowers. Katerina adored watching the horses when they were on the plain, running like the wind, testing their spindly legs, and at the same time strengthening them. When she could stand it no longer, she would leap on Bluefire's back and race along with the colts and fillies.

Each day as new foals were born, Katerina and Katlof were in attendance. "It looks like an especially good year for selling stock. Except for one or two sickly colts, we haven't lost one horse, and with the proper attention, the two sick fillies will be up and around again," Katlof said quietly.

"Father, let me nurse the two sick colts. You know how they respond to me; let me take care of them!" she begged.

"If you want to spend that much time with the animals, of course you may tend them. But as you know, it's a full-time task which must be done with much love and patience," he stressed.

"Just trust me," she said confidently.

"Very well, Katerina."

Every day and every night for weeks, Katerina hand-fed the colts and tended to their every need, sleeping in the barn at night to make sure nothing went awry. Almost a month to the day, they were up on their legs, kicking up their heels with the urge to run. Katerina led them from the barn to the open steppe, where they disappeared like the wind. She had done well; her father would be proud. She had the Kat's touch. As she gazed after them, she noticed a streak of white flash by. It was Whitefire, prancing and running with his offspring. Busy with the ill horses, she had forgotten it was time for Whitefire to perform stud service. The stallion would stay in Volin for two months, and then Stepan would take him back to the Carpathians.

Leaving the barn, Katerina looked toward the compound and saw it filled to capacity with the mares selected for next year's supply of foals. As was Katlof's system, so long as his herd was plentiful and healthy, he divided the mares into thirds, each group going to stud once every three years.

As she watched the men release a mare to run with Whitefire, feelings of desire began to stir in her. It was spring, and the animals, birds, and horses were busy reproducing. She smiled as Whitefire chased a mare behind a small clump of trees. Soon thereafter, the stallion reappeared, reared up on his hind legs, and whinnied triumphantly. It was done: another mare carried the seed of the prized horse.

Strange feelings and emotions began to course through her as she watched the mares, her mind remembering the animal that had raped her. But deep within her she felt a need for tenderness, for love. She wondered if she could love. Was love the same as lust? What the Mongol did to her, was that the way love happened? Underneath it all, was it just a matter of copulation? She couldn't and wouldn't believe that was all there was to it.

That night two lovers stole into the barn under cover of darkness, unaware of her gaze. How sweetly they embraced each other and how passionately they vowed their endearments in husky murmurings. As quickly as they had appeared, they were gone, leaving a wide-eyed Katerina staring after them.

Her heart fluttered in her chest at the thought of the young couple. She wanted desperately to be held, to be kissed tenderly and gently. No man will want me now, not after the Mongol ravaged me, she cried silently. She felt confused and afraid. If only it hadn't happened that way, if only . . .

Forcing her mind to think of other things, she walked back to the hut to tell her father the colts were well and running in the fields, healthy young Cosars.

Excitement began to build in the village as each passing day brought the buyers one day closer. This year the thought of the buyers coming for the Cosars held no appeal for Katerina. Something was missing in her life, and she couldn't come to terms with the alien feeling. Throwing herself into her work, she toiled during the day and then rode Bluefire across the plains for hours to clear her head, and still the aching feeling stayed with her.

Someday, somewhere, she would find what she was looking for, and when she did, she would know it, she was sure of it. As always when the thought entered her mind, the Mongol was right behind, mocking her with his dark eyes. Then she would wonder . . . would she know, would she really know?

Chapter Four

WORD SPREAD QUICKLY through the village—Czar Ivan's emissary would be arriving any day now. To Katlof, he was just another buyer, but his people were always impressed when the Czar's man came to Volin. They knew if it was not for the Cosars, a nobleman would never set foot in this part of the steppe.

Katerina was glad that she had managed to keep outward appearances normal during the past weeks, but inside she was depressed, lonely, and hurt. She hoped her father wasn't aware of her inner turmoil, and since he hadn't asked if anything was wrong, she knew she was playing her part well.

Maybe the arrival of the Czar's emissary would distract her from her thoughts for a few days. She wondered what the man would look like. Would he be any different from the grouchy, businesslike nobles that came before him, who selected the horses, settled on a price, and were gone?

When breakfast was over and the hut was in order, she dressed and headed for the barn. Tending the brood mares, Katerina heard a commotion outside the barn. "Yaschu, what's going on?"

"One of the riders just rode into the village with news of the emissary from Moscow."

"What news?"

"The rider said the Czar's buyer is on his way and should arrive within the hour."

Katerina felt a stir of anticipation, but paid it no mind and went back inside, content to care for the horses.

From outside the barn she heard someone shout, "They're here!" Putting aside her work, she left, looking for her father, and found him standing at the front of the village, waiting for the emissary. Two men approached quickly on horseback. Katerina walked to her home, deciding to wait and watch from there, knowing her father didn't like to be disturbed when he was conducting business.

Katerina's sharp eyes noticed that this buyer was younger than his predecessors. From his horse the emissary looked down at her father and said, "I'm looking for Katlof Vaschenko. Can you tell me where I might find him?"

At the sound of his deep, vibrant voice, Katerina felt her heart pound. She could see him clearly now, in his crimson jacket and black trousers. The shine from his leather boots winked in the bright sunlight as he moved to dismount the graceful brown Arabian. Respectfully, as the Kat identified himself, he removed the pointed black cap resting rakishly on his head. "Yuri Zhuk, emissary to Czar Ivan, and this man is Gregory Bohacky with whom I've been visiting," Yuri said, motioning to his comrade. "Gregory comes from Kiev and is a cousin of the Czar's. He also wishes to purchase pure whites. Gregory will observe the herd now and make his final selection during midsummer," for he must leave immediately.

Katerina drew in her breath as she watched Yuri dismount and walk toward her father. The Russian extended a long, muscular arm and handed Katlof a rolled piece of parchment to read. The Kat raked his eyes over the crackling paper and nodded slightly. He was proud of his rare ability to read, having learned it as a boy from a priest. It had stood him in good stead more than once and he had encouraged most of the Dons to become literate as well.

His voice carried to Katerina. "The Czar shall have one thousand horses by the end of spring, but only if he pays the price I ask. There will be no haggling and no bargaining. Do you have the money with you?"

"Czar Ivan said the money will be paid on delivery of the horses," came the low, husky reply.

"And the Kat says not one horse leaves until the money is paid . . . in advance," came the cold, firm reply.

"The Czar wishes me to remind you that the price is not what was originally agreed on. He wishes to know why the price has doubled."

"The price has doubled because I wish it. If there are more words between us, the price will triple."

Yuri Zhuk, emissary to Czar Ivan, looked at the leader of the Cossack village with smoldering eyes and knew he would pay whatever the amount was for the horses sired by Whitefire. "Agreed," Yuri said curtly. "I'll make my selection tomorrow at dawn, when the horses are at their best."

"The matter is settled then," the Kat said briskly. "The following day you will leave here with a signed contract for one thousand horses. This evening you will have supper in my house." With a curt nod of his head, the Cossack chief walked away, leaving Yuri to stare after him.

Oles, one of the young men from the tribe, told him in cool, jeering tones that he was to remain in the Kat's house until dinner.

Yuri's dark eyes were angry, and his jaw tightened at what he considered the Cossack's crude manners. He straightened his slim shoulders as he followed the Cossack. How sure they were; how confident they appeared. Here he stood, an emissary from Czar Ivan, and he was being treated with thinly disguised insolence and mocking superiority. Tales of Cossack fierceness were widespread, as were the tales of the Kat's horses. The Cossack, in Yuri's view, had no equal. Some people were born to royalty, like himself, while others were born to be a Cossack. Yuri knew instantly he would have given his life's blood to have been born a Cossack.

A wild whoop of laughter split the air. Yuri turned to watch as a group of young Cossacks mounted their horses and rode the length of the dusty road, their weapons thrust in front of them. It must be some sort of drill, he thought to himself. For an hour he watched as horses and riders cavorted on the sleek white horses, animal and rider one, each magnificent beast perfectly attuned to the man on his back.

Weapons drawn, the equestrians charged at each other with split-second timing. A moment before impact, a rider would slide beneath his horse and come up, weapon flicking the air, from the horse's right flank. To Yuri's amazement, no weapon ever touched another, nobody was unseated during the drill. A pity these men did not fight for the Czar. They were a race, a people, an entity unto themselves. No soldier, no warrior, no matter how experienced, would wish to go to battle against a Cossack.

At a sound from behind, Yuri turned to see a girl with hair the color of burnished copper in the doorway of a hut. Her heavily fringed, slanted eyes shone like rich amber. Yuri's eyes widened appreciatively. Cossack women were more beautiful than he had imagined. Her tawny skin intrigued him, as did the doe eyes. Mongol blood must run in her veins, he told himself as he smiled at her and bowed graciously. "Yuri Zhuk, at your service."

Katerina inclined her head slightly, her breath quickening at his show of good manners. Not one of the young Cossacks would bow to her or show her respect in any way. Women were to be used and good for nothing else. It wasn't only the Mongol on the steppe who held that opinion. This man looked at her with approval and liked what he saw.

The thick lashes fell over her high cheekbones as she advanced a step and stood looking up at him. "I am Katerina Vaschenko. The Kat is my father. He asked that I show you around our village before supper, if it is agreeable to you," she said hastily.

"Only if you promise to tell me about the Cossacks." He grinned, showing even white teeth, his voice deep yet melodious.

Familiar with the company of the boisterous, fun-loving Cossack youths, who did nothing but taunt her and tell her wild, gory tales of what they were going to do to her when she came of age, Katerina felt at a disadvantage with this tall, muscular man. Her cheeks flushed a bright crimson as she pictured what he would look like stripped to the waist. Would he be as master-ful and powerful as the Mongol? Would his arms hold her as tightly . . . She shook her head to clear it, and forced herself to look into the Russian's eyes. Her tongue moistened her dry lips as she imagined his nude muscles moving in his powerful back as he hunched his shoulders to make himself more comfortable in her presence. She wanted to feel the wide, sensuous mouth on hers. Swallowing hard, she tried to force herself to ignore such wanton thoughts, but found her-self mesmerized by his dark, smoldering eyes as they stared deeply into hers. What would his lean, hard body feel like next to hers? How would his hands feel on her flesh? Why was he looking at her like that? Surely he couldn't read her mind, or could he? Or was it that he was thinking the same thing? The moment she saw him ride into the village, she knew he was different. She had to do something, say something. How long was she going to stand and stare at him like some ignorant child? "If you'll come with me," she said, her voice soft and thick with emotion.

They walked from one end of the village to the other, each aware of the other, deliberately keeping a space between them. Katerina knew that if her arm so much as touched his, she would crumble and faint. She was petrified at this strange feeling that was taking hold of her.

At last she risked a sideward glance in his direction when he turned to look at a small watering pond for the new colts. A sheaf of dark hair fell low on his wide forehead. His nose was straight and chiseled, his jaw lean and square, with a pronounced cleft in his chin. He didn't have the full cheeks of other Russians, and his skin was weathered but not rough like the Cos-

sack youths'. He sported no beard or mustache, reflecting an individual who dared to defy fashion. Her
heart thundered as she imagined his cheek next to
hers before their lips met in a searing, passionate kiss.

Katerina stumbled and would have fallen if Yuri
hadn't reached out a strong arm to grasp her and bring
her closer till she was steady on her feet. Leaning
against him, her breathing labored, she laid her head
on his broad chest and listened to the furious pounding
of his heart. She raised clear amber eyes and looked
directly into his as the tip of her tongue again moistened her lips, his eyes pulling her into their depths.
Katerina felt him stiffen as she brought her head up
till her face was inches from his. I should do what the
other girls do, flutter my eyelashes, smile, and tease
him with my eyes, she thought. It was impossible, and
Yuri wasn't one of those loutish young boys that . . .

Katerina felt her body forced back slowly till she
was against the wall of the stable. Like a hungry child,
she raised her mouth and waited for the feel of the
Russian's lips. Her body was feverish, and she felt
her breasts grow taut beneath the thin fabric of her
sarafan. She strained toward him and felt a hard yet
gentle hand slip beneath her bodice. Fire raced through
her as she sought to fulfill her newly aroused hunger.
She arched her back, and soft moans escaped her as
she felt the hardness of his manhood against her thigh.
Katerina felt herself soar as her breasts fought and
strained against the fabric that held them prisoner. Her
inner heat threatened to consume her until in the dim
recesses of her mind, she heard her name being called.
She tore her mouth from Yuri's, her eyes glazed and
full of wanting. "I . . . I have . . . I have to . . .
go back." Turning, she tripped and ran, her body
welcoming the light breeze that wafted about her. "Oh,
what did I do? How did I . . . I just saw him for the
first time . . . oh, God! . . . I don't care," she cried as
she raced indoors and slammed the door behind her,
her hands clapped to her flaming cheeks.

Yuri, his chiseled features calm, watched as Katerina

raced back to her father's house. The disturbing ache in his nether regions stayed with him. When it became a violent pain, he would do something about it. For now, it wasn't so uncomfortable that he couldn't live with it. The promise of exquisite release would soon be his.

The meal was silent. Katlof Vaschenko ate the thick cabbage soup without lifting his eyes from the bowl. When he finished, he wiped his mouth on the sleeve of the coarse tunic he wore. He leaned back and eyed the Russian with open suspicion. "There was no need for you to make the journey to this village. The Czar was aware of my demands and agreed to them at the time the mares were bred. When you return to your post to report to the Czar, you will deliver a message . . . from the Kat. No more visits. The horses will be delivered on schedule. For many years now, all of Russia has tried to steal our horses, tried to steal our breeding secrets. I'm the only one who knows the secret," he lied, "and I will carry it to my grave. The crossbreeding of the Cosars has been our livelihood for centuries and will never be divulged to anyone, and that includes the Czar. The stallions are not kept here on the steppe; after they impregnate the mares they are taken away. I'm telling you this so there won't be any need for you to creep among our people, as the last man did, to try to learn by deceit and trickery what isn't to be told. There aren't any stallions here except those that have been castrated," he lied. "Tales of your ferocious Czar have filtered here, and it would be wise if you tell him that the Don as well as the Terek Cossacks are not happy with the tales of his mass murders of people and his lunatic ways. For now, his only thought is to have my Cosars. If it weren't for my horses, he wouldn't have a cavalry. Remind him of this matter when you return."

Yuri's dark eyes narrowed slightly as he watched the slovenly Kat lean back on the rough-hewn chair. The Kat's eyes were cold and unreadable. His body tipped precariously on the wooden chair as he eyed the Russian, daring him to dispute what he said. Yuri felt nauseated as the man's odor reached him. He smelled of stale horseflesh and his own dirty sweat, and the fumes of vodka were strong enough to set the room on fire. His coarse, homespun clothing and mud-crusted boots were those of a fighting Cossack. This fearless leader of men, this awesome breeder of horse-flesh, was no different from his men. He looked the same, he dressed the same, and he smelled the same.

"I shall give your message to the Czar . . . exactly as stated," Yuri said cooly. "I would like to hear the story of the horses—that is, if you wouldn't mind tell-ing me. There are many hours to get through till dawn, when I inspect them." What he didn't say was that he had no desire to sleep in the moldy-looking feather bed that was to be his. Besides, it was something to help while away the time till the old man was sod-den, and then he could take the beautiful Katerina outside to some grassy spot and unleash his violent pain.

With supreme effort he managed to keep his eyes averted from the tawny-skinned Katerina during the meal. He felt the amber, catlike eyes on him, and knew the Kat was aware of it also. He would have to be careful. She was probably being saved for one of those smelly oafs in the horse pens. Yuri's mouth tightened as he visualized her soft, honeyed skin being caressed by some filthy, sweaty hand. He had to force himself to remain seated, his face schooled to show nothing of his thoughts: of one of those rancid, evil faces with the thick, slobbering lips salivating over her naked body.

He was saved from further thought when the Kat got off his seat, pulled aside a curtain, and brought forth a jug of vodka. He wiped his hand across his heavy beard as he plopped the jug on the table, with a dirty hand motioning that Yuri should take the first drink. There weren't any glasses. Yuri raised the heavy jug to his lips and drank deeply.

The older man's eyes registered shock when the young Russian set the jug down, precisely on the same spot he lifted it from. His eyes didn't water, and he wasn't coughing and sputtering.

Yuri grinned as he stared at the Cossack. "My guts aren't on fire. I've been drinking vodka since I was six years old. I admit this," he said, pointing to the jug, "has the kick of one of your stallions, but I've had worse."

The Kat laughed. "When the jug is finished and if you are still on your feet, then, and only then, will I tell you about my horses." He brought the jug to his lips and drank with deep gurgling sounds.

Yuri took his turn, to the amazement of Katerina, who was watching with wide, frightened eyes. Why was her father doing this? Why was he pretending to be this . . . this dirty, unkempt, uncultured man? He was up to something, and she would have to stay in the kitchen till she found out what it was. Surely he wouldn't kill the Russian, or would he? She had never seen him in this sort of a mood before.

Yuri drank and set the jug down, a patient look on his face.

The Kat took another long, gurgling drink and handed the jug to the young Russian. "Drink as I drink," he said harshly. "There's more where that came from. Half vodka and half blood runs in my veins. What runs in yours, Russian?"

"Russian blood," Yuri said curtly as he brought the jug to his lips.

"Fetch another jug, Katerina," her father said, never taking his eyes from the young man sitting across the table from him.

Katerina withdrew behind the curtain and brought out a jug, placing it on the table with a loud thump to show her disapproval. She looked at her father with contempt and at Yuri with suspicion. The Russian didn't have a chance. Her father would probably trick him into confessing an ulterior motive once Yuri could not think logically anymore. She walked from the

room, disgust written in the straightness of her back
and her firm, hard gait. And they said women were
fools!

Katerina looked at the star-filled night and felt saddened. Spring was a time for lovers and she was alone.
The coming months of summer would pass quickly and
soon it would be time to take the mares back to the
Carpathians and settle in for the long, cold winter. I
survived after all; I managed to get through spring
with my secret intact, and I can get through summer
and winter the same way, she thought bitterly. The
thoughts of the new colts and fillies that would be born
did not help to dispel the gloom. What was her father
up to? What did the Russian have in his mind? Why
did she constantly think of the Mongol of the steppe?
What was it about the young Russian that appealed to
her? If only she knew what was in the soldier's mind.
Whatever it was, he would be no match for her father.

Would Yuri seek her out after the drinking was
over? Would he be able to handle himself, or would
he be like the others when they drank vodka for hours
on end? Would he want to make love to her as she
wanted him to? Would he be the one whose eyes
would understand when she told him she was not a
virgin?

Katerina walked for what seemed like hours. When
she returned to the hut, she wasn't surprised to see
four jugs sitting on the table and her father talking
freely of the horses. She let her eyes wander toward
Yuri and then to her father. She closed the door behind her as she gave Yuri one last, lingering look,
which he did not return.

Katerina settled herself on a bench outside the door
and listened as her father disclosed how he came to be
called the Kat.

Quarts of vodka let words tumble freely from the
Kat's mouth. "I'll tell you about my beautiful horses,"
he said, slurring his words. "Do you know how long it
takes and how difficult it is to breed pure whites? Do

you know how many generations it has taken to breed this horse with that horse and end with stallions like Whitefire and his son, Snowfire?"

Yuri drew in his breath and leaned his elbows on the simple plank table, his eyes keen, his ears alert. "Tell me," he said quietly.

The Kat laughed. "First more vodka. I'll drink and then you drink." He reached for the jug in the center of the table. Both men drank heartily, but it was Yuri who replaced the earthen bottle in the same spot it had been taken from. His hand was steady, although his head reeled. "Go on about the horses," he urged.

"It began long ago with the Przhevalski horse and . . . and another horse. Would you like to know what we did?" he baited the young Russian.

"Of course, but only if you want to tell me," Yuri replied nonchalantly.

"Do you wonder how I got to be named the Kat?" Yuri nodded. "My father, his father, and his father before him had a knack for handling stallions. One day my great-great-grandfather was sent to the barn to watch the horses. He was but a lad, and his father told him he couldn't leave until he understood the animals. My great-great-grandfather sat on a stool and watched the horses eat and he watched them sleep. He talked to them as his father talked to them. The story goes that he stayed in the barn for two days and two nights and still he didn't understand what his father expected of him.

"With nothing to occupy his time, save watching and talking to the horses, he noticed a cat wander through the stalls, gently rubbing against the horses' legs and purring softly and contentedly. The stallions quieted immediately, as did the rest of the horses. They lowered their heads to the ground while the cat purred and nuzzled their noses. My great-great-grandfather learned from the cat how to touch and how to speak to them."

"An amazing story," Yuri said quietly.

"And now you wish to know the secret, eh, my

young friend," the Kat said drunkenly. He slapped the Russian on the arm and started to speak. "The secret is . . . is . . ." He stopped. "I'll tell it to you this way," the shrewd Cossack went on. "There is an old Arab proverb that says: the fleetest of horses is the chestnut, the most enduring the bay, the most spirited the black, the most blessed the one with the white forehead. That is the secret, my young friend."

"Is it!" breathed a puzzled Yuri, who dared not ask one question.

"You fool, did you think for one moment that I was so drunk I would tell you our secret? Better men than you, my friend, have tried and died for their efforts. Fool!" He pushed the liquor toward the Russian. "Have a drink."

Yuri rose from the table and walked to the door. As his hand touched the latch, the Cossack thundered, "I said have another drink!"

Yuri turned, his eyes full of hate. "I don't drink with liars," he said softly as he left the room, the latch clicking softly behind him.

The Kat picked up the jug and sent it crashing against the wall. "Fool! Better men than you have tried and died for their efforts, just as you will!" he shouted over and over, until his eyes grew heavy. Finally he lowered his head onto his folded arms and slept.

Katerina sensed Yuri approaching. Drawing in her breath, she turned to meet him and rushed into his arms, welcoming him with her whole being. "I've been waiting," she said simply.

"I know," he said huskily. "I'm here now." He pulled her into his arms in a hard embrace before she could utter another word. His lips crushed hers, driving the breath from her body as she pressed willingly against him. Yuri's arms tightened around her. His long muscular legs, next to hers, drove her back till she rested against the gnarled old tree where she had been sitting. His hands caressed her back, her breasts, the flatness of her stomach. He lifted his mouth from hers and looked deeply into her eyes in the bright moonlight. "You're so beautiful," he said hungrily as his mouth opened her lips, demanding more and still more from her straining body. She felt his hands inside the looseness of her sarafan, her breasts becoming alive under his touch. His strong hands caressed the warm, bare flesh till she moaned in delight.

Suddenly they were on the ground, the grass soft and cool. Fumbling, with shaking hands, she removed her clothing while Yuri did the same. When their nude bodies met, low moans escaped them both as his lips crushed hers, his body pressed hers, demanding more.

Crying softly with desire, she lay beside him as Yuri explored her body, which was pliant to his every demand. Her senses soared and whirled about her as she opened her mouth to his gently exploring tongue, her taut breasts boring into his hard, muscular chest. She moved invitingly beneath him, striving to make them one, always one.

Unable to bear the exquisite torture, she parted her thighs, and he entered her, gently at first and then with deep plunges, her pain a momentary thing as she was caught up in the passion of the pressure within her. Wave after wave of passion engulfed her as Yuri's violent pain was released to meet hers in the cascade of their emotions.

They lay quietly, each content to feel the other's nearness, neither speaking. From time to time Katerina reached out to touch his arm to make sure she wasn't dreaming.

As she nestled herself in the comforting hold of his arm, she said quietly, "I'll miss you when you return to Moscow."

"I'll return for you at summer's end. Promise that you will wait for me."

Katerina looked into his eyes and wanted to tell him of the time on the steppe when the Mongol took her by force. Something stopped her just as she was about to speak. She remembered her own thoughts: when I look into his eyes, I'll know if he is the man who will understand and forgive. Some instinct, some warning, told her that Yuri was not that man. He wanted her, but was it for now or would it be for always? "I'll wait for you," she said huskily.

Yuri raised himself on one elbow. "I've bedded many women, but none like you. I think I loved you the moment I saw you standing in the house, waiting for me. I'll love you forever, for all eternity."

"Where will we go, what will we do?" Katerina asked quietly.

"Don't concern yourself, I'll take care of you. I have many plans to make. When I return, all will be in readiness. Would you like to live in Kiev with a houseful of servants, and have fine clothes and fine food?"

"Oh, yes," she murmured happily. There was no need for her to tell him that in the mountains during the winter months they lived a life of royalty, in the tradition of the Vaschenkos. No need to reveal that her father was not what he seemed. Later she would tell him. Later she would let him know everything except her secret. For now, this was her time—hers and Yuri's.

They slept, their naked flesh entwined on the grassy copse, far from the house.

Yuri's selection of the horses was slow and thorough. Katerina sat, unobserved, willing the tedious process to be over. Unable to keep her shining eyes off the muscular Russian, she followed his every move. All she could think of was the velvety night and how it felt to have Yuri's arms embrace her.

She watched as the tall Russian shook his head over something, his jaw tight and angry. Even from where she sat, she could hear his harsh complaint to her father.

"The agreement was two hundred horses from the stallion Whitefire and the mare Wildflower, not one hundred and fifty, not one hundred, but two hundred. Two hundred pure whites. The other eight hundred were to salve your ego. Do you take me for a fool?"

he demanded angrily. "The purpose of this agreement was for the whites." Angrily he waved a long arm at the black and russet horses that roamed the pens. "What good are they in the snow? The Czar wants only the whites. You agreed, you gave your word. If you wish to renege on the agreement, then I must cancel the bargain we made. Two hundred pure whites or nothing," he said adamantly.

The Kat grinned at the determined look on the Russian's face. "It never hurts to barter. You shall have your two hundred whites—one hundred and twenty-five mares and seventy-five castrated stallions." When the Russian flinched, the Kat roared with laughter. "Does the word bother you, my friend, or is it the act itself? Never mind, it isn't important what you feel. When we return from the Carpathians in April, the horses will be taken to Moscow.

"Oles," he called loudly, "take the Russian to the pasture so he can inspect the mares." His eyes told the Cossack to watch and let nothing go unnoticed.

Yuri correctly interpreted the look and smiled to himself.

He could feel Katerina's eyes on him while he made his selection, nodding as each horse was examined. He could do worse. With a little finery she would be acceptable at court, he mused as he finished his chore.

Katerina, who had been standing next to her father during the counting, looked at him with wide eyes. He knew! Why didn't he say something? What would he do? She watched the Cossack hetman turn and stride away, a look of fury on his bearded face.

How to get through the rest of the day? A walk, a ride on her horse, Bluefire? A nap under the gnarled old tree where she had made love with Yuri?

When the inky black night had closed around her and the birds slept, she settled herself under the leafy tree to wait for Yuri. She felt confused. She wanted him, felt a need for him, and would willingly go with him, yet he wasn't the man she wanted to spend her life with. His eyes didn't return unspoken words. Perhaps there was no such man. Now that her father knew, she felt fear for what he would do to the Russian and terror of what he would do to her. Once he knew she was no longer a virgin, he would lose face with his fellow Cossacks. It would make no difference that he was the hetman. A Cossack girl married a Cossack man, not a Russian or a Mongol. Now, why had she thought of the Mongol? Why did he creep into her mind? She had to stop thinking about that day on the steppe. That time was over. No one would ever know. What did Yuri mean when he said he would return for her? Did he mean to marry her or did he mean they would live together without a wedding ceremony? Men didn't marry women who weren't virgins. Some inner voice whispered in her ear: but the Mongol would. She didn't know how she knew, but she did.

Yuri came to her quietly, his footsteps hushed, his breathing soft. His arms reached for her and held her close. He crushed his face into her wealth of coppery hair and groaned softly. "I've been waiting all day for this moment," he said tenderly. "My body might have been choosing horses, but my mind and my thoughts were on you," he said huskily.

They settled themselves beneath the old tree, Katerina's head on his chest, her breathing tortured as she sought for and found his lips. Hungrily, he crushed her lips to his with a low growl of passion. The kiss was deep, savage in its intensity. They paused only long enough to shed their clothing, their bodies meeting just as passionately, entwining as his hungry mouth once more sought hers. Unable to contain herself, Katerina enticed him by straining against him till he entered her almost brutally. A sheen of perspiration flashed on his muscular torso as he sought for and conquered her, again and again.

Spent, they lay in each other's arms, talking softly. From time to time Yuri kissed her gently as his hand caressed her firm breasts. "When we're together, I shall keep you a prisoner in your chambers." He smiled down at her. Katerina snuggled closer to him, saying nothing. "Spend every waking hour thinking of me," he teased. "When will you speak to your father?" he asked quietly, a sense of urgency in his voice.

"After you leave. I can tell you now that he'll be furious. A Cossack girl belongs with a man of her own kind."

"Girls have a way of twisting their fathers around to their way of thinking. I've seen my sister do it many times," he said with amusement.

Katerina didn't want to discuss her father's reaction. "What do you think of the steppe, and how did you like doing business with the Kat?"

"He is a shrewd businessman. For a while he thought he could outwit me with the whites. I would have canceled the bargain which was made. The Czar agreed to the additional eight hundred horses for the sake of two hundred whites. What good is a black or russet in winter combat? I asked your father for four hundred whites in the autumn of next year, but he wouldn't agree. I don't know what I'm going to do when I return to Moscow and report that he wouldn't agree to next year's shipment. The Czar will be outraged. One stallion out of Whitefire is all I would need to breed my own horses. Think about it, Katerina. We could go to Kiev and breed the horses as your father does here on the steppe. One stallion, that's all we would need."

"No, darling, that is not all you would need. There's more to it than you think," she said, nibbling on his ear. "The breeding of the pure whites is a science . . . a . . . Never mind, it is not for me to say."

"Perhaps, if we were to marry, your father would give us a stallion as a wedding gift," Yuri teased lightly as he ran his hand over her thigh. "I haven't seen the stallions, where are they kept?" he said, crushing his lips to hers. "Tell me, darling, so that when I go back to the Czar I can tell him I've seen the magnificent beasts."

Her senses were reeling, her body was full of desire,

but still something managed to worm its way into her subconscious. "Whitefire and Wildflower are here under guard," she whispered.

Yuri clasped her head in his two hands and drew her to him. "Where is Whitefire?" he questioned.

"Only my father . . ." She felt herself being lifted from the ground as a deep roar of outrage thundered in the quiet night. She saw a heavy pouch sail through the air and land at Yuri's side.

"There will be no horses for the Czar. I'll leave it to you to make a suitable explanation. You have but minutes to ride from this village. One moment longer than I deem necessary and every Cossack in this village will be on your trail. Get dressed, Katerina," Katlof said coldly, "you betrayed us—the Cossack heritage. And for what? For the lust of this Russian. Fool!" He spat angrily. "He holds your naked body to his and questions you about our secret, and for the pleasure of his body you betray us. Don't deny it. I heard him ask you and I heard you answer him." His eyes full of hate, he stood back and spat on her.

Yuri was on his feet instantly, his eyes full of murder as he lunged at the Cossack chief. They tussled on the ground, and within minutes the Russian was pinned beneath the hetman's powerful hands.

"I said minutes and I meant minutes! If you wish to waste them fighting with me, that's your business, but you've been warned."

"Father, you are—" Crack! Katerina stumbled backward, her hand clasped to her cheek. Again she tried. "You're mista—" This time she landed on the ground, sprawling awkwardly next to Yuri, who was struggling to his feet.

"She told me nothing. It's true that I asked, but she divulged nothing," Yuri said harshly. "She's telling you the truth."

"All Russians are known for their lies," the Kat said coldly. "My daughter is my affair, not yours. Never yours," he said vehemently.

His face full of rage, Yuri looked at the Cossack a

moment and then at Katerina. "I meant what I said. I'll be back for you at the end of summer. If you choose to go with me, I'll keep the promise I made to you. If you choose to stay with this . . . this . . . barbarian, then I will understand."

"Take me with you," Katerina pleaded tearfully.

"It isn't possible now. I said I'll return and I will. You must trust me."

"I'll count the days myself," the Kat sneered. He looked down at his tearful daughter and said coldly, "He got what he wanted and he won't be back. We'll count the days together."

Yuri, now fully clothed, jumped upon his horse and rode from the camp. Some distance out, he shouted, "Remember what I said, I'll return!"

The ride back to the village was unbearable. Katerina dared not look back to catch one last glimpse of Yuri, and she didn't dare look at her father. They rode to Volin in deafening silence.

Before retiring, Katlof informed Katerina in as few words as possible that in the morning she would stand trial before the council. Katlof knew what the outcome would be if she was found guilty, but he had to put his feelings aside and allow the justice of the Cossacks to prevail.

A Cossack escorted Katerina into the hall and down to the semicircular table where the men sat. She stood solemnly before her father and the council. Katlof's eyes bored into her as he stood, magnificent in his full-dress Cossack uniform. The somber panel, six men on the left and six men on the right of the hetman, wearing ankle-length caftans, boots and black sheepskin hats, sat and waited. Her father stared at her with loathing as he spoke. "Katerina Vaschenko, you stand accused of breaking the tribal law of chastity, and the tribal law of silence regarding the secret bloodline of the Cosars. Do you have anything to say before we pronounce your sentence?"

"Yes, Fa . . . yes, my hetman, I'm not guilty."

Katlof lost control of himself for a moment. "Not guilty! You, who betrayed your heritage! You, who lay in the arms of a Russian emissary who asked questions that you eagerly answered! You, who in your wild lust betrayed God Himself!"

Within moments she was reduced to jelly, her amber eyes pleading for understanding.

"Papa!" she screamed. "That's not true! I didn't tell the secret! It's true that I lusted after the Russian, and it's true I lay in his arms, but I didn't tell the secret. When Yuri gets to Moscow, the only report he can give the Czar is that he made love to me. Why . . . why won't you believe me?"

She looked at each member of the council and knew that they believed her father. She had been accused, tried, and found guilty by all. The council offered no resistance to Katlof's feelings or his judgments.

"I have spoken with the men of the council and all are agreed: you are guilty. Step forward to hear your sentence, Katerina. It is the judgment of the council that since you broke the law of silence, you will not speak to anyone and no one will be permitted to speak to you. You may stay in Volin and in our hut, and may continue to work with the Cosars. This is your punishment, and from this moment until the Feast of Christmas, silence will be your bedfellow."

Katerina turned and walked proudly away and proclaimed, "I am a Cossack through and through and would never, never, even under the penalty of death, reveal any of our secrets. I have never lied to you, my father. What I say is the truth. If you wish to carry out this sentence because I lay with the Russian, then do so, but it is the only thing I'm guilty of. The mating secret of Whitefire is safe; I didn't divulge it. Be fair and just in your sentencing, Father. Sentence me for what I did, not what you think I did!" she cried brokenly.

Katlof's expression was cold and indifferent. "No more words! Go in silence!" he shouted harshly.

Dejected and alone, Katerina walked from the hall and headed to the barn and the mares. At least she still had the animals; they still loved her.

Spring gave way to summer, and the days passed quickly for the villagers, who were busy with the horses and farms. The grasslands sang with activity. Horses could be seen everywhere on the plains, under watchful eyes. The steppe, now dressed in a myriad of full color, was dazzling to the eye. The tall, swaying stalks of wheat, barley, and oats created the illusion of shimmering gold, while the broad stripes of green-leafed and multicolored vegetables painted a dazzling mosaic. This was what Katerina loved about the steppe. It was a place to be proud of, a place in which to feel deeply about the land and her people. When she was not in the barn tending the horses, she rode or walked through this wonderland of color. With no one to talk with, the time to summer's end was agonizing. Occasionally, when no one was looking, Stepan would slip a note to Katerina, telling her he adored her and was her friend forever. It helped ease the days and her tormented mind. During the day, without someone to talk to, to distract her thoughts, her mind was constantly invaded by Yuri and his promise to come for her. In the darkest hours of the night the slant-eyed Mongol continued to pursue her.

Chapter Five

KATERINA LOOKED AROUND the enclosure that held the alabaster mares and smiled slightly. This was the time of day she liked best: the hour before twilight, which cloaked the bustling Don Cossack village of Volin with its velvety mantle of darkness.

The sweet, pungent smell of horseflesh permeated the air as Katerina leaned into the pen. The fillies and colts trotted to the rail fence, vying for the slim girl's attention. A long-legged colt nuzzled her delicate outstretched hand, looking for an apple. Katerina laughed softly as the young animal's mother gently nosed him away from the fence. Secure in the knowledge that her offspring was taken care of, the mare swished her tail and tried to pry open Katerina's hand. "Very well, you may have the apple, but only because you're so exquisitely beautiful," she crooned, opening her fingers. The mare took the fruit and held it gently in her mouth as she trotted away in search of the colt.

Katerina settled herself on a trough and tried to shake the uneasiness that had settled between her shoulders. Whatever it was that was disturbing her was having its effect on the mares, for they, too, were skittish, and clustered together in small groups. Perhaps a wild animal has worked its way into the pen, she thought nervously. Any other day, any other time, she would have been able to shake off this peculiar feeling, which was becoming more pronounced. The horses gathered closer still, whinnying softly and pawing nervously at the ground, their thick, lush tails swinging furiously.

Did they sense that tomorrow at the first rays of the sun they would start the journey to their winter quarters? That had to be the reason. What other could there be, she rationalized uneasily.

The catlike hazel eyes narrowed as Katerina strained to look deeper into the enclosure to see if anything, save the mares, moved. "Anything on four legs, that is," she said quietly to herself. Her voice was a thick, rich purr. The horses became quiet and began to separate. She leaned back again, her eyes scanning the quiet village. This past month her father had avoided her as if she carried some dread disease. There were no more quiet evening talks, no more camaraderie between her father and herself. He was distant and cold. Somehow, before morning she had to make things right between them, before they began the journey to the House of the Kat. Things had to be settled between them before they were quartered together for the winter in the Carpathians.

She shook her head, and the copper-colored curls, free of their pins, tumbled to her shoulders. She brushed them away impatiently to clear her vision. Her body stiffened at an unfamiliar sound, like that of a knife being scraped against new leather. It made her think of her father's raspy voice when he had sentenced her.

One of the mares kicked up her hind legs and began to circle the pen, snorting and flicking her plumed tail. Papa should be here, he had a sixth sense where the horses were concerned. If something was wrong, he should be told. She knew he was in the barns with the other men, readying the wagons for tomorrow's journey. She postponed the moment when she would have to go to him and tell him something was wrong. How could she bear to see the hurt and the hostility in his eyes? How could she accept the fact that, in his heart, he thought she had betrayed him? She couldn't. She had tried, but her tongue became thick and refused to do her bidding. When she tried to explain, tried to convince him that he was wrong, she was not talking to her father but to the Kat, the head of the Don Cossack village. She wasn't answering to her father but to the chief of the Cossacks.

Katerina blinked, driving the hateful memory from her mind as one of the creamy mares again pranced nervously around the pen, snorting and scraping the dirt in a near frenzy. He should have killed me, she thought bitterly. Anything was better than being ostracized by her own people. With each passing day she felt as if she were dying slowly, inch by inch. Yuri, Yuri, she cried silently. Where are you; why haven't you come for me as you promised? You said you would return at the end of the summer and take me back to Moscow with you. You said you loved me. Is my father right, did you make love to me so I would tell you the secret of Whitefire? Was it true?

"No!" she screamed as she ran from the mares' pen down through the dusty road and out to the fields. She ran till there was no breath left in her body. Twice she fell, and twice she staggered to her feet and kept running. She flew from the eyes, from the horses, from the Kat and from her father. She had to keep running and never stop. When Yuri came, and he would come, they would be gone. Back to the Carpathians, where he would never be able to find her.

She fell to the ground and sobbed, great racking tears that shook her slender body. Finally, drying her face, she sat up and looked around. How long had she stayed here? How far had she come? What did it matter? What did anything matter now? There wasn't one person who cared what she did or where she went. Not any more. She was alone. If she allowed her father to have his way, she would always be alone. Branded a traitor by every Cossack on the steppe, she could never again take her rightful place in the Don village.

Katerina looked at the minuscule stars overhead and knew she had stayed away too long. It was time to see her father and make one last effort to make him understand. There must be trust between us, she cried silently. Still she didn't move. Her eyes closed wearily as she lay back on the thick grass.

The tall reeds were still, their slender shafts straight and supple in the gentle night air. Nothing stirred, save the snakelike movements of the Terek Cossacks as they crawled on their bellies through the shoulder-high stalks. The moment the moon took cover behind approaching storm clouds, the Tereks infiltrated the grasses. Each man crawled with his knife clutched between his teeth. They made no sign, nor did they disturb the graceful lengths of greenery that hid them and kept their presence secret from the Don Cossacks. Each man bore a sense of pride as he crawled. This was the closest any man had ever come to the village of Volin, except for the horse traders and buyers. Gregory Bohacky was right, his timing was incredible. The lonely nights they had ridden to get to the outer perimeters of the village, and then sat sentinel, were finally going to be rewarded. After tonight the village would be no more; the Cosars would belong to the Tereks and then to the highest bidder, Czar Ivan.

Gregory lay still, barely inches from the fences that encircled the compound. Still shielded by the tall grasses, he could hear the men of Volin brawling and shouting boisterously as they consumed jug after jug of vodka. From the sound of the merrymaking, he wagered they had been drinking for days as they prepared for their departure to the Carpathians. He listened for Katlof and smirked when he heard him drunkenly address one of his men. He was the only man to worry about. If the hetman was sodden, the others would be in even worse condition. They would be able to wield a weapon, but not with any accuracy. Gregory knew in his gut that his men could cut down the entire village and be back in their own quarters within a short time.

He cast an anxious eye overhead to see if the threatening storm clouds would continue to give him cover. His long body relaxed in the grass as he pondered his next move.

To his left and standing sentry outside the wall surrounding the compound a guard argued vehemently with a Cossack youth. "Someone has to be alert. What you're doing is a disgrace to the village. All of you are so drunk you can barely stand. You're a disgrace to our forefathers."

"Bah, you talk like an old woman. This is a night for pleasure and celebrating. All the wagons are loaded, the horses have been readied for hours, and the houses will soon be closed for the winter. If the hetman says we can drink, then we can drink," the young man said drunkenly as he brought a bottle to his lips and drank greedily. "The Kat said to bring you this jug, but since you don't want it, I'll drink it myself." The youth laughed raucously as he toppled from the wall, alcohol spilling over his face.

The guard looked at him and felt only disgust. One of the horses whickered, and his head jerked upright. He knew that sound, he had been hearing it for hours. It didn't come from an animal, at least not one with four legs. Should he leave his post and report what he thought he knew? And to whom? he asked himself. The Kat was in no condition to hear what he said, let alone make a decision. One other guard stood at his post on the far side of the compound. Should he venture over there and ask him if he, too, had heard the noise and if he realized what it meant? An ominous feeling crept up his spine. No matter what, a Cossack never left his post. There it was again. The soft whicker and then an even softer one in reply. He peered into the velvety darkness and could see nothing. He looked down at the prone young Cossack and cursed long and loud.

A wild whoop was heard; the guard's hand automatically came up with his sword outstretched in front of him. He was cut down from behind before he could move. Everywhere wild shouts and curses filled the air as men struggled and fought. The Don Cossacks, in their drunken condition, were no match for the trim, hard-fighting Tereks with only one thought in mind: the Cosars!

Katlof reeled drunkenly toward the fire, where his sword rested among the others. His hand reached for his saber; just as his fingers closed over the hilt, he felt a blade strike him across the back between his shoulders. He dropped to his knees. As he cried out to his people, "Run! Hide!" blood gushed from his mouth.

Women and children fell beneath the savage onslaught, the Tereks merciless in their attack. Katlof watched in horror as a small child crawled away from his dead mother's arms toward the fire. He reached out a hand as a wild-eyed Terek scooped up the child and tossed him into the roaring inferno. He died with the child's agonized screams ringing in his ears. It was over in a matter of moments.

Gregory stood near the fire on top of one of the loaded wagons, his arms held high above his head in a show of victory. A wild cry rang out as the men reached to pull their leader to the ground. "Ready the horses and burn these wagons after you confiscate the supplies. We can use them ourselves. And don't forget the vodka, we'll do our own celebrating when we return to camp. We did what no Russian has been able to do!" he shouted arrogantly. "We now own the Cosars. Czar Ivan will be proud of us!" A lusty shout of approval rang through the blood-soaked night.

"Are they all dead?" one of Gregory's men shouted.

"Every last bitch and bastard!" came a hoarse shout in reply.

Gregory smiled to himself as the moon slid behind its hiding place, storm clouds moving on. With a wicked flourish of his sword and a wild cry of victory, Gregory spurred the horse beneath him, his men thundering behind him as they rode victoriously from Volin.

When Gregory Bohacky turned his head, those mounted behind glimpsed his heavily greased mustache. No one ever joked about the corkscrew curl at each end, as Gregory's mustache was his manhood, his pride and joy. Many words were spoken about it in jest behind his back, where he would never overhear, but nobody ever uttered a demeaning word to his face. To his face, only words of adoration or praise, if one valued one's head.

The pale moonlight silhouetted the hard outline of his profile as he looked over his shoulder. A sheepskin hat sat on top his black, curly hair, which circled his chiseled face, emphasizing the small, shrewd blue eyes set upon high-boned cheeks that were separated by a large, aquiline nose. The one redeeming feature that made him attractive to women was his full, sensuous mouth and the voice within. His commands held an authoritative manner, leaving no doubt that he meant what he said. But when he wooed the lovelies of his choice, his resonant voice was a choir singing the Gregorian chants, compelling and hypnotizing, so soothing that surrender was a gift of thanks, gladly and freely given to him. Gregory Bohacky, a warrior among warriors, a man among men, was so respected by those under him that he inspired complete obedience.

Gregory twisted in the saddle, raising his hand upward, signaling his men to stop. "The hour grows late and soon our village will be in view. Our families will be asleep, but tonight when we arrive, the thunder of the Cosar hooves, along with our cries of joy, will awaken everyone. Tonight our mir will ring with joy, music, and dancing, and the vodka will flow like the Dnieper. Tonight we'll celebrate our victory and conquest, stopping only when we all fall unconscious. We have done what others only dreamed of doing—we captured the Cosars from the Don Cossacks!" A loud roar of approval boomed from the warriors, almost stampeding the horses.

"Keep those beauties calm and quiet, my brothers, we mustn't lose them now. As happy as I am, I'll behead any man who lets one horse escape!"

The threat of the Don Cossacks coming after them was as nonexistent as the lives of the people of Volin. Secure in this knowledge, the Tereks broke into a Cossack song of victory, their voices filling the night air with a melody of joy.

Gregory, at the water's edge of the Dnieper, reined in his horse and instructed his men, "As we cross the river, carefully lead the Cosars through the rocks, for lame horses are of no value to anyone. When we are once again on our island of Khortitsa, I'll personally check the animals, and someone will pay with his life if one lame Cosar is found."

Restraining his stallion, Gregory waited on the bank as the Cossacks led the horses through the shallow waters. He smiled to himself as he watched. Never had he seen his rough men handle anything or anyone as gently as they handled the Cosars; not even their women were afforded such tenderness. The mothers of the village would mock us forever if they witnessed this scene, he thought.

As they left the banks of the Dnieper behind, the faint outline of their huts came into view. Gregory felt a warm glow sweep over him; it was good to be home. Returning this time was that much sweeter, for he would be proclaimed a hero. The gutting of Volin and his victorious capture of the horses would have the mir celebrating for days, and the men would talk of his exploits for years after his death. Gregory Bohacky would be a folk hero in Russian history, and the Tereks would sing his praises across the vast, endless steppe of the Ukraine. He trembled as he envisioned his welcome from the moment his stallion's hoof first crossed the village entrance. The anticipation telegraphed itself to his legs as he dug his heels into the animal's flanks, driving him into a full canter. His men sensed his eagerness and rode rapidly behind him, the Cosars driven along with them.

A guard hidden from view called out, "Is that you, comrade Bohacky? If it is, show yourself."

Stepping forward into the light of a blazing campfire, Gregory answered, "Yes, comrade, it is Bohacky."

"What do you bring with you? I see many black objects in the distance," remarked the guard as he stepped from behind the high wooden wall that surrounded the camp.

"Those black objects you see in the darkness are white objects, and those white objects are the famous Cosar horses. The whole lot of them from the village of Volin!"

"You joke, Gregory! It can't be. The Cosars belong to the Don Cossacks. They would never let them go."

"They didn't let them go, comrade, we captured them!"

"But the Don Cossacks? I don't understand, you must be making jokes!"

"Comrade, I never make jokes. The Cosars now belong to the Tereks. The Don Cossacks of Volin are no more! We killed every last one of them. No one will come chasing after us for the horses; we saw to that!"

The guard shook his head in disbelief.

"Are our people asleep?" asked Gregory.

"All is quiet. With only four hours before dawn, the warm beds hold fast our people."

"Comrade, wake them from their sleep and tell, no, shout the good news! Tell them Gregory Bohacky has returned triumphant from Volin with the Cosars! Tonight we begin the celebration. Wake the women and have them prepare food for the victory feast. Wake everyone and tell them!"

"Yes, comrade!"

"Then why are you standing here looking at me? Wake everyone. We'll drive the Cosars through the village to help you. Move, comrade!" he shouted.

The guard mounted his horse, galloping down the roads, shouting as he went, "Wake up, wake up, Gregory Bohacky has returned from Volin with the Cosars! Wake up, wake up! The Cosars are here! Tonight we celebrate!"

The commotion woke Yuri. He arose from his bed, opened the door and listened.

"The Cosars are ours! Volin is no more!" shouted the men.

Yuri couldn't believe what he heard. His mind reeled as he tried to think. "Katerina, I must go to Katerina . . . she can't be . . . I must get dressed."

Within moments, he was outside his host's hut looking for a horse.

"Ah! Yuri, my friend, I see you have heard the good news," shouted Gregory above the din.

"I must have a horse!"

"A horse? You shall have one and anything else you may want this night," exclaimed Gregory happily, as he motioned to a Terek to bring a horse.

"Before I go——"

"Go where?"

"You must tell me what happened at Volin. What

do they mean, Volin is no more?" Yuri asked hesitantly, afraid to hear the answer.

"I am a hero now comrade. You have shared the hut of a Terek legend this summer," Bohacky boasted.

Impatient, Yuri lost control, "I demand you tell me what happened at Volin!"

"I'll gladly tell you. We took the Dons, slaughtered all the people and burned the village to the ground. The Tereks are proud Cossacks now."

"Proud? You slaughter a village and you're proud? What of Katerina? Did you kill her, too? You knew how I felt about her, how could you do this? She was all I had left. Your hospitality is no longer needed by me."

He jumped on the back of the waiting horse and disappeared into the night; the words of Gregory echoing in his head.

Still seated atop his stallion, Bohacky laughingly mocked Yuri's words and said, "Bah, women! Tonight's victory is all we'll ever need." He turned from the darkness and looked at his village and watched as shuttered windows flew open and candlelight peeped out at the night. Heads appeared in windows and hands rubbed away the sleep.

The Tereks quickly donned their tunics as the women scurried for their sarafans, and within minutes the men were out in the village circle, throwing wood on the campfire to brighten the area. Gregory ordered the women to prepare poppy cakes and kasha and sausage, and to ready a sheep and a goat for roasting on the spit. "Bring on the vodka, beer, and forty-year-old mead."

The handful of women in Khortitsa worked feverishly to cook the food for the carousing men, knowing that when they finished they would be allowed to return to their huts. Once inside, they would whisper among themselves of the night's events, not venturing outside until the men had fallen into a drunken stupor.

Khortitsa was a village of men. The women who

were allowed to stay were middle-aged, forgotten and old before their time, forsaken by their husbands for the saber and life of the Cossack. Other tribes whispered about Khortitsa and its savage breed of Cossacks, the misfits of life: the killers, robbers, escaped prisoners, rapists, and political escapees. Khortitsa was a stewpot of vicious, cunning men. Cossacks who lived for the saber and the horse. There were no rules in the village. Rules were made for others, not for the Terek. Freedom was their motto, their life.

The few daughters born in the village were quickly sent off the Crimea for safety, the threat of rape and death hanging over them if they were allowed to stay, but when a male child was born a celebration was held which lasted for three days. When a boy reached eight, a saber was thrust into his hands and his training as a Cossack began in earnest. At the age of twelve, he was expected to perform as well as any man, and when he reached eighteen he was given his fighting outfits—wide trousers of pleats and folds, drawn in with a golden cord, boots of morocco leather, a Cossack coat of bright crimson cloth, and a sash, gaily patterned, into which went an embossed Turkish pistol and a saber. His hat was a black, gold-topped astrakhan cap. In his battle attire he was a Cossack to be feared, and his forging would come in the fires of his first battle.

Campfires burned brightly along the roads of the village as the men ate, celebrated, and drank. The guards watched enviously, knowing their turn would come to join the merrymaking when some of the men sobered. For now their only concern was the safety and well-being of the Cosars in the compound, under heavy guard. They could eat till they burst, but they couldn't drink.

That night, and for several nights thereafter, the Terek celebrated the capture of their golden treasure —the Cosar horses—every pound worth its weight in gold.

Yuri Zhuk lay in the thicket and knew he was dying. Never a religious man, he prayed, in his brief moments of lucidity, that his end would be quick and merciful. A wild fever raged through his body, and his dark eyes were glazed with a thin white film. The pain in his throat and neck was so intense, he began to pound the earth where he lay. He had heard of others that lived with no tongue, but he had no desire to be one of them. He blinked as pain shot up his arm. For a moment he had forgotten the loss of his fingers. Blood spurted from the severed stumps of his hands, and he wanted to cry out, but he didn't. Instead he rolled over and crushed his face into the welcoming dirt, the brush and twigs crackling with his movements. He wanted to savor this moment of clarity before he died. He wanted to remember how it was, and he wanted to remember Katerina's face. If God chooses to smile upon me, perhaps the pleasant thoughts will drive away the pain, he thought as his mind wandered back in time.

What a fool he had been. The moment he rode from the Cossack camp he should have known that they would come after him. How confident, how arrogant he had felt when he had ridden out onto the steppe at the end of spring. There had only been one thought in his mind: spend the summer cementing ties with Ivan's allies on the steppe, get back to Russia, make up some story for the Czar to explain his failure, and return for Katerina.

He knew he was being followed even now, months later, though he heard no sound. The fine hairs on the back of his neck prickled, and that was all the warning he needed. Making camp for the night at the first sign of dusk, he was certain that eyes watched him. Only once in the short time he waited for the Cossack did he have any feeling of panic. He had been trained well in the Czar's army before his advancement to his present position and he would give a good accounting of himself, of that he was certain.

The two Cossacks had ridden boldly into his camp

as soon as darkness settled. The only light was the small, flickering campfire, which threw the two riders into ghastly, eerie shadows. Yuri had waited for what he knew was coming. Oles, the young Cossack from the village, had walked over to the fire and stood looking down at the Russian. From where he lay Yuri could see the wild gleam in his eye as he made a motion for his companion to dismount. When both men stood towering over him, Yuri rose to his feet, his saber held loosely in his hand. "What do you want here at this time of night?" he asked harshly.

Oles and his friend stared at the Russian, their faces cold, dark and forbidding. Yuri felt a twinge of fright. One man he could handle, but two Cossacks was something he hadn't planned on. They would fight by their own rules, not the rules he had been trained under.

"The Kat ordered your death. We were selected to carry out the order. You crept into our camp and tried to steal our secrets and then ravaged the hetman's daughter. Your death is to be slow and painful. The secrets of our village will never find their way to Moscow and that lunatic Czar you serve under. We have finally succeeded in tracking you after all these weeks. Your tongue is to be removed and then your hands," Oles said coldly.

"Secrets be damned!" Yuri shouted. "It isn't Katerina that is making you do this. I didn't ravage her; she came to me of her own free will. I don't expect you to believe me, but she didn't tell me any secrets, and if she had, I wouldn't divulge them to the Czar. I love her and want to marry her. My plans are to return to Moscow and settle things, and then I am coming back for Katerina."

"You lie; all Russians lie. The Kat said you lie, and that is all we need to know. Even if you somehow managed to escape us and return to Moscow, you would be too late. We leave for the mountains on the last day of August. There is no way you could find your way into the Carpathians once the snows come.

You were doomed from the moment you rode into our village."

So intent were the three men on their conversation that they heard nothing until a wild whoop split the soft, dark night. Yuri backed away from the flickering fire as a dozen men converged into the semidarkness with sabers drawn and evil smiles on their faces. Oles swiveled and immediately brought up his saber as he danced around the tiny fire. Iron clanked against iron as the three men fought for their lives. They were outnumbered, and Yuri watched as the valiant Cossacks lost their heads with wicked sweeps of the strangers' sabers. He threw down his saber and waited.

"Who are you?" he demanded.

"Your executioners." One of the men laughed. "Surround him," the leader ordered his men, "and lash him to the horse. Throw those heads into a sack so they can be returned to Gregory."

Katerina jumped to her feet; she had to get back to the village. Her father was right. Yuri had not come and summer was over. Had the Czar put him in prison when he failed to deliver his contract for the pure whites out of Whitefire? Had the Kat sent someone after Yuri and killed him? She would never know. Tomorrow they would go to the mountains, and that would end any remaining hopes.

Her eyes were wild as she looked around the grassy copse and lashed out at the gnarled old tree with her booted foot. Now she would never know if he had lied or not.

It would soon be dawn and time to start for the mountains, and still she hadn't talked with her father. No, there was no point in trying to talk to her father now.

It was a night made for lovers, but Katerina didn't notice the warm, scented air or the star-filled night as the moon crept from behind its hiding place, lighting up the steppe as she trudged along the grassy field. She welcomed the indigo darkness when the moon slipped behind the cloud. The inky blackness was her ally, her confidant.

Blinded with tears, she skirted a small outgrowth of shrubbery and raised her eyes when a high-pitched wail reached her ears. She wiped at her eyes, and for the first time was aware of the smoke on the road and around the pens. They were gone! All the horses were gone! Everyone was dead! All around the compounds and enclosures lay the lifeless bodies of the Cossacks. The buildings were burned and gutted, the stables nothing but smoldering ashes. "Father!" she screamed.

"He's over here."

Katerina whirled at the sound of the voice and ran to where an old woman, leaning heavily on a cane, pointed. She dropped to her knees and gathered her father to her, crying openly. "Tell me what happened —who did this?"

"You know who did this!" the old woman shouted malevolently. "You are responsible!"

"No! No! I was over by the copse. I didn't know. I heard nothing, saw nothing. Who did this?"

"They're all dead! The horses are all gone. Soon I'll die like the others." The old crone cackled as she opened her shawl to show a large, gaping wound in her side. "They thought I was dead when they left."

"Who? Tell me, who did this?" Katerina screamed.

"Your own father said you were a traitor to our people. You ask me who did this? It was the Terek Cossacks that rode into this camp, but it was your Russian that made it possible. With the horses, they could do nothing. Even with the two stallions, Snowfire and Wildfire, they could not breed, but you told the Russian the secret and now it's over. Your heritage is gone! Your father lies dead! My husband and my three sons lie dead!" She coughed suddenly, and a bright stream of blood spurted from her dry, cracked lips. "Look around you, traitor, and see what your lusting ways have done. Bah!" she said, waving the stick she carried in the air. "He did not come for you as he

promised. He will never come for you! Your father sent
men after him when he left here. They were ordered
to cut out his tongue and cut off his hands. Now he
can never tell the secret."

"You lie! The children, the women, where are
they?"

The old woman cackled insanely. "Dead. All of
them. I am the only one left, and soon I will die and
you will be the only one alive. What will you do? How
will you live with this on your soul?"

How can this have happened? Katerina cried silently. "Where were our glorious fighters, where were
all the glorious Cossacks?" she demanded bitterly of
the woman. "Drunk with vodka water? Look at me!"
she commanded the old woman. "They were drunk,
weren't they? Once we started the trip to the mountains, there would be no vodka during the trip and
none at my father's house. Speak the truth before you
die, old woman!"

"They fought superbly," the woman said weakly.
"There was none that did not rise to the battle. They
died valiantly. And for what? To save the horses for
you. For you, because you are your father's daughter." Suddenly she lashed out with her stout stick and
brought it down on Katerina's arm. The pain was ex-
cruciating, but Katerina made no sound as she watched
the old woman fall to the ground.

Katerina crawled over to the old woman and gently
closed her eyes. "I didn't betray my father or my people," she whispered.

There was a chill in the early-morning air as she
waited for the sun to come up. Only her eyes moved.

When the sun was high in the sky and the last drop
of dew was scorched from the lush grass, she still sat.
She stared at her father and at the others and did
nothing. The pain in her arm was wild, and she welcomed it. It would keep her sane and remind her of
what had happened.

She was hungry and thirsty, but still she didn't

move. Food would lodge in her throat and choke her, water would make her vomit.

By sundown the pain in her arm was alive and fierce. Her lips were dry and parched from sitting in the open sun all day. Still she sat, her eyes going from body to body and then back to her father.

At dawn the following day, the stench of the dead bodies forced her to her feet. Hobbling to the water trough, she wet her lips with her hand and smeared water over her face, wiping it on the shoulder of her dress. She had to do something about the bodies. Carefully she explored her injured arm, feeling to see if any bones were broken. She could move it, but just barely. Another day and Mikhailo would know something was wrong when the caravan didn't arrive in the mountains. He would ride down on horseback to see if something was wrong. But the dead had to be taken care of. The bodies would have to go into a drainage pit; when Mikhailo came, he could cover it over and give the necessary eulogy. There was no other way. She bit into her full lower lip till the blood spurted. Her amber eyes went to the pit at the far side of the enclosure and back to the dead bodies. She would have to drag them one by one till they were all taken care of.

A grim look on her face, the cinnamon eyes narrowed against the bright sun, she started her grisly chore. Her arms felt as if they were being pulled from their sockets as she dragged body after body to the pit. Her legs gave out once and she collapsed, falling onto Olga's corpse. She screamed and quickly rolled over as a gurgling sound from the body split the quiet air around her. If there was one thing she could be thankful for it was that Stepan had returned to the mountains to alert Mikhailo of their coming.

This is my punishment for lying with a man, she said over and over to herself as she rose to drag another friend's body to the pit. I am guilty of nothing except lying with a man. I will pay the price because I want to live. "I'll drag everyone to the pit if it kills me," she said harshly as she bent to grasp a pair of feet in her hands.

Some time later, only her father's body remained. Katerina looked down at him, her face expressionless. How could she drag him through the road like a sack of flour? The same way you dragged the others, a voice inside her answered.

Savagely, she bent to grasp the big man under the armpits, her injured arm sending shooting pains down the side of her body. She clenched her teeth and began to pull him down the length of the road. Tears of pain and sorrow trailed down her cheeks as she cried over and over, "I did not betray our people! I harmed no one but myself." Over and over she repeated the words until she came to the pit. "I did nothing, Father," she said quietly as she pushed his body in with the others. "Forgive me for what you thought I did. I forgive you," she cried brokenly as she collapsed at the edge of the cavernous hole.

Mikhailo, the horse trainer from the House of the Kat, found her a day later, feverish and muttering in delirium.

He looked around the devastated village and then at the girl. He shook his shaggy gray head as he picked her up gently and laid her down beneath the shade of a tree and sponged off her dirty face. From his saddlebags he lifted a goatskin and poured a trickle of vodka into her mouth, waiting for her to swallow. Her eyes opened, and at the sight of the old, weather-beaten face she sighed and slept. Mikhailo bound the injured arm in a splint and sat back, waiting for her to wake again.

Angry at what he did not understand, the old man made a small fire and boiled some water. Carefully he added herbs and waited for the water to boil again. When it cooled, he would give it to Katerina for her fever. More than that he could not do.

From time to time he would lay his hand on her brow and then spoon the herb tea into her mouth. She muttered and thrashed about, then would lie still, the dark lashes like smudges of soot on her pale cheeks.

She was sleeping peacefully, a natural sleep; the fever had broken. He walked around the village, hoping that some explanation would rear up at him. From the countless blood-crusted weapons that lay upon the bloody roads, it was evident that the village had been attacked. Who? Was it some nameless tribe? The horses and the mares were gone. Thank God Whitefire and Stepan were already in the mountains. He knew why, there was no point in asking himself that question. There wasn't a man, a Cossack, a soldier of a Czar, that wouldn't pay, and pay handsomely, for the Cosar horses. Men had killed and fought for the horses, and they would kill and fight again.

Mikhailo Kornilo was a small man by Cossack standards, but he was a fighter and had served his tribe well until the day a wild-eyed Tatar severed his leg at the knee with one flourish of his scimitar. Now he had grown stocky with food in his belly three times a day and vodka water at night. He shook his wooden peg leg and cursed all Tatars for what happened. His normally ruddy face was crimson with the expletives he spit out. His straggly gray-and-white beard was sparse as his hands now pulled and tugged at it in anger. His brown eyes traveled around the village and came to rest on the sleeping Katerina. He was her godfather. He remembered how he had dandled her on his knee when she was a baby. Too ugly to take a wife, he had devoted himself to Katlof and his family, and they, in turn, regarded him as one of their own. He gladly would have given his life for any of them, but now it was too late.

One day soon the elder Katmon would die. Already he was preparing for an elaborate funeral. Soon the old man would join Katlof and the other dead Cossacks, leaving only Katerina, Stepan, himself, and the other old people. His eyes lighted for a moment when he remembered that Whitefire was safe in the Carpathian Mountains. If one had to be thankful for small favors, this was the one to be thankful for. Katerina knew the secret. Katerina would rebuild, and he and Stepan would help her. It never entered his mind that the mares were gone, that without Wildflower, the stallion, Whitefire, was just another stallion. He tugged at the straggly beard as he limped back to the sleeping girl.

Three days later Katerina was on her feet, her eyes haunted, her mouth a grim, tight line. "What are we to do, Mikhailo? It will take us ten years to get any breeding stock. Twenty before we have a herd. I've been thinking while I lay here."

"You plan to go to your mother's people, is that what you're going to tell me? I see it in your eyes. You intend to ask the Khan for help?"

"There is no other way, Mikhailo. I must get the horses. How can I live with this?" she said, waving her arm around what had been Volin. "I have to try. If I fail, then that is something else, but first I must make the effort. I didn't betray our people. You say you believe me. That's all I need to know. Somehow you will make it sound right when you tell Grandfather what happened."

"And the Russian?" It was a question that, up until now, Katerina had refused to think about. Now she would have to bring the matter into the open and discuss it with Mikhailo.

"I loved him. He loved me. Nothing you or anyone else says will ever convince me differently. I don't know what happened. I was told that Father sent two of the men after Yuri to slice out his tongue and cut off his hands so he couldn't divulge the secret. Father would never let him go back to Moscow thinking I gave him the secret. He's dead, Mikhailo. And my father killed him just as surely as if he wielded the weapon himself. I have to try to prove to myself that Yuri was not responsible for what happened. Every Cossack on the steppe will think me guilty, and this must not be allowed to happen. I don't know who or why the raid happened, but I will find out!"

"So you will journey to the Khanate of Sibir, and then what? You're a woman, what can you do?"

"As you know, the Khan is my mother's brother. He'll help me. Sit down, Mikhailo, for what I have to tell you will shock you off your feet."

The old man eyed her warily but sat down, his face full of dread.

"We all know that the Mongols' military strength has deteriorated to the point where they are no longer the fierce warriors they once were. I plan to ask the Khan for men from his prisons to take back with me to the House of the Kat. I will work with them through the winter months and make Cossacks out of them. In the spring we will ride out and seek that which belongs to me—the Cosar horses."

The old man shook his head. "Just like that, eh? The Khan will give you the prisoners, criminals of the worst sort, and you are going to train them to be fighting Cossacks! And then you will set out in search of your horses. You're a woman. What makes you think you can do this, and what makes you think you can make the Khan help you? A Cossack is born, you can't create a Cossack."

"Make no mistake, Mikhailo, as sure as the first wild flower blossoms on the frozen banks of the Dnieper River, a new breed of Cossacks will be born," she said savagely.

"I know in my bones the Khan won't help you," Mikhailo said.

"He'll help me," Katerina said coldly. "And the reason I know I will succeed is because I am my father's daughter. Yes, I'm a woman, but I'm also a Cossack. If it comes to money, I will give the Khan whatever he asks. I will do whatever he wants if he agrees to my plan."

"Criminals! The men are criminals! They'll kill you!" the old man said fearfully.

"Mikhailo, you don't for one second believe that a

man, a Mongol, could kill me, do you? Where is the Cossack courage you forced me to cut my teeth on? Have you no faith in my ability? Where else can I get the men? Men that will fight for me? Our village is wiped out; our men are gone. You and I are all that are left, save Grandfather and the elders in the mountains. If you have a better solution I would be happy to hear it."

"I have no thoughts, Katerina. But criminals? How many do you plan to bring back with you?"

"As many as the Khan will give me."

"What if they kill you on the journey home?"

"Mikhailo, they will be shackled together. If I am not worried, then you should not be. It is the only way. I'll leave in the morning, and I'll have to take your horse. When you next see me I shall have my new Cossacks with me. Be gentle with Grandfather when you tell him. Make him understand, please, Mikhailo."

"How can I make him understand when I don't understand myself?" her godfather asked irritably. "Mongols are ugly sons of bitches."

"I hate to remind you, but Mongol blood runs in my veins. You know my mother was a Mongol. I never knew you thought I was ugly," she teased lightly.

"You are beautiful, but Mongols are ugly," the old man said sourly. "All that yellow skin and slanted eyes. Sneaky! Don't turn your back on them or they stick a knife in you. Mark my words."

"Mikhailo, who is better, a Mongol or a Cossack?"

"A Cossack—what sort of question is that?"

"Then you have your answer. I want your promise that you will not worry about me."

"How long?" the old man asked curtly.

"A week's ride each way. Three days at the Mongol camp. I'll be in the mountains before the snows come. My word, Mikhailo, as a Cossack. You'll see me before the snows come. If I'm to get an early start, I must sleep now." She kissed the leathery cheek and lay down. She was asleep immediately.

The sun was coming up and the old man had not closed his eyes once. He watched the sleeping girl who was now a woman with fear in his eyes. She was right; she was her father's daughter. If there was a way to bring the Mongols back to the mountains, she would do it. Never had he seen such a look in anyone's eyes. Not even in Katlof's eyes, and he was the most awesome, the most fearsome of all the Cossacks.

From the time she was able to ride, Katerina had been trained with the others, purely out of indulgence by her famous father. It amused him to see her unseat one of the mighty Cossacks, and then he would sit and drink with her till the sun came up. He would praise her and tell her that she was as good a Cossack as any of his men. Proof of his sincerity was when he bestowed the gelding Bluefire on her when she reached sixteen.

Before it had been for sport, but now it was a matter of survival—Katerina's survival. She was so full of hate and vengeance she would do what she said, and she would win. He was sure of it. When she awoke he turned to her and said, "With your father's death your birthright demands that I now address you as the Kat. You have now been given a grave responsibility, Katerina."

"I knew I was the Kat the moment I walked into the village and saw my father's dead body. There is no need for you to remind me," Katerina said sharply.

Katerina eyed Mikhailo carefully as she swung herself onto the horse. "If I'm to ride all the way to the Khanate of Sibir, these clothes are best. They were all I could find among Stepan's outgrown clothing. A bit small but I'll manage," she said, patting at the skin-tight trousers that covered her slim haunches. "I'll need the boots for the Urals." The old man eyed her attire solemnly and nodded his shaggy head. He drew in his breath as he watched a button pop on the tight-fitting shirt, exposing a creamy expanse of flesh. He was an old man, what right did he have to voice an opinion of her clothing; and besides, he thought sourly, she wouldn't listen to anything he had to say. From this moment on she would listen to no one save herself. He shrugged his stocky shoulders as he watched her gather the reins in her strong, capable hands.

With one deft movement she had the tawny hair in a twirl and bunched on top of her head. "A safe journey to you, Mikhailo, and remember to be gentle with Grandfather." With a light wave of her hand she was off, the thick leather boots spurring the horse beneath her.

Mikhailo watched horse and rider as they rode with the wind. "And a safe journey to you, Kat," he muttered as he watched the young woman rein in the horse at the top of the rise. She looked back and then kicked the horse again. Would she return? Of course she would; she was her father's daughter, wasn't she? And when she did, she would have Mongol army with her as she had promised. No, that wasn't right— she would have men, hardened criminals, that would be trained to become an army. A chill washed over him as he pictured her return to the Carpathians with her band of criminals. What in the name of God would Katmon say when he was told? Be gentle with him, the Kat had said. "Ha!" Mikhailo snorted. How does one tell a sick, dying old man that his granddaughter would be arriving with the first snows with a band of Mongol criminals? How was he to tell him that his son was dead; all the Cossacks slaughtered because of . . . This was no time to think of what had happened or what might happen when he returned to the House of the Kat. For now, he had better get these limbs moving if he expected to make the next village by sunset.

With a last look around the gutted village, Mikhailo squared his shoulders and started down the long, dusty road. By nightfall of the following day, he might be back in the mountains. That was all he would think about on his trek.

Katerina rode the gelding as though she were in training. Her slim body was hunched over, her head almost touching the horse's mane. There was no need to spur the russet horse, for he knew he was supposed to run at breakneck speed till the reins were tightened.

When the sun was high, Katerina slowed the obedient animal and let him nibble at the sea of green grass and drink from a bubbling stream. Shielding her eyes from the strong sunlight, she refused to let her mind think of anything except the horse that was eating serenely beneath her. Her eyes raked the quietness around her as she turned, first in one direction and then in another. She had seen no sign of life since starting to keep close to the high growth, off the main roads. Again she let her eyes rake the quiet surroundings. The feeling of eyes boring into her was so strong that she pulled a knife from her belt and moved stealthily into a pile of brush and crouched down. The horse, finished with his munching, reared his head and pawed the ground. So he, too, knows something is wrong, the Kat thought. An animal? A snake perhaps? Two-legged or four-legged? she mused to herself. A slight rustle to her left and she swiveled, the knife grasped firmly in her hand. Crouching lower, she moved from the thicket to open ground and waited, her breath quickening as the gelding paced anxiously. The amber eyes glittered as she crept toward a dense thicket and lashed out with her booted foot, her knife raised high, ready for a deep plunge.

The sight that met her eyes drove her backward, a look of horror on her face. She ran till she reached a tree, which she clasped with all her being to hold her upright. Breathing raggedly, she closed her eyes, tears streaming down her cheeks. Suddenly she struck out with the knife, gouging the tree, shredding the rich brown bark. Again and again she struck out, till the ripe yellow wood beneath the bark gleamed in the bright sunlight. The blade slipped from her hands, and she crumpled to the ground. Great sobs racked her body as she flailed at the hard dirt.

Yuri rolled over and felt himself retch. Thick red blood poured from the gaping hole in his face. He thrashed about in the thicket, praying he wouldn't choke to death. A sound alerted him, and he lay still. Were they coming after him again? He prayed. He tried to move his neck, thinking he could ease the pain, but the heady scent of the wild flowers near him nauseated him and he knew he was going to be sick again. Don't think about it, think of Katerina, he told himself. Think of her beautiful face; remember how soft she felt in your arms. Remember the feel of her lips on yours. Don't think of the barbaric Tereks and don't think of the hatred they have for Katlof and his Don Cossacks. Think only of Katerina. More blood spurted from his mouth as he opened his eyes and looked up at the bright, golden sunshine. My mind must be playing tricks, he thought as Katerina's face came into his field of vision. The end must be near, and God was rewarding him by allowing him the vision of the Cossack girl. A wild animal sound escaped from his wounded throat as in the last moments of lucidity he realized she was real. He had been blessed with staying miraculously alive until he saw her once more. It was this slender hope that had pulled him through nearly a week of pain and delirium. Disbelief and horror danced in her eyes before she turned and ran.

He must not allow her to think her people had done this to him. Somehow he must let her know that it was the Tereks who had severed his tongue and fingers and left him to die when he would not tell that which he had no knowledge of. If only he could communicate that he had suffered for her love. Even if he had known the secret, he would have carried it to his grave before revealing it. Perhaps she would be able to read these things in his eyes. He prayed again; his eyes closed tightly. When he opened them, she was standing over him, tears streaming down her cheeks.

It was Yuri, but only his dark eyes were recogniz-

able. His face was a mass of dry, caked blood, and
bloody stumps remained where his hands used to be.
Deep gurgling, inhuman sounds escaped from him as
his tortured eyes pleaded with her, begged her. She
nodded slightly to show she understood. Her words
were an agonized whisper: "Did my father's men do
this?" Yuri feebly shook his head. When he closed
his eyes, her knife found its mark.

Her eyes were cold and bitter as she covered his
still body with the brush.

Viciously, she dug her heels into the horse's flanks
and galloped across the grassy turf of the endless
steppe.

For hours she raced the spirited horse. Her frenzied
mood transferred itself to the animal beneath her. She
barely noticed when she left the greenery of the
wooded steppe and emerged onto the vast wasteland of the endless eastern plain, reaching as far as
the eye could see. There was nothing before her but
virgin ground until she reached the Urals. The hot, dry
wind licked at her face as the scorching, relentless
sun beat down upon the tormented woman. She had to
get as far away as she could, as fast as she could. She
would never look back, not now, not ever. All she
knew was that she had one more score to settle.
One more reason for going to the Khan.

If her father's men hadn't tracked Yuri, who had?
Would Yuri lie to her when he was dying? Had she
correctly interpreted the slight, infinitesimal shake of
the head? Hot, scorching tears blinded her as she
continued with her wild ride.

She felt the beast beneath her gradually slow as
she wiped at her glistening eyes. A village. She drew
in the reins slowly and let the horse have its head. The
gelding entered the town at a fast trot and stopped
with no instruction from Katerina. She remained
seated.

A Cossack, who walked with a swaggering gait,
came over. "Welcome," he said gruffly.

Katerina nodded. Her voice was emotionless as she

told him of the raid and the slaughter of her people. The Cossack hetman's eyes widened as he looked at the beautiful woman dressed in a man's clothing. "How could this have happened to Vaschenko?"

Ashamedly, her eyes downcast, the words painfully forced out: "My father and his men were drunk. They never knew what happened." The Cossack shook his head sadly as she straightened up. "I'll be riding for many days, can you spare me provisions?"

The elderly Cossack nodded. He disappeared momentarily into a building, and when he reappeared he held a bulging sack in his hand.

Katerina reached down for the offered food and water, and with a curt nod of thanks was off, riding as though the devil were at her heels.

Several of the men of the village approached the hetman and looked at him expectantly.

"Let her go. She is one of us. There is the fire of hell driving her. Never have I seen that look in anyone's face. Not even in the Kat's."

"Where is she going?" one of the men asked curiously.

The hetman shrugged. "To hell, to put out that raging inferno that is consuming her." Quietly, he speculatively watched as Katerina rode out into the desolation of the steppe. Where is she going? he wondered. Every Cossack needs a tribe. She has nothing, save an aged grandfather and more old men in that mountain fortress. Finding no answers, the hetman let his mind wander to the Terek Cossacks and wondered vaguely if they were responsible for her people's deaths. He knew in his heart that as she made her way across the steppe the other Cossacks would brand her a renegade. There was no place in the Cossack heritage for a rebel, especially one who was a woman.

Chapter Six

FOR THREE DAYS Katerina rode across the parched steppe, stopping only to sleep and to water her horse. On the fourth day she crossed into the Ural Mountains. At the base of the range she stopped the gelding for a moment while she pondered her next move. If I go north where the ridge is narrow and treeless, I'll lose two days. Or I can cross through the southern section, which is ladened with trees and much wider. From here, straight across this end, I could be through the mountains in four days. She frowned. It would be easier riding across the north ridge, and would probably take only a day to cross. I could lose four days getting to and from there, and I might ride into the first snow. She decided on a southerly trek; she would risk the steep terrain and thick forest. The Kat saw a pass directly ahead and decided she would ride her horse through the passes and walk the animal over the precipitous slopes. She dug her heels into the animal's flanks and headed for the pass.

She thanked God for the clothing she wore, and especially for the thick boots. Katerina admitted to herself that she was tiring and in need of more food; her sack was almost empty. The boiled potatoes were gone, and all that was left was a small bit of cheese and a chunk of black bread that was so hard she feared she would crack her teeth on it. The food would be gone by nightfall, and then she would have nothing, with four days of travel still to go. She cursed long and loudly to the animal beneath her. "I can live on my hate for as long as it takes me to reach the Khan," she muttered as she rode through the first pass. Moments later, she was confronted with the first steep ridge. She dismounted and walked the horse alongside her. Finding release from her tension by talking to the animal, she continued with her bitter tirade. "When I find him, and I will, I'll carve his heart from his body and hang it on a spear to dry. But first," she said viciously, "I'll cut his tongue from his throat and cut off his feet. Then I'll cut out his heart." Bile rose in her throat as she remembered the feel of the knife in her hands when she plunged it into the center of Yuri's heart. "There will be no pain in my heart when I retaliate for what was done to Yuri and my people. I'll feel only sweet blessed revenge!"

As she and the horse carefully edged their way up the side of the slope, her thoughts continued. Who was it who attacked Yuri? If only I could rid myself of this anger. Was it Father's men or renegade Cossacks? Poor Yuri, why did they have to be so cruel? When I first saw him he seemed so confident, so strong, but seeing him with Father made me realize there was a weakness about him. Was it because he was so young? Was it because he was unsure of himself in dealing with us Cossacks? Even when he made love to me, our union was strong and good together, but I felt something was missing. That elusive feeling must be what I'm yearning for. What is it? I said I would find it in the eyes of the man I want forever. It wasn't in Yuri's eyes. Perhaps that is what they call love? Is that what is missing when animal lust is not enough? The combination of lust and love together must drive one to the gates of heaven. Someday I'll have this feeling; I'll not settle for anything less.

Her thoughts were so intense, she failed to see a low branch hidden by the stygian darkness. She walked straight into it and fell, her feet going out from under her. Her head reeled as she tried to get up. Was it the fall, or was she weak from too little food? Whatever, she had to stop.

She tied the reins of the horse to a tree and lay

down on the hard, rock-strewn ground. The pain of
the stones beneath her was all she needed to remind
her of where she was and where she was going.

Eventually she slept, the rocks digging into her soft
flesh. When she awoke, she could barely move, the
aching was so intense. She tried flexing her arms and
massaging her thighs, trying to work out the shooting
sensations that were so severe she had to gasp for
breath. Through clenched teeth she muttered over
and over, "I need this pain. If I'm to survive, then I
must have this pain to make me remember."

Twice more she slipped and fell as she made her
way down the mountain grade. The jagged edges of
the rock and the scrubby outgrowth of brush tore at
her thin shirt, leaving it hanging in tatters on her back.

For the next three days and nights she walked her
horse up and down the steep ridges. Whenever a pass
opened up, she rode the animal like the wind to make
up for the time-consuming climbs. They stopped only
to get water from the many streams that trickled
through the range from the many rivers up north.
Straight ahead should be the Ural River, she reasoned
as she rode through the opening of the last pass.
"The Ural River means the end of the mountains;
it's all flat riding from here," she told the horse as they
rested. "We'll pick a shallow spot in the river and be
across in no time. After we skirt the town of Troitsk
we should be on my uncle's doorstep." Reaching
down, she patted the horse on the neck. "My faithful
friend, you have brought me a long way; you have
done your job well, and I'm grateful to you. When
we get to my uncle's camp I'll make sure you are
treated to plenty of feed and water."

She pushed on, and soon the Ural River was in
sight. She did as she promised the horse and found a
suitable place to ford. Weary, almost leaning completely forward on the horse, she spurred him onward.
As they passed the town of Troitsk she found herself
too weak to go on. She stopped the horse and sat lean-

ing forward on the animal's mane. She looked and she listened.

Her eyes burned with lack of sleep and fatigue. Katerina dismounted and waited for the traveler who was approaching so he could make known his name. Barely able to stand erect, she found her vision blurring as the horseman reined in his mount and sat looking down at her in disbelief. She grasped the saddle to steady herself and tried to speak. She wet her parched lips and opened her mouth, but the words wouldn't come. Her head reeled, and she blinked, trying to bring the solitary figure into focus. "I . . . need . . ." and then she remembered nothing more.

The man dismounted, his eyes never leaving the woman on the ground. It could be a trick. What was a woman doing here in this godforsaken place? Who was she and what did she want? Why was she traveling alone? He stood a moment, his hands on slim, muscular hips, his indigo eyes speculative as he continued to gaze at the fallen girl. Impatiently he brushed at a sheaf of rich ebony hair that fell over his forehead as he dropped to his knees for a closer inspection. He frowned at the parched lips and at the dirty sunburned face. Strong, square teeth played with a full lower lip as he narrowed his eyes at the array of yellowish-purple bruises that peppered her arms and back. His mouth was a grim, tight white line as he felt his hands go to the thick, luxurious copper hair. How soft it felt. His sun-bronzed hand traced a gentle line around her soft mouth, and she stirred slightly, moaning softly.

A small dark bird fluttered among the branches of the solitary tree as Banyen Amur sat back on his haunches to wait for her to awaken. He was patient; waiting was nothing new to him. He decided that there was nothing wrong with her, save overexertion. She would awaken soon.

When Katerina woke, she was fully aware of where she was and of the man sitting watching her. She watched him for a second through her heavily fringed lashes and felt her heart begin to pound in her chest.

She watched him a moment longer as his finger trailed over a jagged scar on his cheek. The pounding in her chest lessened as she remembered how he had come by the scar. The thick lashes parted slightly as she took in his appearance. His loose blouson shirt was deep indigo, almost the color of his eyes, and he wore it tucked into form-fitting black breeches. Soft leather boots rode high on his legs, making the muscles bulge with the softness of the richly polished leather. From her position on the ground she could see the questions in his eyes, the puzzled look on his hard, high-cast face. She lowered her gaze to his long, slender, sun-darkened hands, hands that would be capable of gentling a horse or stroking a woman's flesh. Hands that would . . . did . . . Don't think about that, she cautioned herself. Her eyes still narrowed, she watched him flex his shoulders, the muscles rippling and dancing across his chest. Yuri had been a boy compared to this man. A man who had raped her and now didn't know her.

Katerina struggled to her knees and found herself within inches of him. She looked deeply, piercingly, and saw nothing but blankness. A small sigh escaped her as she was again struck by his sun-bronzed skin and the darkness of his hair. Swallowing hard, she fought to speak, hoping he would not recognize her voice. Why didn't he offer her a drink; was he going to make her ask for water? He was waiting; it was evident in the patient look on his chiseled features. He would want to know who she was and where she was going. This was Mongol territory. "I'm on my way to Sibir to see my uncle, the Khan. I have . . . traveled for . . . for many days. I must see . . . I must see him," she said in a halting voice.

"Why?" The one-word question was harsh and cold.

Katerina didn't like the sudden spark she saw flash in the agate eyes. "That's my . . . my affair."

"And now I'm making it my affair," the man said coolly, almost mockingly.

Katerina's body trembled as she tried to speak. "I

must see . . . I must see him . . . I need his . . . his help. Please, you must take me to . . . take me to him." She would have fallen with the exertion of speaking except that he gathered her close and held her upright.

"Weak-kneed females, they're all alike," he muttered to himself as he slung her over her horse's back. He gazed at what instinct told him was a supple, pliant body beneath the thick clothing. One of these days he was going to find a woman to his liking, and then he would do the honorable thing and marry her. "I detest swooning, vapid women," he said to his horse as he gathered the reins in his lean, capable hands. So she would be jostled on the ride back to camp; it wouldn't harm her. It would be interesting to see if she really was the Khan's niece. Knowing the old fox as well as he did, he could almost see him bristle with rage when he, Banyen, dumped her in his presence.

As they rode toward the Khan's camp he wondered why this female wanted to see the Khan. It made him remember when he had first come to the Khan for help, after the Russians had wiped out his family and everything they had. What would I have done— for that matter, where would I have gone—if I didn't have Khan Afstar to turn to? Where would other roads have taken me? What would I be doing this very minute and where would I be if I hadn't come to Sibir? It isn't what I want to do with the rest of my life, and it isn't something I enjoy doing right now, but I have no other choice. Someday I'll conquer all that was lost to me, and I'll command my own camp, he thought bitterly. When I have my lands back again, I'll take a wife so I can have many sons to reign after me. It won't be a question of love, just a matter of choosing someone pleasing to my eye and pleasant to be with, when I choose to be with her, and someone who will be a good mother to my children. No man will intimidate my sons.

A noise behind him caused him to turn around.

"Damn you, get me off this horse," Katerina shouted

to Banyen's back. "Untie me this moment. Wait till the Khan sees how you bring me into his camp. Untie me, you arrogant bastard!" She shouted to be heard over the horses' clattering hooves.

"In good time, all in good time," Banyen called over his shoulder, a wide grin splitting his face. "Didn't anyone ever tell you that all the good things in life come to those who are patient and quiet?"

Katerina clamped her lips tightly. He was right. All good things, like a knife between his ribs, would be worth waiting for. She seethed as she was jostled with the even gait of the horse.

She must be the Khan's niece; there was a certain resemblance that was reminiscent of the old fox. That and her strong language. She seemed to have the tongue of a viper. A match for the aging Khan. He wondered if she would be so feisty when he got her into his bed. It never occurred to him to doubt the inevitable. From the moment he set eyes on her he was relishing the feel of her naked body against his. A little on the scrawny side, but the Khan could fatten her up and then he would take his pleasure. Now what in all hell could she be traveling this terrain for, and what did she want with the Khan? He knew in his gut it would turn out to be something not to his liking.

From her undignified position on the horse, Banyen's muscular thigh and his booted foot were all she could see as she fought to keep her head from bobbing about. Her neck was stiff, and her stomach was beginning to feel queasy. "How much farther is it?" she shouted.

"I thought I told you to be quiet. When we arrive at the camp you'll be the first to know," Banyen called back.

"You insufferable—"

"Bastard." Banyen laughed. "I've been called worse."

"When I get off this horse, I'll—"

"Fall into my arms and kiss me with passion-filled lips." Banyen laughed again.

Katerina smoldered with anger. Hot, searing anger. She would kill him the first chance she got. Perhaps she could ask the Khan to put the bastard out of his misery and save her the trouble. Who was he? What did he have to do with her uncle? Of all the people in the world, why did it have to be him who found her? This was the second time he had humiliated her. There won't be a third time, she vowed silently. His day was coming, as the Cossacks said, and when it came, she would show him no mercy. She would be as brutal and as savage as he was that night on the steppe. And then she would mock and ridicule him as he was doing to her now.

The amber eyes spewed fire as she was untied from the horse. Her knees gave out, and she slumped to the ground. She never knew where she got the strength, but she reached out a slender arm and jerked with all her strength till the tall figure lost his balance and sprawled on the ground. The knife from her trousers was in her hand as she crouched low, her teeth bared in a snarl. Her burnished hair was in wild disarray, tumbling down and around her shoulders. Her arms moved effortlessly as she flicked the air with the slender blade. "I'll grant you it's not much in the way of a weapon, but it can kill if the aim is true," she panted. Banyen nodded, his dark eyes hooded as he got to his feet. "You first, Mongol," Katerina said harshly, "and don't do anything but walk. If the blade doesn't find its mark, it will cripple you, which is just as well. Now move."

Banyen's eyes narrowed till they were mere slits, but he moved. He knew he could take her if he wanted to. She was tired, and she looked hungry; she wouldn't be able to put up much of a battle. He told himself it amused him to do her bidding. He recalled another time when he also had felt amused, and he would carry the scar with him for the rest of his life. She might get one good swing at him and slice him where it counted most. For now he would do as she said. Let her think she had won . . . this time. There would be other times, and he would win then, as he always did.

Katerina squinted in the bright sunlight and was aware of her femininity for the first time since meeting the Mongol. She looked a mess; her clothing dirty and torn, her hair hanging down like a ruffian's. She knew her face was dirty, and for some reason that bothered her. She told herself she wanted to put her best effort forth for her uncle. It wasn't the Mongol; it couldn't be because of him. The other time he had ridiculed her and . . . What did he do, Katerina? she asked herself. "He raped me," she muttered through clenched teeth. He left me to die on the steppe in the freezing cold. No, a small voice defended, he covered you with the sable caftan. She moved closer to the man in front of her and jabbed at his broad back with the tip of the knife. Bright-red droplets of blood seeped through the indigo shirt, turning into blackish streaks. "I told you to move; I didn't say crawl," she said viciously as she jabbed again and then danced away from his muscular form when he turned, his arm out-stretched, to grab at her. "Oh no," she spat. "It's my turn now. If I tell you to move again, I'll throw the knife, I won't just play with it. Now *walk*."

Banyen's jaw tightened as he turned to do her bidding. Damnable woman, who did she think she was talking to? Maybe he should tell her who he was. He negated the idea, knowing she would snigger and certainly never would be impressed.

Banyen stopped and pointed with his arm. "The Khan's tent," he said, bowing low with a flourish.

Katerina couldn't believe her eyes. Never before had she seen anything like this. This flat wasteland, fit only for the sheep and goats that grazed on it, was like the steppe—it went on endlessly. The yurts that stood upon flatland created an illusion of a fantasy-land to Katerina. No matter in which direction she looked, there stood row upon row of ten-foot-tall tents. To Katerina they looked like a forest of trees that had been chopped off on top. The dwellings were cov-ered with felt pieces of all descriptions and sizes, each home reflecting the tastes of its owner. The grandest of all, of course, were the three yurts that belonged to her uncle. They were covered with a high-quality felt, thicker and heavier than the rest. They also were highly decorated on the outside. She wasn't sure whether she had been here before or not when she was a child; she couldn't remember. She thought it strange for men to live out in the open like this. The Cossacks lived out in the open, too, but they had their sturdy huts to go into at night. The yurts looked so fragile, so vulnerable. She realized that on land as flat as this, as on the steppe, someone could easily be seen approaching the camp. At least, she thought, the steppe has flowers, trees, and grass on it. Other than the small tufts of grass that the livestock fed on, this camp was nothing but desert wasteland. The heat in the dead of summer must be unbearable.

She took in all the sights as she carefully watched Banyen out of the corner of her eye. He reached forward to open the closed flap of the yurt for her, but she didn't move.

"You first, Mongol, and no tricks. I am who I say I am, remember that," Katerina said, brandishing the thin blade in his general direction.

Banyen grinned. "Do you want me to announce you or would you rather go in unannounced and have your head sliced from your shoulders? If I'm to announce you, then I should know your name. We strive for formality here in camp," he said, bowing low again.

"You missed your calling, whatever it was. You make an excellent buffoon," Katerina snapped. "Tell my uncle Katerina Vaschenko is here to see him."

Banyen entered the tent and strode over to the Khan, who reclined against a pile of elaborately embroidered cushions. "While riding patrol I came across a female bent on traveling here to the camp to see you. She's weak from hunger, and not too steady on her feet. But that doesn't seem to interfere with her tongue; it's like a viper. She already left me a me-

mento," he said, turning for the Khan's inspection. "She says her name is Katerina Vaschenko."

The Khan rose awkwardly from his comfortable position in his nest of cushions. "Katerina!" His voice was full of shock. "And you say she is alone. Fetch her to me immediately, Banyen! Why did you make her stand outside like a beggar? Fetch her this moment," he said imperiously. Banyen's mouth tightened, but he lifted the flap from the tent and motioned to Katerina to enter.

At the sight of her uncle's dear face Katerina felt tears sting her eyes. She ran to him as she had when she was a child. When he gathered her close, the tears coursed down her cheeks. The Khan, embarrassed at her display of affection in front of Banyen, motioned to him to leave his tent.

"Tell me, child, what is it? What brings you here to my camp? Come, sit here with me and tell me what is troubling you."

Gulping back her sobs, Katerina wiped at her tear-filled eyes. "They're dead. They're all dead. Grandfather himself waits to go to his Maker. Only Mikhailo, Grandfather, and a few of the others are left in the mountains. All of the horses are gone. All of them."

"But I don't understand. Are you telling me all the Cossacks from the village are gone, dead?" he asked in an outraged voice.

Katerina nodded tremulously. "A raiding party. It happened the night before we were to leave for the mountains. I was away from the camp when it happened. When I got back they had all been killed and the horses were gone. I didn't know what to do. Mikhailo came down from the mountains when we didn't arrive on schedule and helped me bury the dead. I came here because I didn't know what else to do. Will you help me?"

"What can I do for you?" he asked quietly as the enormity of what she had said dawned on him. "You have only to ask, but I don't know what assistance I

can offer. Do you want a patrol of my soldiers to help
you find the marauders?"

"More than a patrol, Uncle, much more. Before I
came here I discussed the matter with Mikhailo. In all
truth, he was against my plan, but I managed to convince him it would work. I told him my uncle, the
Khan, would help me. You must help me," she
pleaded. "I have nowhere else to turn." Before she
could lose her courage, Katerina continued, "I want
the men from your stockades, all of them. I want to
take them back to the mountains with me and train
them to be Cossacks. Please, Uncle, don't look at me
as if I'd lost my mind. It will work, I know it will. Give
me the men that have no hope, the men who are
destined for death. Those are the men I want. The
more vicious, the more bloodthirsty, the better. I have
to get the horses back. I can't do it alone. I'll work
with them through the long winter, and in the spring
we'll leave the mountains and we'll find the Cosars.
It's the only way."

The Khan narrowed his oblique eyes as he listened
to his niece plead with him. He loved her and would
help in any way he could so long as he benefited in
some way, he told himself. It had been a long time
since he had seen hate such as hers. He asked himself
where he had seen such a look. Of course—in
Banyen's eyes the day he was brought to the camp.
He rubbed his hands through his coarse black hair,
making it stand out in tufts about his round head, as
he continued to listen to her plead her cause. The
coal-black eyes were shrewd, watchful, and ever speculative. Short, stubby fingers stroked an undefined chin
as he interjected a word from time to time.

"It will work, Uncle, I know it will," Katerina said
vehemently.

"These men from the stockade are the dregs of the
earth. The first chance they get, they'll kill you. What
chance will you, a woman, have against them?"

"I'm a Cossack, or did you forget, Uncle? If there's
any killing to be done, it will be me who does it, not

your prisoners. If you believe nothing else, believe that."

"Listen to me, little one, these men, these prisoners, are due to go to their death shortly. An offer such as you make will mean that they will leave no stone unturned to gain their freedom. Once you set out with them, that will be their only objective. Why do you think they will go with you and train through the long, cold winter and then fight for your cause? This is foolish woman-talk. It will never work."

"I'm telling you it will work. I'll take them, shackled in irons, through the Urals, across the steppe, and up to the mountains. The snows are due soon. Where could they go? There's nothing for them on the outside. They have a chance to regain their dignity and fight for something worthwhile. I'll even agree to pay them so afterward they can begin a new life. As you know, Uncle, the Cosars have bequeathed my family a fortune in gold. If I lived a thousand years I could never hope to spend the fortune that rests in the House of the Kat. I'll pay anything, do anything, to succeed. They have a choice—a new life with me or death at the hands of your men. Which do you think they'll accept?"

Katerina felt a lump settle in the pit of her stomach. She wasn't convincing him. "Very well, Uncle, what is it you wish to bargain for in return for your help?" she asked shrewdly.

The Khan laughed. "You know me well, little one. There is one small request you can grant me. A colt and a filly from Whitefire," he said slyly.

"You know it's forbidden, Uncle. However, I see you will accept nothing less. You drive a hard bargain, but one I'll accept, only because I'm desperate."

"Forbidden by whom? You just told me Volin was wiped out. You're the leader now, the decision is yours alone. Let's be sure we both understand the bargain we're making," the Khan said, standing up, his scarlet shirt and shiny black trousers bright against the dimness of the yurt.

"I understand the bargain," Katerina said coolly. "You also have my word: when the first wild flower sprouts on the frozen banks of the Dnieper in the spring, a new breed of Cossack will be born," she said grimly, her amber eyes flashing.

The Khan looked deeply into her eyes and believed her implicitly. If anyone could do it, she could.

"Sit down, Katerina, we'll have some food and drink. There is much we must discuss." He clapped his pudgy hands, and an old serving woman entered the tent. His tone was husky and guttural when he gave his orders. The old hag looked at Katerina with suspicion as she scurried away to do the Khan's bidding.

Katerina settled herself on the pile of fox and mink furs. "I see that you surround yourself with all the trappings of wealth," she said, looking around at the brightly colored silken hangings. "And a wooden floor," she said snidely. "Not to mention a blanket of sable that stretches from one end of the yurt to the other." She noted that a small fire glowed in the center of the yurt, banked and ready to flare with a shovel of sheep dung.

The old Khan waved his pudgy arms around his yurt and smiled. "It befits my simple station in life. True, a little lavish compared to the other yurts, but . . . comfortable. The season has been excellent for trading the hides and wool from the sheep."

"Your treasury is . . . ample, is that what you're saying?"

"Very much so. I have no complaints. Now tell me, what does an old man like myself need with wealth? I like this simple life and the few little luxuries I allow myself. I'm content. Since you have just agreed to the filly and colt from Whitefire, my happiness is unsurpassed."

Katerina flinched. No matter what she promised, she knew in her heart that she would find a way to get out of the bargain. There was no way he would get the offspring except over her dead body. She forced her face to blankness as she poked at the fire with iron tongs.

Her amber eyes were sleepy, catlike, and the Khan felt uneasy, a strange feeling creeping in and around his stomach. By now she should have been married, with babies sucking at her breasts. Indulgent fathers! he snorted to himself.

"Let us suppose that I agree to what you ask, and let us further agree that you are amenable to bestowing a colt and filly upon me for my generosity, what is your ultimate goal once you train my prisoners for whatever it is you have in mind?"

"I thought it was already agreed upon."

"Ah, Katerina, one should never assume anything until it is a fact—will you never learn? Your father did you no favors by allowing you to be trained with his men. No, it's not definite. Tell me, an old man who is in his failing years, what exactly are your plans? Spare me all the nonessentials. I'm also bearing in mind something Katlof once told me: a Cossack is born a Cossack, there is no in-between."

Katerina clenched her teeth, a bitter, cold look in her eyes. The light breeze that wafted through the tent opening caused the silken hangings to flutter and sway, creating slight rustling noises, a restful sound that was making her drowsy. "I need the men to get the Cosars back. I must have trained men who will serve under me and do as I command them. I'll raid and plunder every village from here to Moscow to get back what is mine. This is the only way I can do it. You must help me, I beg you on my mother's life! I can train the men. I'll make Cossacks out of them or die trying. Believe me, Uncle, I will succeed. If what my father told me was true, your own armies could stand some training. When we rode into your camp it was a sorry sight that greeted me. How did your armies deteriorate so? How did you allow it to happen? Tell me, what's gone wrong?"

The Khan shrugged his ample shoulders as he settled himself more comfortably by the banked fire.

"Men get tired of fighting and want to return to their families. They scatter and come back when they have no more use for their relatives. What you say is true. We've grown fat and complacent." He laughed, patting his ample girth. "For now, there is nothing to fight. Only a foolish man leads men to war for the sake of war. I am not a foolish man. In the ways of women, perhaps," he said, a roguish twinkle in his dark eyes. "Very well, I agree, but with one other condition. I'll send fifty of my best and youngest men along with Prince Banyen. If you are so determined to train the prisoners, then you can give my men some training also. Upon their return in the spring, they will train others. Do you agree to this stipulation?"

The amber eyes flashed warningly. "And this Prince Banyen, is he the man that brought me here?" The Khan nodded. "Tell me," she asked softly, "who is to be in charge of these men of yours? If I agree, then it must be me. I'll not take orders from that . . . that . . . insufferable, that arrogant . . . bastard. Those, Uncle, are my terms. Be sure that your prince understands this, for I have no liking for him and I would just as soon stick a knife through his ribs as look at him."

The Khan's eyes were outraged at her words. "What did he do to you? Tell me and I'll have him whipped. Did he . . . did he?"

"No, Uncle, he didn't. I have no liking for him, it's as simple as that. Before the end of winter one of us will kill the other. I plan to be alive when the snows melt, so be warned. It's my way or not at all. This is your golden opportunity, Uncle," she said in a low, rich voice, hoping to sway him to her way of thinking. "My visit here and my request will serve a twofold purpose. You can rebuild your armies with my help, and you will be the only man in all of Russia that can boast he has foals from Whitefire. A colt that will grow to be a stallion, not a gelding. Think about it, Uncle, before you decide."

"Banyen will be like a devil if I agree to your terms. He has no love for women." He shook his head and laughed. "It will do him good. Perhaps when the snow melts you will be enamored of each other."

"Don't plan on it, Uncle. I've decided the man hasn't been born yet that will be good enough for me, so put that thought from your mind."

"Strange that you should say that." The Khan laughed wickedly. "That's exactly what Banyen said. He said there wasn't a woman in the world that was fitting to share his name."

"Is that what he said?" Katerina snapped.

"As a matter of fact, those were my exact words," Banyen said, entering the tent. "Would you like me to repeat them for your benefit?" His expression mocked her as she looked up at him.

Katerina laughed, a rich, full laugh that seemed to circle the yurt and come to settle around him. The hackles on the back of his neck seemed to rise and then fall against his sun-darkened throat.

"Sit down, Banyen, join us in a light repast. I've just committed you to a mission."

Katerina watched as the agate eyes turned the color of deep indigo at the Khan's words. His muscular body stiffened, and the bronze hands were clenched into fists at his side. His mouth was grim and tight as he waited expectantly for the words he knew would not be to his liking.

"First, allow me to introduce you to my niece, Katerina Vaschenko. She's come here to me for help, and I've agreed to do as she asks in return for two very small favors. You and fifty of our best and youngest men, along with prisoners of her choosing from the stockade, will accompany her back to the Carpathians, where you will all undergo extensive Cossack training. In the spring you will return here with our men, who will train the others. The prisoners will remain in the Carpathians with my niece, who will then . . . That isn't important," he said suddenly. "My niece will be in charge, is that understood?"

"And if I refuse?" Banyen demanded curtly.

"You won't," the Khan said calmly. "You're too good a soldier to disobey an order. If you do, you know the consequences. It's my command, Banyen, and one I won't repeat. My dear," he said as an afterthought, "allow me to present Prince Banyen."

"Nobility and titles don't impress me," Katerina said aloofly. "It's what's inside a man that counts, and you, Prince Banyen, are sadly lacking. It will be interesting to see how you fare in the mountains. Very interesting indeed." She laughed again as she watched his dark hand reach up to touch the scar on his cheek. His dark eyes were murderous as he stalked from the tent, his back straight and stiff.

Katerina's voice was calm, yet the Khan sensed a tone of danger in her softly spoken words. "Who is Prince Banyen? How is it he commands this ragamuffin parcel of men you call an army?"

The Khan sighed wearily. "Kindness, Katerina. Please, kinder words when you speak of my army. We'll rise again as we did before, for this is but a momentary relapse. I have placed all my faith in Banyen to rebuild my army and make them the noble fighters of yesteryear. Banyen's father was the prince of a league, controlling many banners and baks. Czar Ivan, in one of his mad rages, sent his soldiers out, and the Khanate of Kazan was burned to the ground. As a boy, he wandered until he came to Astrakhan, where he stayed until the Khan surrendered, and then he ran away. For years he lived with whoever would have him, until one day my men found him wandering near the Urals, alone and dazed, near death. They brought him here, and to this day I still wonder how he survived. If Kazan flourished, one day Banyen would have been the next Khan, but his entire family was slaughtered and everything lost. He'll do as I say, because he owes me his life, and he needs my help to avenge his people. A brilliant strategist, he's not entirely without compassion. One day he may let you see that side of him. Now he's bitter and angry and has little patience,

but that will change. What I'm saying is not to push
him too far or you may rue the day you did. In open
combat he has no equal, and on horseback the animal
and man are one." He laughed. "And he devours
women the way I consume food. Later, I don't wish to
hear you say you weren't warned. Enough of this,
where is that infernal crone with our meal?" he complained loudly, just as the old servant entered the
yurt. Carefully she placed the platters of roast lamb
and the decanter of wine near the fire, and slowly
backed away.

Katerina drank deeply from the decanter and wiped
her mouth with the back of her hand. She bit into a
plump piece of lamb, and didn't stop till every morsel
of meat was gone from the bone.

"Rest, little one. I have business outside the yurt.
No one will bother you. Sleep," he said fondly as he
laid a gentle hand on her coppery hair.

Katerina needed no further urging. She cradled her
head on her arm and was asleep instantly on the sable
carpet.

Khan Afstar stood with his hands posed on his ample hips, waiting for Banyen to walk toward him. He
didn't like the arrogant gait nor the murderous look in
the young prince's eyes. He schooled his own face to
impassiveness as he looked around the camp at the
multitude of tents that dotted the landscape. Far to the
right of the giant compound, his entire army was garrisoned. Even from where he stood, shading his eyes
from the brilliant sun, he could see that the yurts were
sadly in need of repair. Men roamed about as if they
had no destination in mind. Men should be busy or
they grew fat and soft. What was Banyen thinking of
to let them behave in so aimless a fashion? "What's the
meaning of this?" he demanded, pointing toward the
garrison.

"The men are tired. I gave them a few hours of respite to do as they wished. Not everything can be done
in a matter of a few days. It was you yourself who told

me this. I can't make staunch fighting men overnight
from derelicts who have grown sodden with wine and
rich, spicy food. If they drill too long, they collapse.
All things in good time. When the time comes to storm
Moscow, they'll be ready—you have my word."

"I see by the harsh look on your face you have no
liking for my orders. I have my reasons, Banyen. This
may be my one and only chance to ferret out the
Whitefire secret. I want you to go with Katerina under
the guise of commander of my men. What I want you
to do is gain the secret. I don't care how you do it, just
do it. I have the utmost faith in your abilities. Make
yourself available to my niece. Woo her if necessary,
but don't come back without the answer."

The scar on Banyen's cheek began to throb with the
hard set of his jaw. "And that means another delay.
Very well, I always repay my debts, and this is one
that will be paid first. I am well aware that I owe you
my life. For that I'll do your bidding . . . this time.
But when I return from the Carpathians I'll take matters in my own hands. Perhaps you forget how you
promised me the aid of your men if I took over the
training of your armies. A twofold arrangement, you
said. I'll never forget why I'm a paid soldier in this
sorry excuse for an army. It would be simpler to just
buy your army."

The Khan shook his head. "When will you young
people learn that all things are gained by patience and
timing? Revenge will be yours, but when I deem the
moment is right, and that will be when we lead every
Mongol in Sibir and surrounding territories through the
streets of Moscow. Vengeance will be that much
sweeter, take my word for it."

"If it's the last thing I do before I die, I swear to you
my sword will taste Ivan's blood."

The Khan motioned to Banyen to sit beside him on
a tufted sheepskin pillow. "Sit with me, here under this
canopy, so we can talk. The sun will go down soon,
and the day will get cooler. It's a pleasant hour of the
day to talk and have some wine. Besides, my young

prince, I want to know more about your reasons for wanting Ivan's blood. When you first came to my camp you told me your family was slaughtered and all your father's territories taken away. I heard of the attack, but the details have never been told to me. Do you wish to speak about it now? I never urged you before because, as I just told you, I'm a man who selects his moments wisely, Banyen. You will see how it serves you and how much sweeter the fruits of victory. Now, angry one, tell me what happened to your people," the Khan urged Banyen.

"Why should you be interested?" Banyen questioned sarcastically. "You got my hide tied to a bargain, and I'm without a piece of gold. At one time I could have bought anything, including your so-called army. I don't understand your interest, since my story can be of no value to you."

"Allow me to be the judge. I'm interested for many reasons. I always make a point of being informed of all battles and attacks, it teaches me the ways of the enemy. As for my second reason, if you haven't realized it by now, then you shall. All Mongols are brothers, and when one Mongol gets killed it is a brother that is killed. I wish to retaliate for that injustice. Banyen, if you can put your anger aside for a moment, I'm interested in the attack on Kazan. I would imagine you were quite young when it happened—can you remember?"

Before Afstar could say another word, Banyen raged, "Can I remember? A stupid question! If you saw your mother and father slaughtered, would you forget it? Would you, even though you were only six years old? Spared because some distant Russian forefather let you be born with a different color of eyes than the others," he roared at the Khan.

"No, I wouldn't. Calm yourself, Banyen, tell me how it happened. Perhaps if you talk about it, it will ease the pain a bit. I'm not saying you should forget, or that you could. I'm only suggesting that if you talk about it, it might help."

"It won't help, as I have no wish to discuss it now. End it, Afstar."

"Your trouble lies within you. You are too full of hate and vengeance to think clearly. After a winter in the mountains with the girl, your mind might clear enough for you to realize that emotions must be put aside, for one to think and plan attacks with care," the Khan instructed the wrath-filled prince.

"Speaking of the mountains and my niece, have you mulled over which of the young men you'll take with you? I suggest you choose healthy young men, if there are any, for the winter is harsh in the Carpathians. If the snow starts while you're on your way, half the journey will be made through knee-deep snow."

"When do we leave?" Banyen asked coldly.

The Khan shrugged. "A day or two, perhaps three. My niece needs to regain her strength before she starts out on that arduous trek through the Urals. Patience, Banyen."

Soft gray twilight cast the high-domed yurts into an endless expanse of bubbles. To Banyen's narrowed eyes, it was home, the only home he had known since the loss of his family and estates. He hated the squalor, the undisciplined men in their slovenly clothing, and their rough, crude manners. How was he to make a marching army from such degradation? Perhaps if morale were higher, or some sort of incentive offered, he might have a better chance of succeeding. His chest constricted at what he imagined would happen with his first charge into battle. The men would drop like flies or run with fear. They weren't soldiers, they were inexperienced youngsters. He had to try—what else could he do? He needed the Khan and the Khan's men. He shrugged; there was no point in torturing himself with thoughts such as these. His eyes traveled to the Khan's yurt and the sleeping girl. He frowned. She reminded him of someone. While he might agree to the Khan's terms, that was all he'd agree to. Once in the mountains, he would do as he damn well pleased.

Never would he take orders from a woman, even a beautiful woman. He would conquer her first.

A vision of her crouched low, her teeth bared, the knife thrust in front of her, made him draw in his breath. A formidable enemy, no doubt about that, but he was a man and she a mere woman. He allowed his mind to drift, envisioning her in a silk gown, her hair loose upon her bare shoulders. Of course, he smirked, her eyes would be filled with desire and her mouth would tremble for the feel of his lips. Perhaps this time the Khan was right, and patience was what was needed. He could be as patient as the next man, but when his patience was at an end, it would end.

Chapter Seven

THE DREARY FALL SEASON took its toll on the Czar's patience as he grew bored with the endless array of dinners and affairs. Nothing pleased him, not even his personally selected harem of beauties, who tried to bewitch and tantalize him. "I need something different to entertain me, I grow weary with dinners and women," he wailed. "Does anyone have a new idea for their Czar, something to excite me?" he questioned his gathered nobles.

The room was silent. Suddenly a quivering voice at the rear of the room was heard: "My Czar, the Oprichniks have taken many traitors as prisoners. Perhaps we could have them entertain you, under your supervision, of course."

"Yes, a splendid idea. I will have them perform for me and my subjects. Who is it that speaks? I order him to step forward."

A young nobleman slowly made his way through the crowd toward Ivan. Trying to control his trembling limbs, he bowed graciously before the Czar. "I am the person you seek, Czar Ivan. I pray I have not offended you with my outburst," he said meekly.

"On the contrary, young man, stand before me and let me look at you. You're close to the age of my eldest son, and I would have been proud of him had he made such a joyful suggestion." Ivan beamed. "On Saturday next we will have a mass execution at the Place of the Skulls in Red Square. I personally appoint you to announce this news to the people of Moscow. I want Red Square filled to capacity with my subjects. It is my wish that every citizen attend; if they refuse, they will join the traitors at the chopping block. Be off with you and prepare your announcements, for you have but a week. If the square is filled to my satisfaction, when we return to the palace I will have you dubbed a lord."

"Thank you, my Czar," the young man mumbled, making a low, sweeping bow. "I will not fail you, you have my word."

The days following the Czar's announcement were busy ones in the Kremlin. Ivan was everywhere, joyfully directing the workmen who labored day and night erecting intricate instruments of torture and execution: large pans for frying the victims, huge caldrons of water suspended over faggots, ropes that would cut a body in two when tightened, bear cages, iron claws, pincers, and the gallows.

The day of the execution arrived. When Ivan rode into the square, accompanied by his guards, he was appalled by the lack of spectators, and immediately called for his guards to produce the young nobleman. When the young man appeared before Ivan, fearing for his life, the Czar spoke. "You were instructed to fill this square to capacity and I can count the number of people on one hand. Where is everyone?" he roared.

"My Czar, I did as you directed and made known this day to every citizen. They were told to attend.

However, if I may, my Czar—I have heard talk that the citizenry is fearful of your wrath. Forgive me, Czar Ivan."

"If what you say is true, then we must set the matter straight. Come, you will ride with me through the city while I tell the people they have naught to fear."

As they rode Ivan shouted to the populace in a loud ringing voice, "Good people, come! There is nothing to fear, no harm will touch you, I promise! My word as Czar Ivan!"

Assured by the Czar's words, the people straggled into Red Square.

As the citizenry began to move about, the Czar rose majestically and spoke: "All traitors to death!"

A thunderous roar of approval rose from the crowd, with cries of "Long live the Czar!" The young nobleman smiled contentedly.

Three hundred prisoners, their chains clanking behind them, were led into the square, the majority of them half dead from previous torturing. To win his people over, Ivan dramatically showed mercy to several of the traitors by freeing them, and granted a few others the right to exile.

For the most-hated enemies of the state, Ivan saved the greatest and most extreme torture. One boyar was hung by his feet and cut into pieces. A trusted treasurer was placed in iced water and then in boiling water repeatedly, until his skin peeled off him like an eel, while Ivan laughed in delight.

As the executions continued throughout the day, Ivan's eyes rolled in ecstasy over the pain and blood of the traitors. At sundown Ivan and his son rode to the home of a dead nobleman, where he ordered the man's widow tortured until she told where their family treasure was hidden. Ivan's son then ravished her, giving her fifteen-year-old daughter to the chief guard. Throughout the long night Ivan and his son rode to the houses of the executed nobles and seized their treasure. The wives and daughters of the dead men were given to his guards, who delighted in violating them. Wearied from the ride, Ivan then ordered eighty widows of executed nobles drowned.

For days thereafter, to add to the disgrace of the traitors, Ivan allowed their mutilated bodies to lie rotting in the square. Hungry dogs feasted on their flesh as passing citizens spat contemptuously on them. Finally the Czar ordered his men to rid the square of the foul-smelling bodies.

In a remorseful mood, feeling sorrow for the souls of the traitors, Ivan spent hours in church, praying for their souls, and donated large sums of money to the holy institution. Tiring of prayers, he then went to Alexandrov, where he took to his bed pleading exhaustion.

His days of penance over, Ivan returned in splendor to Moscow, dressed in his finest regal attire. Parading into Red Square with his guards forming columns on either side of him, he rode his stallion up the steps of Terem Palace, directly into the dining hall. Clapping his hands, he shouted, "Tonight I want a feast commemorating my return. Let the cooks prepare the finest in delicacies for my guests. Invite by my special request beggars, thieves, whores, and murderers. Bring them into the palace and have the servants dress them in finery. Inform the boyars they must give their finest clothing to these people, by my order. I want them dressed and seated an hour after dark, at which time we will dine." His announcement finished, Ivan rode his horse down the marble corridors to his bedchamber and dismounted, leaving the horse in the hallway.

That evening Ivan dined among the dregs of Moscow society. "For entertainment tonight I have a surprise for all my noble guests. I have summoned the wives of the boyars to dance for us. Ladies and gentlemen, please direct your attention to the middle of the hall," he cackled, pointing a bony finger in front of him.

Dressed in beautiful gauzy material in an array of

colors, the boyars' wives minced their way around the hall, trying to cover their bodies with their hands and arms. The ladies, aware that the gauze hid nothing, only accentuating their breasts and thighs, danced with their eyes downcast as the male guests leered at them. Thoughts of tasting their delicious femininity was more than most of them could bear. They shouted obscene remarks to the women as they drank and ate like the lowlife they were. Ivan delighted in every minute of it. "These are my people!" he shouted.

With a wave of his hand he dismissed the dancing women, to groans of dismay. "Gentlemen, noblemen, please, I have more to dazzle your eyes. Allow me to present my witches and magicians to mystify you. They will perform feats never before seen by man. Bring on the witches and magicians," he commanded.

At the height of the magic show, his personal messenger darted into the hall. "My Czar, I beg your pardon, but I've come a long way and have news for you."

"You dare intrude during the performance!" Ivan bellowed. "Your news had better be worthy of this interruption. What is it? Tell me at once!"

The messenger rushed forward. "When I stopped in Kiev I was told to deliver this to you, my Czar."

Ivan's eyes scanned the parchment. A loud rancorous laugh echoed above the din as Ivan doubled over in mirth. "I can't believe that God is this good to me. This announcement is the prize that makes my evening complete. Ladies and nobles," he said, grinning sadistically, "let it be known to one and all that Yuri Zhuk, my noble emissary, is dead." He crushed the parchment as convulsions of laughter rocked him. "My emissary was found in a clump of bushes outside Volin, with his tongue and fingers missing. Delightful!" He drooled, his drunken eyes rolling in his twisted face. "Enough, enough of this, back to the witches. Where are my witches? Continue, I order you to continue!" he roared. "Tomorrow I must . . . no, not tomorrow, but soon, I must send for Halya and tell her this delightful news."

On Ivan's orders, everyone drank, feasted, and fornicated throughout the night. Czar Ivan was once again delighting in the affairs of state.

Chapter Eight

KATERINA WOKE ONCE, shortly after midnight. She stirred restlessly and settled her bruised body more comfortably on the plush carpet. Within seconds she was asleep again, this time deeply and totally, a dark-haired man stalking her through snow. She moaned while she dreamed, as she slipped and fell time and again in her struggles to get away from the man bent on capturing her. As always, the moment his hands were within reach of her she woke, her body drenched with perspiration, her eyes wild and haunted, a scream on her lips. She lay back, exhausted, as tears welled in the luminous amber eyes and flowed down her satiny cheeks. One day soon it would be her turn. When that day came she would sleep again, as when she was a child, peacefully and happily. Slowly, as if they had a will of their own, the thick heavy lashes lowered, and she was again asleep, her cheek pressed into the richness of the carpet.

The Khan stood over his sleeping niece, willing her to wake. As if she sensed his presence, the doe eyes opened and she stared up at him, frowning, trying to remember where she was. Recognition of her uncle and the warm closeness of the yurt reminded her, and she struggled to her feet.

"If you have a change of clothing for me I would be

grateful, and I would also like a bath if it's at all possible."

The Khan nodded as he tossed her a vivid striped cotton shirt. "The yurt next to this one has bathwater and a light breakfast waiting. When you've finished, join me and Prince Banyen by the open fire in the center of the compound."

The slim girl worked at her shoulders, trying to loosen the tension and the tightness that had settled over her in sleep. She rubbed at her arms and thighs, trying unsuccessfully to ease the stiffness in her muscles. Perhaps the bath will help, she told herself as she left the tent in search of food and the luxury of warm water.

Not wanting to waste time, she removed her filthy clothing and slid down into the oil-scented water with a thick wedge of goat cheese and a chunk of bread. This was indeed a wonder. Now where did the Khan get scented oil? She suppressed a wicked smile at what she imagined was his favorite pastime.

She ate the cheese ferociously and chewed at the bread as if she hadn't eaten in days. Later she would gorge herself at the noon meal. For now, she needed her wits about her for the coming hours she would spend with the Khan and Prince Banyen. Just the thought of his name and she trembled. The gold-tinted eyes darkened to newly minted copper as she reached for a length of toweling. She stepped from the round tub onto a deerskin. The moment her bare foot touched the fur she stumbled, and would have fallen if she hadn't reached out to grasp the rim of the tub. Don't think about him, she cautioned herself as she pulled on the trousers Stepan had outgrown. The brilliant shirt was tight and felt confining. Her breasts strained against the thin fabric as she tucked the end into the band of the trousers. She longed for a mirror to see the condition of her hair. Sighing, she gathered it into a knot and tied it back with a loose strand of hair from the side of her head. What did she care what she looked like? She was clean, and that was all that mattered.

When Katerina left the bathing yurt she shaded her eyes against the brilliant sun. She looked around to get her bearings and was surprised to see people moving about, their colorful garb dazzling in the shimmering light. They moved slowly, intent on what they were about. Children ran and played, laughing boisterously as they scampered over piled twigs and strewn rock piles. She was surprised when she received no more than a passing glance from the playful children and busy women. She frowned. Where were the men? Katerina squinted against the glare of the sun and saw that at the very outer perimeter of the compound men were drilling with weapons. Horses whickered softly as men climbed onto their backs to ready themselves for a charge. She was puzzled. If the Khan's wealth was as great as she had been led to believe, why was he bothering with this ragtag group of soldiers? Money could buy him a fit and ready army. He was up to something. And whatever it was, it had something to do with her, she knew it just as sure as she knew Prince Banyen had . . .

Skirting the playful children, Katerina picked her way among the yurts, avoiding the chattering women who were busy washing and cooking outdoors. She nodded slightly to the prince and touched her uncle fondly on the arm to show she was ready for whatever it was he had planned. Banyen's eyes raked her as she skipped along to keep up with his long-legged stride. She said nothing, knowing the Khan preferred that she remain quiet. So—he was taking her to the stockade to show her the prisoners. She was shocked but schooled her face to reveal nothing. Never had she seen or smelled such . . . such . . . Words failed her.

"Breathe through your mouth," Banyen suggested.

The stockade ran the entire width of the encampment. It consisted of poles hewn from the nearby forest. The poles, seven feet tall, were crisscrossed by rough-hewn planks. Overhead, animal hides were laced tightly across the tops of the structure to ward off the hot, scorching sun and biting wind, and the snows of winter. Instinctively she knew that in the summer the bodies of the prisoners baked, burned, shriveled, and stank. In the winter they would shake with the cold and turn blue from frostbite. The lucky ones would survive; the rest would freeze and die.

The skin on the men was blistered from the heat, and full of sores. Many were sick and dying. She knew the older men would never live through the winter. Ringlets of dried blood formed clusters around their wrists and ankles where the shackles rubbed the skin.

"Do you wonder why so many prisoners are penned like animals in so small an area? The Khan can only spare a few men for guard duty. You can see it takes at least twenty men to surround and maintain a constant guard. They are relieved of duty three times a day, so sixty men a day are involved in guarding prisoners when they should be doing other things," Banyen said gruffly.

"Why don't you put them to work? Why are they standing so close together? I don't understand," Katerina asked softly.

"Is this what you want, Katerina?" the Khan asked. "Do you still wish my help? There is a tribal meeting I must attend. I'll join you at the noon meal. Be sure, little one, that you know what you are doing," he said, patting her arm.

"I see there are still many questions in your eyes," Banyen observed.

Outraged, Katerina took a deep breath. "I've seen animals treated better. This is . . . this is inhuman. How can one human being treat another in such a manner? They live and breathe as you and I do."

Banyen ignored her words. "As the prisoners die, we move in the outer poles. They are in no condition to attempt escape, not even the healthiest, believe me. If they were fortunate enough to escape, they would be killed instantly.

"It would not be advisable to see them when they are fed the watered-down mush. They fight and kill to get their ration, many times knocking their bowl over in a desperate attempt to get more. They kill to be chosen for work, and they kill for food. They think nothing of slipping their shackled arms around each other's necks and strangling one another for more food. We don't stop them, it's one less mouth to feed. It's called survival," Banyen said coldly. Women! Such outrage over suffering, and yet she recovers quickly enough, he thought. Women always wore two faces. Who was she really concerned for? Was it for his benefit, or did she truly feel sympathy for the prisoners? He admitted he didn't know, and he didn't give a damn.

"Yes, I know the meaning of the word," Katerina said curtly. She knew the Mongols hated to take prisoners, and when they did they were known to be very cruel, but she had never realized just how much so until now. "What did these men do? What crimes have they committed?"

Banyen stepped forward, and with the tip of his saber he pointed at a man and ordered him to speak to the lady. "Tell her why you're shackled and in the stockade."

"Murder."

"And you, what was your crime?"

"I stole horses."

"You?"

"I was caught raiding a village."

"You?"

"Murder."

"Murder."

"Is the punishment the same for all crimes?" Katerina demanded. "The punishment should befit the crime. Tell me, Prince, what is the punishment for raping a woman? Or is it not considered a crime?"

Banyen grinned. "It's no crime. However, we have one here who not only raped a woman, he also killed her. Kostya," he shouted, "step forward."

Katerina couldn't help herself. She stepped near the man and said in a low voice, "Are you here because you raped a woman, or because you killed her? In your mind, what are you being punished for?"

He was tall and fair-haired, with the bluest eyes Katerina had ever seen. His golden beard glistened in the bright sun. His eyes appeared puzzled, but he answered readily enough. "I didn't rape the woman, she came to me willingly. Men have no need to rape, only animals and savages do that. Women are plentiful and willing to fall into a man's arms. While I slept she tried to steal my pouch of coins. I woke and we struggled. She fell and hit her head on a boulder and died. That is why I'm here."

"That's what he says. The girl's father tells another story," Banyen said coolly, stung by the prisoner's words.

"He goes with me," Katerina said softly.

Deep murmurings came from the stockade at these strange goings-on. Who was the woman dressed in man's clothing? Why was she asking questions, and why did the prince look as if he wanted to commit murder? One man after another was called to step forward and state his crime. All spoke readily, their eyes questioning.

"You," Katerina said, pointing a finger at a broad-chested man with small round eyes. She watched the powerful play of muscles on his upper arms and chest as he shouldered his way to take his place near the front of the line. "What is your crime?"

"My family was dying from hunger. I waylaid a wagon full of grain and killed the men who were driving the wagon."

"What happened to your family?"

"They died from starvation. One babe in arms and two barely able to walk," he said simply.

"Your name."

"Rokal, mistress."

"He goes with me also," Katerina said quietly.

"It would appear that you have a soft heart for a sad tale," Banyen said mockingly.

"I have no heart," Katerina said coldly. "But I can judge a man's worth by the look in his eye. Remember that."

Banyen's eyes mocked her. "I'll remember."

The selection continued till the noon hour, when Banyen called a halt. "Enough for now. Tomorrow you can question the prisoners that are working today. I don't want you to come to me later and say you were cheated, that the best had the work detail."

"Tell me, what happens when the snows come and the weather is bad? Where are the prisoners taken then, to which yurt? I can't believe you leave them in the stockade."

Banyen's eyes darkened with rage. "They stay right where they are. Fir branches are tacked to the animal skins overhead and to the sides to prevent the wind from driving at them full force. They huddle together for warmth."

"That's inhuman. An animal is treated better than that," Katerina said viciously.

"They should have thought about the matter before they committed their crimes," Banyen said coolly. "I repeat, I didn't say I approve. It is the way of the league. Only the Khan can change the rules."

"It's wrong. The punishment should fit the crime. These men have nothing to look forward to but their death. It's inhuman." She spat.

"How generous you are with other people's lives. If you were slain, I wonder what would happen to your killer?"

Katerina's eyes darkened. "I wonder how you would survive if you were shackled as they are for a crime that doesn't warrant death—let us say, raping a woman, leaving her to die."

"Again, let me repeat myself. Rape is not considered a crime," he said coolly, his eyes mocking her, daring her to retaliate.

"The price you put on women—they are worthless,

is that what you're saying?" Katerina asked dangerously.

Banyen shrugged. "A woman is a woman. For
some strange reason that I can't fathom, a woman
places a very high price on her virginity."

"Not half as high as the price a man places on his
genitals. Once a woman's virginity is gone, it's gone.
If you were to take away a man's ability to rape a
woman or make love to her, he would die of shame."
Katerina laughed. "He would simply lie down and die.
Women rise again and again." Suddenly she stuck out
her booted foot, catching Banyen behind the knee. He
went down, his hands outstretched to break his fall.
Katerina stood aside, her hands on her slim hips,
laughing in delight. "The position becomes you, grovel-
ing in the dirt. It's where you belong." Turning, she
walked slowly back to the yurt, her slim haunches
swaying seductively before Banyen's murderous eyes.

Katerina's nerves were on edge; the days were passing too quickly. She knew she had to make fast work
of her selection or she would get caught in the snow
and ice when she went through the Urals. Still, she
forced herself to make a slow, thorough appraisal of
all the men. She couldn't afford any mistakes, now or
later.

For three days she stood near the stockade, breathing heavily through her mouth as man after man
stepped forward. She let her eyes measure his form,
his muscular capability, and the tilt of his head. She
listened with a keen ear to his crime and stared deeply
into his face with eyes that were keener and sharper
than her ears. She also watched Banyen, covertly. His
agate eyes gave away his feelings. When they lightened
she knew he approved of her choice; when they darkened to indigo she knew he didn't approve. For the
past three hours his eyes had remained a deep, dark
shade of blue, which not only amused her but delighted her. She watched carefully to see if any of the
prisoners would reveal some feeling about the prince.

Only Kostya, the first man she had chosen, revealed anything, and she was uncertain what name to put to his expression.

Banyen was impatient with her lengthy, time-consuming choice of men. He listened with half an ear as Katerina ordered one of the men to flex his arm as if in preparation for a weapon thrust. He saw her eyes narrow, and mentally calculated where the weapon would have landed. He fixed his sights on a point to the far left of the stockade, where Katerina's gaze also rested. She nodded. His impatience quickly turned to anger as she continued with her methodical system of choosing an army. "One would think you were choosing prize cattle for showing," he snapped.

"Not cattle. Human beings that are being treated like cattle."

Banyen ignored her words. "The noon hour approaches and the sun will be unbearable. Make fast work of the last or you'll be standing here alone."

Katerina swiveled till she was facing him. "Don't ever make the mistake you just did. Don't ever tell me what to do. Do you understand? You're here by sufferance. Remember that. You do what I tell you, not the other way around."

Banyen's eyes became mere slits as he noted an amused look in some of the prisoners' faces. Kostya eyed him strangely, as he always did, and the man named Rokal was grinning. He knew he should say something, do something, but he held back. Let her think she had him in her power. If it amused her to humiliate him in front of the prisoners, let her; his time would come. When he took her, he would do it in front of the lot of them. Then she would see how her animals would come to her aid.

"Is that something else I should remember? The list grows overly long," he said arrogantly.

"Whatever pleases you," Katerina snapped. "Remain quiet so I can finish with my selection."

"You have only to command and I will obey," Banyen ridiculed as he slouched against a gnarled tree trunk. Why was she so hostile to him? He'd done nothing to her, save sling her across the horse's back and bring her into camp. What was that strange look in her eye when she stared at him? He could feel the animosity every time she was near him. Was it just him or was it all men? What was the reason she disliked him so? He corrected his thoughts: "dislike" was too tame a word. Did she hate all men? Evidently not, he answered himself. There had been an approving look in her eye when she chose Kostya. Did she fear men? No, he answered himself again. If she feared men she wouldn't be standing where she was now, with the plans she had in mind. No, it was himself. Why?

His mouth tightened as he watched the swell of her breasts, the sway of her hips as she walked up and down in front of the men. He liked the look of her long legs in the tight-fitting trousers. Those legs, he knew, could be pliant or firm, whichever she chose. She could be soft and she could be hard. He didn't know how he knew, he just did. Katerina Vaschenko had passions that he would wager had never risen to the surface. He grinned. He was just the man to unleash them and bring them to a roaring, tumultuous conclusion. His eyes widened slightly at Kostya's look. He's thinking the same thing, Banyen fumed. Bastard!

An hour past noon Katerina finished her selection. She had her hundred and fifty men. She fixed a steely eye on Banyen and walked away from him. Tomorrow the prisoners would be readied for the trip back to the mountains. One more day and she would leave the camp. She turned as she heard footsteps behind her. "Women walk behind men," Banyen said through clenched teeth.

"If there was a man about, perhaps I would do as you . . . suggest. Seeing nothing more than a prince, I'll continue as I am. Furthermore," she said, turning, "I walk behind no man . . . or prince. Why don't you go about your . . . duties and leave me alone."

Damnable woman! He wanted to grab her by the

long, shining hair and pull her to him till he felt her body grow soft with desire. Why in hell did she have this strange effect on him? What was there about her that intrigued and heightened his desire? He wanted her, but he had wanted other women, too. What made this one so different from the others?

A smile tugged at the corner of Katerina's mouth as she imagined the look of frustrated outrage that would be settling over his face. He wanted her, she saw it in his eyes every time he looked at her. "Good," she muttered to herself. Men filled with passion became reckless, foolhardy. Her eyes were merry as she shortened her stride and wiggled her hips seductively. "I hope his eyes fall from their sockets," she muttered through clenched teeth.

"Come with me, child, I want you to see the sun come up over the Khanate. It's a beautiful sight, and I wish us to view it together. There are several things I want to discuss with you."

They walked slowly, uncle and niece, through the compound, where everything was quiet and still. A new day will begin soon, Katerina thought. And what will it bring? she questioned herself.

The Khan pointed a pudgy finger to the east. "A new day, for both of us."

Katerina looked at the huge orange ball covered with what looked like gossamer wings and sighed deeply. "It's been a long time since I saw anything so beautiful," she said huskily. "You're right, Uncle, this is a new beginning."

"Child, tell me your reasoning as to why you didn't want the prisoners told of your plans. It would seem a little late to tell them on the morning they are to leave. Banyen does not approve, but then, of late Banyen approves of very little of life's goings-on. He's been here two years now, and I still don't know him. Your reason?"

Katerina shrugged. "Would it have made a difference? They have no choice. They go with me whether they like it or not. This way they have less time to worry on the matter. I expect no trouble from any of them. Your prince is the one that worries me," she said sharply. "I'm giving the men a chance to live, why would they reject the offer? Is there something you know that you aren't telling me?"

"No." He raised his round head and looked at the huge ball rising in the sky. "Another week and you'll be in the Urals, and that, my dear, is when your problems begin. You can't beat the snows. It's too late."

"There's no cause for worry, Uncle. I've gone through the snows before. Mikhailo knows I'm coming. He'll string the pass with bells, as he's always done. You must have faith in me; I'll succeed. Now tell what else is bothering you. I see many questions in your eyes."

"Your assurance that you intend to give me the colt and the filly."

"But that was understood and I gave you my word," Katerina said glibly.

"What is this hostility you have for Prince Banyen? I want to understand what it is—"

"Don't press me, Uncle. I loathe his mocking eyes and his arrogance. I detest his manner in regard to women, myself in particular. Evenly matched, I know I could bring him to his knees, and I think he knows it also. Time will tell. I warned you when I first came here that I will not allow him to interfere with my plans. If I have to kill him I will." Her hazel eyes were pinpoints of flame as she gazed at her uncle. "If you think he can ferret out the secret of Whitefire, think again. Because we are flesh and blood means nothing when it comes to the horses. One wayward move on his part and he dies, is that understood, Uncle?"

The Khan cringed at her words. He shrugged. Banyen was a man and she was a woman. He knew in his heart which of them would win. "Understood," he said softly. "Look," he said, pointing his arm in the direction of the stockade. "Banyen is preparing the prisoners. By the noon hour all will be in readiness. The food sacks were made up last night, and the barrels of water are being loaded on the wagons now. Blankets and carpets will also be given you. Does it meet with your satisfaction?"

Katerina nodded assent. "It's time then for me to speak with the prisoners. If you don't mind, Uncle, I prefer to do it alone, but before I do that, there is one other question I want to ask you. This . . . army you have garrisoned here, is this the army you plan to use when you attack Moscow? I overheard you talking to one of your tribal elders about the high price you've been paying for soldiers. Where are these soldiers and how many of them are there? If you're buying an army, why is Prince Banyen working and training these men? What does it mean? If he's needed here with your men, why are you sending him to the Carpathians with me? No lies, Uncle, I want the truth from your lips."

"You are your father's daughter, there is no doubt of that. You pick at something as a dog picks at a bone. Leave me to my reasoning, whatever it may be. I've agreed to your demands, and other than my two small requests, I have not badgered you." Suddenly there was a ring of iron in the jovial voice. "Leave it, Katerina. Go, talk to your men, and then join me for breakfast in my yurt."

Katerina agreed and strode off, her back stiff and straight, her thoughts whirling. The old fox was clever, and sly. What was he up to? She would watch Banyen as carefully as he planned to watch her. Sooner or later he would give away his plans. Men were fools in that they thought women were stupid.

Her voice was sharp and clear when she spoke to the prisoners. She fixed her eyes on Kostya when she spoke, and was pleased to see the light of interest in his eyes. "You men have been specially chosen by me to travel to the Carpathian Mountains. With the Khan's permission, I'm giving you back your lives. I'm going to train you to be Cossacks through the long cold winter. I warn you now that there will be no escape from the House of the Kat. You will all remain in your chains until we get to the mountains. Once we are there, your irons will be removed and you will walk about as free soldiers. I ask that you give me your loyalty, and in turn I will feed you, clothe you, and pay you an adequate sum of money that will be yours to do with as you see fit. What you did in the past does not interest me. It's what you do in the mountains that concerns me. It won't be easy, I can tell you that now. I'll talk with you again when we get to the House of the Kat." Loud murmurings and buzzings followed her as she strode from the stockade. Her step was light, purposeful, as her stride lengthened. She could almost feel Banyen's glittering eyes boring into her back.

Perhaps it had been a mistake to let him see her hostility. Sooner or later he would begin to wonder why she felt as she did about him. Certainly her past actions were too strong to be laid to his tying her to a horse like a sack of flour. She would have to temper her tongue and be careful when she was around him.

Breakfast was a somber affair. Strong, bitter black coffee, pungent goat cheese, and round, flat bread spread with honey were offered to her by the Khan, whose face was a study in blankness. Katerina wondered if he was already regretting his bargain. She remained quiet, her thoughts on Banyen and the long trek back to the mountains. She suddenly felt uneasy. It wasn't the thought of taking the prisoners, shackled as they were, nor the fifty men from the Khan's army with her, it was Banyen. Her uneasiness increased with each mouthful of food she swallowed. Her eyes fell to the sable carpet, and automatically she withdrew her booted foot till it rested on the plank floor of the yurt.

Prince Banyen led first one prisoner and then another from the stockade. He himself saw to their manacles and brought each man towards the wagons with a terse order to remain quiet and be still. Low-voiced murmurs reached his ears as the men conversed and speculated in low whispers. It was Kostya who voiced the question aloud to one of the others.

"There's more to this venture than the woman told us. After she trains us to be Cossacks, what is it we're to do? That, my fellow prisoners, is the fly in the honey pot. Still, she's given us back our lives. How many of us do you think would survive the first cold spell and snowstorm in this stockade? For that we should offer thanks."

"She's a woman, and we number a hundred and fifty men," a prisoner named Dmitri said in a low whisper.

Rokal grinned, showing short, stubby teeth. "Look over your shoulder, my friend, and tell me what you see."

"There will be no chance for any of us to escape," Kostya said softly. "And why should we? The woman promised us food and money to do as she asked. I for one have no wish to die in the snows. Let us agree among ourselves that we will give this venture a chance."

"I vote with Kostya," Rokal said softly. One by one the others by the wagon agreed.

The man called Dmitri, his eyes nearly closed against the brightness of the day, watched as Banyen's men readied themselves for the trip. Kostya is right, he decided. Later, when the snows melted in the spring and he had good food in his belly, along with gold in his pocket, would be time enough to get free. For now he would agree. Beyond that, he would make no promises, to the woman or his fellow prisoners.

The sun beat down upon the tiny crystals of silica, heating them, making the temperature rise to a hot, uncomfortable degree. Everyone felt the effects of the heat, including the animals. The wagons stood like sentinels, waiting for the horses to be harnessed to them. The prisoners stood shackled together on the hot sand, waiting. The Mongol soldiers who comprised the guard were busy preparing their horses and wiping away the perspiration that ran freely down their bodies. The remainder of the soldiers fastened the last of the ropes, securing supplies and foodstuffs aboard two wagons. A caravan of ten wagons, two hundred men, Prince Banyen, and one woman waited, poised on the brink of success or failure.

The Khan, with Banyen and Katerina, watched the final preparations from under a canopy, escaping the onslaught of the hot sun. "Katerina, one would think from the feel of this heat that you should have the usual ride through the Urals. Banyen and I know, however, that this is not the case. The Urals are tricky and treacherous this time of year. You feel the sleighs unnecessary trouble at this time, but I assure you, once into the Urals you'll thank me for my foresight. Word reached me several days ago that the northern ridge is deep in snow, and your only chance is the southern ridge, even if it is longer. You still might have a chance to bypass the worst of the accumulation. The men are almost finished, so if there is anything else you need tell me now," Afstar said, concerned for her well-being. He knew her journey would be a difficult one.

Katerina's heart pounded as she looked at the caravan, and a momentary panic gripped her. Was she capable of the task that lay before her? Could she handle two hundred men and Prince Banyen? Were Mikhailo and the Khan right? Could she accomplish what she intended? Then, as a Mongol soldier brought up her horse, the Cosars and Volin flashed before her. No matter what, nothing would ever stop her from avenging the demise of her people and returning the Cosars to their rightful home. The image she had of her father lying dead with the others, the huts burned to the ground, was all she ever needed as a source from which to draw her strength. Each time the scene flashed before her, unbounded power soared through her body, energizing her very being with unparalleled confidence. She knew she could do anything.

Reaching for the reins of the horse, she turned to

her uncle. "I can't think of anything else that's needed, everything has been checked. If we've overlooked anything, it won't matter once we're on our way. I thank you, Uncle, for all you have done for me, and for all you have given me. Most of all, I wish to thank you for believing in me and what I must do. My mother would bless you many times over if she were here. She would be very proud of her brother." Putting her arms around the Khan, she embraced him tenderly and kissed him on the cheek. Once again she looked him in the eye, and said, "With all my heart, my people, who are no more, and I thank you."

Katerina mounted her horse, her seat relaxed, her cat eyes sleepy and lynxlike as she waited for Banyen's signal to start the small caravan. A patrol of twenty soldiers was to lead the way on horseback. The remainder of the soldiers would ride in the wagons behind the prisoners, Katerina would ride behind Banyen. "Are you ready?" she asked him.

Banyen's stallion stood before him, waiting. The prince reached out his hand to the Khan. "I'll not give speeches of thanks. I merely wish to say I'll be back in the spring. When I return, I wish to hear news of preparations for our attack. I need say no more. Farewell, my friend." He released his hand from the Khan's and leaped onto his horse.

Afstar looked up at both of them with worry in his eyes. "You embark on a difficult journey. You'll need all your strength and will. Katerina, you especially have a long journey, as yours doesn't end with the Urals. Good fortune to you both."

"We'll succeed, Uncle, never fear. There is much to do, and it will be done," she said, with such confidence that even Banyen almost believed her. "Give the command to move," Katerina ordered Banyen, "for we must make the Ural River by nightfall. Once again I bid you farewell, Uncle. Banyen will bring news of my progress to you in the spring." Katerina dug her heels deep into the horse's flanks, the animal responding immediately, with Banyen close behind.

He looked at Katerina's easy, relaxed position in the saddle and felt desire rise in him. The tight, confining shirt she wore was open at the throat, revealing a deep cleavage as her breasts rose and fell rhythmically with her steady breathing. He let his gaze linger on the slight spread of her thigh in the form-fitting trousers. Long and supple. His heart pounded in his chest when he thought how she would feel next to him, her flesh as naked as his.

Katerina felt his appraisal of her and stared pointedly into indigo eyes. She allowed a small smile to tug at her lips as she returned his bold look. She motioned him with her finger to come closer. Suspecting a trick, Banyen held his whip loosely in his hand, ready to strike out if necessary. Katerina leaned closer till she was barely inches from his sun-darkened face. "I know how to kill just as you do. I can do it quickly and silently and not shed a drop of blood, or I can arrange to have your blood flow like a river . . . Remember what I said, Mongol, this is no game we're playing. When this is over, there will not be a prize for the winner."

Dark eyes scoffed at her words, confusing Katerina, throwing her off balance. She had threatened to kill him and he accepted it lightly. Suddenly she felt vulnerable and weak beneath his gaze.

"Do my ears deceive me, are you threatening me? Never mind, I know a threat when I hear one. Answer one question for me, woman, why do you have such . . . an unreasonable hatred for me? I had to tie you to the horse when I brought you to camp. If I had set you upright, you would have fallen and possibly killed yourself. If you recall, you were in a greatly weakened condition. I see no hatred in your eyes for these . . . scum," he said, pointing to the prisoners, "nor do I see anything but fondness in your eyes for the Khan. I and I alone am the recipient of your hatred. Why?"

Katerina stared deeply into the indigo eyes for barely a moment, willing him to remember. She saw only blankness. "You really don't know, do you. A pity," she said, straightening her slim body on the horse. "One day possibly the answer will come to you. When it does," she said, wagging a finger playfully at him, "it will be too late."

Banyen's face filled with rage. What kind of riddle was that? Damn fool woman! Did she think he was a mind reader? Why couldn't she just tell him whatever it was? Oh no, beat the bush, go around it but never through it. He squared his broad shoulders, gave her a last scorching look, and rode to the front of the twenty-man patrol. With a brisk wave of his hand, the small caravan began to move.

The prince rode silently ahead of his men, his anger driving his thoughts back in time to the rage he had felt as a boy of six. He lay face down in the dirt, left for dead, as Ivan and his troops stormed Kazan.

Scared, every muscle in his body still, he dared to move his eyes. When the cannons had finished, and the village had been leveled, he watched the soldiers ride in and slaughter every last person, including his mother and father. He watched as Ivan and his men feasted on goats and sheep afterward, and for sport used the bodies of children for target practice. Banyen's anger turned to revenge as he thought of Ivan. The sound of a voice startled him.

Katerina turned in the saddle and waved to Afstar. "My promise, Uncle, when the first wildflower sprouts on the frozen banks of the Dnieper, a new breed of Cossack will be born!" With a last wave of her hand, she spurred the horse forward and raced to take her place behind Banyen.

The Khan patted his ample girth, a smile on his lips. He had lost count of the times he had seen the wild flowers poke through mounds of snow, only to darken and die within hours. His dark eyes became hooded as he recalled a lone sprout that had survived long after the others were nothing more than brown specks in the smooth, unblemished snow.

Chapter Nine

❊❊ ❊❊ ❊❊

HALYA ZHUK PACED her luxurious bedchamber, a furious look in her eyes. Something must have happened to Yuri, he was weeks overdue. Angrily she thrust out a satin-slippered foot and kicked at the dressing table. Bottles and jars teetered precariously as she continued to jab the table. It was Ivan's fault. Each time she questioned him he grew angry and hostile. And yesterday, in one of his insane rages, he had said Yuri was dead and it was no great loss. He acted as if he knew something he wasn't telling her. Yuri couldn't be dead, not her baby brother.

She flung herself on the high bed, scalding tears seeping into the rich brocade of the coverlet. If Yuri was dead then nothing mattered. She would go back to Moldavia to be with her aging parents, if they were still alive. And that's another thing, she thought as she sat up in the bed. How many times had she asked Ivan to send a messenger to her home to find out the condition of her parents? He promised, then did nothing. What if she returned only to find them dead? Another attack of weeping seized her. What should she do? "I don't want to become Czarina, not any more. I just want to leave here and go where people are sane and normal. I don't want to sit next to him. He's ugly, fat, and disgusting." She hiccuped. "I can't bear to have his cold, flabby flesh next to mine, and I can bear to . . . to . . . I hate him!" she cried passionately.

The week before, when Ivan had returned from Alexandrov, he had been stranger than ever. The great palace buzzed about his bizarre behavior. One of the boyars said Ivan ordered a sleigh with seventeen hundred gold plates to be driven to Alexandrov. Afterward, he immured himself in a ramshackle hut. On his return to Moscow he insisted on the right to judge and punish traitors, and also to form a state within a state, if the people wanted him to stay.

The Prince of Moscow, as he rendered himself, now paid homage to a Tatar called Semyon Bukbulatovich.

Halya had seen Ivan only once since his return, and had been shocked at his appearance. His clothes hung on his slovenly body, which reeked of wine and sweat. She gagged when he gathered her in his arms, murmuring insane things. In desperation, Halya filled him with liquor till he fell unconscious, then crept from the room, her ears burning with his decadent words. He was crazy, and she had to leave now, before he took it into his head to kill her.

Halya looked around her elegant room, and at the rows of elaborate gowns that had been sewn for her when Ivan claimed her for his next wife. Every jewel imaginable had been added to her coffers to enhance her beauty. Anything she fancied was given to her upon a simple request. *Can I give up all this richness?* she wondered, looking around at the magnificent tapestries that adorned the walls, and the thick, colorful carpets that covered the marble floor. The elaborately brocaded silken drapery on the high windows and bed were such as she had imagined existed only in fairy tales. Coffers for her rings, pendants, and bracelets rested on finely made tables. All the boxes were of solid gold and lined with rich, thick velvet. Sometimes, when Halya had nothing else to do, she amused herself by the hour playing with the gems, lining them up on the bed. They were hers for her willingness to do whatever Ivan asked. When she left she would take them with her—nothing else, just the gems. Jewels could buy anything and were an acceptable bribe when one was needed. They had been earned by the use of her body. Yes, they belonged to her, and she would never part with them.

Halya left the bed and stood on a small carved stool to peer out the small window. Dusk. She hated this time of day, for as night fell Ivan began to grow restless and make demands on her. His day at an end, and his belly satisfied, he would begin to think of the ache in his loins. A bellow would go up, heard all over the palace, and within minutes two of his trusted guards would be at her door, informing her that the Czar demanded her presence in his chambers. Please, not tonight! she prayed silently. Please, not tonight!

Her slender shoulders shook and heaved with her unchecked sobs as she stepped down from the casement. In her heart she knew there wouldn't be a reprieve for her this evening, as it had been over ten days since he had summoned her to his rooms. She didn't know which was worse, the acts she was forced to perform or the dread of anticipation.

Shortly after sunset, the moment she dreaded arrived. A knock sounded on her door. "The Czar desires your company this evening," a guard said imperiously.

The moment the door closed, Halya threw the bolt and tore through her room, plucking first at one gown and then another from the deep recesses of the wardrobe. Finally she settled on a seagreen silk, cut low over her breasts, adding a string of emeralds around her neck as she preened before the glass. She looked beautiful and Ivan would appreciate her, she was sure of it. Carefully, Halya arranged her hair into deep swirls, allowing one long curl to drape her shoulder. When she remembered how Ivan liked to wind his fingers around the curl and force her head down between his legs, she shuddered. Tossing the lock of hair over her shoulder, she gagged and swore never to do that again, never, never again! After tonight she would do as she saw fit, and would answer to no one. She would start a new life, but only after she had found out about Yuri.

Slowly she walked to Ivan's bedchamber. Inside the room, she found him completely nude, dancing obscenely in the center of a ring of naked women. She gasped at the sight, afraid to make a sound.

"Would you care to join us, Halya?" He drooled as his grotesque body was eagerly caressed by the laughing females.

"Perhaps another time, dear Ivan," she said hesitatingly. She prayed that he would not ask her to disrobe and perform humiliating acts in front of the other women.

"Yes, another time," he said threateningly. "I have other plans for you tonight." A sadistic sneer formed on his twisted mouth as his mad, glazed eyes rolled in his head. Halya trembled at his words.

With a vague wave of his bejeweled fingers, the women were gone. Gathering a robe around him, he picked up a rolled parchment from a nearby table. "I have news for you of your brother, Yuri." An evil grin quivered on his lips, the madness still lingering in his eyes. "I have word of the hero you call your brother, the boy I called a man. You were right—he was a boy. I must tell you the results of his journey."

Ivan played with Halya, watching her every expression, delighting in the intensity of her anticipation. "This message has been in my bedchamber for several days now . . . no, not several days, but two weeks . . . no, a month. Yes, that seems more like it. A month ago my personal courier brought this missive to me." Ivan waved the crackly parchment in her face, taunting her with its contents.

Desperately trying to control herself, Halya asked calmly, "Has my brother served you well, my Czar?"

A roar of mad laughter split the tense air, sending icy shivers down Halya's spine. "Oh yes, my lovely one, he has served me well." Knowing this was the moment to inflict the most pain, Ivan seized it. "He served me so well that he died for me." The twisted mouth in his demented face spewed forth an evil, demonic laugh, wrought from the center of the earth.

Halya fell back in shock at the sight of Ivan's face

and the sound that emanated from it. A moment later she lay faint on the floor.

The sight of her body, collapsed, threw the Czar into a dance of delight, and another heinous laugh gurgled out of his throat. Sitting down beside the princess, he stared at her unconscious form. A variety of noises and movements befell him, as though he were possessed by a demon.

Halya stirred. She sat up, supporting herself on one arm, and beheld the transformed face of Ivan before her. Controlling her instinct to run, she fought the urge to vomit. Never had she seen such madness as that which played on the face of Ivan. Trembling fearfully, she rose to her feet.

"Go to your room now and change for my banquet. Within minutes I want you at my side in the common hall. I want everyone to see my whore sitting next to me."

Halya flew from the room, relieved to be away from him. Running through the hallways, she sobbed uncontrollably as she thought of Yuri. Inside her chamber, she slammed the door and cried out with anguish, "Yuri, oh, Yuri! My brother dead! How? Why? Now I have no one!" she cried brokenheartedly, collapsing on her bed.

A knock at her door made her remember Ivan's order. "My princess, Ivan is calling for you, you must come!" her maid begged, running into the room.

"Quickly, help me change my gown," Halya said, motioning the girl to hurry. "Fetch me the black dress and slippers. Tonight is a sad night, and black fits my mood." She felt dead, drained of all emotion, detached. Ivan would not bother her this night. A numbness settled in her, freeing her from everything but thoughts of Yuri and her hatred of the Czar. Dressed, she walked down the long corridors to the hall, vowing Ivan would find his death at her hands.

When Halya's escorts seated her next to Ivan, she was stunned to see an unkempt, filthy man with a curled mustache sitting in the place of honor, on the

Czar's left. Her eyes widened at this strange behavior. It could only mean that Ivan was up to some dastardly thing that would bring harm to someone. Dear God, she prayed, please don't let it be me. She forced a bright smile and spoke lovingly to Ivan, who looked at her as though he had never seen her before. Her stomach churned as she watched him pick at a stray thread on his elaborate crimson robe. The thread seemed to annoy him. Unexpectedly, he ordered one of the guards, standing behind his throne, to cut the sleeve from the robe immediately. The guard blinked, grasped a long-handled knife, and slit the rich fabric from shoulder to wrist. Ivan took the sleeve and tied it around the head of the man seated next to him. He laughed and sat back in his high gold throne, the saliva dribbling down his chin. The boyars sat mesmerized at his lack of manners and lowered their eyes to the gold plates in front of them. A few of the women smiled at his wicked display, immediately sobering at a well-placed kick under the table by a husband.

The man at Ivan's left felt embarrassed and confused, for he knew he was the object of ridicule, but he was powerless to do anything about it. He suffered in silence, the offensive sleeve of scarlet tied rakishly to his head. He reached down and picked up a piece of meat, intent on bringing it to his mouth.

Ivan slapped the meat from his hand and stared at him. "Were you born in a stable, sir? I eat first, to be sure the food isn't poisoned. After I have eaten, the boyars eat, and then you may, if there is anything left. I'm not ready to dine yet, so you'll have to wait until I give you permission. I may not sup at all this night. I see nothing on the table that pleases me," he said petulantly.

Halya watched nervously. No one ate, no one made a motion that could in any way be misconstrued by the Czar. When he said nothing tempted him, then nothing should tempt them. If there was one among them who was starving, he would starve. Halya looked at her own plate and closed her eyes. She knew if her life depended on it she couldn't eat.

Suddenly Ivan stood up and bowed before his guests. "I called you all here today for a reason," he announced. "I wish you to pay homage to this man," he said, pointing to his left. "He's here on a matter of business, business that could well mean that . . . Never mind, there's not one among you that can be trusted with such important news. Rise," he commanded, "and bow to my new envoy. Another day I'll tell you his name and where he comes from."

"From the look of him, he came from the nearest pig trough," came a low, muttered response.

"Who is it that dares to speak when I'm talking, and dares to make such an offensive remark to my newly appointed envoy? Speak, or all of your heads will be severed. On the count of one, the man responsible had better step forward. One!"

Four boyars immediately stood and pushed forward a rotund man who was trying to pull away, his hand reaching for his wife.

"Remove his head and place it in the middle of the floor," Ivan ordered. "I'm hungry now, I think I'll have some meat." He stretched his bare arm toward a heaping platter of lamb and withdrew a large chunk. His eyes focused on his bare arm, then moved to his new envoy's head and the sleeve that was tied around it. He ripped it from the envoy's head and stuck his arm into it. When the heavy silk slipped to his wrist in a bunch, he frowned and chewed on his meat. The envoy sat stunned, as did Halya, who feared her deep breathing would be the subject of Ivan's next attack.

The large room was silent as a guard walked slowly to the center of the hall, a large domed platter in his hands. Quickly he set the platter down and stood back to await further orders. Ivan continued to chew, his vision cut off by the assembled boyars at various tables. "Is it ready?" he called, stretching his neck.

"Yes, my Czar, it is ready," the man replied.

"Good. Remove the cover and let us feast our eyes. Did he bleed much?" he asked casually.

The guard knew the expected response by heart. "Like a pig, my Czar," he said as he lifted the lid and exposed the severed head. Gasps rang out through the hall.

"You may leave," Ivan said imperiously.

The new envoy turned in his chair and closed his eyes. Halya clamped her teeth together and forced her hands to remain still in her lap. What would he do next?

Without warning, Ivan stood up and waved his arms, the fallen sleeve dangling over his long, thin fingers. "The dinner is over! Place your tax monies in the basket with your names and lot numbers. And no cheating," he said, wagging his finger playfully in the air. "Take the food away," he ordered the servants. "They don't deserve fine food served on my priceless plates. Send it all to my quarters and I'll feast by myself."

Halya sat, hardly daring to breathe, waiting for Ivan to leave the room. Not till she was sure he was far down the corridor did she move, and then she ran as if the hounds of hell were on her heels. Out of the corner of her eyes she noticed that the slovenly dressed man with the curled mustache wore a deep, perplexed frown on his face. Who was he, and what was he doing here? What manner of envoy was he, dressed like a beggar with dirty, mud-caked boots and filthy, baggy trousers?

On and on she raced, till she came to her room. She skidded to a stop, almost losing her balance in her haste to enter and lock the door behind her. Quickly she slipped the cover from the thick, fluffy pillow and started to throw her jewels into it, helter-skelter. When the coffers were empty she tossed a few pieces of underclothing into the sack and tied the end into a stout knot. She then stripped off her gown and pulled out a pale lavender afternoon dress with simple lines and folds. In an instant she had it over her head and quickly grabbed a matching cape. She had all she needed; she was ready to leave.

Halya dropped to her knees at the side of her bed and bowed her head. With all her being she prayed for guidance and strength to do what she had to do.

While Halya prayed, Gregory Bohacky, the new envoy, exited the dining hall behind the grim-faced, muttering boyars. Carefully he avoided the severed head on the large gold platter. His stomach heaved as he made his way through the corridors in search of the room a guard said was to be his. He walked for what seemed a long time, till he came to familiar surroundings. A flash of scarlet and a loud bellow caused him to stop in his tracks.

"Enter, my envoy," Ivan called in lordly fashion. "We have much to discuss. Let's do it now so you can leave at dawn. Tell me, how did you like your first state dinner? Wasn't it interesting? I find if one takes control of the situation one doesn't get kicked from behind. Sit, and tell me of the Cosars and how we'll do business. I see by the look on your face you were not successful in gaining the secret. It's of no importance now, as long as you have the horses. The sum agreed upon was six chests of gold, I believe. Am I right?"

"No, Czar Ivan, you aren't right. The horses are worth their weight in gold. There is now a price on my head, as well as that of every man in my tribe. That, and that alone, has made the price double," he said bravely. "I had to slaughter the whole village of Volin to get those damnable animals, and I expect to be well paid! If not, there are other buyers. Don't be hasty and think you can kill me, for if you do, and I don't return when expected, the horses will be moved. It was arranged before I journeyed here. If you agree to do business, then the Cosars will be delivered on schedule. Half the money now and the other half on delivery, as agreed two years ago."

"That was two years ago, and this is today. My treasury is not as great now as it was then. We must renegotiate the terms."

"There will be no bargaining. I have stated my price and it is the only price I'll agree to. Take it or leave it."

"You drive a hard deal. To think that after I made you my special envoy you have the audacity to try to cheat me. I'll call my Oprichniks—yes, I'll call them and have you beheaded." He reached out and pulled a long velvet rope. The sound of a gong thundered in the room and into the outer corridors. A guard opened the door and waited expectantly. "Fetch your leader for me immediately," Ivan ordered.

Gregory felt fear gnawing into his chest as his breathing became strained. Ivan was insane, incapable of being reasonable. He had to leave and get away from this lunatic whose spittle was drooling down his chin. He thought quickly, and his eyes narrowed as he looked deeply into the insane stare of the Czar. "How would you like to see the stallion Whitefire? I rode him here myself so you could be the first and only man to claim he saw the famous stallion." He made his tone purposely light, almost cajoling, in the hopes of diverting Ivan from thoughts of his murder.

"Is what you say true?" Ivan asked excitedly. "But of course, my envoy, I wish to see the stallion. Where did you stable him?"

"If the Czar will stand on the balcony, I'll get the stallion and ride him beneath the window. You'll be able to boast what no man has ever boasted. If you like, I'll let you ride him," Gregory said enticingly.

"Yes, yes, that's what I want to do! A night ride on Whitefire. How wonderful you are to suggest such a thing. I knew I made a wise choice when I appointed you my envoy," the gullible Czar said happily, forgetting the order he had given a minute ago. "Go, ready the stallion, and I'll change to suitable clothing. As we ride through Moscow, you shall go ahead of me and announce to one and all that I ride the stallion Whitefire. Agreed?"

Gregory nodded and immediately left the room, his throat dry and his head reeling with his near mishap.

How much time did he have to ride away before the lunatic sent someone after him? Not long, he surmised. He vowed to ride like the wind.

Ivan set about changing his robes to clothing more befitting a ride through the streets at night. He carefully chose a tunic of lemon yellow, trimmed with black braid. He preened like a peacock in front of the mirror and then sat down to wait. What seemed like hours later, he called for one of his guards and ordered him to the stable to find Gregory and see what was causing the delay. When the guard returned a short while later, Ivan knew by the look on his face that Bohacky was gone. He cursed long and loud, to the discomfort of the guard, who feared for his life. In a rage-filled voice he ordered the guard out. "He shall pay with his life for his treachery!"

Irate, Ivan slammed the door and bolted it. His eyes full of madness and hate, he shouted to the guards outside, "No one nears my door tonight!"

Until dawn, unholy screams, low moans, and demonic laughter emanated from behind closed doors, ringing throughout the palace. Then all was silent.

Chapter Ten

AS THE FIRST DAY of their journey began, Katerina felt the need to assert her leadership of the caravan immediately or else her raw recruits would easily turn to a more powerful person to be their commander. While she and Banyen rode up ahead, Katerina turned to him, her eyes narrowed against the glare of the sun, and said, "I don't care for this arrangement. Have your guards change the position of the wagons so the food and supplies come first. They must be where we can see them at all times. Place two wagons of prisoners next, then a wagon of soldiers, the prisoners, the soldiers again, the last wagon of prisoners, and then the sleighs. Put six guards on horses in the rear, five spread out on each side of the caravan, and another four behind the supply and food wagons. I hope the two soldiers in charge of each wagon are trustworthy and know how to handle the wagons. Do you approve? Before you answer, let me tell you, whether you like it or not, that's the way it shall be!" she said with grim determination.

"Why do you bother to ask if you have no intention of changing anything?" he questioned, with a look of arrogance on his face.

"I owe you no explanations, I ask you out of courtesy, and to see if you agree with my methods," she retorted, just as arrogantly.

"The arrangement will do," he said sharply, not wanting her to know that he couldn't have planned it better. She does have a brilliant mind, he thought. But it belonged in the body of a man, not a woman. If she were a man, she would be someone to reckon with, a leader among men. With a mind such as hers, bolstered with such zeal, there would be no stopping such a person. Without realizing it, Banyen stopped his horse as the thought struck full force: there'll be no stopping her! His mouth hung open as he shook his head, his mind racing. I sit here and describe the qualities of a man among men, a leader among leaders —I sit here and describe a woman! He was thunderstruck. He muttered, "I can see my work is cut out for me. It should be an interesting winter."

"Banyen!" Katerina shouted at him. "Why did you stop? What's the matter? Is there a problem? Banyen, what is it?"

Her voice brought him to his senses. He spurred his stallion with a vengeance, the animal breaking into a gallop. In moments he was alongside Katerina. "There's nothing wrong, I just got caught up in determining the best way over the mountains," he lied. "We have four hours of light left, do you think we'll make the river before then?"

"When I rode from the Urals to Sibir it took about that long, but with the wagons, I don't know. If we reach the river after sunset, it won't be too bad, the land ahead is all flat. Our problems begin when we try getting those confounded wagons up and over the mountains. Why I ever let my uncle talk me into using them I'll never know. I still think horses would have been better. Even with shackles, the prisoners would have managed. If their leg irons were off, with enough chain between the wrist shackles, it would have worked. I think my uncle preferred to give me ten wagons rather than two hundred horses. Tell me, Banyen, does he even have that many horses?" she asked seriously.

"I never took an accurate count. A good source of strong men and fast horses is what he needs to rebuild his army and I have no doubt he'll find them. He is a shrewd man, and an excellent trader backed with a wealth of gold and jewels. When I return in the spring, I know Sibir will be greatly changed. Enough of this talk," he said suddenly, realizing there was much work to be done, "we have to get these wagons moving." He broke away from Katerina and rode down the length of the caravan, shouting at the drivers to keep the wagons going as fast as they could.

The Kat rode her horse to the side of the road and stopped. She sat and watched as the wagons rolled by, trying to determine the pace, trying to estimate how much time would be needed to get from one place to another. The sun was sinking lower in the sky; only two hours of light were left. Her first calculation had been right—they would make the Ural River an hour after sundown. Not too bad, she thought. It will take an hour and a half to eat and bed down, giving all but the guards a good night's sleep.

Banyen rode up to her, the men and wagons moving to his satisfaction.

The Kat turned to Banyen. "After we have eaten and all is secured, we must talk about getting the wagons over the mountains."

"Do you have any ideas? If so, will you handle it like the wagon arrangement? Ask my opinion when you've already made up your mind?" he baited her, with a sneer on his lips.

"I have several suggestions, but I would like to hear your opinion, what you think best," she said, controlling the anger in her voice. You sarcastic bastard, she thought. A man always has to act like a man, never like a human being, she told herself. Whacking her horse on the haunches with her hand, she sent him pounding ahead of the caravan, leaving Banyen behind. She rode the horse hard for a mile or two, trying to rid herself of the aggravation the Mongol stirred within her. Why did she let him get to her? Her mind went back to that day he had forced himself on her. If she were truthful with herself, as hateful as that act was, she couldn't deny he interested her. The question kept returning. What would it be like to make love with him if he were tender and caring? No doubt he kept many women happy with his slim, muscular body, his good looks and willing mouth. Anger coursed through Katerina again. She had to stop thinking about him, there was a caravan to get through the mountains to the House of the Kat. A winter of training unruly prisoners, trying to make Cossacks out of them. This wasn't the time to act like a woman; she had to be the Kat first, last, and always, until her people had been avenged and the Cosars returned.

As fast as she rode away from the caravan, she returned. The river was now in sight, and they would soon be at its banks. The darkness brought to a close the first day of their journey. Katerina trotted by Banyen's side as they headed for the river, enjoying the warm night air, lavishing in it, knowing that, once into the mountains, heat would be a matter of clothing, not the season.

Once again she and Banyen rode the length of the

wagons, making sure everything was in order. Satisfied, they ordered the men to make camp for the evening.

The banks of the Ural River glistened with the dancing flames of their bonfires. It reminded Katerina of fireflies dancing in the summer night. She watched as the soldiers made the prisoners line up in an orderly manner to receive their ration of food. If all else fails, Katerina thought, I'll have the satisfaction of knowing I freed men from inevitable death and have given them the right to live, eat, and sleep like normal human beings. I'll have given them an ample supply of food so that no man goes to sleep hungry, and blankets to protect them against the night air. Compared to the stockade, where conditions were hopeless, this camp and the comforts she could provide would bring no complaints.

The prisoners and guards ate as Katerina and Banyen waited by the fire for their food. A middle-aged man from the Khan's camp served as the cook for the group, helped by a driver on the food wagon. The ration passed out was the same for all: one cold boiled potato, a chunk of black bread, a wedge of cheese, and a piece of marinated lamb. The only luxury in camp was two skinfuls of wine, a present from the Khan to Katerina. The cook handed them their food in shallow wooden bowls and left.

Banyen motioned to Katerina to move closer to the fire, where it was warmer. "The nights are cool and will be getting cooler," he said quietly.

Katerina took his suggestion and started to eat. Pulling a goat-skin from behind her, she offered Banyen a drink. His nearness bothered her. The scent of his body hovered over and around her, his lean hardness stirring her as she watched him carefully. A long arm reached for the wineskin. Tapered fingers touched and quickly withdrew. Slowly she inched away from him, afraid of what might happen if she were to feel the length of his body against hers.

Banyen smiled knowingly, aware of her discomfort. "Don't worry about the others watching us drink," she said, trying to ease the tension. "They sit far enough away. I don't wish to make them envious. Let's discuss how we'll take the wagons over the mountains."

"You know more about that than I do, you just came through the Urals. You could tell me how steep they are, and if the rocks and trees will be a problem," he said as he chewed on a piece of lamb.

"The real difficulty is the inclines. Some mountains have gradual slopes loaded with rocks and trees, while the others are steep and clear. We must be prepared to deal with all the elements. If the snow starts, the wagons will surely slip and slide. Tomorrow we go through the first pass, and should reach the mountain ridge around noon. It's the largest and the steepest. It will probably take us two days to get to the top. Do you have any suggestions?" she asked Banyen, who had listened attentively.

"Yes, I suggest we cross the river first." He laughed.

"I thought we were going to be serious about this," Katerina fumed.

"I am serious," he went on. "I think we should cross the river first. Was there a shallow spot you rode through?"

"Where I crossed the water would be too deep for the wagons. My horse had to swim."

"In the morning I'll test a few spots, and pick one for the wagons to cross. If we unload them, with just one driver and a team of four horses, we should get them most of the way. We'll tie ropes on each wagon and put five men on each rope. With the horses and men pulling, we should be able to get the wagons up the mountain. If we find snow, God help us." He sighed, reached for the wineskin, and took a long drink.

Katerina finished the last of her food, put down the bowl, and watched Banyen drink. Full and warm, she longed for a good night's sleep. She asked Banyen for the wine and took a short sip. Afterward she moved to get up. His strong hand reached out to grasp her slender arm. "What is it? I'm tired and wish to sleep. A busy morning awaits us," she said harshly, pulling away from him.

The wine, the warmth, and the sight of Katerina's tawny hair glistening in the light of the fire aroused desire in him. "Katerina, we've a long journey, the fire is warm, and the nights are lonely sleeping by oneself. Join me here and we'll share the delights of the night together," he muttered, his voice mellowed from the wine and his deep, dark eyes heavy with sleep.

"You fool, you're full of drink. Sleep it off by yourself, for when I stay with a man, he'll be sober and full of passion, not half drunk and half asleep." She pushed him over with her foot and stalked off into the darkness to her bedroll.

Dawn found Katerina and the cook quickly moving from wagon to wagon with the allotted pieces of bread. Eager to get an early start, she had awakened the cook and told him to distribute the food and make quick work of it. When the task was finished, she walked to the fire, now glowing red embers, and looked down at Banyen. She nudged his torso with her foot. "Get up, we've got to get the men up and moving." Her words went unheard. Once again she poked him, on the other side, but this time a little harder. The pressure of her foot in his back finally roused him.

"What's the matter?" Banyen muttered, sitting up and rubbing the sleep from his eyes. He looked up and saw Katerina standing over him, her hands on her hips.

"Tonight you'll be given one drink of wine and that's all. I have no time to wet-nurse a man who downs too much. There's much to be done, and you need a clear head to do it. Now, get up and get to the river and douse yourself with water. You were supposed to be up before everyone this morning, checking the river for a suitable crossing spot, and you lie there like a wounded animal. While you're there, find the place for us to cross, if it isn't too much trouble," she ordered sarcastically.

Banyen stood up, called a soldier to roll up his blanket, looked Katerina square in the eyes with burning hatred, then stalked off toward his horse. There was no need for words; his expression said it all.

His head pounding with every step he took, Banyen made his way to the bank. The dark eyes closed slightly when he saw Kostya, stripped to the waist, dousing himself with the icy water. Gingerly he dropped to his knees and began to scoop small handfuls of water to his face. He flinched at the stinging coldness.

"Better to do it all at once," Kostya said helpfully. "One good dousing and the pain in your head will subside, and that tight feeling in your shoulders will lessen. Your mind will clear with the shock of the cold water."

"I had too much wine," Banyen mumbled as he continued to dabble the water on his face and neck.

"I noticed." Kostya grinned. "Here, let me help you," he said, drawing Banyen to his feet. "Stand fast now, and don't move." Quickly he thrust out his arm and grasped Banyen around the neck, at the same time wedging his knee in the small of his back. He jerked the prince backward and released him. "How does your upper back feel now?"

Banyen flexed his arms and shoulders, staring quizzically into bright blue eyes. His headache gone and his back normal, he spoke quietly. "Why did you do that?"

"You were suffering. I would be less than human if I didn't offer to help you. Today is a day when all of us will need every ounce of strength we have. How can you do your job if you aren't fit? I didn't do it for thanks. If you need my help again, you have only to ask me. There is no thought in my mind to escape, so rest easy. I made a bargain with the woman, and I'll stick by it."

Banyen nodded as he watched Kostya walk back to

the camp. "Damnation!" he exclaimed. He believed every word the prisoner said, and was also freed from last night's overindulgence. His head was clear, and his back felt better than it had in months.

The camp was bustling. By the time Banyen got back, all was in readiness.

"I've found the place to cross, so let's be on our way, if it's convenient for you," he mocked Katerina.

She held out his piece of bread. "Here, take this, it will quell your fermenting stomach. You'll have to eat it as we ride."

Banyen rode to the head of the caravan with Katerina at his side, his head throbbing once again. When they were in position, he shouted back to the drivers to follow him.

They soon arrived at the fording site. After a quick inspection by Katerina, she nodded approval for the wagons to move. One by one, they labored through the water, creaking and groaning as they tilted and slid on the slippery moss-covered rocks. It took more time to cross than Katerina had anticipated; valuable time was lost again. She knew she couldn't beat the snow. Angrily she urged Banyen and the men to speed up their pace. Katerina was well aware that the men were in no hurry to go anywhere. They were out of the Khan's stockade, and that was all that mattered to them. They were free of that hellhole.

Two hours into the first pass, light snow began to fall. Katerina's heart sank. *If it starts this early into the Urals, once we leave the mountains the snow will be waiting on the steppe.*

"Banyen, we must keep moving at a faster pace if we are to make the first mountain by nightfall," she said harshly. "If you have a keen eye, you should have noticed the flurries. Light snow now means we're bound to reach heavier snow as we go along. We must keep these men moving, keep after them, they travel as if they have all the time in the world."

"You're overly concerned, I think," Banyen said. "We're moving right along, and if we push them they

might get angry and rebel. Besides, to go much faster
would be risky for the wagons."

"I just knew you wouldn't agree with me," she said
with indignation. "I'll find a way to get these men to
move more rapidly, there must be something that will
bait them to hurry. I'll be back shortly, I'm going to
ride up ahead to see how things look." A sharp kick in
the horse's sides and she was off, cantering down the
pass. "I can't let him make me angry," she muttered as
she rode hard, trying to rid herself of the resentment
she felt toward him.

"A rider coming in the distance," called one of
Banyen's soldiers.

"Keep the wagons moving," Banyen ordered. "It's
the girl returning."

Katerina brought her horse to Banyen's side. "The
big mountain is just ahead. From what I could see,
the lower slope is still clear of snow, but there's no
way of knowing what we'll reach a few hundred feet
up. We must make our best time on these flats. While
I rode I also came up with an idea to entice these men
to work harder."

The moment the high mountain loomed before them
the men began to grumble and groan. They knew immediately they were in for a hazardous climb.

Katerina ordered the men to form a line and pro-
ceed slowly up the mountain. "You prisoners will
leave the wagons and travel by foot, climbing and de-
scending. If a wagon gets stuck, or slips, you men will
lend a hand any time it is needed. You will put your
backs to pushing and pulling when necessary. Banyen,
post a guard to watch over them, and at the first wrong
move, cut down the troublemaker. This caravan will
get through to the Carpathians, even if it means many
of your bodies will be strewn along the way to prove I
mean what I say!"

The wagons were emptied, and the trek up the
mountain began.

Two hours before nightfall of the following day, the
top ridge of the mountain was in sight. Suddenly a

whirlwind of snow unleashed its millions of silent, devastating crystal flakes. It was man against the elements.

"If we push hard we can make the summit tonight. We should be able to make camp before the snow creates any problems. Hurry! Otherwise you'll taste your first uphill battle with snow, making everything twice as difficult. You made good time until now, and I'm proud of what you have accomplished," she said, her voice full of praise and encouragement for the men.

Banyen sat in his Mongol saddle and watched in amazement as Kostya and the other men put on a show of superhuman effort.

At nightfall the wagons lined the upper peak, while everyone made ready for their well-earned meal. The bonfires on the ridge cast a magic glow that encircled the mountain. The glowing fires of red-yellow reflected their dance onto the millions of tiny crystals that fell heavily from the heavy skies. Steam rose as the flakes hit the fires, creating the illusion that the breast of the mountain was heaving in its sleep.

The company ate, some quickly, the smarter ones slowly. Everyone was anxious to get to sleep, their bodies spent from the uphill climb.

Each fire was sheltered by a lean-to. The guards, who had built them, huddled beneath, keeping watch. The camp was quiet except for Banyen and Katerina, who sat conversing by the fire. Secure in their plans for the downhill trek, Katerina offered Banyen his one long drink of wine. When he finished, she bid him good night and crawled under her blanket next to the fire. The prince, in no mood for another scene, quietly made himself comfortable by the crackling flames. He watched the sleeping girl, somehow drawn to her in spite of her roughness. Why? Why did she intrigue him? Certainly she was beautiful, shapely, and desirable, but so were other women. What lay beneath the outer shell?

Many nights had been spent in the arms of welcoming, soft women, women eager to please him. Would Katerina ever be so willing? Why in the name of God did he desire a woman who dressed and thought like a man; yet, in her own way, was more of a woman than any who had lain with him.

Morning found everyone huddled beneath their blankets, covered by cold white snow. Katerina woke to find Banyen sitting by the fire, chewing his piece of bread.

"You're awake early," she said, startled to find him out of bed. "I see you're eating already. Is the cook also up?"

"Yes. But the men are still asleep. It's just you, me, and the cook. Now what do you think of the drunken Mongol?" he asked.

"I think you're doing what you are supposed to do. If you want applause, you've come to the wrong place," she replied icily. "Get on with it, wake the men. I want those wagons going down the mountain as soon as possible."

When the men had finished eating, Banyen called for their attention. "Listen to me carefully. The wagons must go down the mountain in single file, one at a time, ten lengths apart. That way, if one slips the others will not be caught in the slide. We'll try the first wagon with the horses, no ropes, and see how it goes. If the wagon slips we'll have to use the ropes. They'll be tied to the back of each wagon, and we might need one or two up front. Several men will handle each rope, pulling back so we can ease each one down the slope. The unloaded wagon will go first. Bring it up here and harness the horses. Tie the ropes on now, for once it begins to slide it's too late. You prisoners, divide into groups to walk alongside the wagon, and be prepared to grab the ropes. Number one wagon, move!" he ordered the first team.

Slowly and carefully the wagon edged its way down the steep grade. The driver strained, leaning far back into the seat, the horses almost sitting on their haunches. Gingerly the animals descended in the ankle-deep snow. One by one they made their way, driver and team working together.

Katerina called for the food wagon to be brought forward. As it pulled up, she warned the drivers and the men on foot, "If this wagon goes careening down the mountain we'll eat snow all the way to the Carpathians, if we don't freeze first. I trust you all agree." The team prepared to go downward. "One moment, I've changed my mind." At the sound of Katerina's voice, the men stopped in their tracks. "I've decided to send a sleigh wagon down next. If the weight of the sleigh causes the wagon to slide, and the horses can't control it, we'll know how to handle the supply wagons. Bring that wagon around to the front," she ordered the drivers. Katerina could see the concerned look on the faces of the two drivers.

"Listen to me," she addressed the men on foot. "You must hold the ropes immediately, so take your positions now. If the wagon goes out of control, release the ropes and save yourselves. You drivers, cut the horses free, then jump. I don't want any men or animals killed. We can manage without a wagon, but I need every one of you." With a wave of her hand, the wagon moved ahead.

Banyen and the others stood on the edge of the crest, watching the agonizing descent. The men strained at the ropes as the wagon, horses, and drivers eased slowly down the decline. Katerina turned to Banyen. "I wish my uncle had never given me these damn wagons. If we were on foot we'd be down near the bottom for all the time the first wagons are taking. I'm sorry I consented to this madness." She held her breath as a wagon slipped momentarily.

Suddenly the air was split with a loud, bloodcurdling "Yeow-ow-ow!" Those on the ridge watched in horror as the wagon gave way. The men holding the ropes tried desperately to let go, but they were caught and went cascading down the mountain. The drivers leaped from the wagon, forgetting to cut loose the horses. The animals and men struggled for their lives. The screams of both could be heard everywhere as the wagon reeled into a fir tree, splintering to pieces. The sleigh broke loose, tumbling down the slope. Three prisoners, still tangled in the ropes, were smashed against trees and rocks, until all that remained were broken, lifeless bodies.

Katerina turned her back on the tragic sight, kicking out at the rock next to her. "I knew it, I knew these damn Mongol wagons were a mistake. Now I've lost three men and four horses."

Kostya made his way down the slope behind Katerina. Working side by side, they freed the wounded who lay trapped beneath boards from the heavy wagon. Using all his power, Kostya freed one of the men, only to lose him to a dead horse that slid down the snow, dragging the man down with him.

Stunned at the tears that glistened in Kostya's eyes, Katerina laid her hand on his arm. "There was nothing you could do. There's no time to dwell on the matter, others need our help." Her own words were tortured, a look of agony covering her delicately boned face.

"Nor can you blame yourself for what happened," he replied. "Each of us must do the best we can." Bright blue eyes stared into Katerina's. "The men will not blame you for this. You have my word."

Katerina nodded but said nothing, her throat constricting at his words.

Diligently they worked together with the help of the other prisoners, binding wounds and helping them to safety. Perspiration dripped from Kostya's face as Banyen put his arm around him to lead him away. "It's finished. You have to rest, or you'll be no good to us the remainder of the journey. A few moments to sit and you'll be as good as new." He grinned into the blue eyes. "Call it an act of human nature, mine."

Banyen and Katerina agreed that it would be madness to send a second wagon down with the sleigh aboard. Four mounted soldiers were ordered to secure ropes to the sleigh and loop the ends to their saddles. That done, they started down the hazardous mountain.

While the others watched breathlessly, the sleigh and soldiers made it safely to the bottom.

Katerina was beside herself as she realized that the day was passing and all they had accomplished was the descent. She had figured a day, but she had hoped for better time. Again she cursed the wagons.

The prince walked alongside her and tried to calm her. "Don't worry, we'll get these down shortly, and the worst of it will be over. Tomorrow, if a pass is ahead, we'll make up for lost time."

"Damn those wagons!" she hissed again. "Three men, four horses, one wagon, and one sleigh, gone. Damn . . . damn . . . damn! Are the last two ready to go?"

"Yes. We've added more ropes and more men to hold them."

The extra hands and ropes proved effective. The last of the wagons went safely down the mountain.

The Kat announced that they would make camp for the night at the base of the mountain. Every man was hungry and tired from the grueling day. As quickly as possible, the fires were made and the food was prepared. The men ate, the horses were bedded down, and soon the camp fell silent. Neither Banyen nor Katerina was in the mood for conversation. They were spent, their only thought of rest.

The next week was a repetition of small ridges and long passes. Up one mountain and down another.

Katerina was relieved when they finally approached the pass that led out of the Urals. Quietly she checked with the cook on their food supply, and found they could spare some extra for each man. A small reward, she thought happily.

That night they camped at the mouth of the pass. "Men, listen to me. You see the snow is with us every day, and it will get worse. We've been through hard times, and we still have a hazardous journey ahead. If the drivers of each wagon can keep the horses at a lively pace, I promise all fifty kopecks."

Wide grins and shouts of approval went up over the

camp. Katerina smirked to herself. Men would do anything for money. The following morning would be their true test: the crossing of the Kama River.

The Kat watched through half-closed eyes as she got to her feet and took her place at the end of the line to await her dinner portion. The meal over, the fires roaring brightly in their efforts to reach the sky, she sat back and closed her eyes. She was jarred from her light sleep by a shout from the cook, who volunteered to play a tune for the men on his balalaika. She listened while he played and sang songs of the Russian people and their land. Tears burned her eyes at the haunting, beautiful words. When the cook finished his tune, he played another. This time he sang of the flowers and the sweet song of the nightingale. He stopped playing for a moment, reached out his hand to draw Katerina to her feet, and motioned her to act out the scenes as he played. Caught up in the moment, she agreed, and began to move her hands gently to the music as she had done before, as a child.

Banyen and the others watched, enthralled by her slow, rhythmic movements to the sound of the balalaika. She smiled, her small teeth pearl-white in the orange glow from the fire, her movements sure and relaxed. Banyen stared, never having seen her like this before. Suddenly he wanted to reach out and clasp her to him, to take her slender, swaying body in his arms. He wanted to feel the warmth of her beneath him while he released his aching loins into her. The welt on his cheek began to throb as he watched the men leering at her. He was sure they were all thinking the same thing, just as he knew he needed to take another breath to live. He hated it. The wound ached again, making his cheek twitch as he placed his index finger over it, trying to stop the pain. What was bothering him? Jealousy? He had never been jealous of a woman in his life. His dark eyes scanned the men around the campfire, and he knew he had to do something before . . .

Banyen stood up. "The hour grows late. The men need their sleep," he said curtly.

A loud groan of dismay circled the fire. It was the Kat who seconded Banyen's words and gathered up her bedroll. "The prince is right. The cook will play for us another time, and then we'll all dance. Tomorrow you'll thank Prince Banyen for his foresight." She unrolled her blanket, spread it by the fire, and lay down. The only sound heard throughout the camp was the crackling of the fires.

Banyen lay awake long after everyone else was asleep, his mind refusing to let him rest. The vision of Katerina dancing left him only with the thought of conquering her so that his body would be appeased. He wanted to reach out, here and now, and take her. Blood coursed through him, keeping alive the fire in his loins. Wondering about the taste of her lips, he thought of the ways he would make love to her. He imagined how she would feel in his arms, the softness of her body and the firmness of her breasts against his chest. Rolling over onto his belly, he willed the ache to subside. The men looked asleep, but he wondered if they too tossed with an ache in their groin. Frustration gave way to exhaustion, and he slept.

As dawn broke through the darkness, the camp stirred. The men got up and ate. Some were already at work. Katerina and Banyen discussed the best way to cross the Kama River.

"I know the Kama is treacherous and deep, but I think crossing over the ice would be the quickest and easiest way to get to the other side. I'll test the ice by walking on it, and if it holds me I'll go out on my horse," Katerina said.

"I disagree with you. I think we should find a shallow area," urged Banyen.

Katerina ignored his words as she tested the ice around the banks, satisfied with its thickness. Cautiously she edged out onto the ice-covered river. She walked a third of the way without hearing or seeing a crack. On her return she trod briskly, stopping now and then to jump up and down, testing the ice. At the bank of the river a soldier waited with her horse. Once again she ventured across the ice, this time a little farther. Satisfied, she turned the horse around and headed back.

"I have no doubts the ice will hold the wagons, no doubts at all. It's strong enough to hold anything."

"In the middle of the river the current moves deep and fast, and the ice doesn't get as thick as at the edges. I'm telling you, it won't hold."

"Line up the wagons and prepare to move. An empty wagon will go first, followed by the ones with food and supplies. After that, move the wagons with the men. If the ice should give way, it will happen before the men go out. Now move them onto the ice," Katerina said forcefully.

Cautiously the empty wagon crossed the river. Katerina turned to Banyen and gave him a satisfied smile. Next, the food wagon eased over the ice. Once past the center of the river, the other bank in sight, the cook heaved a sigh of relief. The supply wagon followed. As it crossed the middle of the river, hairline cracks, invisible to the eye, started to form.

"Next," called Katerina, ordering the wagons filled with the men to go. "Stay two wagon lengths behind each other. There is nothing to fear. You see how the ice holds. Remember, two lengths behind."

As the wagons began to move, the guards on horseback trotted along. When they reached the middle of the river, the ice began to rumble. "The ice is cracking!" the prisoners shouted in unison.

All eyes were on the frozen river, watching as a horse in the first team lost its footing and fell to one knee, dragging down three other animals. As they fell, a loud thundering crack ripped through the air. The first load of prisoners reached the bank just as the ice behind them cracked and split asunder. The river's mouth, wide open, swallowed the men, horses, and wagons into its mad, rushing, carnivorous depths.

The death cry of the men and horses clawed at

everyone's ears. As men and animals struggled to get out of the icy water, their screams tore at Banyen and Katerina. The Kat headed for the shattered ice, shouting for the others to try to save the men.

Banyen rushed after her, shouting. "No! You'll only waste more lives. You can't save those in the water. When it's this cold they can only survive for a minute. Katerina, do you hear me? Only a minute. The men in the water are dead men. Let them go and save the others."

Katerina stopped in her tracks. He was right.

"Get that sleigh and the other wagons off the ice quickly! Back them off carefully!" Banyen shouted, his voice full of authority.

Banyen could see apathy overtaking Katerina. She stood on the bank, helpless, motionless. Her head dropped down on her chest in defeat. He quickly grabbed her arm and pushed her toward the rescue party. "Katerina, there's much to be done and we need everybody's help. Take the reins and lead the horses onto the bank," he ordered, trying to bring her back to her senses. "You had to let the men in the river go. I'm not coldhearted, but I've seen men drown in the rivers before in the winter. There's nothing anyone can do, they die quickly. They don't suffer. We have to help the living. Some of the men left hanging on the ice need a fire to dry their clothes and warm their bodies. The horses have to be dried, too. Then we must regroup and set up camp, for this day is lost."

She was totally to blame, and he wouldn't let her forget it, but now was not the time; he had to get her back to work. "Katerina, have your men start large fires. Do it!" he shouted, giving her a vicious shove. "The prisoners are looking at you, you're their leader, give them their orders."

Slowly she turned to the men and without emotion ordered them to make fires. Little by little she busied herself, until she gradually had worked off the lethargy.

Banyen was busy helping and directing. "You,

guard, ride up the river and look for a shallow spot to get these four wagons across. When you find such a place, get back to me. I want to make camp on the other bank by nightfall."

Darkness found them camped along the opposite bank, huddled around the fires, feeling the cold more piercingly this night than any other.

Katerina was furious with herself. *Another day lost and it's my fault. By the time we reach Volin, the snow will be falling and knee-deep on the ground. Each day counts, each day makes the trip to the Carpathians more difficult. The wagons will slow our progress as they slip and slide in the snow. Perhaps there'll be some sleighs left in Volin and we can use them instead,* she thought.

Banyen wanted to chastise her to her face, but he knew the wrong decision and the deaths of the men and horses were punishment enough. But when he could he would lash out at her, this Cossack girl, and teach her that stupid womanly pride had cost them time and lives. She would pay when the delay caught them in the heavy snows of the Carpathians.

Katerina called the cook and one other driver, and after supper that night they checked the remaining wagons and sleigh to make sure they weren't damaged. She shook her head as they walked, muttering, "Four men, one wagon, one sleigh, and four horses lost on the mountain. Now two more wagons, eight horses . . . a total of ten guards with their horses and thirty-five prisoners, all dead." The men walking with her heard her but said nothing. Everything looked in order. She prayed silently that the rest of the journey would be accomplished without the loss of more lives. From here to Volin the land was level, the glorious flat steppe. The only enemy left to fight would be the heavy accumulation of snow between Volin and the House of the Kat.

As they made their way back to camp she knew that within four days they would probably be near Volin.

Banyen and the men were asleep when they returned, exhausted from the tragic day. This was one day none of them would ever forget, not even the rough, hardened prisoners. She laid back by the fire, curling up to keep warm under her blanket. As her eyelids grew heavy, the thought of arriving in Volin comforted her. The thought of the steppe also made her feel a little better. She had cursed the flat, desolate plains during the winter for their endless snow and icy cold, and in the summer she had cursed them for their heat. This night Katerina found she loved the plains, their vast, barren emptiness. It would mean no hills, no rivers, no death. Straight ahead was Volin, waiting. The picture of home faded as her cinnamon eyes closed and the pain of the tragic day was lost in sleep.

Chapter Eleven

KATERINA TRIED TO FORCE HER EYES to remain open in the swirling storm, to no avail. It was up to her now, her and the lead horse. The Khan's soldiers and Banyen couldn't help her now. Their fate would be decided by the horse. She would have to trust to the animal's blind instinct in getting to the pass. If Mikhailo had had the foresight to bring extra horses and sleighs to Volin, then he would have strung the pass with bells in anticipation of the heavy snows and her late arrival. Somewhere out there in the vast, all-consuming whiteness was the pass that would take her to the House of the Kat. She closed her eyes, the driving blizzard coating her thick lashes. She whispered encouraging words to the horse, aware that the animal couldn't hear her in the blizzard that raged around them.

They rode for hours, the animals straining to pull their heavy burdens through the deep snow. Katerina sat huddled in the sleigh, her ermine cape and heavy fur rug pulled tightly around her. For the first time she felt the faint stirrings of panic. What if this mare that Mikhailo had brought missed the pass? She, Katerina Vaschenko, would be responsible for the deaths of all these men. How confident she had been! How glibly she had assured the Khan that she wouldn't have any trouble getting back to the Carpathians. And she wouldn't have, if it hadn't been for her stupidity on the Kama. She paid for that daily. The presence of the Mongol was her reminder of it all. She felt his closeness in the sleigh they shared and was surprised that he made no snide remarks concerning the snow and the fact that they were two days overdue. Was that why he was quiet and not baiting her with his testy remarks about her abilities?

She was numb with cold, all feeling gone from her legs and feet. Dear God, help me, she prayed silently. Don't let us freeze to death.

Through the loud winds she thought she heard the high, clear sound of a bell. Where did the sound come from? It couldn't be from the horses' harness; the bells were too tiny, and the sound would be lost in the force of the driving wind. Katerina sat upright, and felt Banyen also straighten from his slumped position next to her. She stared into the white void of nothingness. It was a bell! Thank you, Mikhailo, she sighed. When the horse heard the bell he would know he was near the pass and close to home and a pail of oats. Once through the pass, he could find his way back to the House of the Kat blindfolded.

Squirming deeper into the fur lap robe, Katerina let her tired body relax. The snow was needle-sharp as it stung her face and beat against the sleigh. She was so tired, so very tired. All she wanted to do was sleep, but she knew that if she allowed herself the luxury she would never wake. She felt Banyen stir, trying to make himself more comfortable. Think about Prince Banyen, her mind shrieked, that will keep you awake. Think about that time on the steppe when he raped you and left you lying there with nothing more than a cape to cover your nakedness. Think about him sitting next to you. Think how it will feel when you finally get your revenge.

Her mind wandered as the horse strained and heaved to pull the heavy sleigh. The driving, pelting snow and ice were Banyen's hands forcing her back, back, back, till she sprawled on the sable blanket. The force of the wind was his hot, searing breath as he leaned over her, closer, closer, always closer, till he smothered her with his heavy body. The fir tree overhead with its swinging, dipping branches, which beat against the sides of the sleigh, was his heaving, thrusting body. The low-slung branch that reached out its tentacles to strike her full force across the side of her head was her shock of pain. She screamed as she lurched and fell against Banyen.

Banyen reached out an arm protectively to grasp her slim body. His eyes took in the fallen branch, and his hand felt warm stickiness on the side of her face. Damnation, this was all he needed. His hands explored her face, roughly at first, and then more gently as he felt the gash on her cheek. How smooth and satiny her skin felt beneath the ermine hood. The thick lashes fluttered against his hand as he brushed her hair from the wound. "A limb from one of the firs dropped on you," he said softly. "You were just stunned. Your animal has entered the pass, the bells are clear now, and the snow is not quite so thick." He gathered her close, his hands inside the ermine cape encircling her body. How vulnerable she feels, how cold, how defenseless, he thought as he brought her nearer to him, his own cape open so that their bodies met in warmth. "An old Mongol custom—two bodies together for heat will allow us to survive," he said huskily.

Katerina was too tired to resist, too weary to care, and she decided she liked the feel of him. For now, it was all that mattered. How gentle his hands were. For the first time in days she felt warm. She burrowed her head in his chest, her eyes sleepy and relaxed. She felt his hands cup her face gently as he lowered his face to hers. Katerina parted her lips as his full mouth settled possessively over hers. She felt light, soft nibbles against her lips. The pressure of his lips on hers was increasingly demanding, persuasive. Her breathing became his as he explored her moist mouth with his searching tongue. His hands on her body inside the fur cape were hypnotic, touching her intimately, spreading fire throughout her body. Her arms moved naturally to encircle his broad back, the black-tipped hood slipping from her head. She felt his hands cradle her head as her wealth of copper hair fell over their faces. His lips ground against hers hungrily as she eagerly gave him the sweetness of her mouth. She began to moan softly as his hands tantalized her with their gentle, sensuous caresses. The warm feel of his body and the rippling muscles beneath her hands so delighted her, she crushed her lips against his, demanding he return her ardor. Her heart pounded with exquisite torture as she heard him emit low animal groans of passion. His hard mouth was devouring her as his embrace became more urgent, more frantic. "I knew I could melt that cold, icy reserve of yours," Banyen panted heavily as his mouth came down against hers, crushing her, driving the breath from her body.

The sleigh lurched as the words penetrated Katerina's mind. Knew . . . he knew he could . . . ! "Damnable devil!" she screeched as she pushed with all her strength. Banyen was flung over the side of the sleigh into the swirling drifts. "Walk!" she screamed into the void. "If you try to get back in this sleigh, I'll kill you!"

Tears trickled down her reddened cheeks as she straightened her clothing and drew the ermine cape over her head. Her chest heaved at his remembered nearness, the feel of him. How could she have let it happen? How could she have been such a fool? She was tired and weary, numb with cold, she defended herself. Her defenses were down, she had been vulnerable, but thank God she had come to her senses. It wouldn't happen again, she would make sure of that. For a brief moment the thought saddened her, and she quickly thrust it from her mind. There was no room in her life for men and passion. She had a mission to fulfill, and when she accomplished that . . .

Katerina wondered vaguely what time of day it was. Here in the pass, with the low-slung pine trees, it was too dark to tell if it was evening or late afternoon. It really doesn't matter, she told herself. It was just something to think about so that the damn Mongol wouldn't invade her thoughts again.

The sound of the bells was clear, more distinct. The worst of the storm must be nearing an end. The lead horse seemed to be going faster. Did it mean he was almost through the pass, or was the snow less deep? No, the storm was abating. She could see the horse's broad back in the flurry whiteness. She could even see the bells strung across the evergreen trees. "Another hour," she shouted, "and you shall have the warmest blanket and the biggest pail of oats I can find!" The horse whickered in pleasure at her words. The matched blacks snorted and strained, their glossy hides snow-covered, making them look spectral in the dim light. Katerina had done it. She hadn't let the snow defeat her, or bury her beneath its blanket of coldness. Banyen had been wrong. He had said they would die and it would be her fault. Wrong again, Mongol!

Banyen seethed and smoldered with anger as he trudged through the knee-deep snow. He clutched at the second sleigh in line to keep from falling. He stumbled along as the sleigh half dragged him through the deep snow. His arms felt as if they were being pulled from their sockets. By God, he would kill her the first chance he got. Damn the Khan and his orders! But first he would torture her and taste her body, he promised himself.

The storm seemed to be letting up, and he noted that the sound of the bells was clearer, more distinct. It couldn't be much farther. He cursed Katerina and all Cossacks for their bloodthirsty ways. They were as bad as Czar Ivan. Thoughts of the Czar and how he planned to kill him kept Banyen going. Hatred could make a man endure and survive anything. Vengeance was a balm to the soul, food for the heart. He prayed that when the day arrived for him to kill the Czar, Ivan would be lucid. There would be no pleasure in killing an insane man.

As he trudged forward, he forced his mind to think of Ivan and the atrocities he had committed. The vision of his parents' savage slaughter floated before his eyes. It was true that he had been a child at the time of their death, but it was a sight that would stay with him for the rest of his life. As he grew older, the Czar and his activities had become an obsession with him. He would ferret out any and all tales of the mad Czar and relish what he would do in retaliation. How could a man, a Czar, cut the eyes and tongues from people's heads and laugh? How could a man, a Czar, string small children up by their feet so the swordsmen could practice, using their bodies as targets?

Perhaps the Czar's insanity stemmed from his boyhood, when, it was said, he was sequestered with a dimwitted brother and a monk who tutored them. The story was told that Ivan blamed the boyars for his parents' death, and when he had himself crowned Czar he began waging his war against those boyars whose power equaled his own.

Banyen's mind filled with hatred for the man he had sworn to kill. It would be an act of goodness, for he would rid the world of an insane, murderous madman, whose touch wreaked havoc on all nations within his reach.

Just let him meet me face to face so I can drive my saber through his heart. "God, grant me Ivan is sane when vengeance is mine," he muttered as he slipped in the snow, his mind not willing his feet to do his bidding. Regaining his position by clutching the sleigh, he failed to see the huge walls of the fortress looming in the distance. Each step was made with hatred and vengeance, hatred for Ivan, and hatred for Afstar's niece. "God grant me the will, the strength to do what has to be done," he muttered over and over as he continued his trek.

The lead horse snorted to show they were approaching the huge fortress known as the House of the Kat.

Katerina sat up straight, her eyes searching the dimness around her. They were home! We made it through the snow! she thought happily. Soon she would look upon her aging grandfather for the first time since the raid on Volin. How would he look, and how would he feel? Would he blame her?

The heavy, monstrous doors swung open, and the crimson sleigh, followed by the others, entered the deep cavernous underground stable. The tinkling bells on the horses' harness sounded merry and cheerful in the dim, cold expanse.

Katerina clambered from the sleigh and wrapped her arms around Mikhailo and Stepan, who stood waiting with raised lanterns.

"So you thought I wouldn't make it! Thank you, Mikhailo, for stringing the bells."

The old man looked at the young woman with respect in his eyes. "I knew the snows would come early, my bones felt it. I was worried, and so was Stepan, who helped me."

When all the sleighs had been placed side by side, and the horses taken to their stalls, the heavy doors were closed against the swirling, biting snow.

Other lanterns were lit as Katerina, Mikhailo and

Stepan walked among the shackled prisoners. It was Katerina who spoke first, her eyes on Banyen. "Your shackles will be removed. Sleeping quarters have been provided and blankets await you. Food will be brought to you soon. You, Prince Banyen," she said coldly, "will remain with the men."

The thick ermine cape trailing behind her, Katerina entered the dank tunnel that led to the main part of the house, the eyes of all the men on her back. Kostya's eyes were heavy, almost sleepy-looking; Banyen's were narrowed and speculative. When he turned, he felt Kostya's gaze on him. A grin tugged at Kostya's mouth as he held out his hands for the shackles to be removed.

Upstairs, the old man sitting near the fire warming his brittle bones, a yellow cat in his lap, looked up with rheumy, watery eyes at his grandchild. He watched as she tossed her fur cape on the table, her coppery hair tumbling over her shoulders, the golden-flecked eyes like tapered candle flames in the dim, shadowy room.

The blazing fire in the hearth drew her to the dancing, flickering light as a moth to light. She rubbed her long, slender fingers as she stared at her grandfather, wanting to throw her arms around him and tell him how sorry she was. There were so many things she wanted to say to the old man, but she remained silent, waiting for him to acknowledge her in some way, to show he didn't fault her for the slaughter in Volin.

Katmon's head trembled as he stared at the slim girl, willing her to speak to him. When she remained quiet, he spoke, his voice thin and reedy.

"You're not to blame, little one. What will be will be. Mikhailo told me of your trip to the Khanate. I applaud this action on your part. I pray in this frail old heart of mine that I'll be here to see if you succeed in the spring."

Katerina dropped to her knees. "Zedda, I was afraid to speak for fear I would see anger in your eyes, anger that I . . . I see no forgiveness in your eyes either, and that makes me happy, for I know truly in my heart that you don't think me guilty in any way." She laid her coppery head on her grandfather's bony knee and felt tears sting her eyes. How wasted he was since she last saw him. How weak. His voice trembled like that of a frightened child. She felt the gnarled hands stroke her hair with tenderness. "I'll make it come right, Zedda, you have my promise. I'll get our horses back, every last one of them. My word as a Cossack, Grandfather."

"I know that, my child. You're Katlof's daughter, and for that, and that alone, you'll succeed. Now you must eat and sleep. We'll talk more in the morning. Your room was readied by Stepan days ago, and a roaring fire has been going since then. Eat, Hanna made thick potato soup for your arrival. There is also fresh-baked bread and plenty of hot tea."

"Well then, I'd better do as you say or Hanna will give me no rest." Katerina sighed with amusement. "I believe that no matter how old I get, she will always nag me as though I were still a child." Katerina patted the elderly man fondly on his arm and sat down near the fire to dine. From time to time she watched the aging man as his transparent lids quivered and then closed over the faded eyes. How sad he must feel in his heart, she thought, to lose his only son to marauders. How unbearable to know all the horses are gone from Volin. The first time in their history, the Cosars were stolen by murderers and thieves.

She finished her simple meal and looked around for Mikhailo or one of the others. Of course—they were all with the prisoners, helping to get them settled. Zedda would be all right alone, dozing by the fire. She added another log and tucked in the lap robe a little tighter around his stick-thin legs. She kissed him lightly on the forehead and left the warmth of the kitchen.

Katerina shed her rough clothing and donned a warm woolen nightdress. She climbed into the high feather bed and was surprised to feel the heated rocks at the foot, where her feet rested. Dear Stepan, he thought of everything. She lay back, sleepy and contented. She had done well. There was respect in Mikhailo's eyes, and the old man in the kitchen loved her. She knew her father couldn't have done any better than she in bringing the wagons through the mountains and down through the pass. Yes, she had done well!

When Katerina woke, she had no idea of the time. The fire still blazed brightly in the silent room. Sometime shortly before dawn, she wondered if Zedda would be awake. If not, she would kiss him lightly on the cheek and he would open his eyes as always when she ran to him with a bad dream. He always made the villains in her nightmares disappear with a few carefully chosen words and a gentle smile. Perhaps his magic would work again even though she was grown.

Quickly she wrapped herself in the white-and-black fur and raced down the cold corridors till she came to the kitchen. Zedda was awake and staring into the flickering flames, his hand resting on the yellow cat's head. Turning his head at her entrance, he motioned her to sit next to him. "A bad dream Katerina? Tell your Zedda all about it." He smiled.

"No nightmare this time, Zedda, I just couldn't sleep. I think I'm too tired, if that's possible. My stupidity on the ice torments me. Once I gave father my promise that I would never fail again, but I did."

"We're all human and vulnerable—you're no different from your father. Tell me now, when there is no one to hear us, how did my son allow the village to be raided. What was his mistake?"

"Mistake?" Katerina said, puzzled.

"Yes, your father did something that permitted the raid to take place. An error in judgment perhaps, just as you say you made on the ice. There isn't a person on this earth who at one time or another doesn't make a mistake. Unfortunately, this time it cost Katlof his life and his people's. Now, tell me what he did."

"The men were drinking the night before leaving

for the fortress. On several occasions I noticed Father wasn't able to consume the vast amounts of vodka he used to. He would reel drunkenly and sometimes fall asleep. If the men saw their hetman so, they naturally assumed they could do the same. Only two guards were posted along the camp. I haven't any other explanation for you, Zedda."

"It's not for me that you must provide the answer. It's for yourself. Your father was not perfect, and neither are you or I. It is to be hoped that we learn from our mistakes. Remember your father as he was and how he loved you."

"He hated me in the end, Zedda. I can't forget his words to me. I tried to tell him, but he wouldn't listen."

"Your words were heard, and they ate at his heart every hour and every minute of the day. I say this to you in truth, little one. You must believe me! Your father loved you with all his soul, no matter what you did or didn't do. He was hurt and bewildered by what he didn't understand. In time he would have come to his senses and made things right between you. Believe that."

Katerina laid her head on the old man's knees, tears trickling down her cheeks. "I want to believe it, but he's gone. He never had reason to doubt me. I never lied to him, Zedda, just as I have never lied to you!"

"We'll talk more later. My eyes grow heavy, child," he said drowsily.

Katerina reached out her arms as her grandfather gathered her close to him, stroking the rich, coppery hair. "You must believe," he said sadly. "Always believe in what you do." The paper-thin eyelids closed as his bony hand dropped into his lap.

Quietly she got to her feet and walked back to her room, feeling better for having talked with him. Not once did he say a word about his grief over the loss of his son, she marveled. "His only concern was for me and my feelings," she said out loud. Her step lightened as she entered her room and crawled beneath the downy comforter on the bed. For a little while she could sleep; maybe this time her dreams would be pleasant.

An hour before dawn, Katerina climbed from her warm nest in the high bed. As she scurried to the fire to dress she looked longingly at the heavy pedina that had covered her. She couldn't afford to sleep another second, she had to dress and have her morning meal before the others were wakened. It would be a long, tiring day, the first of many in the coming winter months.

Katerina quickly donned a thick black body garment. Throwing the ermine cape around her shoulders, she descended the wide stone steps that led below.

Inside the cozy kitchen, she looked for her grandfather. She found him in the same position he was when she left him during the night, only this time the big yellow cat purred contentedly in his lap. She smiled a greeting and immediately began to flex her arms and legs, the way Cossacks do when warming up for a saber drill.

"Have you spoken to Mikhailo, Zedda?" she asked.

"He and Stepan just left to see to the men and give them their morning meal. Mikhailo said you made wise choices of which he approved. For him to make a comment like that he must have been truly impressed. My old friend mentioned that there were a few among them who might give you trouble, but he felt sure you and the prince could handle it. Tell me, little one, how many men did you lose coming through the Urals?" He leaned back, the words costing him dearly. When he had his breathing under control he opened his eyes, waiting for her answer.

Katerina, alarmed at his ragged breathing, trembled and fought the urge to run to him and cradle the shaking white head to her breast. She knew how he hated open displays of emotion, so she remained seated, her breakfast untouched.

"I lost thirty-five of the prisoners and ten of the

soldiers. It was my fault. I tried to rescue them, but it was a foolish thing to do—an impossible task. We worked doggedly to try to split the ice and rescue them, but they were already dead and washed away by the strong current. We lost two days because of the accident, that's why we were late coming through the pass. I'm to blame, Zedda, not Banyen."

"Why do you dislike the prince?" the old man asked sharply, aware of her hostility at the mention of his name.

Katerina's mind raced. "Because he's arrogant and selfish. He mocks me every chance he gets with words, and with his eyes. My mistake on the ice convinced him I will fail. He hates me as much as I hate him."

The old man sighed and shifted so the cat could snuggle deeper into the crook of his arm. Fire and ice, he thought, and they'll be together for the entire winter.

"I'm the Kat now, Grandfather, and I won't let him forget it, not for a moment, for a day, or a month. Never!"

The aged Cossack leaned forward, jostling the yellow cat from her comfortable position. "Such hatred for a man who is arrogant and selfish! You lie to me, granddaughter, there's more to it than you're telling me."

"I don't wish to discuss it, Grandfather. For now, those are my reasons."

"Be wary, child. If what Mikhailo tells me is true, this is a man who will bring you to your knees."

"Not to my knees, Zedda, my back!" Katerina muttered quietly. "I'll remember what you said."

"Why weren't you born a boy?" he grumbled. "Things would be so simple if you—"

The honey-colored eyes sparked, and Katerina's full, sensual mouth tightened into a grim, hard line. "You haven't said that to me in many long years. I've made one mistake, but I've done nothing wrong. I've trained as well as the men in Volin. I've managed to bring one hundred and fifty-five men through the

Urals during winter, and you tell me he's a man that can bring me to my knees! Hear me well, Grandfather, the day will never come when any man can conquer me." Her voice was so quiet, so deadly, that the old man shuddered in his warm, cozy chair near the fire.

Katmon's tone was petulant. "When are you going to start thinking about taking a man? I think you need someone to warm your bed at night. I wanted to see grandchildren before I die."

"Then you'd better plan on living many long years," Katerina said bitterly.

Whatever retort the old man was tempted to make went unsaid as he noted the narrowing of the catlike eyes. Whatever was bothering her wouldn't last forever. Katerina finished her breakfast in silence.

"Zedda, would you like to come with me to the arena and watch?"

"Bah! I've no desire to see grown men cry with your wicked ways. Mikhailo and Stepan will give you all the help you need. I wish you well."

Katerina advanced near the fire. "Your mouth tells me you wish me well, but your eyes say you hope I'll fail. Speak the truth, Zedda."

"Yes, that's what I wish. To see you fail just once."

The titian eyes were stormy as Katrina gazed at her grandfather. He was an old man; already he had lived more years than a man had a right to expect. She loved him dearly, and would gladly lay down her life for him if necessary, but he was wrong, and she wouldn't fail—she couldn't.

Chapter Twelve

KATERINA WRAPPED HERSELF in the white ermine and, with a last fond look at her aging grandfather, left the comfortable kitchen.

She shivered inside the enveloping warmth of the rich cape, not with cold but with dread. How would it go? How receptive and dedicated would the men be? And Banyen, what of the prince? Again she shuddered, remembering the feel of his lean, hard body next to hers. Her cheeks flushed as she remembered how she had responded to his mouth on hers and strained her body next to his. It wasn't the men Katerina dreaded meeting, it was the prince, she admitted to herself.

She descended the cold granite steps to the huge arena below the fortress, noting the beads of ice on the rough gray stone walls. Her breath whirled and eddied around her in the crisp, chill air. For one brief moment she wished she were back beneath the soft pedina on her bed, with the fire blazing and her sleep untroubled.

The moment her foot touched the last step Katerina heard the babble of voices and knew her recruits were finishing breakfast and soon would be ready to start the morning drill. Perhaps they would be relieved that their shackles had been removed and would work diligently. She hoped none of them would give her trouble that required strong measures be taken against them. In her gut she knew it was going to be the prisoners against the prince's men. Banyen would fight her every step of the way. He would give nothing, and she knew instinctively that he wouldn't compromise in any way. In the spring would come the day of reckoning. He was a man and she was a woman. Men were entitled to their thoughts about women, just as women were entitled to theirs about men. And men, in her opinion, were good for only one thing: to help women bear children. That was the one thing women couldn't do alone. Since she had no intention of having a baby, now or later, she had no use for Banyen or any other man. She laughed delightedly at the thought. Somehow she must manage to voice her opinion to the Mongol and see his reaction. He would be livid, she knew, sputtering with rage, his indigo eyes dark and full of murder: hers!

She thrust open the door to the great arena that ran the entire length of the House of the Kat. Even with the brightly lit sconces, she couldn't see to the end of the vast underground cavern. The plank tables had been cleared away by Mikhailo, and now all that remained were the prisoners and soldiers stamping their feet and wrapping their arms around their chests in an effort to keep warm. All were clad in heavy fur coats, hats, and high boots.

A monstrous fireplace with whole tree trunks blazing was the only heat the room offered. Katerina walked over to the blazing fire and stood with her back to the dancing flames. She looked around at the men with clinical interest. She noted that Banyen stood in front of his men, who were off to the side, separated from the prisoners.

Katerina pierced him with her gaze. "It's you against me, is that what you're trying to say? The prisoners are my men and the soldiers are yours. Is it to be a test?" When he didn't answer, Katerina smiled. "They're babies." She smiled again as she looked at the youthful faces. "When a general goes to war, he should have men fighting at his side, not infants that need a wet nurse." Guffaws of laughter erupted from the prisoners as the soldiers tried to kill her with their eyes. Banyen refused to be baited and remained quiet.

Katerina dropped the ermine and waited a moment for the shock to register in the men's eyes. She knew how she looked with the body garment, the one-piece uniform the Don Cossacks were noted for, cleaving to her slim body. Each curve, each limb cried out starkly. If I stood here naked in front of them I doubt I would get more of a reaction, she thought. Katerina heard the indrawn breaths and noticed the looks of approval in the eyes of the prisoners as well as the soldiers. Banyen's face was a study in nonchalance, appearing impervious to her lithe body. She shrugged as she called Mikhailo to her side.

"Issue each man a body garment, and see that they move briskly. You too, Prince! We all wear the same attire," she said coldly. "This attire has always been made expressly for and given to each youth the day he began his training for the Cossack army. This year, because there aren't any Dons, you men from Sibir will wear them."

The agate eyes were darkening at her words. "I refuse to wear that ridiculous clothing," Banyen said savagely.

"Either you put it on under your own power or someone will help you," Katerina said threateningly. "You do what I tell you, not the other way around. Make fast work of it, for we are already behind with our drilling." Katerina glided to the front of the clustered prisoners. "These are my men, those are yours. Either you do what I tell you or my men will help you. As you can see, you're greatly outnumbered. Move!"

The Mongol's eyes narrowed till they were mere slits. He looked around, and Kostya's face was the first thing that came into his line of vision. A sly smile was on Kostya's mouth. Damn woman, she was right, he was outnumbered, and a good soldier always knew when to retreat. For now, he would do as she said and don the crazy costume she wanted him to wear. Later, he would strangle her with it.

Katerina suppressed a laugh when Mikhailo led the men back into the cavernous room. All appeared self-conscious and were holding their hands over their male organs. She waited till they were in line before she moved. Lightly, a saber held loosely in her hand, she literally danced in front of the men. "Welcome to the House of Vaschenko, or"—she let her eyes wander down the straggly line of men—"the House of the Kat. That is the name you've been whispering among yourselves, isn't it? Yes," she said, answering the unspoken question, "I'm the Kat. It would appear that you respect the title but not the person who owns it. You will, in time. From this moment on we will be together for sixteen hours every day for the next six months. We will work with the saber from dawn till noon. From noon till twilight you will work with the horses that will be assigned you. At sundown you will have your evening meal. You may eat as much as you wish at that time, and be advised, after today it is the only time you will be fed. Is that understood? A good Cossack can go days without eating, and if he has food he gives it to his horse first. Remember that. You come second.

"After your meal we'll work with the lance and the horse till the moon is high in the sky. Then you will sleep. A good Cossack can go for days without sleep, also. That is another point I want you not to forget.

"If for some reason your performance is judged poor, you'll spend your sleeping hours practicing your weakness. I said I would train you to be Cossacks, and that's exactly what I'm going to do. I'm going to work you till you think you'll fall in your tracks. Every day for as long as you're here you will curse me and hate me with a passion you didn't know existed. You will think and plot my death a thousand times over, and when you believe you have picked the right time and place, I'll be behind you, not in front of you.

"There are a few of you who'll be tempted to escape this fortress. Don't! I'll come after you and I'll find you, and then you'll force me to make an example of you in front of the others. There is no escape from the House of the Kat. An hour outside and your ears will drop from your head. Your eyeballs will freeze in their sockets. I have no wish to see any of you die," she said, looking directly at Banyen, "but if you insist on leaving here, be warned—it can't be done.

"The only link to the world below the mountains is our trained falcons. We have two birds. One is kept here, and the other is quartered in Kisinev. If help is needed, or someone wants access to the mountains, one of the birds is sent. I'm telling you this so you'll know if you have any plans to leave here, it can't be done. No one save a Cossack can survive this weather. At January's end the blizzards come, and they last till March. You must believe me when I tell you that at such time even a Cossack can't survive. You've been warned, and more than that I can't do."

One of the young soldiers standing near Banyen, little more than a boy, spoke haltingly. "I'm cold and I didn't get enough to eat, I'm hungry."

Katerina laughed, the sound bouncing off the thick stone walls, and raising the hackles on the boy's neck.

"In the House of the Kat we don't complain . . . ever. We don't whine like new born puppies. You are a babe; where do you fit into the Khan's armies? As a matter of fact," she said loftily as she walked in front of Banyen's men, "I've never seen a larger group of infants in my life." While she spoke to the young boys, she was looking at Banyen, the amber eyes mocking and scornful.

"I'm no baby," the youth said belligerently.

"Your name," Katerina said coldly.

"Igor."

"If I say you are, then you are," Katerina said dangerously. "Mikhailo, hand this . . . child a weapon.

Now tell me you aren't a babe with a sword in your hand. When you make a statement, be prepared to defend it . . . to the death, if necessary. Now tell me, are you a baby or not?"

"I'm no babe," the young voice cried defiantly, the blade held awkwardly in his thin hand.

"And I say you are," Katerina said, slicing down the front of the heavy fur coat, and with catlike speed she had the sleeve in tatters with her quick, cutting motions. "When are you going to fight for your words?"

Igor's eyes sought out Banyen's and pleaded with him to interfere on his behalf. Kat correctly interpreted the look and spoke. "Each man stands alone in the House of the Kat. A Cossack never asks or accepts help from another. A Cossack stands alone except for his horse. His animal is the only friend and ally he has," she said coldly.

Tears of rage burned in the youth's eyes as he lashed out with his sword, his movements clumsy and uncoordinated.

"Bah, you're impossible! Resume your place in line. I have no more time to spend on these childish games. I'll find a wet nurse for you unless the prince can make a man of you.

"Mikhailo!" The one word was an iron command. "Lock their furs away."

The Kat stifled her laughter as the men continued to hold their hands over their groins. All of Banyen's men—or youths, as she preferred to call them—wore sullen, angry looks. The prisoners wore puzzled, questioning looks on their broad faces.

"We're ready to begin," the Kat said in a clear, high voice. "Mikhailo, the music, please. You're going to learn Russian dancing. Form two circles and dance like this," she said, leaping into the air, twisting her body in a whirling motion, landing gracefully on her feet. "On your toes, and pretend you are holding a basket of eggs on your head. On the count of three." The Kat turned her head to hide her grin as the men leaped and cavorted through the air, their arms and legs flying every which way. A soldier named Vladimir protested as his feet left the ground and he ended in a heap.

"I came to be trained as a Cossack, not to learn to dance. Dancing is for women," he said vehemently.

"You're right, you're no dancer. I assure you, this is necessary. I care nothing at all about what you think. It's what I think and what I do that's important! Every Cossack goes through this phase of training. It will limber your muscles and enable you to move quickly and effortlessly. Now try it again."

"No!"

"Very well." The Kat sighed. "Mikhailo, take him to his quarters. No blanket and no dinner tonight. Perhaps he will develop a craving for the dance by tomorrow. Why are all of you staring?" she asked coldly. "I thought I told you to dance."

"But there is no music," one called Igor complained.

"If there's no music and I tell you to dance, what should you do?" the Kat asked coldly.

"Pretend!" cried a young voice from behind Banyen as he leaped wildly in the air, coming down with a thud. Banyen grimaced at the look on the Kat's face, and at the looks his men were giving him.

"Eggs, remember the eggs!" the Kat shouted as she walked among the men, the tip of her saber tapping this one and that one to show he was doing something not to her liking.

Mikhailo returned, and within minutes his fiddle was active. Katerina leaned against the wall as she watched Banyen leap into the air, his long, muscular legs doing exactly what they should be doing. His performance was almost as good as her own. She felt smug as she watched him help his men. The youths smiled crookedly, their eyes fearfully on the Kat.

As the noon hour approached Katerina signaled for Mikhailo to stop the music. She motioned for the men to fall into columns and stand at attention. She spoke briskly as she walked up and down among the straggly lines of prisoners and soldiers.

"Today is not an indication of what is to come. Today I'm judging you on flexibility and coordination. Timing and exact movement are extremely important. You must learn this or you could die. A good Cossack has a seventh sense. When you leave here, it will be honed to a sharp point. Your life will depend, at one time or another, on this new sense you're going to develop, always remember that. Your dancing leaves much to be desired. In time, with practice, you will improve. Now, cross sabers. Mikhailo will issue each of you a weapon, and you'll practice with a partner. I'm going to divide you into groups of fifteen men each, and you will have a leader whom you'll obey. The prince will do the same." She signaled to Banyen to begin choosing his men.

Katerina looked over the men she had come to know a little better than the others. Her first choices were Kostya and Rokal, then two others. She debated before she made her fifth, and final, choice, finally deciding on a tall, dark-skinned Russian.

Katerina's eyes danced when she saw Banyen's choice was a youth named Gogol and his second choice the boy Igor.

"Saber tips in place," she called loudly. "I have no wish to see the lot of you bleed to death, not today. Tomorrow you will remove them and slice at each other to your hearts' content. If your skill as a dancer improves, you'll be able to make your feet do what your mind tells you. Tomorrow," she shouted to Banyen, "your man who has been sent to his quarters will cross sabers without the tips. Is that clear? If he bleeds to death for some clumsy movement, it is on your head, not mine."

Lithely Katerina danced out to the middle of the arena and motioned for Mikhailo to join her. "A brief demonstration," she said, removing the saber tips. Deftly she backed off and flexed her legs, her slim body a study of perfection in the brightly lit center of the room. She brought up the saber and touched the tip of his weapon and shouted, "Begin!" Metal clanked against metal as she danced and reached, always finding her mark. Her movements were well practiced as she fluidly moved out of Mikhailo's reach. Twice the point found its target, Mikhailo's heart. The Cossack laughed as he moved clumsily, trying to get out of her way. She would advance, bring up her weapon, and slice up and down, her wrists barely moving.

Banyen watched, mesmerized as she leaped and thrust. He told himself her slim body had something to do with it. No woman could handle a weapon as she did. He understood her theory of dancing and crossed sabers. Grudgingly he admitted she was right. A body in good condition could handle anything—he was the living proof. Now all he had to do was convince these babes, as she called them, that he approved of what she was doing, without losing their respect. Damn, why couldn't the Khan have assigned him men instead of these raw recruits?

Her exhibition at an end, the Kat told the men to pair off according to their leader's instructions. She sat down near the blazing fire next to Mikhailo and watched as the men struck out with their heavy weapons. "What do you think, Mikhailo, is there any hope?" she asked softly, her eyes on Banyen as he lunged out at one of his men. His movements were sure and flexible, his weapon finding its mark each time. Not so the boy he was fighting with, who thought the weapon was something to hold across his chest for protection.

"In time they'll be all right, Katerina. Miracles do not happen overnight, nor in a week. The prisoners seem agreeable. I've heard no grumbling from any of them. They take orders well, but I expect trouble in the next few days."

"It is sure to come. For now, the lot of them are biding their time, waiting to see what's going to happen. Wait till they get one meal a day and then have to give up their sleeping hours to practice mastering their imperfections."

"The one called Kostya, I see the way he looks at you. He also seems to be the spokesman for the others. I've noticed the way they listen to him and look to him for some sign that they should do what he wants. I saw him give a slight nod of his head when you told them all to dance. He approved, and that's why there was no grumbling among the others. I noticed this, and so did the Mongol prince. His eyes hold cold murder, but for whom I don't know."

"For me, Mikhailo. If there is murder to be done, it will be me that commits the act. And it will be his body that falls to the ground, not mine!"

At the end of the second hour Katerina called a halt to the saber drill, and Mikhailo gathered the weapons and stockpiled them in the dim recesses of the cavernous room.

While Mikhailo tended to his duties, the Kat informed the men that their leaders were to follow Mikhailo to the underground stables, where they would select the horses and bring them back to the arena. "The rest of you may now take a rest period."

Deliberately, the Kat waited till the men filed behind Mikhailo, and found herself walking next to Kostya. She sensed the stiffening of his shoulders as she brushed against him going out the wide stone archway. She quirked an eyebrow and looked up at him. His bright blue gaze pierced her, but his stride never faltered as he continued to hold her eyes with his own. She searched for an expression, some sort of indication of what he was feeling, but his features remained blank, unlike Banyen, whose face and eyes were an open book. She felt puzzled but said nothing. She liked the feeling being near him gave her. There was hidden strength in his strong, sinewy arms, and his broad chest looked just right for a woman to be cradled against. She blinked. Now why had she thought of something like that? She wanted to say something just to hear his voice, but she remained quiet, some instinct warning her that this was not the time to speak with the Russian. She made a mental note to find a spare minute as soon as the men were on a strict schedule. Yes, she would make the time and use it to her best advantage.

She looked up as Mikhailo indicated a halt and opened the doors to the underground stable. She found herself staring into indigo eyes that spoke of many things, one of which was her death. She smiled to let him know she correctly interpreted his thoughts, and spoke softly so her words would not echo in the stillness around her. "I'll always be behind you, Prince Banyen. It promises to be a long, cold winter, so it would be wise if you diverted your thoughts to some other form of torture."

Banyen's tone was just as soft when he replied. "You can only be behind me if I go to the front, and I have no intention of doing that. It would be wise if you remembered that." The indigo eyes lightened as he gave her a low, defiant bow to allow her to precede him. A slight nick with the tip of her saber into his broad back and he entered ahead of her, an arrogant smile on his lips. He told himself it amused him to allow her her little flights of fancy. If she thought she could win out against him, let her. When he ceased to be amused, he would change things. He was a patient man—at times.

The stable was warm and moist with the horses' deep, even breathing. The sweet, pungent smell of horseflesh was like a balm to Katerina as she walked among the animals, patting them gently on the muzzle or stroking their flanks. The horses whickered softly as she cooed tender words to them. Their ears recognized the soft words of the Kat. Immediately they calmed as the men walked among them.

"I'm going to allow you to choose the horses yourself. I do, however, want to remind you that the animal you choose will be with you for the balance of your stay here in the mountains. Your life could well depend on the animal you choose, so be selective. Choose it as though you were choosing a woman."

Her eyes were banked fires as she watched first Banyen and then Kostya walk among the animals. Both men seemed to know what they were looking for. Their selection was slow, methodical, and thorough. In the end Banyen chose a gelding and named him Vengeance. Kat smiled into his eyes and waited for Kostya to choose his horse. He picked a mare and said he would call her "Horse" until he could think of an apt name. For some reason, Banyen's eyes were furious, his mouth a grim, tight white line in his handsome face. Kostya grinned as he continued his selection for the men who were training in his group.

Why do the men rub each other the wrong way? the Kat wondered as she walked among the horses. Was it because of her? Or was there some other reason, a reason that had to do with the Mongol camp, when Kostya was a prisoner and Banyen his guard? They were like cat and mouse. She was unsure which was which. Sooner or later she would find out, she told herself. She leaned against a bale of hay, her long, slender legs planted firmly on the floor. They were both handsome men; both had lean, hard, muscular bodies. Both had keen intelligence, and while Banyen was the more verbal of the two, the Kat felt instinctively that Kostya's actions would speak louder.

The stable was too warm for her liking, and she wished they would hurry up with their selection. She wiped impatiently at a loose lock of coppery hair with a slender hand, her eyes on the two men. She looked around and was surprised to notice that she was the only one with beads of perspiration on her brow. Her amber eyes grew stormy as she continued her scrutiny of Kostya and the prince. They were both having an effect on her, and one she couldn't deny even to herself. Kostya with hair the color of wheat, and Banyen with hair the color of raven's wing. Day and night. Did she want either of them?

The remainder of the time until dinner would be

spent with each man acquainting himself with his horse. They mounted and dismounted, getting the feel of the steed that was assigned to them. The Kat watched carefully through the long hours for any sign of dissension between animal and man. As Mikhailo entered the stable to let them know the hour for supper was at hand, she relaxed. The first day seemed to be going well.

Mikhailo motioned her to come near him and informed her in a low whisper that her grandfather requested the company of the prince at his supper table. The Kat was shocked at the request.

"And he said that he was appalled at your lack of manners!"

"Royalty does not eat with the common soldier?" Katerina asked snidely.

"The words are those of your grandfather, not mine. He's insistent, Katerina, that your Mongol prince dine with us each day, and not in our work clothes. He had Hanna get out the best dishes, silver, and the linen napkins and cloth. He told Hanna to serve in the kitchen because he is not well enough to entertain in the dining hall. Perhaps it means he's feeling better. What do you think?"

Katerina's amber eyes smoldered hotly. "What it means is I'll be forced to eat next to him every day if Grandfather doesn't change his mind. The prince should remain with his men. I'll try to convince Grandfather he is making a mistake."

"Save your breath. He wants to hear strange voices. He wants to hear new things, see new people. How can you deprive him of this small pleasure?"

"Very well, you've made your point, Mikhailo. But don't expect me to help with the conversation. And," she said emphatically, "I have no time to dress for dinner. A quick wash is the best I can manage. If you can convince the prince, more power to you, Mikhailo. With Grandfather's failing eyesight, I doubt he'll notice. And if he does, tell him I'm exercising my womanly prerogative."

Mikhailo shrugged. "It's time for the men to eat. How long do you wish them to remain at the table?"

"An hour, or a few minutes longer if you think it is advisable. What did Hanna prepare for the men?"

"A thick potato soup with chunks of lamb slowly simmered for many hours, black bread with yellow butter, and rice custard with raisins for a sweet. There should be no complaints." He grinned. "And she followed your orders so that the men could eat as much as they want." Katerina nodded as she left him to go to her room and freshen up before her dinner with the prince and her grandfather.

She felt her eyes smart as she picked up her small hand mirror, a gift from her father on her fifteenth birthday. Her cheeks were flushed, and the amber eyes were bright and shiny. Carefully she brushed her coppery hair till it shone in the dim lamplight. She whisked the stray strands away from her brow and hoped they would stay in place. She bit into her full, ripe lips so they would appear rose-colored. Satisfied with her appearance, she blew out the candles and left her high-ceilinged room to make her way to the kitchen.

Large oval windows were cut in the solid stone wall that led to the bottom of the circular stairway. Katerina stopped once to look out. All she could see was thick, swirling snow. A drift that looked as sharp as a razor's edge reached as high as the third window. She wondered which of the men would be the first to try to escape through the deep, suffocating accumulation. She sighed. They would have to learn by their own mistakes. Katerina knew they didn't believe her when she told them what it was like outside. Her father had said if you tell a man the truth, sooner or later he will learn to know that what you say is correct. It takes time, he had explained, for one person to trust another. Once trust is established, then everything settles into place. He was right; only time would tell. And for now, all she had to do was get through a dinner sitting at the same table with Banyen.

When Katerina entered the large, warm kitchen, Banyen stood up and greeted her with a show of respect. Her grandfather remained seated at the huge table. Hanna stood nearby, waiting for Katerina to be seated. Her rosy cheeks and wide smile made Katerina grin. Already Hanna was matchmaking—she could tell by the bright, twinkling eyes. Hanna approved of the prince, and it was obvious in the way she served him the biggest bowl of soup and the largest slice of her hot bread. The bright yellow turnip was mashed to perfection, with a round mound of butter nestled into a hollow. She ladled out the turnip on Banyen's plate and gave him a toothy smile. Katerina grimaced and looked down at her own meager allotment. She watched disgustedly as Banyen fell to his food as though he had never eaten before. He smiled at Hanna and praised her cooking, saying it was the best he had ever tasted. Hanna, beside herself with happiness, added another thick slice of lamb to his plate and then retired to the stove.

"I'm honored to have you visit my house," Katmon said in a frail voice. "Allow me to apologize for entertaining you in the kitchen, but these old bones of mine demand heat, and the dining hall is full of drafts. Tell me of the Khan and of Sibir. Did my granddaughter tell you that her mother was a Sibirian Mongol and that she and the Khan were brother and sister?"

"The Khan told me all of the facts," Banyen said quietly. "There is no need for you to apologize to me. I also prefer the warmth and closeness of a kitchen. Many times when I was a child I ate in the kitchen with my parents and the cook, in our fortress where two rivers came together. I'm not sure I remember it clearly, for I only knew my parents a short time. They were slain by Ivan and his Russians." He felt his blood begin to boil, so he looked around the room and commented on its size and its cleanliness. He smiled. "Your kitchen is one of the best I've sat in."

Katmon pushed his half-eaten food away and leaned back in his comfortable chair, the lap robe pulled tightly around him. His pet cat jumped onto his lap and snuggled deeply into the robe. "Do you think you can survive the winter here?" he asked in a reedy voice.

"Yes, I can survive in this house, as can my men. In the spring we'll all be here."

Was she mistaken, or did he stress the word "we"? Was he implying that if anyone tried to leave it would be the prisoners and not those directly under his command? Probably, for everything he said or did seemed to have a double meaning.

Her grandfather's next statement stunned Katerina.

"My granddaughter fancies herself the next savior of the Ukraine in that she can train these men and regain the Cosars. Do you think she can do it?"

Katerina seethed and fumed as she waited for his reply. When she heard his terse, cold "No" she wasn't surprised.

The old man chuckled, enjoying the prince more each time he spoke.

"Savior! Hardly," she protested to her grandfather. She fixed a steely eye on Banyen and said, "According to the Radziwill Chronicler, in 6453, by the old Russian calendar, there was a great Russian heroine named Olga. When her husband was killed, she used her wits ingeniously and avenged his death. She tricked his killers into a bathhouse, locked them in, and burnt it to the ground. There are some women," Katerina said coldly, "who will do whatever is necessary to survive and to avenge a wrongdoing. Do you remember the story, Grandfather?" she demanded, her eyes on the Mongol.

Her grandfather answered with a light nasal snore. Banyen's eyes mocked her as he continued to stare at her.

"Since you seem so well versed in the Radziwill Chronicler, perhaps you are familiar with this verse," Banyen said sotto voce. "In the winter, the Cumans came to Kiev and captured many villages beyond Kiev, returning with much booty to their land. Glebe,

Prince of Kiev, was ill, so he sent his brothers Mikhalko and Vsevolod to pursue the Cumans. Mikhalko, obedient, went after them and overtook them. God helped Mikhalko and Vsevolod against the pagans. Some were killed and others taken prisoner. They took their own prisoners, who were four hundred in number, from the Cumans. They sent the prisoners back to their own lands, and they returned to Kiev praising God and the Holy Mother of God and the Holy Cross. Old Russian calendar 6679," he said arrogantly.

"Bah, all that means is that you can read or someone told you the story and you remembered it," the Kat snarled. "Dinner is finished. We have a long night ahead of us; let's get on with it," she said, getting up from the table. "You first, Mongol, remember what I said—I'll always be behind you." She followed him down the cold, dank tunnel that led to the underground arena.

The flickering candles lent themselves to eerie shadows that played on her nerves as she kept her distance, the cloak wrapped snugly around her. "To the left," she said as Banyen came to a stop. Almost colliding with him, Katerina backed off, but not quickly enough. Suddenly she found herself imprisoned in hard, muscular arms. Her face was cupped in strong yet gentle hands as his head came down to meet hers. She struggled feebly as she tried to free herself from his grasp. The feel of his moist lips on hers sent her mind reeling, and she became limp in his arms, responding to him as she had on the day of their arrival.

His lips were hungry, demanding that he be satisfied by her. Slowly she strained toward him, willing him to demand more of her so that she could feed his insatiable appetite. Her lips parted, and she tasted his sweetness as she felt his hands explore her body beneath the ermine cape. Her hands found their way to his thick, cropped hair, and she ran her fingers through it, moaning at the desire that washed over her as she crushed her lips into his. Everything was forgotten, all the promises, all the dire threats she had made in silence against him. All she wanted now was to be near him, to have him be part of her. He whispered soft endearments that were barely audible as he blazed a searing trail from her mouth to her neck to her breasts. His hands were tender yet searching. Low animal sounds erupted from his throat. Nothing matters, she told herself as she sought the devouring lips and the delicious feel of his body next to hers. Wave after wave of desire rose in her as she felt him stiffen against her.

"Later," he whispered. "Later I'll come to your room," he breathed raggedly. "Later we'll be as one," he said, tearing his mouth from hers.

She stared at him with glazed, passion-filled eyes. In that moment she would have promised him the moon if he had asked for it. Shaking, she straightened herself and drew the ermine around her slim body. He wanted her, needed her. God help her, she also craved his total embrace—but she knew that when he came to her room she wouldn't open the door. Not to this Mongol! Never this Mongol!

Banyen positioned his men with their assigned horses and lances and put them through their paces. While they were slow and inexperienced, he was satisfied with each man's performance. Not so with the Kat as she singled out man after man with the tip of her lance. Once Banyen ground his teeth together when she drew blood from a sharp-tongued soldier. Her rejoinders were just as caustic as his epithets.

Kostya wasn't having any trouble with his small column of men. They did his bidding, their movements were sure and precise. Banyen's eyes narrowed as he watched Katerina look at Kostya with approval. She smiled and said something that sounded like congratulations. Kostya nodded, his bright eyes appraising and full of . . .

Banyen shook his head to clear his thoughts. He berated one of his men for a senseless mistake.

The prince's gaze traveled back to Katerina as she slouched against the wall next to Mikhailo. What was there about the Cossack girl that could stir him as she did? Why did his senses get the better of him when he was near her? Why did he want *her*? A woman was a woman. He liked the sweet, heady fragrance that she exuded, and he liked the feel of her slim body, covered though it was by her heavy clothing. And her incredible eyes—he had never seen any like hers. One moment they were like ripe, golden apricots, and the next they were raging volcanoes. He had to have her, and he meant to have her, and the sooner the better. But even though he had told her he would come to her room this night, he knew he wouldn't. He would make her wait, wait till she craved his body, till the desire rose in her eyes for all to see.

A wild thought stormed its way into his mind, and he stiffened. What if the bastard Kostya got to her first? Even from this distance he could see that there was only one emotion exuding from the Russian. He bristled with anger at the Russian's fitness. Stronger, better men had broken in the Mongol stockade. What had kept him alive and in condition? He had seen men beg and cry to be freed from their shackles, but not Kostya.

It was true, Katerina had a keen eye for a man's worth, but he knew in his gut she had made a mistake with Kostya. A sly look settled over Banyen's face. Let her learn from her errors; he owed her nothing except the promise he had made to her, that he would have her one way or another.

Kostya could feel the Mongol's eyes on him and knew the prince was filled with rage at his ability to carry out his orders so well. He smiled to himself. There was a lot to be said for hearty peasant stock. It was to be a contest between himself and the Mongol, but not for the obvious reasons. Who would get the Kat, the Mongol or himself? He was no fool, even if the Mongol thought otherwise. Hadn't he seen the approval reflected in the girl's face? Hadn't he felt her tremble at his nearness when they came through the archway? Time was his answer. Let the Mongol plow ahead like a bull and antagonize her every chance he got. It would be he, Kostya, who would win out. All he had to do was wait and bide his time. All things came to those who were patient. The Mongol was not a patient man; this he knew from his months in the stockade. He was tense, taut, as if ready to spring at a moment's notice. True, a formidable enemy and one who would give a good accounting of himself, but with a few weeks of the Kat's rigorous training Kostya would also be someone to seriously contend with. It would be interesting to see which of them won.

Katerina continued with her nonchalant pose against the wall as she whispered to Mikhailo, "A wise choice, don't you agree? Look at their eyes—they're like two fighting cocks. One won't let the other get ahead of him. Which do you put your kopecks on, Mikhailo?"

"The Mongol," Mikhailo said curtly.

"The Mongol!" Katerina exclaimed in surprise. "Why?"

"Several reasons," Mikhailo said harshly. "He's a man, the Russian is but a boy compared to him. True, they both have strength to their bodies, and both have a certain arrogance about them, but it's the years of experience the prince has behind him in the ways of the world that will drive him to be the victor. The question is, what will he win, Katerina? Observe his eyes and you'll see that I'm right. I see things in him I saw in your father and in your grandfather. Heed my words, Katerina, for I speak the truth."

Katerina was stunned at his words. "How can you say a thing like that? He's nothing like my father. And my father is dead because he made a mistake and thought he was infallible. No man is above that," she said gruffly.

"Not this man, Katerina."

Her honeyed eyes glinted angrily as she listened to the Cossack. She wouldn't, she couldn't admit that his words shook her to the core. How could he be so confident? She hated to admit it, but she knew the old man was right; she sensed it, felt it, every time she was near Banyen. "He's an animal," she seethed under her breath. And she would treat him as such. Kostya, on the other hand, was a . . . Yes, she asked herself, what is Kostya? She felt drawn to him for reasons she couldn't explain. Yet he showed nothing when he was near her, just that piercing gaze that was completely devoid of any meaning. Banyen's eyes spoke of many things . . . things she had no wish to see.

Shortly before midnight Katerina called a halt to the drill and ordered Mikhailo to collect the weapons and take the men to their quarters. "And," she said harshly, "I have no wish to hear that the Mongol is to be quartered in the big house. He stays here with his men, and you'll place a guard on the door and bolt it from the outside. Royal blood means nothing in this house; please tell him that for me."

Katerina neither spoke to nor looked at the men again as she left the vast arena. She had no desire to look into piercing blue eyes or smoldering, angry, dark ones that plotted against her.

She stopped in the kitchen before retiring to her room, and was surprised to see her grandfather still awake near the blazing fire, the cat clutched tightly in his bony hands. His eyes were bright with questions, but he waited for her to speak.

Katerina poured herself a cup of strong tea and sat down on the hearth. "It went well. Tomorrow, when their bones and muscles ache, we'll see how proficient they are. They all made wise decisions on the horses. I anticipate no great trouble, at least nothing that I cannot handle with Mikhailo's help."

"When are you going to tell them why they're here?" the old man demanded. "A man has a right to know what's in store for him. Withholding your reasons could well be your undoing. What will you do if, after you've trained them, they refuse to fight for you? What will you do then? These are not weak-kneed

people but strong, virile men. Think on that while you
sleep tonight. A man has a right to know what's in
store for him," he repeated in his frail voice. "What
you're doing is a magnificent thing, but what good will
it do you if the men don't choose to fight with you
when the time comes? You must be fair, your father
taught you well. How can you be so shortsighted?
Don't let it all be for nothing." The paper-thin eyelids
closed, ending the argument. He was asleep.

Zedda is right, Katerina thought wearily as she
rubbed at her temples. Tomorrow she would explain
to the prisoners her reasons for bringing them to the
mountains and what she expected of them. Tomorrow was another day. If only she had the Cosars, none
of this would be necessary. Who had them? And what
would become of them? Would they be scattered and
sold to the highest bidder?

Katerina poured herself another cup of the scalding
tea and carried it with her down the long corridor and
up the steep curving stairway to her room. She set the
cup on the hearth and added several logs to the already blazing fire. The high bed, with its thick, downy
pedina, looked inviting. What would it be like to roll
and move around in the big bed with a man she
loved? Katerina blinked as she realized where she
was, and quickly raced to the door and threw the bolt.
The sound was comforting in the quiet room—a balm
to her tightly strung nerves. Did she really want the
Mongol to come to her room? Did she want to lie with
him?

She sat down near the hearth and drew her legs up
to her chin, her arms clasped around them, a red-fox
blanket covering her like a waterfall. How could she
respond to Banyen and still feel such hatred toward
him for what he had done to her on the steppe? Tears
gathered in the titian eyes as she remembered the time
she had spent in the barn watching the young lovers.
And then a picture of Yuri flashed before her. Even
the embraces with Yuri hadn't been right. She hadn't
felt the way the couple obviously had. What she had

had with Yuri was passion; there had been no love. She knew that now. A meeting of the bodies for release was all it had been. If he had returned, would she have gone with him? No, she answered herself. There was no point in thinking about Yuri. Yuri was dead, killed by her own hand. She had put him to death to ease his suffering, just as she would put to death a wounded animal that had no hope of living.

Tomorrow was another day. Dawn would come before she was ready for it. She had to sleep. God, if it were only so simple. Just get into the bed, close her lids, and sleep. She raised her eyes to look at the icon on the wall over her bed. She bowed her head and prayed silently. She prayed to God to free her mind of her torturous thoughts; she prayed for peace of spirit and soul; prayed for the hatred to leave her; and she prayed for love somehow to find its way to her heart. So many things to ask for; surely He would answer at least one of her pleas.

Katerina let the fur lie carelessly across the bench that stood near the hearth and shed the thick body stocking. She stood naked for a moment in the chilly air and again wondered what it would be like to lie next to a naked man who loved her as she would love him. She shook her head, freeing the coppery hair from its pins, and donned a woolen nightgown. Sliding beneath the thickness of the pedina, her eyes closing . . . No sooner was she asleep than she was racing Bluefire across the steppe, his hooves crushing the white earth with his long-legged gallop. Strong, sinewy arms reached for her as she tore over the snowy fields, her breathing coming ragged and harsh. Would he catch her. Ride . . . ride . . . ride . . . faster . . . faster . . .

Katerina sprang out of bed in the morning, anxious to get the ordeal of informing the prisoners over with. After a quick breakfast she summoned Mikhailo and told him to get all the men assembled in the training arena immediately. Shortly thereafter, the Kat stood before the prisoners, legs astride, hands on hips, waiting for them to line up in formation.

"Men, I have ordered you here a little earlier this morning because I want to tell you why you're here and why you're training so hard. My village was raided, and my father and all the people were slaughtered. The raiders got what they came for, the sought-after Cosar horses. I can't bring my father or the people of my village back, but I can get back the horses. That is why you're here, and that is what you're going to do," she told them with a vengeance. A loud moan of dissatisfaction was heard from the multitude. "Save the moans for your sore muscles. Like it or not, the horses will be found by us and brought back to the Don Cossacks. Now, go have your food and be back here ready to practice hard and long. Eat hearty," she called to them as they filed out of the arena.

Chapter Thirteen

THE WHITE CARPET OF SNOW across the vast, endless steppe continued its relentless path into the fir-covered breast of the Carpathians. The massive fortress loomed like an intruder on the crystalline accumulation, trapped by the dense, mammoth evergreens. Winter had come in all its intensity to the House of the Kat.

Winter months in the Carpathians were well-waged wars between the harsh, ferocious winds that swept through everything and everyone and the cold, insidious, sparkling crystals that fell gently and constantly from the skies.

The snowdrifts hugged the walls of the fortress tenaciously, pushing and climbing their way to the second-story windows of the structure. All garrisoned within its cold walls shivered as the wind howled its song and shook the mighty walls with its breath. The monolithic trunks and branches of the giant firs accompanied the savage winds, hitting and striking against the thick gray stone of the dwelling, filling the interior with ghoulish, eerie sounds that chilled the dwellers to the bone.

The House of the Kat was no match for the clutching, all-consuming white giant that ruled the winter. The King of the North held fast its inhabitants, closing them off, making movements into or out of the fortress impossible. They were isolated and locked in for the winter. The smothering whiteness would take its toll on each of the hostages within the House of the Kat, but in a different way for each.

The tiny, shiny brass bells strung in the green, snow-ladened branches of the firs dared to sing out their merry melody to the stark, endless void. The whipping winds urged their constant activity, sending out their cheerful sounds to fall on the deaf ears of space. No human or animal moved to hear or applaud the mellow-sounding courage of the bells. During the reign of the King of the North, no man made the journey through the pass to the cavernous underground arena and stables that housed the Mongol prince and the prisoners from Afstar's Khanate of Sibir.

The training of the recruits and Banyen's men was long and seemingly endless. The prisoners worked diligently with something close to vengeance. Not so with Banyen's force. It was a contest of wills, and Kostya drove his men with quiet looks and a grim, tight line around his mouth when they did something he disliked. It was evident to Katerina and Mikhailo that the men respected him and even liked him. Banyen, on the other hand, drove his men unmercifully as he followed Katerina's orders. The young men serving under him resented Katerina and at times openly refused to follow her orders, which Banyen issued through clenched teeth. One night in the cold, bare room with no blanket and no dinner was all they needed to renew their hatred of her. She watched them through catlike eyes as they murdered her time and time again in their minds and hearts. Banyen remained aloof, and often openly ridiculed her with some snide remark or blatant show of contempt. Still, she admitted to herself, he didn't defy her; he did as she ordered even though he didn't like it. She felt in her bones that he was playing a game with her—a game that he intended to win. And Kostya, what was he planning?

She felt drawn to the tall, quiet man with the piercing blue eyes and found herself making excuses to talk to him, complimenting him on his skill or just standing near him, feeling the power his body exuded. And when she found herself standing next to him, she would feel Banyen's eyes on her, arrogant and mocking. She, in turn, would give him her sleepy Kat gaze and toss the heavy, burnished hair till it fell winsomely over her high cheekbones. Banyen would then shout at his men, and a look of cold, deadly hatred would settle over his handsome features. It was a game they played, and Katerina knew instinctively that if she wasn't careful the stakes would be something she was not prepared to lose. Kostya would watch the little byplay with an amused expression and smile down at Katerina, his white teeth gleaming in the dimness of the cavern. The three of them were playing a game, and each knew the unspoken rules. The only question in their minds was: what was the prize at the end of the game? Was it the Cosars, or was it Katerina?

Katerina led her horse to the water trough and watched him drink thirstily. Her back stiffened as she felt Banyen bring his stallion up next to her. Her eyes were quiet and languid when she looked up at him. Why hadn't he come to her room last night, as he promised? She would not have opened the door, but this way, she felt humiliated and embarrassed. He had said he would come and there were no footsteps in the great hall that night. Another game, cat and mouse. Well, she was no mouse, she was the Kat. This was the first time today that she found herself so close to him, close enough to smell his heady body scent, to feel the heat his lithe, muscular body gave off. Her hand trembled slightly as she grasped the reins of her horse and led him away from the trough.

Kostya waited a moment before he too brought his mount forward. His movements were slow, almost calculating, as he swaggered slightly, his bright gaze searching and alert. He nodded briefly to Banyen and let his gaze drift to the Kat, who was staring at him openly. She liked the way he carried himself, almost effortlessly, as though he moved to music. Banyen stalked and prowled, his eyes those of the hunter, his actions those of a killer bent in getting his prey. With Kostya present at the water trough, there was no way Banyen could talk to the Kat, even if it was only to needle her. His dark eyes smoldered with rage as he led the stallion back to his perspiring men.

Kostya grinned as he led his horse away and settled himself next to Rokal. "A small breathing spell," Kostya said, a smile in his voice.

"Best be careful, my friend," Rokal said quietly. "The Mongol knows how to kill. Read his eyes and don't say you weren't warned."

"I was warned back in Sibir, Rokal. If it comes to a personal battle between the two of us, I can give a good accounting of myself, have no fear. Those days in the stockade were not meant to be forgotten."

"He obeyed orders, Kostya, remember that. Back in the stockade, he had no stomach for what he was forced to do. Here it's another story. He wants the woman. You want the woman. Somebody's blood will flow, and, my friend, I feel it will be yours."

Kostya laughed, a sound that reached Katerina and Banyen. Both of them looked up to see the man's shoulders convulsing.

Katerina looked at Mikhailo and realized she liked the sound of the rich laughter the prisoner exuded. The stocky Cossack's face wore a strange look as he watched Katerina, a feeling of dread settling over him.

He, too, knew trouble would come soon. Which of the men would be the one to bring matters to a head? And was it just Katerina that was at the bottom of whatever it was that was bothering the two men? The old man's gut told him there was more to it than a woman. Katmon was forever telling him stories of how men made fools of themselves over women and lost not only their manhood to them but their dignity and their wealth. All for a woman. Never having had one of his own, Mikhailo found it hard to accept the elder's words. A woman was a woman! But Katerina was different. He didn't want to see her a pawn between these two, didn't want to see her hurt.

"You're too young for all this responsibility and too innocent to be wounded in the heart and soul. Why must it always come down to survival? Which of you will be the survivor?" he asked.

"Is there doubt in your mind, Mikhailo? I will, and so will the others. Life is a matter of strategy and endurance, and there are none among us who wish to die."

Mikhailo shuddered uncontrollably at the determined look in the Kat's eyes, the same expression she had had when she announced a new breed of Cossack was soon to be born. "But, Katerina, hatred will cloud your thinking. When you hate, you cannot love," he said shortly.

"Love!" she cried. "I have no time for love."

Fear crawled into Mikhailo's chest as he blinked his heavy-lidded eyes. "Someday you will want it," he said softly.

"Perhaps, Mikhailo. Do you suppose there is a man somewhere who will understand me? Will he look into my eyes and see my love reflected in his? Is there a man who will smile at me with humor and hold me close in the darkest hours and tell me nothing matters but me?"

Mikhailo frowned. "Somewhere, Katerina, there is such a man, and you will search each other out." He patted Katerina fondly and walked toward Banyen.

Banyen watched the short, stocky Cossack approach him. His hand went instinctively to his right cheek, where he fingered the hateful scar. As always when he was angry, the damnable thick red welt throbbed. If he ever came across the bitch that did this to him, he would wring her neck without a moment's hesitation.

Mikhailo's voice was thick and guttural when he addressed the Mongol. "Your man, Igor, needs much preparation. Neither Katerina nor myself care for his insolent attitude. You'll bring him into line or he will be spending many long, cold nights alone. It could be the death of him."

Banyen's fingers continued to caress the swollen scar as his eyes raged at the Cossack. He knew the old man spoke the truth. His only defense was that they were boys. It took awhile for a boy to become a man. However, he said nothing to the Cossack, but nodded his head to show that he was in agreement. Igor needed a tongue-lashing, and perhaps a swift kick from his boot. His surly, untamed mouth could be the end of all the youths if he didn't shape up quickly. Another night or two without dinner and the thick woolen blanket just might do the trick.

Banyen motioned his men to fall into formation behind him as Kostya and the men assigned to him mounted their horses and took to the center of the arena. The Russian divided his men into groups of seven, and lightly touched his horse's flanks for the animal to move backward. Banyen watched carefully as the men settled themselves on top of the horses and then spurred their mounts forward, their lances thrust in front of them. He was shocked when no one was unseated, all weapons clasped firmly in hand. Grudgingly he admitted that Kostya would have made a good general. He had the ability to make men do what he wished just by speaking. As yet, the prince had seen no man give him an argument. How, Banyen wondered, was he delegated to be the leader of the prisoners? Did they have some sort of unspoken agreement between them? What was there about the fair-haired Russian that gave the prisoners such confidence? Was it, could it be, that he was their friend? If so, that might account for their seemingly implicit trust in the blue-eyed man. His face contorted in rage as he saw Katerina walk over to congratulate Kostya.

Now it was his turn with his men. He felt a coldness settle over him as he signaled his men to take to the center of the arena. He knew in his gut that he couldn't hope to do as well. They would try, and that was all he could hope for.

He was right. They were clumsy and awkward, their movements unsure, their weapons held loosely in lax fingers.

"Enough!" yelled Katerina. "We have no time to waste with this childish foolishness. Prince Banyen, you will assign all of your men to their quarters for two nights. If they wish, they can practice throughout the night. When I set eyes on them again, they had better be prepared to meet with the prisoners in the center of this arena, and there will be no safety tips on the weapons. If they get wounded and die, it will be their own fault. One more mistake and your men will be turned out into the snow. It makes little or no difference to me if they die of cold or not!" The titian eyes spewed sparks as she stared at Banyen. "And," she said emphatically, "if they go into the snow, so do you." Turning on her heel, she left the arena.

That's what she should do, pray that they failed so she could send them all into the frozen landscape. How would the Mongol fare? He had left her to die in the snow, and she could do the same if she had to. Soon it would be her turn to wreak vengeance on him. All good things came to those who waited. And she would wait and wait and wait! Soon it would be her turn.

Katerina had just folded the blanket from her horse and laid it on a tack box when she felt a presence near her. She whirled, thinking it was Banyen stalking her again. "Kostya!" she said breathlessly. "What are you doing here?"

"Mikhailo sent me for additional blankets. Where are they kept?" he asked as he deliberately brushed near her. His bright blue eyes were expressionless as he stared at her, waiting for a reply.

Katerina pointed to a chest in the corner and moistened her dry lips with her tongue.

The silence between them seemed more eloquent than words could ever be. When Kostya held out his hand, she reached out her own delicate one and felt him draw her to him. They walked hand in hand to the dimmest corner of the stable. Katerina drew in her breath and felt the man next to her tense at her intake. He, too, seemed to have trouble with his breathing. She was conscious of his height, of his nearness, and of his maleness. His arm around her shoulders made her tingle with the contact of his flesh. In the murky light they stopped their initial, tentative gestures. She felt her body move into the circle of his arms. His mouth became a part of hers, and her heart beat in a wild, untamed, broken rhythm. In their yearning they strained together as they mounted obstacles of the flesh and worked to join blood, flesh and spirit.

In the quiet of the stable they devoured each other with searching, hungry lips.

His touch was gentle as he tore his mouth from hers, his breathing ragged and harsh. It was Katerina whose sensibilities returned first, and she stepped back from him, her eyes sleepy and almost content. Her passion-bruised mouth tasted sweet to her tongue as she licked at her lips in an effort to calm herself. She was alive! Her response to Kostya was what she had needed to prove that her body could respond to someone other than Banyen.

Kostya's touch was barely noticeable as he pulled her to him again in a hard embrace. Katerina, in control of the situation, demurred and moved farther away from his touch and his sinewy arms.

"You're right, this isn't the time and the place," Kostya whispered. "There'll be other times, other places. The winter will be long and cold, and one we'll endure together. It's been a long time since anyone stirred my blood as you just did," he said huskily. With a last lingering look deep into her eyes, he backed off, but not before he tenderly ran his finger down the length of her satiny cheek. The feel of his lean finger on her flesh was more shocking than the touch of his lips upon hers. She felt desire wash over her as he left the large, dim confines of the stable. Did she want him or did she need him? She admitted to herself that there was a difference. Sooner or later she would explore this feeling that was engulfing her.

Banyen stepped out of the shadows and watched through hooded eyes as Katerina stared after Kostya's retreating back. His tall frame was concealed by the heavy stone columns in the stable and by the stalls covered with brilliant blankets. What was the girl thinking; what was she feeling? Did she compare Kostya to him? Would she remember the kiss they shared in the sleigh? He didn't know why, but it was suddenly important to him to find out. He wanted to know—no, he *needed* to know which of them she preferred.

The angry, crimson welt on his cheek began to throb as he watched Katerina lay her cheek against a horse's head. Even from where he stood in the shadowy light, he could see the dreamy look in her face. Damnation, what and who was she thinking about? His loins took on an ache that threatened to erupt into fullblown pain. His strong hands gripped into fists at his side, and he clenched his teeth in frustration. He had raped a woman once. Would this one submit to a small taste of lovemaking, or would she have to be raped like the girl in the snow?

Hunter and stalker that he was, he moved lightly to the heavy wooden doors and closed them quietly. He slid the bolt with barely a sound. Slowly, insidiously, he crept up on Katerina and stood behind her. His hands reached for her thick, coppery hair, but before he could touch the gleaming strands, she turned, her eyes wide and staring. What was it that he read in their flaming pools? He said nothing as he twined his hands in her rich wealth of hair. Gently he drew her to him, then forced his parted lips upon hers in a savage, demanding kiss that she returned in kind. Unseen stars exploded overhead, falling, falling, until they settled like a cloak over Banyen. "Tell me," he said huskily, "that I don't stir your blood. Tell me and I'll leave you here and never seek you out again."

He kissed her eyes, her mouth, her cheeks, the hollow of her throat, and she felt a raging fire engulf her as she burrowed her head against his chest. It made no difference that he was the Mongol from the steppe. She wanted him. She needed him. She moaned softly as his mouth crashed down on hers in a savage, blazing kiss of passion. The banked fires began to smolder and burst into flame as she felt his searching hands explore her body through the thick clothing. His touch was scorching, searing, as her own hands ceased to tremble, and she caressed his high cheeks and ran her hands through his lustrous raven hair. Moan after moan escaped her as she strained against him, her mouth mingling with his, her tongue searching, darting to conquer his.

Within moments their clothing lay in a heap on the rough granite floor. Banyen spread his burnoose on the sweet-scented straw and gently lowered Katerina onto the lushness of the warm sable.

A thin streak of moonlight filtered through the high, narrow window that was not covered by the drifting snow. Banyen drew in his breath in a ragged gasp as Katerina's body was bathed in silvery radiance. His face was inscrutable in the faint rays, but his gaze was almost tangible; she felt it reach her, touch her, and was aware of the all-consuming fire that raged through her.

Katerina's response was unwavering as she stared deep into his oblique eyes. She was hypnotized by them as she felt his mouth crush hers. Her body took on a will of its own as Banyen caressed and explored every inch of her bare limbs. She moved to the rhythm he initiated and felt him respond to her in a way she had never dreamed possible. Searing flames licked at her body as she sought to quench the blazing inferno that engulfed her. He kissed her small ears, her eyes, her moistened mouth as he murmured tender words of love, as his hands traveled down the length of her, arousing, teasing her till her breath came in short gasps and her body turned beneath his touch.

His lips clung to hers as he pressed her down onto the softness of the rich fur. He buried his hands in the sparkling coppery hair, twining the thickness, holding her head still as he kissed her savagely. Katerina strained against him, her nude, rounded breasts flattening against his hard, muscular chest as she responded to his passion with an urgency that demanded release. He caressed her again and again, cherishing her, desiring her, imprisoning her body with his hard, muscular strength.

He felt the softness of her flesh grow warm and taut beneath him; his hungry mouth worshipped her, tracing moist patterns on her creamy skin. His dark head moved lower, grazing the firmness of her belly and down to the silky smoothness between her thighs. He parted her legs with his knees and felt her respond to him, arching her back to receive him. Her parted lips were a flame that met his raging, tumultuous mouth. She welcomed him, accepted him, his hardness, his leanness, his very maleness, as he drove into her. The unquenchable heat that was soaring through her beat in her veins, threatening to crescendo into a raging inferno of flames.

He lay upon her, commanding her response, and she offered it, writhing beneath him, exulting in her own femininity as she caressed his broad back and crushed her lips to his. The sound of her own heart thundered in her ears, or was it Banyen's that beat and roared about them?

Her breathing ragged and gasping, she opened herself like the petals of a flower. The searing, scorching aching erupted within her, consuming her in an explosion that matched his.

Banyen opened one sloping azure eye and gazed longingly down at Katerina. Her long-lashed lids remained closed, her breathing slow and regular. Sensing his inspection of her, she opened her eyes and stared deeply into his dark, oblique eyes. Words at the moment weren't necessary. Banyen slept then, his dark head cradled against her breast. Katerina lay quiet, body and mind at peace for the moment. How vulnerable he looks in sleep, she thought. Defenseless, almost like a child. What was it her uncle said? Yes, that he was a compassionate man and perhaps one day he would allow her to see that side of him. She raised her eyes and looked at the bright shaft of moonlight. Were the stars out? Was there a brief respite from the heavy, suffocating snows? She stirred slightly on the sable burnoose, the sweet scent of the straw teasing her nostrils. The slight stirring of her body made Banyen tighten his hold on her, and he sighed contentedly in his sleep.

How had she allowed herself to forget what he had done to her? Was it because she wanted to see if he . . . It didn't matter now. She had lain in his arms; she had matched his ardor and his flaming passions and had been satisfied. The brief interlude with Yuri had been nothing compared to this wild, savage lovemaking. Katerina did not believe she could ever look at Banyen again after this. Her hand reached up to stroke the still discolored welt on his cheek. Even after all these months it had not completely healed. She dug her teeth into her lips till she felt the salty taste of her own blood. Yet she didn't have the will or the power to take her hand away. Instead, she smoothed the ebony hair from his high forehead. She loved the shape of his eyes, and slowly bent over and lightly brushed her lips against the lids, feeling him stir against her with her touch. Gently she let her long, tapered finger trace the shape of his eye. Again her lips delicately caressed his lids, and she suddenly found herself pinned in a hard embrace.

Katerina pushed Banyen away from her, completely unashamed by her nudity. "No! This is not to happen again. We're both to look upon this as a moment in time between two people caught up in something they had no control over, Banyen. There'll be no more times. A meeting of the flesh, isn't that what men call it? Nothing more and nothing less."

Banyen nodded. He would agree to anything right now. Fully satiated, he boldly watched her as she dressed in front of him, not caring to avert his attention.

Once fully clothed, she stared down at him. "Remember, a meeting of the flesh, nothing more." Her eyes lightened till they were the color of taffy. To Banyen, they were the most beautiful eyes he had ever seen.

The moment Katerina walked through the door, he felt more alone than he had ever been in his entire life. He knew that if the stable were suddenly invaded by every recruit and every man under his command, he would still be isolated among the babble of voices. There was only one body that could communicate with his, and she was gone. What did a promise mean? Promises were made and broken. He owed her nothing. Well, Banyen conceded, maybe his body; she had seemed to like it well enough. He laughed, a deep, full, rich sound in the quietness. The laughter, however, was hollow to his own ears, and he sobered.

He lay back on the sweet straw and remembered the feel of her lips on his eyelids. Now why had she done that? And why had she let her fingers caress the damnable scar on his cheek? Evidently she had thought him asleep when she touched him so gently. No one had ever stirred him in quite that way. He was confused by the meaning of it. He told himself he had bedded enough women to know the answer, but he didn't. No woman had ever moved his heart in that way before. The action was tender, the way a

mother would caress her infant. He sneered as he got
to his feet and dressed. He was no child, and the Kat
was hardly maternal. The fleeting instant puzzled him;
it was something else for him to think about.

When Banyen left the warm, fresh-smelling stable,
the first person he saw was Kostya, returning with a
pile of blankets. He gave the Russian an ear-to-ear
grin and saluted him with a mocking finger to his forehead. He had won! The blue eyes were unreadable as
the prisoner stared after the strutting Mongol.

Chapter Fourteen

"THE WITCHES are out, the witches are out," Ivan
chanted gleefully as he ran up and down the marble
hall outside his quarters. "A banquet, we must have
a banquet to celebrate!" he shouted as he began to
shred a drapery with the tip of his staff. "Ready a
banquet, now!"

"My Czar, are you aware of the time? It's past midnight, and the ovens are banked for the night. There
isn't any food prepared," a guard bleated fearfully.

"Roast swan, roast peacock and sturgeon. Prepare
enough for three hundred of my favorite guests!" Ivan
continued to shout, ignoring the fearful guard. "We'll
have the bears and entertainment fit for a Czar. See
to it, my good man, within the hour. Ring the bells,
wake everyone and tell them I wish their presence in
the banquet hall. Tell the nobles and boyars to dress
in their finest, and have the women arrive nude."

"My Czar, at this hour . . ."

Ivan wrenched his staff from the tattered drapery
and with one swing of his arm thrust it into the

guard's throat. "The hour doesn't matter," he said. "A celebration is what I want, and I have decided to prepare it myself. Now that you're dead, you won't be able to attend. A pity, you would have enjoyed the bears," he said, leaning over the body and dipping his bare toe in the man's blood. Languidly he traced a picture of a bear, and stood back to observe his handiwork. "Marvelous!" he shouted shrilly. "It looks just like my pet bear!"

Banging his staff against the stone walls, he made his way to the kitchen, walking drunkenly on his heels so the remaining blood would not drip on the floor. From time to time he stopped and squinted at the red substance congealing on his toes, and laughed delightedly.

Inside the cavernous kitchen, he poked and prodded everything in sight with the tip of his staff. "Roast swan!" he shouted at the top of his lungs. "I want roast swan for my celebration!" He yelled again. When the game did not materialize, he lashed out at the fire in the oven, by pitching his staff into its depths. Angrily he sat down in the middle of the floor and crossed his bony legs, chanting of witches and traitors.

A startled cook and two servants, who jutted their heads fearfully into the archway, were stunned at the sight. Ivan rolled over, banging his head on the hard stone. "I want swan and pheasant and sturgeon for my celebration."

"My Czar, when is the celebration to take place?" the cook asked uneasily.

"You ask when! How dare you ask me when! Now! The celebration is now! Wake everyone and tell them to assemble in the hall. Be sure to tell the boyars and their women they must arrive in a cart. It will be pulled onto the main floor by my bears. See to it!" he shouted as he staggered to his feet.

The two servants ran from the room, their faces masks of fear, to do his bidding.

"My Czar, your head is bleeding," the cook said hesitantly.

"Bleeding, bleeding, you say? I have no blood, how can I bleed? What manner of fool are you?" he demanded, his eyes wild and staring.

"A mistake, my Czar, it must be the firelight," the cook said as she hurried into the storeroom.

When the cook returned, Ivan was again sitting cross-legged in the middle of the floor. He craned his neck to watch the cook as she began to pluck the feathers. "No, no, don't you know anything?" he grumbled as he again got to his feet. He reached an emaciated hand toward the cook and clutched at the bird. Without a moment's hesitation, he flung it into the oven. "That's how you roast a swan, my good woman, don't you know anything? Can't you see the feathers will burn right off? Then the meat will get done. Why must I do everything?" he pouted childishly. "Fetch me the pheasant and I'll show you how to roast it also."

The stench from the smoldering feathers sent the cook gasping from the room, her hand to her mouth. She returned in a moment, handing the freshly killed pheasant to the Czar, and stood back respectfully to await his further orders.

"Wrap this bird in a wet cloth and let it steam in the oven."

"Be . . . before or . . . or after removing the feathers?" the cook asked, her face blank and unreadable.

Ivan sighed wearily. "Good woman, how did you become chef in this palace? With the feathers, of course. I happen to like wet, juicy feathers. Everyone does. Order my throne to be taken to the banquet hall, and see to it that the Princess Halya is present. The pheasant is for her, a special tribute before she leaves the palace. This celebration is in honor of her departure." Suddenly he brought his hand up to his mouth and laughed wickedly. "No, no that isn't why I'm having the celebration, it's for the arrival of the witches."

He shrugged. "It makes no matter. Halya is a witch too. Tend to the matter," he said regally as he hopped from the room on one foot, his skinny arms stretched straight out in front of him.

Tearfully the cook ran from the room to do as instructed, the pheasant clutched to her bosom.

Petrified with fear, Halya entered the banquet hall and took her place next to Ivan. She remained quiet, her body trembling at the insane expression on his face.

"Halya, my love, how nice of you to attend your going-away celebration. This party is especially for you. I want you always to remember how generous I have been to you. Tonight you will see my trained bears lead a cart of naked women around this room. The boyars and nobles will be dressed in their finest in your honor. I do hope you appreciate all the trouble I've gone through on your behalf. Why," he said, wide-eyed, "I even roasted the meat myself. Kiss my ear, darling Halya, to show your thanks."

Halya swallowed hard and bent over, her lips brushing against his ear. "This is a great . . . great honor, Ivan. May I ask where you are sending me?" she said fearfully.

"Never ask me anything, for if you do I shall tell you a lie. I feel like sending you away, so that is what I'm doing, but I want you to have this party before you leave. Later, if I have a mind to, I'll tell you why. Sit quietly now, for the bears will arrive shortly, and noise disturbs them."

Halya clenched her teeth so hard she thought her jaw would crack. God in heaven, what was he doing to do?

Ivan stood up as a steady stream of boyars and nobles entered the room dressed in their regal attire. At a wave of his bejeweled finger in the air, the nobles and boyars sat, their eyes anxious and fearful. When all was quiet Ivan rose to his feet and shrugged his skeletal shoulders.

"We are now going to have a parade, which I will lead. Princess Halya will judge who is the finest. Following me will be the bears with the cart of women.

After the cart, you'll all fall into place and we'll circle the hall. I will sing." He clapped his hands loudly as he jumped from the dais and landed with a thump on the marble floor.

"Bring on the bears," he cackled gleefully.

Halya sat rigidly in her chair as the bears, led by a trainer, entered the room. Merciful God, she prayed, whatever he plans to do, let him do it quickly before I collapse. Ashamed and humiliated for the naked women, she lowered her eyes and stared at the floor.

"Enough!" Ivan shouted. "The parade is now over." Waving his arms wildly, and hopping about on one foot, then the other, he made his way to the cart. He eyed one woman lustfully and, reaching out, pinched a rosy-tipped breast till the woman screamed in pain. His eyes widened, and before she knew what was happening, he lifted her bodily from the cart and flung her in the face of the closest bear.

Halya retched as the bear clawed at the woman's flesh, chewing into her shoulder, mutilating the pinkish-white skin.

When the woman's screams had faded, Ivan pursed his mouth and looked around at the seated nobles and boyars. "You may each pick a woman and fornicate here, where I can watch you. This must be a memorable evening for the princess. I want her to leave with happy memories. When I am seated, you will commence with your lustful ways."

Silence rang in Halya's ears, as no man made a move to leave the table. The women cowered, their arms crossed over their naked breasts. She knew that the moment Ivan sat down the men would do as he said, and the women would gladly surrender themselves, fearful lest their end be the same as the dead woman's. Her stomach heaved as first one man and then another got to his feet, eyes downcast.

Ivan squirmed in his chair, his eyes dancing in glee as he watched. Harsh guttural sounds escaped his drooling mouth as he stood up for a better look at something that pleased him. He clapped his hands and shouted his approval of the orgy going on beneath the dais.

"Tell me, Halya, have you ever been so stimulated? I must plan more celebrations like this. I've outdone myself this time, don't you agree?"

"But of course, Ivan, but then, you always arrange everything so perfectly. You must be very proud of yourself," she managed to say quietly, her stomach heaving at the words.

"That's very generous of you, Halya. And for being so gracious, I'm going to tell you where you are going when you leave here tomorrow. You are going to Volin, the village I sent Yuri to, to finish his mission. My darling Halya, did I neglect to tell you your brother is dead? No, no, I told you. Well"—he shook his head—"I can't be expected to remember everything. No weeping, Halya, you must be strong about our parting. Remember, your brother died for me." He sighed wearily at the tears in Halya's eyes. "You must uncover the secret of the Cosars. I will give you one month to do what he couldn't do. Yuri had a mission to fulfill, and he failed. You may redeem him in my eyes. If you succeed, I'll give you a medal. I decided to give you an award instead of taking you for my wife. Thank me now, Halya," he said childishly.

"Th . . . thank you, Ivan."

"I want the secret of the Cosars. Remember to find out how they breed the horses, I must know! Now, do you understand your mission?"

So that's what it is all about, those damnable Cosars of the Cossacks. Yuri is dead, and this is no time for grief. I've been through that already, the first time he told me of Yuri's death. For now I'll smile—anything until tomorrow, when I leave this godforsaken place. Once gone, she told herself, I won't return. Never! No matter how many men he sends after me, I'll run till I drop in my tracks, or I'll kill myself first. I will never return!

"Well," the Czar demanded, "do you understand?"

"But of course, Ivan, I understand perfectly. I have

never failed you before, and I won't now," she said in a choked voice.

"Who is that man with the ugly face?" he demanded.

"Kubitsky," came a soft reply.

"Give him to the bears to play with. His ugliness upsets me," Ivan muttered as he tossed his rings into the center of the circling bears. "Now bring on the feast!" he roared in a deep-pitched voice.

Halya watched with horrified eyes as a servant set a platter before her. "I prepared it myself, especially for you," Ivan said happily. "Remove the cloth and eat all you want, dear Halya."

Gingerly, her hand trembling, she inched the cloth away from the mound on the platter. She drew back in horror at the smell and sight of the baked pheasant. Unable to restrain herself, she ran from the room, sobs tearing at her throat.

Ivan stood and stretched his scrawny neck till he could see all of the assembled boyars and nobles. "The princess was overcome with happiness," he babbled. "Women are like that at times. All four of my wives acted the same way. Now we'll share her special dinner," he said, pointing to the wild game. "The servants will serve you as much as you want, and eat heartily," he cackled, wagging a bony finger in the air. "I'll leave you to your merrymaking. With me gone, you may do as you please. Enjoy yourselves. I'll leave the bears for you to play with, so they won't become lonely."

"God help me!" Halya screamed as she ran down one hall, and then another, till she came to her room and quickly threw the bolt. She grabbed the pillow sack, still filled with her jewels and clothing, which she had hidden away in a cupboard. This time, even if Ivan had already posted a guard at her door, she would escape. He had stopped her the last time, but this time he couldn't. She was on a mission for him, had been told to leave. Nothing could stop her.

With the help of a young guard she had befriended, she made her way to the stable. The soldier kept watch as Halya saddled a sorrel horse. Mounted, she thanked the man and disappeared into the night.

Halya felt safe now that she rode freely, her security in the sack tied to the saddlebags. She had the next thing to a king's ransom riding with her. Jewels could buy anything. Could they buy a life? She wondered.

Halya rode steadily, stopping only to eat and to feed and rest her horse. She rode for many days before she arrived at a small village. She reined in her horse and wiped the snow from her forehead with the back of her hand. She knew she looked terrible. Carefully she smoothed the golden hair back from her brow and tucked in the stray tendrils, and then smoothed the gown beneath the lush cape she wore, trying to free it of the wrinkles that clung to it. More than that she couldn't do. Perhaps the peasants would allow her a bowl of water to wash with. They might even have knowledge of Yuri.

She knew instinctively that the men advancing on her were Don Cossacks, and just possibly they would help her. If not . . .

Halya waited patiently atop the horse for the two men to approach her. She knew that if she made a move to dismount she would be pinned from behind and dragged God only knows where. The men stopped some distance from her and waited for her to speak. Halya leaned over and raised her hand to show that she was a friend.

"I'm on my way to Volin in search of my brother, Yuri Zhuk. Could you tell me how much farther it is and if you have news of him? He traveled here in late spring to purchase horses and has not been seen since."

The Cossacks looked at Halya and her fine clothes and the sleek animal she rode. They exchanged blank looks and said nothing.

"I mean you no harm. My parents are old and they want news of their only son. I myself come from a village no bigger than this, and I know that news travels from one village to the other. I want nothing more than information. Please help me," she pleaded.

The taller of the two Cossacks advanced another step and looked up at Halya. She was indeed a beautiful woman. What harm could talking with her do? he thought.

"The village of which you speak is no more. Marauding Tereks killed the villagers and burned it to the ground. I've heard that the man you speak of rode from Volin with no horses, and the contract he desired canceled by the Kat. None from my village saw the man you speak of, but if he has not returned since late spring, then there is little hope. A lone man is not safe on foot when the Tereks take to the road. And you, my fine lady, should also be warned."

"Are you telling me that the man known as the Kat is dead?" Halya asked in a shocked voice.

"That's exactly what I'm telling you. The Kat and all his people. The only person to escape the slaughter was his daughter, who was not in the village at the time."

"Where can I find the Kat's daughter? Perhaps she'll know something of my brother if she lived in the village when he arrived to negotiate the sale of the horses."

The two men looked at each other again. The spokesman debated a moment before he spoke. "She's in the mountains at the House of the Kat." He held up a large, beefy, dirty hand and motioned for Halya to remain quiet. "In truth, I don't know if she is there now or not, but it was the custom for the Kat to take his people and horses back to the mountains at the end of the summer. We haven't seen her since she rode from here after the slaughter. There is nothing we can do to help you."

Halya shivered inside the silver-fox cape and wanted to cry. To have come so far only to find nothing . . . She bit into her full lower lip. She wasn't beaten yet!

"Tell me, how can I get to this House of the Kat you speak of? Is there a sleigh or a wagon I could buy to make the journey? It's not for myself, you understand, it is for my old parents, who love their son." Tears gathered in the sea-green eyes and trickled down her cheeks. She reached out a slim hand in entreaty and knew she made an appealing picture. Stronger men than these two had been captivated by her winsome ways; they would be no different.

The younger of the two Cossacks spoke hastily. He, too, had a mother who fussed and fretted over him when no one was around. "We might be able to send a message and . . ."

The first Cossack was also smitten by the sparkling tears. "Dismount and come with us. There is a way for us to let the people in the Carpathians know that someone wishes to travel to the mountains. It may take a couple days for a message to get back to us, but it is the best we can do for now. Snow will come shortly, look overhead," he said, waving his arm upward.

"Oh, thank you!" Halya said gratefully as she slid from her mount.

"See to it, Basil," the first Cossack said quietly. "I'll take the lady into my hut and make her comfortable."

Halya blanched but followed him. She knew what was in store for her, but she also knew she had no other choice. She would do whatever was necessary to find news of her brother. She wondered if Ivan knew the Kat was dead. Did his death mean there were no more horses? Please let Yuri be alive, she prayed silently as the Cossack motioned her to sit at a worn bench. He generously poured her a steaming cup of tea and placed a chunk of dark bread in front of her. Halya smiled gratefully as she nibbled, and wondered how long it would be before he told her to remove her clothing.

Basil trudged through the snow to the barns at the end of the village. There he opened the door to a small makeshift aviary and reached out for one of the falcons. His thick fingers were cold and numb, but he managed to scribble a message and attach it to the bird's leg. With luck the bird would cover the distance by sundown. By noon tomorrow he would have an answer. He felt envy and lust rise in him for his friend Kusma's good fortune. He wondered if his good friend would share her. A good Cossack did not keep his wealth to himself. Basil could only hope that Kusma would feel charitable toward him. It had been many long days since he had seen anyone as pleasing to the eye as this lady. He knew her skin would be like a flower petal, and her lips would cling to his as she whispered sweet words of love and passion. He groaned in desire as he removed the hood from the falcon's head and set the bird free.

All he could do now was wait for several hours, and then he would bravely stroll over to Kusma's hut and demand that they share what should be shared. He wouldn't take no for an answer.

Mikhailo deftly placed the falcon on a perch and covered his head before he removed the capsule from its leg. Unable to read the scrawled words, he set out in search of Katerina.

Banyen and Kostya both watched as she reached for the paper and scanned its contents. She frowned, her amber eyes turning the color of cinnamon as she stared at Mikhailo. Biting her lip nervously, she reread the message. She carefully folded the tiny piece of paper and stuffed it into the pocket of her trousers. With a puzzled look on her face, she left the arena and strode back to the kitchen. She poured herself tea from the samovar and marveled at the thick, syrupy consistency of the liquid. Hanna must have made it days ago, she told herself.

Katerina withdrew the note and scanned the contents again. What should she do? Should she allow the girl to come to the mountains; and if she did, who was to fetch her? If only Oles hadn't died in the slaughter. She would have to send Mikhailo or Stepan, or go herself. She could ignore the message and forget

about it. It would be best to send another message with
the falcon denying the young woman permission to
come to the mountains, saying there was no one to
fetch her. What could she possibly want? Did it have
something to do with the horses? Didn't Yuri mention something about having a sister? It could be a lie,
a trap of some sort. She would have to go herself.

Quickly she negated the idea. Stepan would have to
go; Mikhailo was needed here. She didn't dare leave
the men for the journey. Twice now she had sensed
Banyen's presence when she went to Whitefire's stables. No matter where she went, no matter what she
did, his eyes were always on her. Stepan would have
to take two of the stallions, because none of the other
horses would stand the trip. Only the stallions could
maneuver in the deep snow, which they loved.

What would happen if she did allow the woman to
come to the mountains? Would it cause a problem
with the men? She admitted that that, more than anything else, that was what was bothering her. How
would the others react to another woman? A woman
who, as Yuri's sister, would undoubtedly be beautiful
and wear fine clothes. Envy ate at Katerina as she
stared at the message. *I could just send word saying
Yuri is dead and let it go at that. It would be a cruel,
hard blow to the woman, but then, why should I care?
I don't know her, and I owe her nothing. But if she really is Yuri's sister, I owe her an explanation of his
death. It was by my hand that he died. She deserves
to know how and why. I, likewise, am seeking answers to my father's death,* her niggling inner voice
urged. *I won't be satisfied till I have the answers I
want. Perhaps the woman feels the same way.*

Katerina shuddered as she gulped at the bitter substance in her cup. She knew that if her father had
lived he would have denied permission for the woman
to come to the mountains. But he was dead, and it
was her decision. Right or wrong, she would tell her
the circumstances of Yuri's death. Perhaps it would
ease some of the guilt she carried within her. Yuri's

pleading eyes flashed before her, and she cringed. Would the woman understand and forgive her for what she had done?

When Mikhailo and Stepan entered the kitchen, they found Katerina staring into her empty cup, the small piece of paper clutched in her hand. Katerina raised her eyes and nodded. "You will go, Stepan. You'll ride Wildfire, and Darkfire will be saddled for the woman to ride on the return trip. Send the message and dress yourself warmly. Tell the Dons to take the woman as far as Volin and have her wait for you. Under no circumstances are you to go to their village. Volin, that is as far as you go, do you understand? If you sense a trap or a trick of some sort, send the horses back alone. I'll come for you in the sleigh. You'll need eyes in the back of your head, my good friend. I hope you can do it with no harm to yourself."

"What you mean is, can Wildfire do it?" interjected Mikhailo. "Of course he can, and Stepan can make the trip as well."

At the confidence expressed in him by his friends, Stepan gained a new aura of dignity. He had no doubts about himself either. After all, he had made a similar trip with Wildflower some months before.

"What does she want? Why would anyone come here in the dead of winter?" asked Mikhailo.

Katerina shrugged. "We'll know as soon as Stepan returns with her and not a moment before," she said quietly, her eyes sober and reflective. Although no one mentioned it, Katerina knew that Stepan could easily be caught in a blinding blizzard. She pushed the thought away. Stepan was an excellent horseman, with a superb, specially trained mount. Despite the rapidly approaching period of horrible storms, her childhood friend would be fine and would return with Yuri's sister, though it would likely take much more time than usual.

"Dress warmly, Stepan," Katerina said with a fond pat on his arm. "I'll get the horses ready and food ready. And remember, do not attempt the trek back to the mountains unless the weather permits."

Katerina made sure Banyen was occupied in the center of the arena when she went for the stallions. If he saw them on her return, it would be all right, but she didn't want him following her and watching her press the secret catch. *If he hasn't seen me already,* she thought grimly. *Bastard, he had eyes in the back of his head.*

At the last minute Katerina negated the idea of saddles. Wildfire would make better time without the heavy leather on his back. Darkfire, on the other hand, needed the extra weight, and she chose a saddle with care, testing it before she placed it on his back. The stallion nuzzled her, and she laughed. "You know, don't you. A trek through the snow and you'll show us all who can survive out there in that vast white world, but remember, my friend, it's Wildfire that you follow. On your return you shall carry a beautiful lady. I'm trusting you to give her a comfortable ride, and no playful tricks, do you hear?" she said, stroking the horse's sleek flanks. It was Wildfire who gently pushed her away from Darkfire and waited patiently for the girl to respond to him. "You're to take Stepan safely to Volin, and no antics in the snow. This is business, Wildfire, and we have no time for playing. You'll ride like the wind and bring my guest safely to the House of the Kat and," she gurgled, "don't lose Stepan. He's not used to your spirited ways. No saddle, just a blanket for you." The stallion reared back and shook his great head at her words. Katerina knew he understood every word she said and would do as she instructed.

Katerina led the stallions down the long stone passageway and out to the main stable, where she waited for Stepan. Banyen strolled nonchalantly up to her and ran a hand lovingly over Wildfire's back. His voice was sincere when he spoke.

"Never have I seen more magnificent animals. You

have every right to be proud of them, and I can understand your obsession with getting your Cosars back."

Katerina stared at him, expecting his arrogant, mocking eyes to belie his words. Instead, she read only respect and open admiration in their depths.

"I would give my life for these animals."

Banyen nodded. "I believe you would. I understand what you're saying. Perhaps it won't be necessary to give your life for them. You have others inside the arena who will do that for you." The old scoffing look was back as he stroked Darkfire.

"No one will give his life for me. Why do you think I'm training these men? Certainly not for myself. I have no wish to see any of them die. I see that you don't believe what I'm saying. And I care even less what you think."

Mikhailo and Stepan watched their friend and the prince a moment before joining them. "Good, you didn't give him a saddle. This animal," Mikhailo said, assisting Stepan onto his horse, "detests anything save a human being on his back. We bow to his wishes." He laughed into Banyen's face.

Banyen nodded curtly and walked away, his back stiff and straight.

"Did you make a mistake, little one? Do you think it wise for the Mongol to know of the stallions?"

"Mistake? Hardly, Mikhailo. I'm sure he knew they were stabled here before today. Those damnable slanted eyes of his see everything." Smiling at Stepan, she said, "A safe journey to you, my friend," then flung open the wide oak doors.

Wildfire reared back and preened before Katerina, then thundered through the portal, Darkfire on his heels. Katerina laughed. They were like children, waiting for a romp in the snow.

When the heavy doors closed against the snow and cold, Katerina walked slowly back to the arena in search of Banyen. A confrontation. She would ask him what he intended to do with his knowledge. Why skirt the problem? She would ask and he would lie, and she would tell him that he lied. Whatever happened, she would let him know she didn't trust him.

Taking her position in the arena, Katerina watched the men go through their drills and exercises. The longer they kept at the rigorous training, the more proficient they became. Afstar would have no complaints when Banyen returned in the spring with his band of soldiers. No complaints at all, she thought smugly. She waited patiently for the drill to be over before she sauntered over to where the prince stood and motioned him to follow her out of earshot of his men.

"I want to settle something with you, clarify it for your ears," she said shortly. "Now that you know the stallions are here, and I suspect you have known for some time, I want it understood that if you ever go near them or try to take them from here, I'll kill you. No one takes what is mine. I told you once before, I give only one warning."

"Those stallions are your whole life, aren't they," Banyen said softly. "There are other things in life besides horses. When this is all—"

"When this is all over, I'll be the same. Yes, the Cosars are my life. It's a life I chose, not a life that was forced upon me. If you think for one moment you could get the stallions from here, forget it. They would kill you if somehow you managed to get by me. They know where they belong."

"A horse is a horse," Banyen said curtly.

"Just as a man is a man," Katerina snapped.

"Let us not forget that a woman is a woman," he retaliated.

Katerina laughed, the shrill sound bouncing off the thick granite walls and raising the hackles on Banyen's neck. "This woman says those horses will kill you if you try to take them from the stable. Once you didn't heed my words. You would be wise to listen to me now, before you make elaborate plans to take them from this fortress."

"Why would I want to take your horses? You did promise the Khan that you would give him a colt and a filly. Are you telling me now that you are not a woman of your word?"

Katerina flinched at his mocking words. How true they were. Bastard, she seethed. He knew she had no intention of giving Afstar anything.

The catlike eyes narrowed and flamed at his words. "Only time will tell if I keep my word," she said insolently, leaning back against the wall, her long legs thrust in front of her. Completely aware of the picture she made, she thrust out her chest, and watched one of the buttons slip and then open on her coarse shirt. She made no move to close it, and laughed again when she saw Banyen's eyes become clouded. "Thoughts such as you're having now will one day be your undoing." Katerina straightened and slowly buttoned her shirt, her eyes glittering. "No more Mongol." She let her eyes travel across the room to where Kostya was standing. "Suddenly I find that I prefer Western eyes and hair the color of summer sun." She laughed again as Banyen murdered her with his dark gaze.

Chapter Fifteen

DAYS LATER, shortly before dawn, while the great fortress slept, a thrashing, tormented Katerina was wakened by the howl of the wind and the icy snow that pelted the windows. She wiped her perspiring brow and then shivered as she curled herself into a tight ball for greater comfort. She knew she would never be able to get back to sleep with the raging blizzard that beat at the fortress. She shivered again. The Mongol had invaded her once more, chasing her like a wild animal. She had been so sure, so confident, that after their hours of lovemaking he would cease to stalk her. She shouldn't have allowed it to happen. Katerina tried to tell herself it was because Kostya had kissed her, setting her body in motion and then leaving her. She chided herself for being so vulnerable; for responding willingly as soon as she felt a man's body. How had she let him touch her, caress her naked flesh, and then answered his urgings in a way that she had never thought possible? She had desperately wanted the person who had raped her, and had reveled in his flesh. God, she cried silently as she buried her head in the downiness of the quilt. She couldn't let it happen again. She couldn't let it happen with Banyen, and she couldn't permit it with Kostya, either. All she had to do was avoid looking into those sapphire eyes and she would be safe. Concentration on the matters at hand would solve the problem. Thinking only of the horses and training the men was to be her life for the next few months. When it was over she could ponder about herself and what she was going to do. For now, she would have to be strong and not give in to these strange, wonderful feelings that were happening to her.

Katerina withdrew her finely boned hands from the comforting warmth and rubbed her temples. Her face felt hot, flushed, and she knew that the room was chilly, for she could see the misty vapor from her mouth. If her grandfather was awake, she could talk with him the way she had as a child when she was troubled.

Katerina jumped from the bed and quickly dressed. She splashed cold water, which had a film of ice over it, on her face and drew her breath in with the shock of the freezing wetness on her steaming face. Quickly she brushed out her coppery hair and pinned it haphazardly atop her head. Reaching for the ermine cape, she flung it over her shoulders and tied it in place.

Katerina rubbed a cheek against the rich fur, and for a moment her cinnamon eyes glazed over, reminding her of another gentle touch. Clenching her teeth, she ran from the room, along the long, icy corridor, and down the steep, curving stairwell. She continued to run till she came to the vast kitchen.

Only a pale lamp burned, and she could see without straining her eyes that her grandfather slept peacefully on his cot near the blazing hearth. His affectionate cat purred contentedly as Katerina prepared herself a cup of dark tea. There would be no talking after all, she mused as she sipped at the fragrant brew.

Katerina stroked the saffron ball of fur and listened to her purr her happiness at having attention paid to her. Her eyes raked the high ceiling of the kitchen, with its fragrant herbs and spices hanging in ropes from the rafters. Huge copper pots and skillets hung next to the dancing flames and gave off a subdued sparkle as the flickering light cast its eerie shadows. Large balls of cheese were strung from heavy, knotted ropes next to cooking utensils and gave off a tantalizing smell. How carefree she had been in this big old kitchen when she was a child. Her eyes went to the tall, thin windows that stretched from the low beams to the base of the wall. Her favorite window seat was still there. She remembered the day her father had built it and said that it was just for her and had a chest to keep treasures in when she wanted to play near the great fire. Her eyes took on a faraway look as she continued to look around the enormous room. Long, heavy wooden shelves dotted the sides and were stacked with dishes and everyday tools. Here and there a green plant rested, thanks to Hanna's tender nurturing. It had always been a happy, comfortable place to be. Now, she thought sadly as she glanced about, it held approaching death, secrets, and hostility. Now it was just a place to get warm and a place to eat. It would never be anything more. When had she outgrown this favorite hideaway? She had to stop thinking about things like this. She had to do something active.

The horses! Of course—she would go to the stallions' quarters and see how they fared. There was no one up to see her at this hour, and anyway, an observer would have no idea where she was going. Gaily Katerina set her heavy mug on the worn table and left the coziness of the kitchen. She needed to see all that was left of the Cosar bloodline. Perhaps when she looked at Whitefire and Snowfire she would regain her perspective. Dejectedly she shook her coppery head. What good were the stallions if the mares were gone?

Stealthily Katerina crept through endless corridors and passages till she came to the underground stable. Cautiously she looked over her shoulder and listened carefully for some sound, anything that would alert her to another's presence. Hearing and seeing nothing to alarm her, she inched her way over to the thick, heavy cupboards that housed the blankets and utensils for the animals. She stood on her toes and reached into the farthest corner of the top shelf. Her long, slender fingers fumbled for the catch that would release the monstrous shelf. Standing back, she waited for it to move on its well-oiled hinges. Quickly she stepped through the secret entrance and pressed another catch for the opening to close. Her lamp from the kitchen held high, she made her way down another long, narrow passageway, barely wide enough for a person to lead a horse. Gradually the tunnel sloped, and the Kat knew she was within sight of Whitefire's special stable.

The purebreds sensed her presence, and a low whicker reached her ears. She knew the noise wouldn't carry beyond where she stood; the walls and ceilings were thick and soundproof.

Her hands trembled as she slid the heavy wooden bolt on the stockade grill that separated the lengthy tunnel from the stallions' quarters. She would find peace and quiet for her troubled feelings here in this remote cavern. Just the feel of the horses beneath her hands was all she needed to make her aware of who and what she was. Quietly she prayed that the same feeling would come over her again today.

"Mikhailo," she called softly, "it is I, Katerina. I've come to see the stallions. This is the first chance I've had to come down here since I got back from the Urals. Tell me, how are the animals?"

Mikhailo's gentle hands stroked Snowfire's sleek hide. "All is well, Katerina," he said quietly as he peered at her in the dim light. "These magnificent animals, what good are they without the mares? I think they sense something is wrong. Snowfire has been especially skittish the past several days," he remarked, rubbing the back of his neck.

"How is Whitefire?" Katerina asked anxiously.

"Calm, and that's what worries me. The other stallions always sense his moods and act accordingly. He's quiet, almost placid, and Snowfire is the skittish one."

"Did you change their feed? Are the fires kept regulated? Perhaps it's the hay, or the fact that Wildfire and Darkfire haven't come back yet with Stepan."

"None of those things, Katerina. Even down here in the bowels of the fortress they know there is a fierce storm blowing outside. Maybe that's what is bothering them," he said, in a tone that conveyed his doubt.

Katerina sensed the agitation the old man was trying to keep hidden from her, and a small flurry of panic settled itself in the pit of her stomach. "They aren't ill, there isn't any sign of something being wrong, is there?"

The Cossack stroked his chin, his eyes thoughtful. "No, nothing visible. I've stayed with them as much as I could and had Stepan or Hanna sleep with them when I had my other duties to tend to. But it's hard, Katerina. I tend your grandfather, the men, and the horses. The others help a great deal, but it's much work. Stay with the horses, I must tend the fires," he said, giving Snowfire a gentle pat on his head.

Katerina watched him walk away with a frown on her face. She sensed that something was wrong with the stallions. Dear God, don't let anything happen to them, she prayed silently. Gently she walked between the animals, crooning soothing words to their ears.

Whitefire whickered softly and tossed his great head as he reared back on his hind legs. He came down gracefully and nudged her shoulder playfully with his head, his silky mane swishing across her face. Katerina laughed. "You want to play, is that it? Don't they have time to play with you? They're busy, you know, keeping this place just right for you. All of you," she said sternly, "are upsetting him. You have to treat Mikhailo the way you treat me." Katerina smiled as she fondly petted Whitefire, to Snowfire's chagrin. The stallion tried to nudge Whitefire away from the slim girl so he too could rub his face against her shoulder. "You're jealous," she giggled.

Katerina continued to comfort the noble horses, touching this one and that one, talking softly as she laughed openly at their display of affection. "I'm the guilty one; I've neglected you and I'm sorry," she said, clasping Whitefire, her favorite, around his thick neck. "I, too, have my problems, that's why I'm here. I knew if I came to see all of you I would get my wits back. Listen to me," she cried in a tormented voice. "I swore if he came near me I would kill him. Then my body betrayed me, and I allowed the Mongol to make love to me." Tears welled in the amber eyes, and a sob caught in her throat as she clung to the stallion. "I don't know what to do. He has a hold over me that I cannot explain. When I'm near him I feel calm, and at the same time so full of . . . of . . . It's like when I come to you and talk to you and you become calm. That's what Banyen does to me. Yet he raped me brutally, and left me to die in the snow, and still I can feel something for him that I can't explain. I want him to stroke my head, as I stroke yours. I want to hear the soft words of love and yearning. I want . . . I want him near me, and yet . . . yet it can't be."

Whitefire picked up his foreleg and gently tapped on the floor as he tried to free his head from her tight grasp. He advanced a step and pushed her backward until she toppled onto a pile of yellowed hay. He continued to nudge her till she saw that he wanted her to lie down. Katerina laughed, the tears glistening in her eyes. "Sleep won't make it go away. I know, you want me to stay here, but I can't. I have things to do, and I must get the mares back. I know you understand what I'm saying. I'm doing it for you and the others. I'll retrieve them, you have my promise. I'll come back tomorrow and every day after that.

"Mikhailo, are you here? There's nothing wrong," she called. "They missed me, that's all. I've been so busy with the men and worrying about Grandfather, I neglected the most important thing of all. I'll come back each morning around this time. You're not to worry, Mikhailo, everything is fine. Look, see for yourself," she said, getting up and pointing to the animals.

Mikhailo's old eyes danced with glee when he saw that she was right. The stallions were quiet, all signs of skittishness gone. The touch of the Kat, he marveled. Who would have believed it, and yet he had seen the same thing hundreds of times. Yet each time he saw it he marveled at the way the girl had with the stallions.

Katerina brushed the hay from her clothing and, with a last caress to each of the stallions, left the hidden stable and made her way back to the underground cavern that housed the other horses. She stood a moment and listened for some sound on the other side of the wall. Satisfied, she pressed the catch and waited for the heavy shelf to swing back. She walked through the opening into the darkness of the stable and again closed the hidden door.

She remained still, checking the area as her eyesight adjusted to the darkness. This was her life. How could she, even for a second, have forgotten? She couldn't, she wouldn't, let Banyen into her life again; and as for Kostya, he had no place there either. Only the horses mattered! Always the stallions, never Mongol princes or blond, blue-eyed Russians.

Day by day the tension and hostility increased in the training arena. The recruits worked tirelessly, mastering all that Katerina set before them. The Mongols, under Banyen's command, came into their own. It seemed to Katerina that overnight they lost their youthful looks and childish, willful ways. They were now strong, muscular young men with keen eyes and coordinated movements. Their chests broadened, and the sinewy muscles in the calves of their legs gripped the horses' middles as if soldier and animal were one. Another few weeks and they will be an even match for Kostya and his men, Katerina thought. She watched Igor take to the middle of the arena. Without a second of wasted time, he charged at Rokal and unseated him with no wasted motion. Katerina watched as Banyen nodded approvingly. Grudgingly Katerina complimented Igor with a slight inclination of her head.

So far she had been able to successfully avoid staring into the Mongol's oblique eyes. She made sure that she was never near him or alone with him at any time. Always Mikhailo was at her side. During the dinner hour she was forced to share with Banyen, she sat by the hearth and gulped down her food and immediately returned to the arena, leaving him to converse with her grandfather. She wondered what they spoke of at such length.

Kostya looked for and found ways to be close by, and at these times she would force herself to be cool and aloof, to show that he was of no concern to her. Since the day in the stable, he had lost his appeal for her. She found that standing next to him was like standing next to one of the other prisoners or next to Mikhailo. One full, rich taste of the prince was all she needed, and nothing else would satisfy her.

Mikhailo, too, nodded approvingly at the Mongol's men. Everything seemed to be working well, just as Katerina had said. The only thing that worried him was Katmon, who had taken to his bed and was slowly dying. Katerina wore a haunted look in her eyes each time she sat near his bed. He knew without asking what was bothering her. She didn't want her grandfather to die until she proved to him that she could re-

gain the Cosars. The old man knew in his heart that
she would be successful, but the Cossack also knew
he would never convince the girl. In her own way she
was blaming herself, and nothing short of regaining
the animals would satisfy her.

Then there was the prince, who also sat at the
feeble man's bedside. They had long conversations
about Russia and the Czar. Katmon listened while
Banyen did the talking. The relationship bothered
Mikhailo, and it annoyed Katerina. More than once
Mikhailo had seen Katerina stalk from the room, her
eyes spewing flames, to the amusement of the prince.
Why did it always have to be a contest between them?
A contest where there would be no victory for the
winner. His bent shoulders shook as he made his way
back to his position against the damp stone wall.

The ensuing days were nerve-wracking for Katerina. While everything regarding the prince and the
recruits seemed to be going well, the dread of her aging Zedda dying alone in his room made her pace the
arena, her long, supple legs tense and straight. The
bright amber eyes were cloudy and sad as she let her
mind drift from time to time to happier days when she
was a child and her grandfather held her on his knee
and told her stories of the brave and fierce Cossacks
of his day. She couldn't let him die without telling him
what was bothering her! Was his mind lucid enough to
understand? Could she convince him that she would
get the Cosars or die trying? Should she tell him about
the night on the steppe with the Mongol? What would
he say? Her trim body shuddered with the thought as
she lifted her eyes to meet Banyen's stare. His gaze
was deep, penetrating, willing her to . . . No, she
wouldn't look at him. She had no desire to be devoured by the indigo eyes that belonged to him as he
wanted her to belong to him. Not just for now, for this
short time here in the mountains, where the cold
seeped into one's bones and virtually froze the blood
in one's veins. She didn't know how, but she knew that
he wanted more than she had to give. She was part of

his overall plan. It had to be the horses, the stallions. Afstar must have made some sort of bargain with him. The wily, foxy Khan would leave no pebble unturned if he thought he could get the stallions. And if Banyen could manage to get them for him, so much the better. Blood meant nothing to Afstar; family meant nothing. Only owning the Cosars would satisfy him. Over her dead body, and, if necessary, over Banyen's.

When the evening meal was over, Katerina sat back in her grandfather's chair near the fire and sipped at her steaming tea. She refused to meet Banyen's eyes or to talk to him. They had eaten in a silence she had insisted on. Once she had raised her eyes and been aware of the angry red scar on his right cheek. She could almost feel the pain in his lean cheek; and for a split second she fought the urge to reach up and touch it, to make the throbbing cease. Instead, she lowered her lids and finished her dinner without comment.

The yellow cat, at a loss without her master, jumped up on Katerina's lap and began to purr. Absent-mindedly Katerina stroked the soft fur, her thoughts on the man seated at the table. Three more long, arduous months to be gotten through. Could she do it? She had to do it; she had no other choice.

Katerina finished her drink and set the heavy cup on the hearth. Gently she put the cat on the floor and got up. Banyen watched her through narrowed eyes as she adjusted the black-tipped cape. She was going to go to her grandfather, as she did every night after the evening meal. She would sit near his bed and whisper soft words that held no meaning. Three times Banyen had stood outside the door and tried to hear what she was saying. The words were indistinguishable, but his ear picked up the torment in her voice. What was it about the girl that . . . ?

"I'll wait here for your return. I promised your grandfather that I would read to him from a book I brought with me. That is, if you have no objections," he said quietly.

Katerina shrugged and left the room. At this point if Zedda wanted the Mongol to read to him, who was she to object? One always acquiesced to the dying.

The thin, frail body beneath the thick pile of bedding shocked Katerina, as always. He had been a strong, robust man; a man of strength and character. Now all that was alive to her eye were the faded, pale eyes of the man in the great bed. The paper-thin lids fluttered at her approach, and he smiled weakly. She bent over the bed and kissed his dry, wrinkled cheek. "We must talk, Zedda. There is much I want to say to you. Listen to me and don't try to talk." The old man fluttered his lashes to show he understood, and Katerina began to speak. "I want you to die with the knowledge that I'll get the horses back. I won't just try, I'll do it—that's a promise I make to you!" She bent closer to the bed. "I have never given my word to you or Father and gone back on it. I will regain them and bring them here, where they belong." The sparse lashes fluttered again, and there was a question in the faded eyes that Katerina understood. "All is going well in the arena. The Mongols have come into their own, as I knew they would. The prince is a mighty leader and will one day be victorious, this too I know. I realize that in the short time he has been here you have grown fond of him and enjoyed his company, and yet at the same time you have felt guilty because of the way I feel about him. You can't understand my hatred of him. The day I returned from Volin with the men, I wanted to tell you, but I couldn't. I don't know if you can really understand me now, but I have to talk about it. I have to say the words."

The old man's lashes fluttered madly, and he tried to withdraw his arm from beneath the covers. The faded eyes wavered and settled near the doorway, where a shadow loomed. He had to stop her from what she was going to say. He thrashed about feebly on the bed.

Katerina's strong arms lowered him gently back

against the thick softness of the bed. She spoke softly, the way a mother would speak to a sick child. "You must not move about like this; it isn't good for you. Just listen to me, Zedda."

Resigned to the inevitable, Katmon Vaschenko closed his eyelids and waited for the words that he didn't want to hear, the words that he knew in his heart would change the life of the Mongol standing close by.

"Do you recall the day Stepan took the mare back to Volin?" Not waiting for a reply, she continued, "I set out after him to bring them back. I knew the boy would make it back to Volin safely with the mare, because he loved the horses as you and I both do. I could have stayed here, but Father was so angry, and in his own way he blamed me for allowing Stepan to take the horse. I told myself that I had to bring them back or at least make sure they were safe and sound. It's the only defense I had. On the way, once I got to the steppe and I was so cold and so hungry, I allowed myself to become trapped. I rode into a Mongol camp, and when I tried to ride out, there was this . . . this Mongol that followed me . . . and . . . he followed me and I tried to get away . . . but every time I ran he caught me . . . and he . . . and he . . . raped me like a wild animal! He tore the clothes from my body and left me to die in the snow. No, no, that isn't quite true—he threw a sable burnoose over me and then he left me. I can't sleep at night, he stalks me in my dreams the way he stalked me on the plains. I can't get it out of my mind. When the others came back to Volin, I more or less had myself under control, and I don't think Father suspected. Who," she cried brokenly, "would want me after that? You know that all Cossack girls are to be virgins on their wedding night. I was coming to some manner of peace within myself, and by that I mean I managed to get through the days, and while the nights were and still are a horror, I have survived. The Mongol who raped me is Prince Banyen, and he doesn't even realize that I am the one. He looks at me with blank eyes and with lust, but he doesn't remember. Tell me, Zedda, how does a man do this to a woman and then not remember who she is? You're a man, tell me so that I can understand," she pleaded.

Katmon lay still, willing her to think he had fallen asleep. She would rest easier if she thought she spoke to an empty silence. He forced his lids to remain still until he felt her move and leave the room.

Banyen stepped into the dark shadows outside Katmon's door and watched as Katerina left, the tears streaming down her cheeks. He wanted to run after her to tell her he was sorry, that if it took him the rest of his life he would make it right for her. He wanted to tell her all those things, and other things too, things a man only told a woman he . . .

A low gurgling sound drew him into the room, forcing the thoughts from his mind. He looked down at the elderly man with the tortured eyes and nodded slightly.

"Tell me how this happened. I want to know before I die, Banyen," Katmon gasped.

Banyen's eyes locked with those of the old man. "A man is bound at one time or another in his life to make a mistake. Raping your granddaughter was mine, and one I will have to live with for the rest of my life. Would it make your death any easier if I told you I love Katerina?"

"If you speak the truth, then yes." Katmon whispered.

Banyen's hand caressed the scar on his cheek, his eyes still held by those of the dying man. "There is no need for me to lie to you. I knew the moment I saw your granddaughter that somehow, some way, we would meet again."

"And yet you took the one thing that was hers to give the man she loved. A Cossack woman is taught to value her virginity from an early age." The old man gasped, his face deathly pale, as he tried to continue speaking.

Banyen laid a gentle hand on Katmon's shoulder, forcing him back against the mound of pillows. "Don't speak, save your strength," he said softly.

"Bah, save my strength—for what? My time is near, we both know it, so there is no need to pretend. I want your promise, Banyen, that you will take care of Katerina and make it right with her. Women don't understand . . ."

"You have my word. Listen to me, Katmon. We have spoken many times after the evening meal, and I have come to treasure those talks. Never once in all that time did I lie to you. I understand that those times we spoke of Russia and the Czar are different. I could have made up stories just to please you, but it is not my way. Even now I could try to defend my actions that night, but there is nothing to defend. I was wrong."

"Will you tell her that you know she is . . ."

"Is that what you want? For if it is, then yes, I will tell her. If you will, I would prefer to do it in my own way when the time is right, if ever there is such a chance. Trust me, Katmon, I will make it right, but in my own way."

Katmon nodded weakly, his eyes closing wearily.

"She's like no other woman I ever met. She has spirit and courage, more than some men. I find myself admiring these traits in her, which somehow amazes me. I never thought of a woman in this way. To me a woman was someone . . ." The words stuck in his throat, and Katmon felt a smile tug at the corners of his mouth at the Mongol's discomfort.

"You'll do, Banyen. When a man can admit that a woman has a special place in his mind as well as his heart, they belong together. I can go to my grave knowing you will do what is good. When . . . when I am gone . . . you must . . . comfort Katerina."

"If I can, I will," Banyen said quietly.

Long after the old man's breathing had stopped Banyen continued to read aloud from his book, his tone soft and full of emotion and regret. Emotion because a life was gone, and regret that he didn't know the old man in happier times, when he was full of life and living. It was a strange feeling that engulfed him, a feeling that was alien to him. He had to seek out Katerina and tell her and the bandy-legged Cossack, Mikhailo. But first he had to sort out his thoughts. The torment he had heard in Katerina's voice, the torture in her eyes—how was he going to live with that? She hated him, and yet she had given herself to him—and probably detested every minute of it, he thought bitterly. Still, he hadn't forced her that day in the barn, and her passion was as fiery as his own. She despised him for his savagery on the steppe and for the fact that he didn't even remember who she was. Women are like that, he told himself; they would hold hatred and bitterness for as long as they lived. If he was any judge of women, she now believed she had him where she wanted him. That was it, she only gave herself to him so that he could see what . . . A chill washed over him. She would kill him and do it cheerfully. The vision of her crouched low, her teeth bared in a snarl, ready to spring at him with the long knife clutched in her hand, swam before his eyes. How could he make it right with her? Why had he given the dying Cossack his promise? Only Katerina herself could absolve him. And in his gut he knew she would never again come to him— willingly or unwillingly.

Banyen closed his book quietly and laid it on the table next to the high, old-fashioned bedstead. He looked down at the peaceful face and felt saddened. He hated death and dying. In that moment he found out something about himself. If he could have breathed his own life into the old man, he would have done it without hesitation. He would have given anything not to have to see the look in Katerina's eyes when he would tell her Katmon was dead. And the look she always carried in her eyes when she stared at him, remembering, remembering, always remembering that he was the one, the one who . . . This was no

time to think on matters such as these. It was over
and done with. All he could do was go on from here
and try to do what he promised.

"Damnation!" he cursed as he lashed out with his
booted foot at the wooden frame of the bed. Pain,
hot and searing, ripped up his ankle as he thrust his
fist into the heavy text, sending it flying across the
room. Satisfied with the aching in his foot and in his
tightly clenched hand, he gritted his teeth and strode
from the room.

He refused to allow the shooting sensations to slow
his progress along the endless corridors and passages
that led to the underground arena, where he knew he
would find Katerina and Mikhailo. The pain was a
scorching reminder of what he had done and what he
had to do. "Pain be damned," Banyen snarled as he
forced open the heavy oak doors that opened into
the cavernous arena. His eyes sought Katerina's, and
he motioned her to come to him. For a bare moment
she hesitated, and then she ran to him, correctly in-
terpreting what she read in his face. Quickly she raced
past him down the hall, her feet barely touching the
hard, earth-packed ground. On and on she ran till she
came to her grandfather's room.

Seeing his peaceful face, his arms folded across his
chest, she dropped her head to the covers, and great
sobs wracked her body.

Banyen and Mikhailo stood in the open doorway
and listened to the heartfelt wailing that shook the
girl's shoulders. Banyen twisted his hands and shifted
from one foot to the other while Mikhailo let silent
shudders course through his body. Both of them
wanted to go to the bereaved girl, but something held
them back. This was her own private grief, and nothing either of them could do would help her.

Katerina lifted her head from the bed and slowly
got up. She stood a moment looking down at the face
of her grandfather, and then she turned and saw the
two figures outlined in the doorway. "Leave me with
what is mine. He was all I had left. Now there's noth-

ing. I'll see to the preparations myself," she said, tears streaming down her cheeks.

Banyen slowly entered the room and stood towering over her, his dark eyes staring into her tear-filled gaze. His heart thundered in his chest as he made a move to reach out for her. Sensing his intention, Katerina moved backward, her full, ripe lips trembling, the gold-flecked eyes sparkling with her tears. "Leave me with what is mine," she whispered.

Banyen stared at her another moment, the wicked scar pulsating in his cheek. Then he turned and, with a motion to Mikhailo to follow him, made his way back to the arena.

Katerina removed her ermine and set to work. Tenderly she removed the old man's nightdress and set about washing his body in preparation for his simple funeral. The tears were now dry on her tawny cheeks as she cleaned and dried his thin body. At least she had this; with her father and the others she had just . . . just . . . dumped their bodies into a pit. Surely God would forgive her for what she did that day. Every man, no matter what, deserved a decent burial. Slowly she dressed the limp body in his Cossack uniform and buttoned the rows of shiny gold buttons with shaking hands. She set the pointed fur cap on his head and felt tears prick at her eyelids. It was an effort, but she managed to pull the shiny, soft leather boots up his legs and tucked the black trousers into them with no wasted motion. Every Cossack went to his Maker with his boots and cap. Frantically she searched the room till she found his saber, and with a quick swipe of a cloth from the chest she laid the weapon next to him. His cap, his boots, and his saber. All she had left to do was light the candle and kneel down to say her prayer. Her hand was steady now as she lit the long, tapered candle in its ruby container. She dropped to her knees, and in a hushed voice she said her prayer and asked God to help her. How peaceful her zedda looked. His spirit was probably riding through the heavens at this moment, his and those of a thousand other Cossacks just like him. She knew in his first charge through the skies he would meet her father and they would be happy.

Katerina sat quietly, her mind blank, as she waited for the others to come and make their pilgrimage past the bed. At dawn the body would be taken to the vault under the fortress, where her grandfather would rest till the snows had gone. Then he would be interred in the great stone building that rested under the fir trees, where her mother and hundreds of other Vaschenkos rested.

All through the night she sat as the few remaining elderly Cossacks filed past the body, their eyes deep and sad. Each patted her shoulder in passing, their only show of grief. This was the last of the Vaschenkos. Only Katerina remained, and she was a woman. No son would bear the name of Vaschenko ever again. It was over, their eyes said, the old leader was dead and the horses were gone. There was nothing left save the fortress, the four stallions, and Katerina. It was the end for all of them. What good were the magnificent horses without the mares, and what could Katerina possibly do? Still, they stayed drinking their vodka, as was the custom when a Cossack died. Time and again they toasted his death and his ascent into the heavens.

The moment the taper gave out its last sputter the men stood, carefully lifted the body from the bed, hoisted it high above their shoulders, and carried the former hetman to his resting place in the fortress.

The procession was solemn, and Katerina made it with dry eyes. Once she closed them to ward off fresh tears, when they placed the body on the high marble table and then covered it with a sable blanket. Here he would rest till spring, when he would be lowered to his final resting place near his wife and Katerina's mother. Is it the end, can it be possible? she thought wildly. No, never—she had given her word to succeed, and she would. Now more than ever, she couldn't fail! She wouldn't allow herself to, not while there was a breath left in her body. She prayed to God and thanked Him as she made her way back to her room for the impulse that had led her to tell her grandfather what she wanted to do before he died. If nothing else, she was thankful for that one small favor.

Back in her bedchamber, she built up the dwindling fire till the logs snapped and crackled, their flames dancing and licking at the sides of the great oven. She sat huddled near it, the plush fur securely wrapped about her. She stared into the fire for hours, until her eyes began to smart from the smoke and the flying minuscule embers.

Now she was alone, more alone than she had ever been in her entire life. She was the last of the Vaschenkos. There would be no one to carry on except her; even if she should marry someday, the children she bore would not carry the name of Vaschenko. In one way it was the end, she told herself, but in another it was a new beginning for all of them. She had to do it for herself now that she was the only one left. And she would survive. The Kat always survived.

Chapter Sixteen

✿ ✿ ✿

AS THE DAYS PASSED, Katerina's grief lessened a little. She kept herself busy with her training program. The men performed with skill she never thought imaginable in so short a time. It was almost as if they were trying to prove something. But to whom, she questioned? To her or to themselves? Whatever, the strict, structured routine she had laid out for them was finally paying off. There wasn't one among them whom she would be afraid to have at her side. Even Banyen's men were now on par with the prisoners. Each time they met for a practice battle, the match was a draw.

Katerina felt unnerved as she watched the men go through the paces Mikhailo laid out for them. Something was bothering her, and she didn't know what it was. Banyen seemed to be respecting her period of mourning, and not by look or action had he done anything to unnerve her. Kostya was intent only on perfecting his skill. While he looked at her longingly, he made no overt moves in her direction. Were they all biding their time? Were they waiting for something to happen . . . to her? What was it? Her stomach churned as she let her eyes sweep the arena and finally come to rest on the boy named Valerian. No, he was no longer a youth, but a man. A man with cold, hate-filled eyes. If eyes could kill, I would drop on the spot, she told herself as she stared at him. He hated her almost as much as she hated Banyen. He was acting like a wounded wild animal, as her grandfather used to say, which meant he was up to something. She continued to watch him as he, in turn, tracked the men, his eyes circling the room and always coming to rest on the door frame. Surely he wouldn't be so foolish as to try to escape. He could go nowhere in the freezing cold. Her glance strayed to Banyen, who was leaning nonchalantly against the wall, his eyes on the center of the arena, finally flicking to Valerian. He, too, sensed the young man's intent. The lynxlike eyes narrowed as she watched him. A vision of a trapped animal in a snare came to her mind when she watched his movements, jerky and uncoordinated. She was jarred from her thoughts as a shout went up from the center of the arena. One of the Mongols' spears had found its mark in the shoulder of the prisoner named Chedvor. Katerina raced to the man's side and sucked in her breath at the sight of the spurting blood. Mikhailo was on his knees, trying to stop the flow.

Katerina bent over the injured man and spoke softly. "You'll live! Another inch and the point of the weapon would be resting in your heart. It was a careless mistake on your part, one you already regret. Your opponent was younger by ten years, leaner and faster; remember that the next time you take to the ring. Never assume, never prejudge. Your wound will be taken care of, and then you'll return here and work with your horse. A very poor performance on your part," she said coolly.

The fallen man tightened his lips against the pain, his eyes full of shame. She was right. His opponent was younger, less experienced, and . . . What does it matter? he told himself. He carried the wound; he would make doubly sure it never happened again. Hurt by a damn slant-eyed Mongol, he thought bitterly. If it was the last thing he did, he would straighten both his eyes. He lay back while the men carried him on a litter to Mikhailo's small room, where he would be cared for. A glass of vodka to bolster his strength and he was back in the arena, leading his horse through her paces, his eyes angry and belligerent.

Banyen called Valerian's name and waited for him to work his way to the front of the line. Katerina frowned when she heard his name called a second and a third time. Suddenly it was quiet; even the horses had stopped snorting and pawing the ground at the sound of Banyen's harsh voice.

Katerina walked over to the prince, her eyes cold and hard. In her gut she knew he was gone. "If one of you doesn't speak up within the next few moments, you'll remain in your quarters for a full ten days. On the count of three someone had better speak and in a clear, loud voice. One, two, three!"

"He left," Igor stated simply. Too well he remembered the lonely, cold nights in his room, and he had no wish to repeat the experience for even one night, much less several. A man could die in that barracks with no blanket and no food, only water that turned to ice.

"Where did he go?"

"He said he was leaving this damnable fortress, and he said he would take his chances on the outside."

"Fool!" Katerina spat. "Now, I'll have to go after him and bring him back. This is your fault, Banyen," she snarled, "he was your man, you're responsible for him. I should make you go out in the storm and fetch him back, but then I would only end up going after both of you. When I bring him back, he gets ten lashes and three days in his quarters, understood?"

Banyen nodded. What else could he do? She was right, as usual.

He would have left the moment Cheduor was wounded and all ran to the center of the ring. A thirty-minute head start as of this moment. She needed time to get Whitefire and . . . She met Mikhailo's gaze and held up her index finger to show she meant the number one stallion. He frowned and tightened his lips, but he left to do her bidding.

When Mikhailo returned and nodded to Katerina, she secured the fur cape and left the arena, the others staring after her. Someone should stop her, Banyen thought, and it should be me, but she surely wouldn't thank me for interfering in what she calls her business. He motioned for the others to continue with their drilling while Mikhailo took Katerina's work.

A few moments later, standing in the open doorway, he backed off as a wild thundering shook the thick stone walls. A blur of white raced past him and down the long, endless corridor. It was Katerina on an ivory stallion, her cloak flying out behind her. Never had he seen such speed in an animal. It could only be Whitefire! He gasped. What an exquisite animal! So he too was kept here after all, like the other white stallions he'd seen. The question now was where they were stabled and how he could get to them. He shrugged; all he had to do was wait for her to return . . . if she did . . . and watch where Mikhailo took the horse. After that he could . . . He smiled to himself as he sauntered back into the arena to watch the next match.

Outside the great fortress, Katerina gave Whitefire his head and let him go. If there was another horse within ten miles, Whitefire would find it. This was what he liked best, the thick, swirling snow that made him and the whiteness one.

With both hands clutching the horse's thick mane, Katerina felt the great stallion swerve to avoid a thick clump of something and then hurtle down a steep grade. The snow-robed trees stood sentinel as she let Whitefire take to his stride. She should have brought something to cover her face; already the snow spray the horse kicked up was caking on her face. The force of the cold, freezing air was making it difficult for her to breathe. She crouched lower, burying her head in the horse's ice-crusted mane.

The stallion moved effortlessly through the large drifts for what seemed like forever to Katerina. He knew where he was going, to the grove of firs; that was where another horse would shelter until its rider could get his bearings. The moment the copse came into sight was when she heard the sound—a horse's soft whicker, which was pure delight to the numb girl. The cold was having its effect on her now as Whitefire cantered into the darkness the firs afforded. Katerina sat up, her breathing ragged, as she watched the horse look around. A light tug on the mane and he was off, surefooted as a dancer.

Deftly Whitefire trotted around a huge tree and worked his way through what looked like a narrow tunnel. In another few moments the animal would be out of the grove. Where was that stupid man? She called out, but her voice was harsh and sounded like a croak to her own ears. "Find him, boy, he's got to be here somewhere. I heard his horse. You can do it, Whitefire," she crooned. The stallion reared up his head at her words and snorted, his great hooves thumping the ground.

Suddenly Whitefire bolted forward, and Katerina felt her neck snap backward. Recovering, she crouched low and let the stallion have his way. He headed straight for the opening at the end of the aperture and was again in the open. He was going so fast it was impossible for her to see if there was a shape ahead of her or not. The horse swerved to the right, throwing her off balance as he again picked up his long-legged race to catch whatever it was that was eluding him and causing the woman on his back such anguish. Katerina was completely blinded by the spray from the horse's hooves. She gasped as the animal skirted another evergreen, this one so close she felt the branch brush against her head, knocking off the hood of the cape.

Whitefire snorted and slowed, rearing back on his hind legs. Katerina lifted her head, and there was the sorrel, with Valerian struggling to climb into the saddle. Whitefire brought his front legs down with a thump on Valerian's shoulder, sending him sprawling into the deep snow.

Katerina shook her head to clear it and slipped from the stallion's back. Valerian was all right, shaken and fearful but able to stand.

"You'll ride the stallion and I'll ride the sorrel. One false move on your part and Whitefire will send you to your death. Understand?" Katerina demanded in a harsh voice. "I warned you that if you tried to leave I would fetch you back; still, you had to try. At best you could have gone another mile and then you would have frozen to death. Look at the sky, you fool, more snow is already on the way. Now get on my horse and make quick work of it." The moment the man climbed on the stallion, Katerina slapped his flank and yelled, "Go, boy, straight to the stable!" She climbed onto the sorrel and followed the racing steed in front of her.

The moment the fortress came into view Whitefire slowed his breakneck speed and trotted along daintily as he waited for his mistress to catch up.

Katerina slid from the stallion and pounded on the

great doors that opened into the underground stable. Whitefire pranced inside, snorting and throwing his head back to show he had done what was expected of him. The long white plume of his tail swished as Mikhailo pulled Valerian from his back. The old Cossack's eyes were wide and angry at the man's condition.

Katerina nodded. "There is no way he can live. Place him on a litter and take him to the kitchens; it's the best we can do for him. Have the men take the litter through the arena so the others can see what happened to him. Perhaps now they'll believe me. Do it now, Mikhailo," she said firmly, her voice cold and hard, her amber eyes points of flame. "It was so unnecessary, so needless. He is so young to die, he hasn't even lived. Men can be such fools," she spat as she climbed onto Whitefire's back to lead him to his private stall.

Banyen stood looking down at the man in the warm kitchen. Valerian's eyes were glazed and unseeing, his lips purplish, his skin a faint bluish white. He is the next thing to dead, the Mongol thought bitterly. A stupid mistake and one he is paying for with his life.

Banyen looked up at a sound he heard and turned to see Katerina. Her face was unreadable.

"It would be wise if you informed your men that escape is impossible. He'll be dead shortly. A low price for a life, wouldn't you say? I warned you in the beginning. His death is to rest on your conscience, not mine."

"It pleases you, doesn't it? It pleases you that you were right and now you can walk into the arena and know that the others will look at you and fear you as some . . . paragon who is never wrong," he said harshly.

"You're free to have your own thoughts, whatever they may be. I can live with what I've done and . . . and have no regrets. I could have left him out there to die, but then, I'm not a man and I couldn't leave an animal to die if it was in my power to help him. His death is his own undoing."

"A pity he can't appreciate your words," Banyen said bitterly.

"Yes, a great shame he didn't heed my words, the words of a woman who has lived here all her life and only tried to warn him and the others by giving them the benefit of her knowledge. Now he'll never know the truth. Sometimes an example has to be made for others to learn," she said expressionlessly as she turned on her heel and left the room.

Valerian struggled for his last breath just before dawn, and Banyen covered his face with a coarse blanket and bowed his head. Another life was gone—would there be others? Three more long months to go through. Who among the others would die?

Rage coursed through him at his inability to do anything to stave off what he considered to be the inevitable. He hated this helpless feeling!

Valerian's death did nothing to enhance Katerina in the eyes of the Mongols. It was obvious they blamed her for his death, and it was also obvious that it was Banyen to whom they now looked for direction, totally ignoring any and all orders from Katerina. Mikhailo told her it was a wise person who knew how to retreat. She made no threats against them and bowed to their demands. She wouldn't admit that the young man's death had shaken her. She hated the look in the Mongol's eyes, and she dreaded the indigo scrutiny of Banyen. Most of all, his words haunted her. Was he right? Did she want to be some kind of savior?

The close confines of the fortress were beginning to bother her, and whenever that happened she went to the stallions. Here in the warm, steamy, sweet-smelling stable she could pour out her heart to the animals and forget for a time where and who she was. She owed Whitefire the biggest carrot she could find and . . . and what else did she need, her mind questioned. She shook her rich, coppery curls till they were free of the knot on top of her head and sat down in Whitefire's stall and waited for the horse to come to her. He nuzzled her head and shoulder gently, showing her he understood she was troubled. Daintily he backed off and looked at her with huge chocolate eyes. His well-shaped head tilted to the side as if he were waiting patiently for her words. When they came, he shook his head and advanced a step and again nuzzled her.

Katerina's tone was soft, almost heartrending in its simplicity. "What else could I have done? I warned him, I warned all of them, and because I am a woman they ignored me. There is no other answer. The man is dead and they blame me. The prince blames me; he says I'm now happy that I proved myself right in the eyes of the men and that it took the senseless death of Valerian to make this so. How can I take the blame for something that isn't my fault? We rode out, you and I, and we brought him back; there was nothing else to do. And now he lays next to Grandfather, waiting for the snow to melt for decent burial. I've already done something I swore I wouldn't do, and I hate myself for it. I compromised myself and didn't punish the others when they refused to follow my orders. The Mongols will listen only to Banyen now. I don't know if it was the right or wrong decision; I only know that I could not bear to see the look of blame they held in their eyes for me. They *all* think it's my fault." A lone tear dropped to her tightly clenched hand, and she looked at it in surprise. Tears were for children and frail, sickly women. She was neither, she told herself. She was the Kat.

Gregory marveled at the Cosars' slim-legged beauty. "Each of you," he muttered, "is worth his weight in gold, and if I can't figure out what to do with you, all my dreams will be nothing but clouds drifting in the wind." His mind raced with the gruesome thoughts of Ivan and the scenes he had witnessed in Moscow.

He squared his strong, muscular shoulders as he

stroked one of the white geldings. "You may be a pleasure to look upon, but I would much prefer to look at gold and kopecks," he said harshly as he left the animal's pen.

As Gregory walked along the snow-covered road, he noticed that the Terek village was settling down for the night. The full moon was low in the east, casting shadows on the earth, multiplying the Cosars to twice their number. Fury ate at him as he lumbered along, anger at his circumstances, hatred for Ivan and his irrational mental condition. The Czar was obviously insane—a lunatic, as the people said. He feared Ivan would remember how he had tricked him. If he did, he would probably send men after him and his band. He flinched as though from a wound and continued his walk. The Czar would conveniently forget the bargain they had made. Could Ivan even remember the original plans, conceived nearly a year ago, when he was lucid? Gregory recalled there had been a fanatical light to his eyes even then, when he made his proposal. He had been blunt to the point of insult.

Gregory could still hear the Czar's words: "I'm fully aware of your love of vodka, women, and parties. For this you need many kopecks, and your village is poor. I can promise you more gold than you ever dreamed possible. And all you have to do is secure the breeding secrets of the Whitefire bloodline. Failing that, I'll settle for the horses themselves." They agreed and the bargain was sealed within moments.

"He thought me a fool," Gregory muttered. "He came to me because no other Cossack would give him the time of day when the sun was high overhead." Gregory knew his reputation as a ruthless, vicious fighter must be well known if it had made its way to the Czar's ears.

Gregory's mind continued to race. There were other people who would pay handsomely for the Cosars. Afstar, Khan of Sibir, was busily buying men and horses. There would be no haggling with the old Khan;

he would agree, as would many others, to deplete his treasury for the Cosars.

Satisfied that the cold, starless night held no surprises, he settled himself on a fallen tree trunk and lit his pipe. When he had it going to his satisfaction, he puffed contentedly. He needed time to ponder and decide which choice would be the wisest. His decision made, he watched as the spirals of smoke circled overhead. It would be the Khan versus Ivan.

The quiet night, his short walk, and the comfort of his pipe helped settle his speeding thoughts. Now all he needed was a woman and a jug of vodka and he would be completely at peace. A vision of a long-legged beauty in the next village floated before his eyes. He could almost feel the softness of her proud, high breasts and her sensuous lips on his.

Stuffing the smoking pipe into his shirt pocket, he made his way to the stable and led his horse out into the snow-covered compound. He looked around the village and waved to one of the guards. "There are other things in life beside gold and horses." He laughed as he took off down the long, winding road.

Chapter Seventeen

✿ ✿ ✿

THE MOMENT THE LAST of the vicious storms abated, Kusma readied the sleigh and personally escorted Halya to Volin to meet the guide from the mountains. Halya shivered inside the luxurious silver-fox robe she wore as she strolled among the gutted huts in Volin. She turned to look at Kusma and demanded to know what had happened to the village. Kusma himself looked around and felt saddened.

"So many of our people died here for the horses. It's always the Cosars. The Kat and his horses was a living legend, a legend that now ends. Perhaps one day this village will be rebuilt and it will live again."

"How will this happen? Who will come here to live, and if there are no horses, how can they live?" Halya asked as she drew the rich fur closer about her.

"Other Don Cossacks will leave their villages. Wanderers will settle here, and if Katerina Vaschenko makes up her mind, she will bring the elder Cossacks from the Carpathians and they will make this village live. As to the horses, I have no answers for you. Perhaps there are more of the magnificent whites in the mountains." He shrugged as his eyes took in the vast terrain around him. "We Cossacks live one day at a time. In our own way, we are fatalists."

Halya smiled. "I can understand what you say, for I, too, am a fatalist. What will be will be. One can move in one direction, but if it's not preordained, it will not happen." Quickly she changed the subject and smiled again at the muscular Cossack with the dark eyes. "You have my thanks for arranging this meeting. I don't know what will happen or if I will hear good news or bad news when I meet this woman you call Katerina, but I want to thank you from the bottom of my heart. It means everything to me."

Kusma grinned. "You've thanked me adequately already. I shall not forget. Mount up, your guide approaches. Can you hear the horse?"

Halya narrowed her eyes and squinted against the brightness of the blazing snow. She shook her head.

Kusma laughed. "From boyhood the sound of a pounding horse is one of the things a Cossack listens for. We do it unconsciously. One would think there is nothing to hear in deep snow, but the ground gives off its sounds. Many dispute this, but within minutes you will see a rider approach. Turn your eyes to the end of the village and you will see that I'm right. It appears that Stepan is eager to leave my brother's shelter to take you back to the mountains."

Halya laughed outright when she shaded her eyes with her hand to see a streak of ivory whip down the road and come to a roaring halt bare inches from her mount.

Stepan drew in his breath at the sight of the beautiful fair-haired woman atop the sorrel. His eyes sought Kusma's. The man shrugged elaborately, a shrug that clearly stated the woman was now Stepan's problem. Mine and Katerina's, he thought sourly.

"I will stable the sorrel in my village and you can claim him on your return," Kusma said to Halya.

He motioned Halya to slide from her horse and mount the white stallion called Darkfire. With a long, lingering look around the gutted, snowcapped village, Stepan patted Wildfire on his neck, and the horse reared back and took off, his hooves sending the thick snow backward. Darkfire, in his wake, thundered and pounded after the lead stallion. Halya hung on to the reins, positive her neck would be jarred from her shoulders.

For two days they rode, stopping only to feed the animals and for a brief rest. No words could be spoken between Stepan and the woman, and Halya felt uneasy at his strange silence. Stepan felt nonplussed. While he was not experienced in the ways of women, he knew she was going to be a problem for Katerina and the prince. And the one with the flower-blue eyes. Poor Katerina. Just as the Mongol and Katerina were fire and ice, this woman would be nothing but trouble compared to the Kat. Already he could see Prince Banyen taking her to his bed and ravaging her, the way men like him did. She looks so delicate and so pretty, he thought. One would want to cradle her fair head to his chest and whisper sweet, soft words in her ear. Poor Katerina. Would she come out second best with this woman? It was a mistake. He grimaced as he remounted and waited for Halya to do the same.

An hour before they cleared the pass, snow began to fall and the sky was black and ominous. Wildfire kicked up his heels and snorted in delight. It was impossible, but Stepan swore that the animal's stride increased with the swirling snow. Halya, petrified, clung to Darkfire's mane for dear life, trying desperately to understand how the animal beneath her could travel at such an ungodly speed in the deep accumulation.

Wildfire reared up and brought his hooves crashing against the stout doors of the underground stable. Daintily he backed off and waited patiently. When the doors swung open, he rose again on his hind legs and snorted long and loud, the conquerer returned with his bounty.

Katerina raced into the stable and immediately threw her arms around Wildfire's neck. "You did it! I know I could depend on you. It took a long time, but you succeeded. Good boy!" she crooned as she tightened her hold on the horse's neck. "And you, Darkfire, I see that you didn't unseat your rider." She rubbed her cheek against the horse's head and whispered soft words. The stallion wickered in delight as the woman slid from his back. Stepan led the animals away with a last fond pat from Katerina, who then turned to Halya. "Welcome to the House of the Kat. Come with me and I'll give you some hot tea."

Halya nodded. She was so cold. She wondered if she'd ever be warm again.

In the large, cozy kitchen, she let the fox cape slide off. Katerina drew in her breath. How beautiful she was, with her golden hair awry, stray curls clinging to cheeks flushed rosy red. Emerald eyes sparkled as she looked around before sitting down on the bench. Her voice, when she spoke, was soft and melodious.

"I'm Halya Zhuk. Princess Halya Zhuk," she corrected herself. "I want to thank you for allowing me to come to this fortress. I seek information about my brother, Prince Yuri Zhuk, who was sent to your village of Volin in the spring of last year. I know he is dead, but I wish to find out how he died, and why, and who killed him," she said sadly.

Katerina's hand trembled as she poured tea into a mug for the princess. She heard the words and she understood them. A princess. A beautiful princess like in the stories her mother used to tell her. Banyen was a prince. A handsome prince in the same fairy tales. And according to the ageless fables, they would live happily ever after. Now she understood the look in Stepan's eyes. He pitied her and felt sorry for her. I must be ugly, she thought, if Stepan is worried for me. She forced her hand to be steady as she set the cup in front of Halya and then sat down to still the shaking in her legs. How beautiful her hair was, all bright and shiny like golden summer wheat. And her dress— never in her life had Katerina seen anything so pretty. Katerina's long, slender hands stroked her coarse, tight-fitting pants, and she suddenly wanted to cry.

"Will you help me? Do you have information about his death? Was anything said to you about his killers? I must know," Halya pleaded, tears glistening in the bottle-green eyes.

Katerina swallowed hard. She would have to tell her. Tell her that her brother was dead by her hand. She cleared her throat and spoke quietly. "You must realize now that you're here you will have to stay until spring. The snows, the worst of them have already started and last till March. Until now the snow has been intermittent, but this is the blizzard time. There is no way I can send you back, for to do so would only endanger the animals. We'll make you comfortable and do our best by you."

"I understand, and I cannot ask for more. I am truly grateful that you allowed me to come here. I mean you no harm and will do nothing to make or cause you trouble. But you must tell me what you know of my brother. I sense that you know and that you don't wish to speak of it. Please, I implore you."

Katerina decided she liked the princess even though she envied her rich clothing and beautiful face. How she felt about her brother was love, the same kind of love Katerina had felt for her father. She nodded slightly. "Your brother came to our village in the late spring, as you said, and bought many horses for the

Czar. My father, in a fit of anger, canceled the contract. I cannot lie to you and make up some excuse about why he canceled it. He found . . . he saw your brother and me . . . what I'm saying is that your brother and I made love and my father came upon us. He misunderstood. Yuri tried, as did I, to explain to him that what he thought he heard was not . . ." Katerina raised her hands helplessly. "He canceled the contract, and I was brought before the Cossack council and ostracized. Yuri left to return to Moscow with the intention of returning for me at the end of the summer. He never came. I waited and waited. The night before we were to leave for the mountains I was away from the village, and it was raided, all of our people killed and the horses stolen. There are those who say your brother was at fault and there are those that blame me. It was not your brother's fault. Nor was it mine. I don't know who did it, but I plan to find out. Your brother did nothing wrong except to make love to me, if that's wrong. Sometimes I no longer know what is right and what is wrong."

"But Yuri never returned to Moscow. Where did he go, what happened to him?" Halya asked anxiously.

Katerina moistened her dry lips and reached her hand across the table and touched Halya gently. "Listen to me. After our village was gutted I left for Sibir. I was watering my horse when I heard a noise in a clump of shrubbery. When I investigated, I saw your . . . your brother. He was without a tongue and without fingers. He was near death. I don't know who it was that . . . I asked him if it was my father or my people and he shook his head no, but he couldn't tell me who did it. His eyes pleaded with me to kill him. I did. I'm sorry, but I could not let him lie there and suffer and die such a wretched death. I couldn't let the vultures circle overhead for him to see. If I had to do it again, I would." Tears streamed down her cheeks as she waited for Halya to comment.

"Thank you for telling me. No, you couldn't do less. Did my brother love you?" she asked huskily.

"He said he did, he said he would return for me and we would go to Kiev to live," Katerina said simply.

"Then you are as much my sister as if he married you," Halya said, getting up from the table and coming to put her arms around Katerina's neck.

Silent tears coursed down both their cheeks, and it was Katerina who smiled tremulously and said, "I never told anyone. I couldn't. I never killed anyone before. I don't know how I managed to . . ."

"Don't speak of it any more. It was what Yuri wanted. I don't blame you, and therefore you must not fault yourself. It's over, and hopefully one day we'll find the person responsible and then it will be righted. Let us speak of other things. Tell me of this giant fortress surrounded by monolithic trees as far as the eye can see. Tell me of those beautiful animals we rode here. Allow me," she said, pouring Katerina tea and more for herself. "Drink this and we'll both feel better." Katerina nodded gratefully as she sipped at the scalding liquid.

It was Banyen who found them laughing and giggling like two schoolgirls when he arrived for the evening meal. Katerina watched as his eyes traveled over the princess approvingly.

There was no mocking look in his eyes and no sneer on his full, sensual mouth as he stared at the princess. Katerina watched as his eyes traveled the length of her and came to rest on her full breasts, which jutted from her lavender gown. It was obvious that he liked what he saw, and it was just as clear that the princess liked him also. She smiled warmly and introduced herself, to Katerina's discomfort. The green eyes sparkled and her moist lips parted, showing perfect white teeth. Banyen bowed low over her hand and then brought it to his lips. Bastard! Katerina seethed. He could charm the skin off a snake.

Dinner was a miserable, torturous affair for Katerina. She felt out of her depth as the princess charmed Banyen with amusing stories of her life in Moldavia and of the great Terem Palace in the Kremlin. Banyen sat like a lovesick boy, drinking in every word she spoke. Even to Katerina's untrained ear it was evident that they had much in common. It bothered her and she didn't know why. Lost in her own miserable thoughts, she was jarred from them when she heard Halya ask how Banyen got the scar on his cheek. She smiled coyly and said she was sure it was a fierce war wound. Banyen smiled sickeningly and said yes, that was how he got it, from a fierce soldier bent on cutting him down. Katerina almost gagged at the blatant lie and rose from the table. Banyen's eyes laughed at her as she tucked the coarse shirt into the band of her trousers, her breasts jutting forth with her tense, muscular movement. She matched his look and said coolly, "Another time you can regale our guest with tales of your . . . heroics. For now, you are to take the center ring with one of the recruits." Furious with herself, she continued, "It would be interesting to know how the fierce . . . soldier came out during the battle."

"Second best, of course. I won, I always win." He laughed as he reached out a firm hand to help Halya to her feet. "If you have no objection, we can have the princess observe my expertise."

Having Halya in the arena was the last thing Katerina wanted, but she gave in and nodded. Halya smiled as Katerina strode ahead, she and Banyen following in her wake. Damn! Why did he always manage to get the best of her? She prayed that it would be Kostya who met him in the middle of the ring, and she prayed that he would run the bastard through till his blood ran like a river.

The great cavern rang with sounds of laughter and hoarse shouts. This was the drill they had all been waiting for, the Mongols versus the prisoners. The men themselves were to pick the contestants, based on skill and expertise with both horse and weapon. Katerina drew in her breath when she noted that it *was* Kostya who had been chosen. She knew without a doubt that it would be Banyen that the Mongols selected.

With great care and a solicitous attitude, Banyen

fetched a low barrel for Halya to sit on. He gave her
a low bow and marched away to ready his horse.

Katerina positioned herself near Mikhailo to show
she had no favorites.

Rokal stepped to the center of the ring and spoke in
a loud voice. "We have chosen Kostya to represent us
in the drill. Presenting," he shouted, waving his arms
in the air, "Kostya, drill captain of our group." The
men cheered his speech, and he withdrew as a Mongol
stepped forward and in the same words introduced
Banyen. While Banyen's men cheered, their enthusiasm was muted.

Her eyes on Halya, Katerina was puzzled when she
saw the young woman's hand go to her throat, and
all color drain from her face. Surely she wasn't one of
those squeamish females who fainted at the show of
a little excitement. Katerina watched intently to see
where her gaze traveled. Kostya! Why would the sight
of the blue-eyed Russian bring such a look of dismay
to her face? Katerina swiveled to pay closer attention
to the blond atop his mount, and watched as his eyes
traveled the length of the arena and came to rest on
the princess. Katerina frowned when he tensed in the
saddle and jerked the reins.

Banyen, impervious to what was going on, smiled
confidently to all who looked on. There was no doubt
in his mind who the winner would be. Things were
definitely improving in the fortress. A beautiful woman
and a chance to show the steely-eyed prisoner that he
was a fighting man despite his royal title.

Mikhailo also watched the byplay between the princess and Kostya. "I knew she would be trouble the
minute I laid eyes on her," he said harshly.

Katerina nibbled on her lip as she watched Kostya's
horse back off daintily and then wait patiently for his
rider to give his first order. Her amber eyes grew wary
as she saw his hand tremble slightly when he maneuvered the lance in his hand. What did it mean?
Was she so beautiful that men . . . And that stupid
Banyen, he was still smiling in the princess's direction,

his seat lofty, his bearing regal in the saddle. Jealousy ate at Katerina as she watched both men stare at the princess. Damn! she seethed. Mikhailo was right. When you make a mistake, Katerina, you make a good one, she told herself.

Banyen's steed made his way to the center of the ring. The muscles trembled beneath the animal's hide, a sign that he was impatient to begin. On Mikhailo's count of three, Banyen, who had resumed his place at the far end of the room, charged forward. At what should have been the moment of impact, Banyen transferred the lance from his right hand to his left. Kostya rode straight as if to take the lance full in his chest, but instinctively swerved out of the way at the last split second. A wide grin spread across his face as he reined in the horse in preparation for a second charge. Again Kostya rode straight toward Banyen, but this time the Mongol anticipated his move and kept the lance poised in his right hand. Kostya, intent on his maneuver, slid sideways just as a scream ripped through the arena. The princess toppled from her barrel into a heap on the floor. Both men wore stunned expressions as they stared deeply into each other's eyes. Neither moved or said a word. Katerina walked over to the fallen woman and stood looking down at her, her eyes turning the color of cinnamon as she pondered what to do.

"She fainted," Mikhailo said gruffly as he bent to pick her up in his powerful arms. His gait with his wooden leg was uneven as he carried the woman from the arena.

Katerina resumed her position and motioned with her hand for the drill to continue. Kostya's mouth was a grim, tight line and Banyen's dark eyes were hooded as they charged at each other time and time again, neither man unseating the other. "A draw!" Katerina shouted. She swaggered over to the two men and looked up at them, her hands on her hips: "It's fortunate for all of us that this was a drill. If you had been in battle and the scream of a woman could divert you, then your life would be gone. Both of you are fools. I thought you were men. Boys! Babies! Infants! We're talking about your life and you stare at me as if I were some species of fly. Am I right or am I wrong?" she demanded loudly. "Answer me, for I want your men to know what manner of fearless leader they train under. Ask them," she said, pointing a finger, "who among them would agree to ride with you knowing a female shriek could divert you?"

Kostya and Banyen both looked to their men and were not surprised to see all of them lower their heads, refusing to meet their eyes.

"A Cossack has no time for thoughts such as both of you are having. For a faint you would have lost your lives. All these months wiped out for one careless, stupid mistake."

Katerina forced herself to stare into the Mongol's eyes, her own bitter and hate-filled. Kostya gazed at her shamefaced as he slid from his horse and walked to his men, who avoided him by moving away in small clusters, their voices subdued and quiet. Banyen's men moved to the end of the arena and busied themselves with their weapons.

Angry at herself, angry at Kostya and Banyen, Katerina stalked from the room. She would get to the bottom of whatever it was that had startled the princess and put an end to it. Why had she allowed the woman to come to the mountains? What a fool she had been.

The deep, ridged scar on Banyen's cheek throbbed painfully as he reached up to remove the saddle from his horse. Damn her soul, she was right! Why did she always have to be right, and why did he always have to be the recipient of her wrath? If she were within a hair's-breadth of him now, he would choke the life from her body. It was that damnable Kostya who was at fault. He should have killed him when he had the chance, the opportunity, but he held back. He told himself wanton killing was not in his nature. Yet that shriek had startled him also. Fair was fair. How could he kill when he was as much at fault as the Russian?

Sometimes it paid to be truthful with oneself. Like now, he thought bitterly.

Christ, she made so few mistakes! Was she human or was she some kind of devil? He reached up to still the pain in his cheek and remembered who it was that was responsible. A feeling of shame settled over him as his rough kneading of the wound relaxed its throbbing. The Khan would be furious if he knew what was going on. Outclassed and outsmarted by a woman. A woman who hated him . . . totally. He knew one day she would kill him if he weren't careful. True, she had allowed him to make love to her, allowed him to hold her in his arms, but now that he thought about it, it was not quite right. She had done it for a reason. Well, this time she had made an error. Why had she allowed the princess to come to the fortress? She was a beautiful woman, pleasing to the eye with her softness and her voluptuous body, but there was something about her, the look in her eyes . . . it was as old as time itself. A look she could never rid herself of. She had been careful to skirt around the edges of what sort of life she had while living in the palace. Was she Ivan's mistress? Of course she was, he answered himself. He had seen women like her before, and while they performed well in bed, that was all they did. They were dull-witted, placid, content only when their favors were repaid with gems and money. Nothing had any meaning to women like her, everything they did was calculated and planned. No, he didn't need a woman like her. But, on the other hand, if she had news of Ivan that could help him, then he just might have to . . . He shrugged as he left the arena, Mikhailo staring after him.

Katerina stood looking down at the supine woman on the hearth, her head resting on a large goose-down pillow. She was awake and staring into the fire.

"I made a mistake in allowing you to come here," Katerina said matter-of-factly. "Your actions almost got the two best men killed. It was a senseless thing to do. It was a drill and both men were evenly matched. From now on you will only be allowed in this kitchen and in the room next to mine, where you will sleep. Do you understand what I'm telling you? From this moment on you are to have no contact with any of the men. I can't afford any mistakes. Why did you shriek like that? Tell me, so that I'll understand. Are you so naive that you didn't think, weren't aware that a disturbance like that was harmful to the men participating in the drill? If the prince hadn't held back at the last moment, Kostya would be dead."

At the sound of Kostya's name, Halya moved her head and stared up at Katerina. "I'm sorry," she said, struggling to a sitting position. "I owe you an explanation for my behavior. I was startled when I saw Kostya. We played together as children in my home in Moldavia. While I was of royal birth, he was a peasant, so our playful years were forced to end with my father sending him away. I was sixteen and he was seventeen. I was sent to Moscow with my brother so that . . . it isn't important why I was sent. When I learned that my father was sending Kostya away, I ran to him one night and we made love. It was the most beautiful thing in the world to us. We swore that one day we would be reunited and live happily ever after. Children say things like that, only we meant it, and after that night we were no longer children. I loved him then and I love him now. While I lived in the Terem Palace and was Czar Ivan's mistress, I had only one thought and that was to marry the Czar, thinking that somehow Kostya would hear of my marriage and come for me. I've done many things in my life that I'm not proud of, but with only one thought in mind—that somehow Kostya and I would be reunited. If it required the use of my body, then so be it. One only gives that which one wants to give, no more and no less. I've lost Yuri and I've found Kostya. My life is complete."

Katerina looked at the wide-eyed woman in front of her and felt a chill wash over her. If only life were so simple. In her own way she was glad that it was Kostya Halya loved and not Banyen. Banyen was a part of her whether she liked it or not.

Halya stared at Katerina, a strange look on her face. "Please tell me that you don't . . . that Kostya . . . please tell me . . . I have to know," she pleaded, the grass-green eyes moist with unshed tears.

"I have no feelings for Kostya, and he has none for me. Another time we'll speak of him and the reasons why he is here. I have much thinking to do. I want your promise that you'll not seek him out or do anything foolish."

"You have my promise," Halya said happily. "I'll do and say whatever you want as long as I know that he is here. I was going to go back to Moldavia and inform my parents of Yuri's death and make a new life for myself. At first I had many plans, each more difficult than the last. There is one other thing you must know. I left the Terem Palace with the Czar's permission, but a day early. A young soldier helped me escape. I'm sure as I sit here that he planned my death and was due to execute it shortly. He's a madman and I could no longer live under the same roof. If I were to tell you the things I was forced to do, you would die of shame. But I'm alive, and that is all behind me now. Now I have Kostya. There really is a God." She smiled. "Every day from the day we were parted I prayed, and He has finally answered my prayers. Now I must pray anew that Kostya feels the same way I do."

"Come, I'll show you where you are to sleep and let you turn in for the night. You look tired, and this has been a day of days for you. I think that you'll sleep happily and have dreams that only young, foolish girls have," Katerina said, her voice hard and bitter.

Halya regarded her uncertainly, was unable to fathom her tone or the look in her eyes. What was eating at the girl? Surely she spoke the truth when she said she had no feeling for Kostya. It must be the

Mongol. Did she love him or did she hate him? Whatever, who was she to judge or assume anything?

While the two women talked, Kostya settled himself in the cot that was his and sighed deeply. It was impossible, Halya here in the fortress! How? Why? Feelings long submerged surged through him till he had to gasp for breath. He buried his face in the bedding and let his mind race. He had thought he would never see her again. God, how he had searched, day after day, month after month, year after year. And she was finally here, so close he could almost touch her if he wanted to. How did she feel? Did she still love him? Only thoughts of finding her had kept him alive in the stockade.

Katerina paced her room, a deep frown on her face. She was tired but knew she would never sleep. How was she to keep the princess locked up or, barring that, out of sight? What in the name of God was she to do with her for six weeks? What would Kostya do if at the end of the winter Halya . . . She would have to talk to Kostya and see if his promise still held. What will I say to him? she thought nervously. She knew in her heart that she couldn't force him to help her at the beginning of spring. Idea after idea raced through her mind, only to be rejected. Perhaps tomorrow she would be able to think more clearly.

The fire crackled as flames leaped up the hollow chimney, sending tiny sparks out onto the hearth. Katerina sat down and drew her legs up to her chin. Every problem had a solution. If she appealed to the princess, it would help. What if Kostya really did leave? If he did, the others would go with him, and there was nothing she could do about it. The promise of gold and dignity would not go far when he left. She had to talk to him, and plead and beg if necessary for his help. "It can't all be for nothing," she whimpered as she hugged her knees, a lone tear trickling down her cheek. Tomorrow she would talk with Kostya and promise him anything so long as he agreed to her terms.

Curling herself into a tight ball, she cradled her head in the crook of her arm atop the red-fox throw and was instantly asleep. From time to time she moaned softly as she raced across the snows, the slant-eyed Mongol in her wake.

When Katerina woke in the morning, she was exhausted as thoughts of what she had to do plagued her.

Her simple but hearty breakfast over, she ordered Stepan to fetch Kostya to the kitchen. While she waited, she paced the flagstone floor, her thoughts whirling. God, what was she going to say and do when he stood before her? By now all the men knew something was wrong and were no doubt speculating wildly as to what it was all about. And what was the bastard Banyen thinking? No doubt he has it all figured out, she thought bitterly.

Stepan escorted a perplexed Kostya into the vast room and discreetly withdrew as Katerina held out a mug of hot tea and told him to sit down. "I must talk with you, and there's no other place where we would not be overheard. I want you to listen to me carefully, because you are the only one who can help me. Back in the Khanate when I chose you to come here to the Carpathians, I did so for one reason. I sensed in you an honesty. And when you said only savages and animals rape . . . What I'm trying to say is your words rang true, and I knew that whatever your best was, you would give it to me in exchange for freedom. Was I right, was my judgment of you accurate?"

"You judged me correctly."

"Now that the princess is here, what does this do to my judgment? Will you stay with me after the winter is over? Will you keep your end of our bargain? Wait," she said quietly, sensing he wanted to speak. "If you leave here with Princess Halya in the spring, the others will go with you. I need you to help me regain the Cosars. Without you and the men, I'll never see them again. Tell me, are you a man of your word? That and that alone is what I want to know."

"Yes, I am. I'll do what I can to help you. I promised to keep my end of the bargain and I will. So will the others."

Katerina nodded, her eyes lightening to ripe apricot, as she listened to him talk.

"I've searched for Halya for years, and finding her last evening was so unexpected that I was shaken to the core. I love her and I always will. Suddenly it was too much for me. I was free from the damn stockade, my life more or less back on an even stride, and there is Halya to add the final meaning to my life." He looked around, almost expecting to see her sitting in the kitchen. "I understand that it's not good that she's here. I must see her and speak with her. That you can't deny me. If you do, then our bargain is over. After I talk with her and I explain, I'll do what you say. I also understand that you want no more meetings between us. I agree. It wouldn't look good for the men, and I have no wish to disturb them. What is good for one is good for all."

Katerina nodded. "There are those here in the fortress who think I have no heart, that I'm not compassionate. Today is your day. Yours and the princess's. Come, I'll take you to her. Just remember that a bargain is a bargain. If you should default, you'll leave me no other choice. I'll have to kill you and make it look like an accident so the men will not revolt. I want that understood, Kostya."

"I understand. If this were another time and another place, perhaps we could . . ."

"No, your princess would always stand between us. Rarely does one find true love, and when one does, it's not wise to tamper with the . . ."

Kostya smiled. "There is great understanding in you. I sensed it the first time you ever spoke to me. I have you to thank for my life and for my . . . love. I'll not abuse your generosity, you have my word."

"It grows light. Let your face be the first thing the princess sees upon awakening. Remember, only this one day, no more."

"You have my word."

Chapter Eighteen

THE TROTSNIK TAVERN on the outskirts of the Terek camp shook with raucous laughter as the Terek Cossacks danced and drank late into the night.

They raised their mugs of kvass, first to one servant girl, and then to another. When they tired of toasting the women, they toasted their own fierceness and virility, laughing wildly and stamping their booted feet.

Gregory Bohacky, in a near stupor, climbed on top of one of the tables and began to dance, a bottle of wine balancing precariously on his forehead as he crouched low, his arms crossed over his broad chest. The music played wildly as the drunken Cossack thrust out one leg and then the other, finally falling off the table to land in a bevy of servant girls who were laughing as loudly as the men. Gregory lay on the floor, a wide grin splitting his face, his knees drawn up, feet flat on the floor. Two women perched themselves on his knees. The woman who could maintain her balance would be the fortunate one who would make the short ride back to Khortitsa and his bed for the night. The girls laughed and squealed as Gregory stamped his booted feet, trying to unseat each woman who clasped her arms around his muscular leg.

Gregory lifted his haunches and gave his right leg a mighty thump on the floor. One woman fell, amid loud shouts from the Cossacks. The other, Sonia, remained atop his knee, shouting that she and she alone was the victor. Gregory was pleased, for of all the women in the tavern, Sonia was his favorite. She could drink, dance, and make wild, passionate love better than any other woman he knew, and when the night of lovemaking was over she didn't cling and weep like the others. She dressed, kissed him soundly, borrowed a mount and rode back to the tavern to wait for another time when Gregory would seek her out.

At the height of the din, Gregory gathered her close and whispered in her ear. She laughed as she waved to the other Cossacks and winked lewdly at the woman who had toppled from his leg.

Sonia giggled as Gregory tried to mount his horse. On his third try he seated himself, and reached down for the laughing Sonia and pulled her up next to him.

Back in his hut in Khortitsa, they tore off their clothes and tumbled into Gregory's rancid, filthy bed. Their lovemaking was wild and fierce, with Gregory shouting lewd endearments to the grinning Sonia.

Later, relaxing in the aftermath of his proven masculinity, the woman draped across his chest, he became aware of a loud clamoring outside his home. Angrily he stalked to the window. Who would dare to disturb him at this hour? A small group of villagers were wildly gesturing and shouting. He peered into the darkness, seeing nothing to warrant the excitement the men were making. He dressed quickly and stormed outside, shouting to be heard over the excited men.

Holding up both hands, he demanded silence. "You, old man," he said, pointing to a half-dressed Cossack, "what is it, what's going on?"

"It's the Russians from Czar Ivan, they are here for the Cosars. Look, Gregory," he babbled excitedly, "at the end of the road, do you see the coach?"

"Of course I see it, you fool, do you think I'm blind? Did they say why they arrived so early? They weren't due for another month. It's a trick of some sort. Post guards and surround this coach, and at the first sign of a trick, kill them!" he said harshly, striding toward the waiting coach.

"Explain yourself!" he bellowed to a soldier standing guard at the doors of the coach.

"Basil Makoviy, representative to Czar Ivan. I've

come for the Cosars. Your gold is in the coach, full payment as agreed."

"Bah! I made no agreement. I told the Czar I would give him my decision in one month. I didn't say I agreed to sell him the Cosars . . . You made your journey for nothing."

The soldier was unimpressed with Gregory's words. He opened the door of the coach and pointed to six chests that rested on the floor. He nodded slightly, and one of his men opened a chest. Gregory blinked at the gold coins that sparkled in the glowing torchlight. Another nod from Makoviy and all the chests were opened. "My orders were to deliver the money to you and return with the herd. Those are my orders," he repeated.

"And what will you do if I order my men to take this gold and kill you? I'm the leader of this camp, and I give the orders. Your Czar be damned! I made no bargain with him," Gregory said harshly.

"The Czar has given us a certain number of days to reach here and return with the Cosars. Men were positioned along the route we followed and they are reporting our progress to Moscow. The last messenger was sent back to the Czar the moment we rode into this camp. If we don't return on schedule, this village will be nothing more than a memory. Do you understand me?"

Gregory's heart pounded in his chest, and sweat dripped from his forehead. He knew he had to make a decision, and he knew that if he didn't strike a bargain with the Russian his own men would kill him and take the gold for themselves. What good were horses when there were six chests of gold? "Agreed!" Gregory shouted, to the approval and wild stamping of his men.

The Russian nodded and spoke quietly. "The Czar was sure you would agree. We'll make camp here for the balance of the night and start our journey back at dawn. See that the herd is ready at sunup," he said briskly as he ordered his men to unload the chests of

coins. "A wise decision on your part. If you had refused, as I said, this village and all your people would
be nothing more than a memory. A very wise decision."

Gregory strode into a circle of his men and laughed
loudly. "I said the Cosars were worth their weight in
gold, and now we have the gold to prove it."

The men added logs to the campfire in the circle
and brought out containers of vodka to celebrate. "To
Gregory!" they chorused.

Chapter Nineteen

AS THE ENDLESS back-breaking days dragged on, Banyen became hostile and intense, his dark eyes brood-
ing and hate-filled, while Kostya drove his men to a
near frenzy, his own bright gaze smiling and alert.
They were like oil and water. Banyen would sneer,
one large fist pounding into the other, when one of
his men fell short of the mark. Kostya would laugh
and make his man do it over to his satisfaction, his
mind on other things. Anger was a waste of time, and
for now there was none in him. He could, at this time,
even be charitable and forgive Banyen his rough treat-
ment of him in the stockade. Rokal was right, he
merely followed orders, and a good soldier always followed orders and gave the best that was in him. He
owed Katerina the best that was in him, and he would
keep his promise. Halya understood and promised to
wait for him back at her home in Moldavia at winter's
end. For once fortune smiled upon him, and he had
no desire to tamper with God's work. He would do as

he had promised and be happy doing it so long as he knew Halya and he would be together.

The days were just as endless for Katerina. She watched the men for hours on end, finding no fault with their performance. They were as near to being Cossacks as was humanly possible. Even the Mongols gave an excellent accounting of themselves. The Khan would find no fault with her training. Banyen, she admitted, bothered her. His indigo gaze was angry and hostile each time he looked at her. Did he think that the princess had been brought here for his personal enjoyment? Katerina smiled.

Banyen was unable to fathom why Halya was secluded from the others. He ate alone with Mikhailo while Katerina dined with the princess in her room. He wondered if she had something to do with the horses. It was possible Ivan had sent her here. How was he to gather news of the Czar if he couldn't talk to Halya? It disturbed him that some manner of conspiracy was going on and he had no clue as to what it was. Sooner or later he would have to make a decision about the stallions. Now that he knew they were in the fortress, all he had to do was follow Katerina on one of her early-morning jaunts and find out exactly where they were sequestered and then decide what to do. How many more days was he going to wait before he made any of his decisions? Not long, he promised himself; winter was slowly coming to an end and before long the perpetual snows would cease, and he could think about the vast outdoors and the chances he would have to take if he decided to take the stallions.

Christ, he ached with wanting a woman. Not just any woman, he told himself, but the Kat. He wanted her, desired her more than he had ever wanted anything in his life. He rubbed at his throbbing cheek and felt his fingers go to his eyes. She said she preferred Western eyes. She said she preferred hair the color of winter wheat. Was he so ugly that his dark hair and slanted eyes offended her? No, he told himself,

Katerina had only one reason, and he doubted he could ever make it right with her. His dark eyes became hooded as he watched her throw back her head and laugh at something Kostya said. Rage surged through him as he thrust out his booted foot to kick at the low oak bench where saddles were piled. The pain in his foot made his eyes smart with the pain. "Bitch," he seethed. Skinny, scrawny, bitch, how could she have such an effect on him? He stormed from the arena to the corridor, where he saw Katerina walk each morning before the others were awake. He would search the stable till he found what he wanted, and the first person who tried to stop him would find his hands around their neck. After that, they would be dead.

Banyen investigated methodically, the way he did everything. "Somewhere there must be an entrance to another room. I won't give up till I find it even if it takes all night." Already he had spent hours, and still he was no wiser. "It has to be this room. She went in two hours ago and still hasn't come out," he muttered in frustration. "The only thing I haven't done is tap the walls to see if they're hollow. And what will I do if I manage to find a secret opening?" he asked himself, shrugging his shoulders. If I just knew where to enter the room, that would be sufficient for now, he tried to convince himself.

This area, what was so special about it? Katerina had said it was off limits to any and all people in the fortress. Later he would decide what he would do. For now he wanted to see if what she said was true, that the animals responded only to her. If there wasn't any way he could handle them, then there would be no point in doing anything or making any sort of plans. One step at a time, he told himself as he began tapping the thick stone walls.

While Banyen hunted his way around the underground chamber, Katerina stirred restlessly and finally woke, her amber eyes smarting from the smoke that was whirling about the room. She struggled to her feet and added another log to the fire and sat down, shivering from the cold. Tears gathered in her eyes as she leaned back against the large fireplace, the ermine cape wrapped tightly about her. She admitted to herself that she hated her circumstances, the position she was in, the beautiful princess and the damn Mongol. She hated everything and everyone. All she wanted to do was lie down and sleep forever; she was tired, very tired. Somehow, somewhere, her hatred had waned and been replaced by strange, unfamiliar feelings. She needed to talk, and decided to seek out Mikhailo. By now he would be up preparing tea for himself. She dressed quickly and ran to the kitchen.

"Katerina, what is it?" he said gruffly as she threw herself into his arms.

"Help me Mikhailo!" she pleaded. "I have so many peculiar feelings that my mind cannot deal with." Tears formed in the gold-flecked eyes and trickled down her smooth cheeks.

"Is it Banyen or Kostya?" Mikhailo asked, seating her near the fire.

"I don't know. I haven't any experience in the ways of the world, like the princess."

"What do you feel for Kostya?"

Katerina answered honestly, "I have no feelings for him."

"Then it's the prince that's making you unhappy. Do you feel drawn to him?"

"Yes, Mikhailo," she said unhappily. "Soon it will be spring and he'll leave. What will I do, how will I feel when that happens?"

"I have no answers for you, Katerina, you must search and find your own answers."

Kat wiped her tears with the back of her hand. She couldn't allow any man to come into her life, consuming her to the point where there was no room for anything else. That couldn't be love. Love was understanding and forgiveness.

"What is it, Katerina? What is tormenting you?"

"Can a person love and forget something . . . something terrible? No," she answered for the old man. "It's possible to forgive, but one never forgets. Never!" she exclaimed, jumping to her feet. "Never!"

"What is it, tell me!" the Cossack said, drawing her to him.

"Nothing, Mikhailo. Don't concern yourself. I'll go and visit with Stepan and the stallions."

Mikhailo nodded. The stallions would work their magic and comfort her as he couldn't.

The moment she stepped into the stable, she heard a sound. Standing in the darkness, she watched Banyen rapping on the walls, an iron bar in one hand and a lantern in the other. She remained quiet as he slowly worked one side of the chamber and then another. From time to time he cursed softly in the dimness and moved on, the iron bar clanking and grazing off the rough stone. Her eyes narrowed as she watched. What would he do if he found the latch that opened the door? Would he walk through, or would he wait for another time, a time when the snows had gone, and would he try to lead the stallions from their home? Her heart felt heavy as a deep sadness settled over her. It was always the horses; it always ended with the horses.

Katerina stepped forward boldly, her boots making no sound on the hay-strewn floor. Banyen, intent on his search, did not see her or hear her till she reached up a slender arm and pressed the latch at the top of the shelf. "Is this what you're looking for?" she asked quietly.

Stunned, Banyen dropped the bar he was holding and stared at her. "Yes. I would never have thought of looking there. Why is it that the walls give off no echo?" he asked, hoping to wipe the look of defeat from her face. She shrugged as the shelf moved, and motioned him to precede her down the narrow tunnel.

Banyen drew back, hating the expression he saw on her face. "There's no need for you to take me. I would never have found it on my own."

"Eventually you would have, or watched me, and

sooner or later you would have discovered their stalls. This way, I'll give you a tour of the stallions' quarters and you'll tell me what you plan to do. Note, I said 'plan,' not 'do.' There's no way you'll ever take these stallions from their home. I have no intention of parting with them. What do you think you could do? They are worthless to you without the mares. Is it possible that you believe that I'll regain the Cosars and that way you'll have the breeding secret? Fool!" she said softly. "I'm the only one who has the secret, and I would die before I gave it to you. A stallion is a stallion, a gelding is a gelding, and a mare is a mare. There's no way you could succeed. And another thing, as long as we're discussing the horses, let me tell you that I lied to my uncle. I am not going to give him a colt and a filly. The only way he could get the animals is to kill me, and even then I would fight and kick to the death."

"Yes, I know of your intention. The Khan himself was aware that you lied to him. It amused him to watch you barter the one thing you held dearest for his help. He would have given you assistance for nothing, he has no need of the horses."

"You lie. If what you say is true, then why are you seeking out the stallions? Do men ever tell the truth?" she asked in a tormented voice.

"About as often as a woman tells the truth," Banyen said coolly.

"Why should women be any different from men?" Katerina asked, just as coolly.

"It takes a strong, honorable person to tell the truth. I need you," he said simply.

Katerina's heart leaped in her throat at his words. She stopped and stared into his eyes.

"Even from here I can smell the fragrance of your desire." He made no move to touch her, but stood still, returning her deep gaze.

"No," Katerina whispered huskily.

Banyen's voice was deep and sensuous when he answered, "Lie to me, but don't lie to yourself. You

want me, desire me as much as I want and desire
you."

"No," Katerina whispered again, backing off a step.

"Look at me!" Banyen ordered. "Tell me what you
see in my eyes. Put a name to it. Do it," he said, advancing until he was mesmerizing her with his nearness. Still he made no attempt to touch her.

Katerina swallowed as she gazed at him. "I don't
know what it is," she moaned.

"It's the same thing that is mirrored in your eyes.
You must be the one to give it a name." Unexpectedly, the red welt on his cheek began to throb,
and he fought the urge to reach up to still the pain.

Katerina saw the muscle in his cheek begin to twitch
and, without meaning to, reached up and laid a gentle
finger on the angry, throbbing welt. The words tumbled out.

"I did that to you, but I'm not sorry. What you did
to me that night on the steppe was brutal. I can forgive you, but I'll never forget."

"If I say I'm sorry, will that help? If I grovel at
your feet, will that make any difference? I can do anything but undo what has been done. I'll devote the rest
of my life to helping you forget," he said, reaching out
to gather her in his arms. He took her in the damp,
clammy tunnel, and afterward he stared deeply into
her eyes. "What we just did was savage and animal-
istic. Now I'll make love to you the way a man makes
love to a woman. Come!"

If Mikhailo had stood in front of her and said the
Cosars were standing at the doors of the fortress, she
couldn't have cared less. All she knew was she had to
follow him, she needed to follow him as surely as she
needed to breathe. She nodded, moistening her lips
as he wrapped his arms around her. "The stallions,"
she whispered inanely.

"I don't care if I never see the stallions. You're the
only thing that matters to me." Suddenly he stopped
and spun her around by the shoulders. "You want to
hear the words, is that it?" He shook his dark head,

an amused light in his slanted eyes. "I can't undo the time on the steppe. What I did was awful. I ask your forgiveness. You belong to me now and forever, so that might ease your feelings about what I did to you." His face took on a dejected look as he stared at her, hoping against hope that his words were meaningful to her.

She felt a slight trembling in his arm as he drew her to him. Not trusting herself to speak, Katerina laid her head against his broad chest and sighed deeply.

He led her gently from the tunnel.

The blazing fire snapped and crackled, sending sparks shooting out of the cavernous depths of the enclosure.

Naked flesh met naked flesh. Savagely, beneath the gossamer tent of her cascading hair, his lips met hers in a searing, burning kiss that sent a dancing line of white fire coursing through her body. He allowed his touch to become gentle, stroking her skin with tender, teasing touches, stirring her to heights of passion she had only dreamed of. Katerina stirred as he smothered her with kisses, pulling her to him, closer, always closer. Her passion heightened, she was totally aware of his maleness, his lean, hard, muscular body next to hers. Husky murmurings filtered throughout her being as he stroked and caressed her breasts with his gentle touch. Moaning in ecstasy, Katerina strained toward him as desire rose in a tide, threatening to engulf her.

Strong arms encircled her more tightly as she felt the rippling muscles beneath the broad expanse of his back. Her tone was low and throaty as she called his name over and over, bringing her lips to meet his, searing and scorching his very being with her nearness.

Banyen released her for a mere moment, looking deeply into her eyes. A low moan of passion escaped his mouth as he tore at her, his lips searching and hungry for her sweetness. His hold became tighter and tighter; Katerina clung to him, reveling in the feel of him, cherishing this moment of time, remembering it,

burning it into her very soul. She knew without a
doubt that this Mongol would love her and cherish
her for all eternity.

She stirred slightly, moving her head from the hollow in his neck, and reached up a slender finger to
trace the outline of his oblique eye, her own eyes
moist and full of love. Gently she traced the deep-
ridged scar before she brought her lips to meet his,
her long, slender body straining toward him.

Katerina knew in that one sweet kiss that she could
never belong to anyone save Banyen. Without doubt,
without reservation, she gave herself to him.

Spent, they lay in each other's arms. Quiet, rapturous words were whispered, words that only lovers use.

Banyen lay studying her beneath hooded, slanted
eyes. She was beautiful, more beautiful than he could
ever have imagined.

Katerina moaned, delighting in his touch, feeling
him against her, aware of the comforting weight of
him. He twined his fingers through her hair and lifted
it off her neck and shoulders, as she suddenly realized
the stroking she felt were kisses, warm and moist
across her shoulders and the nape of her neck. A
barely audible groan escaped his lips as he brought
his head to the curve of her throat.

Drawing in her breath, Katerina turned, encircling
him in her arms, offering her mouth. She felt his powerful hands in her hair, his lips burning hers. She drew
his head gently into the cradle of her hands and lowered it to her breasts, her body arched beneath him.
She needed him, wanted him, as she was sure no
woman had ever wanted a man.

When he pulled away from her, she clung to him,
forcing him back with her passion-filled lips, gentling
away his reserve and hers with bold, intuitive caresses
of her tongue.

Banyen's mouth was on her throat, her breasts,
drawing moans from somewhere deep within her soul.
Her senses soared, making her lightheaded with passion, bringing her to the borders of lust, as she an-

swered his caresses with her endearing embraces, responding to his kisses with animal passion she had never dreamed she possessed. She sought for and found the most rapturous caress, reveling in the pleasure she gave him.

Banyen rejoiced to find his passion matched by hers, delighting in her moans of exquisite joy as her body welcomed his.

White flames of passion raced through her veins as she sought to extinguish the scorching fire engulfing her.

"Have me, have me now!" she urged.

Banyen moved his head slightly to stare down into her eyes. Her words were softer than the muted sounds of the sparks in the fire, echoing in the fullness of his heart, filling him with a fierce protectiveness toward her that left him gasping for breath. He had never heard the words spoken before. An ever-surging tide of ecstasy swept over him as he once again crushed her to him, mouthing the words aloud that she wanted to hear, needed to hear. She was his, now and forever more.

As the heavy snow continued to fall, word came by falcon from the village of Kisinev that Ivan's madness had worsened. The word spreading throughout Russia told of Ivan wandering through the palace howling so loudly his cries were audible to people outside.

Several weeks later, a second message arrived that read:

Czar Ivan forsakes Christianity, seeking comfort in the prophesies of witches and magicians who were brought to Moscow from the far north where paganism still flourishes.

The last message received in the fortress read:

The peoples of Russia say each day Czar Ivan commands his servants to carry him, sitting in a chair, to his treasury. While his attendants stand and watch, he plucks jewels from their coffers and puts them against his skin. Ivan fancies the jewels change color, proving that he was "poisoned with disease."

Katerina turned to Mikhailo, "I understand the Czar still has moments of rational thinking. If he were completely insane, the boyars would have taken over his rule."

"You're right, Katerina, the man is mad, but still strong enough to rule. We all know his days are numbered," Mikhailo said dourly.

Chapter Twenty

❦ ❦ ❦

THE DAYS THAT FOLLOWED were happy days for Katerina. The men were honed as sharp as a razor's edge. They were indeed Cossacks to be proud of. Happiness radiated from her whole being. Just being in the same room with Banyen, meeting his warm gaze, was all she needed to complete her joy. Passion-filled nights were sweet at the end of a long, hard-working day. She cherished the warm, tousled look of the man next to her on awakening. There was no one in the whole world that was more exultant than she was unless it was Banyen, she told herself. He, too, took on a fine-honed look. His mocking arrogance was gone, in its place a fierce protectiveness to Katerina and all in general.

Banyen watched his men, a smile on his face. He was proud of them. Totally untrained when they arrived at the fortress less than six months ago, now they were efficient soldiers he would be proud to fight with and serve with. He told himself he was a happy man. There was nothing he lacked. His eyes swiveled to where Katerina stood next to Mikhailo. His deep scrutiny made Katerina aware of him, and she looked up and smiled sweetly. How he loved her! Six months ago he would have laughed if someone had told him he would love a Cossack woman, a woman who wore men's clothes and looked like an angel. He blinked and turned from her silent gaze, his loins taking on an ache only she could quell. Was it only hours ago he had felt her next to him, her head cradled against his bare chest? It seemed like an eternity. He wished it were night so he could gather her close to him near the fire and make love to her. A love that she returned with every fiber in her body.

Another week and he would leave this vast fortress. The feeling saddened him, and a light film settled over the agate eyes. What would he do without her? How would he get through the days, and what was he going to tell the Khan? The truth, of course. She would wait for him, she promised. She said there were things they both had to do, and until their lives were straightened out they must make the best of it. A vision of her lying dead on some endless plain rose to haunt him. What she intended was for men, not women; not his woman. He understood and knew there was nothing he could do to stop her. She had to do what she had to do, just as he did. She said she understood, and he could do no less. Would he ever see her again once he left? What would life be like without her? His stomach lurched, and he forced himself into a false calmness. It would work out, it had to. Rarely did one find happiness such as his, and when one did, one treasured it.

A week. Seven days.

His thoughts suddenly turned to the princess and his intention of seeking her out and talking with her about Ivan. Somehow he had become lax, his thoughts only of Katerina. He would do it the first chance he got. He needed all the information he could get on Czar Ivan. The princess was the only one he knew who had left Moscow recently. Her information, whatever it was, would be the most recent. Katerina had told him of Halya's search and her love for Kostya. He was happy for the prisoner. Now he could understand what had kept him alive.

With two days to go till Banyen's departure, Katerina's eyes took on a haunted look, and her body trembled and tears burned at her eyes. What was she to do without him? She wanted to run, seek him out, throw herself into his arms and tell him the horses didn't matter, nothing mattered except being with him. She did nothing but look at him longingly and cry in his arms at what their parting would mean.

Over and over Banyen promised his return and a full, happy life, telling her he wanted a dozen female children, all to look like her.

On the eve of the departure of Banyen and his Mongols, Katerina instructed Hanna, the cook, to prepare a feast to be served in the arena. Mikhailo was to see to the tables and the music. She would be generous and allow the princess to attend and sit next to Kostya. They deserved this special occasion. Not once had either one of them complained of their separation, abiding by the bargain they had made.

As the hour of the feast approached, Katerina raced to the kitchen, imploring Hanna to help her with her dress. "It hangs here and there," she cried frantically. "You know I am all thumbs with a needle, you must do it for me now. The meat can cook itself."

Deftly Hanna pinned, tucked, and sewed, and an hour later she had the bronze-colored gown fitted on Katerina's slim body. She shook her old head and wished she were fifty years younger. The girl was beautiful, and would turn more than one head. The old cook pursed her mouth and told Katerina she was more lovely than the princess would ever be.

Katerina laughed delightedly as she poked her head into her wardrobe and withdrew the soft silken slippers

that matched the gown. Was it only a year since she
last wore the garments and shoes that rested in the
depths of the cupboard? Momentarily tears glistened
in her eyes as she remembered the formal evening
meals in the great dining hall, where her father and
grandfather dressed in traditional Cossack uniforms.
What would Banyen think? He had never seen her in
a gown before. Would he like her? She surveyed herself in the long mirror, turning slowly to see how the
gown swirled around her feet. She knew she looked
well, the low cut of the bodice showing off her tawny
shoulders and the swell of her full, round breasts. The
long, full sleeves, gathered together at mid-arm, fell
in soft graceful folds at her wrist, accentuating her
long, slender hands.

"My hair, what should I do with my hair?" Katerina squealed. "I can't let it just . . . hang. Hanna,"
she pleaded, "do something."

Hanna sighed and worked industriously with the
long-handled brush, swirling and pinning until she had
the effect she wanted. Wispy fringes of the coppery
hair framed Katerina's face becomingly, while the
wealth of her hair was set into deep curls, one cluster
draped over her bare shoulder.

"Pinch your cheeks for color," Hanna gurgled, "and
you will stir every man into a frenzy." Katerina
hugged the old cook, making her laugh as she struggled from the girl's tight grip. Her iron-gray hair,
pulled back into a tight knot, freed itself from its pins
and tumbled down to her waist. Her bright gaze was
merry as her round body shook with happiness for
Katerina. She had never seen her so happy or so
beautiful.

"Wait, wait, tell me, what are you serving for our
feast?" Katerina called excitedly.

Hanna pretended forgetfulness. "Black bread and
jam. Silly girl, I'm preparing just what you told me
to prepare. Roast lamb and duck, three vegetables
from the winter cellar, and fresh popovers with honey
and jam. Boiled potatoes in butter with herbs and

spices, seasoned the way you like it, and a soup—barley with carrots and cabbage. Rice pudding with raisins for a sweet. Wine and vodka till the jugs are empty. Does it meet with your approval?" She laughed.

"But of course. Did you cook enough? Will there be enough for the men to eat as much as they want? Training is over, and this is a day I want them to remember."

"They can eat until the moon is high and still there will be food left for another feast. There is no cause for worry. Mikhailo tells me the men are bathing and dressing in their best, which was laundered by me days ago."

"Do I need a jewel?" Katerina shrugged. "What if I did, I have none," she said, her eyes dancing. "I can barely contain myself, Hanna."

"I noticed," the old woman said tartly. "Rest now, so that you are not tired when the feast begins. A little sleep," she coaxed, "like when you were a child."

"Very well." Katerina acquiesced for the old woman's benefit, but she knew she would never be able to sleep. All she could think of was Banyen and the look in his eyes when he saw her in the bronze gown.

The raucous shouts and the sounds of merrymaking ceased when Katerina and Halya made their entrance. For the first time in her life Katerina felt beautiful, and the men's looks of approval proved it to her. Her eyes immediately sought out Banyen's, and she felt a warm glow spread through her as his dark blue eyes softened and a smile tugged at the corners of his mouth. She wanted to run to him and throw herself into his arms, but instead she seated herself next to Mikhailo and Halya.

"Katerina," Halya whispered, "what is the matter with Kostya? He looks ill to me. Is something wrong, is there something you aren't telling me? Even from here I can see the flush on his face, and it isn't because I'm in the same room. He looks ill to me," she said fearfully.

Katerina stared across the room and felt frightened at Kostya's reddened complexion. "Perhaps a small fever, he could have become chilled. I'll have Mikhailo see to it," she said. She beckoned Mikhailo and whispered in his ear, cautioning him to be discreet when he spoke with Kostya.

"Do you have medicines here in this fortress?" Halya demanded harshly, her lips trembling, her eyes fearful.

"Of course we have medicines here in the fortress. Mikhailo is as good as any physician. He can even pull teeth with little pain to the patient," Katerina said confidently. "You must not show your alarm to the others. I'm sure it's nothing more than a small temperature that will abate by morning. Kostya has been working hard, and I'm sure the reason is that with his strenuous work he could put you from his thoughts. It's his way of making the days go faster. Nothing is going to happen to him, I give you my word."

The princess nodded, but the look of worry did not leave her face. She nibbled at her food and refused to take her eyes from Kostya.

Mikhailo returned to the table and bent over to whisper in Katerina's ear. "The man is ill. Not only does he have a raging fever, but chills also rack his body. He refuses to leave until the meal is over. He agreed to bed down in the kitchen, where it is warm. I told him I would tend him and that it was best he remove himself from the others so he does not infect them with his illness. A day or two and he'll be on the mend," he said, a ring of confidence in his voice.

"The best time for you to take him to the kitchen will be when Stepan begins playing his fiddle. By then the men will have much vodka in them and they won't notice his departure. Tell Kostya that later the princess will come to sit by his side."

Halya nodded her thanks when Katerina explained what Mikhailo had said.

Katerina pushed thoughts of Kostya and his illness

from her mind. Nothing could spoil this last evening with Banyen. God alone knew when she would see him again. Impatiently she waited for the meal to be over with so she could sit next to Banyen when Stepan began to play. Her eyes sought out Banyen's, and she smiled, her whole face alight with happiness at just knowing he was in the same room. Don't let anything spoil this night, she prayed silently.

As soon as Hanna and several of the elderly Cossacks who lived in the fortress cleared the table, Stepan, resplendent in his full Cossack uniform, walked to the center of the arena and brought his fiddle to his chin and began to play a rousing Cossack song. The men stomped and stamped their feet, their hands clapping wildly. Out of the corner of her eye Katerina watched Mikhailo and Kostya leave the room. A sigh of relief escaped her as she noticed that no one paid any attention to the two men's departure, everyone busy singing and dancing in accompaniment with the music.

Banyen excused himself to his men, who paid him no heed, and worked his way among the laughing, shouting men, who were demanding that Stepan play louder. He stood looking down at Katerina, who smiled into his eyes. He seated himself in Mikhailo's chair and immediately searched for Katerina's hand beneath the tablecloth. He leaned over slightly and spoke softly. "This night is ours. In all of Russia there is none more beautiful than you."

Katerina forced her voice to remain calm, but there was nothing she could do to still the trembling in her body. "You'll be gone from here and from me by sunup tomorrow. I don't know when I'll see you again." Impulsively she tightened her grip on his hand and stared into his eyes. "Don't go, Banyen. Please don't go."

Banyen's heart pounded in his chest. "I have to go to Sibir, you know that. There is nothing on this earth that could keep me from returning to you. I'll come back to you, you have my promise. I couldn't live without you," he said tenderly.

Tears misted in Katerina's eyes. She had heard those same words once before, a long time ago. Yuri spoke them to her when he left Volin, and now he was dead. Dead by her hand. A deep shudder ripped through her body at the thought, and Banyen felt saddened. How he loved her. What else could he say to her? How could he prove to her that he would return? It always came down to words. Words he did not know how to string together. Surely she understood his feelings. Didn't actions speak louder than words? "I love you, for now, for forever more," he said huskily.

Katerina's amber eyes glistened with tears. "I know, I understand; it's just that I'm acting like a female. You are my life," she whispered.

"If you don't stop looking at me like that, I'll drag you by the hair from this arena and then what will the men think?" he teased.

Katerina shrugged. "Who cares? I only care about you. Tonight I don't even care about the Cosars, just you."

"We must talk of other things or I'll carry you from here. Tell me, what is wrong with Kostya? He looked sick to me when we entered the arena this evening. Where did your man take him?"

Katerina frowned. "Mikhailo said he has a raging fever and his body is racked with chills. Mikhailo is ministering to him in the kitchen, where the heat from the fire is constant. We couldn't take a chance of him infecting the others. Especially your men, as you leave tomorrow. You have a long ride ahead of you, and nothing must go wrong."

Banyen and Katerina sat watching Stepan as he fiddled away, his eyes merry and his fingers flying with the bow. Banyen leaned back on the rough chair and let his eyes travel to Halya. He *had* to talk with her before he left. What was wrong with him? For days he had promised himself that he would seek her out, but there hadn't been time. He had to do it tonight, before he left, or he would never do it.

Mikhailo walked back into the cavern and, with a nod to Katerina to show that Kostya was resting, strode to the center and took the fiddle from Stepan and began playing. The young Cossack raised his arms and started to dance. The faster Mikhailo played, the faster Stepan's feet flew, up and down, up and down, his feet shooting out in front of him precariously. The men shouted encouragement as he continued with his wild dance.

Katerina felt Halya rise rather than saw her move to make her way to join Kostya. Her eyes were on the dancing Stepan and Rokal, who suddenly entered the middle of the ring. Mikhailo's fiddle stopped, and Stepan stood up and bowed low, a wild grin on his face.

Rokal shouted to be heard over the wild clamors of "More, more!" "My mother used to call me a dancing fool!" He laughed. "What this Stepan can do, I can do. Play, Mikhailo!" he shouted imperiously. Full of vodka and good food, Rokal steadied himself and began to imitate Stepan's movements, to the amusement of his comrades. Seeing that his legs were going in different directions, Rokal sat down in the middle of the floor, a look of defeat on his face. Suddenly he grinned and jumped up and raced to the table where Katerina sat. He pulled her to her feet. "You promised, back in the Urals, that you would dance for us again. Now is your chance. Music, loud music," he ordered Mikhailo.

Banyen grinned at the look on Katerina's face. She had promised, and now she had to dance. Good. This was the perfect time for him to seek out Halya. She would be with Kostya. Katerina wouldn't miss him, and he would be back by the time she was finished with her dancing.

No one paid any heed to his leave-taking; all eyes were on Katerina and Mikhailo.

Banyen crouched down in the kitchen and looked

at Kostya's flushed face. The man was lying on a sable carpet and covered to his chin by another length of fur. The princess sat next to him, tears streaming down her cheeks.

She looked up at Banyen, despair written on her beautiful face. She stood up and brushed her hair from her forehead. "One moment he is lucid and the next he's . . . he . . . It's been so long, and now when I've found him, he . . . It's so unjust. What if he dies?" she wailed.

"He won't," Banyen said, quietly. "He's survived worse than this. Mikhailo says the fever will abate by morning. Believe the old man. Katerina says he is well versed in herbs and medicines. You must believe and have hope. If you don't, you can't survive. Katerina told me of his search for you and you for him. He will survive."

"If I could only believe that," Halya whimpered. "It can't all be for nothing. I don't want to live if he dies. I couldn't bear to go through endless days knowing I would never see his face again. I just couldn't." Suddenly she threw herself into Banyen's arms and sobbed brokenheartedly. Banyen was jolted backward as she flung herself at him. He reached out to grasp her waist in order to break his momentum, and Halya came to rest against his chest, his arms around her to still her shaking and trembling.

Awkwardly he mouthed soothing words of comfort, and gradually felt her relax against him. His arms still around her, he gently pushed her a little away from him and looked down at her. "It will be all right. Nothing is going to happen to Kostya. He's young and strong and if he could survive the winter here in the fortress, he can survive this illness. I've seen fevers such as his many times in the Mongol camps, and it's a temporary illness. Believe me, he'll survive," he said, patting her on the cheek the way an indulgent father would pat a child.

Halya smiled tremulously and reached up and kissed him lightly on the mouth.

Banyen blushed and turned to see Katerina standing in the doorway. He blinked at the look on her face. She didn't think, she couldn't think . . . To his tortured eyes she resembled a tapered candle flame ready to spring to life. He watched as she swallowed hard and ran from the room.

"Oh, God! Oh, God! Oh, God!" Katerina whimpered as she ran down first one corridor and then another till she came to her room. Panting, she raced inside, slamming the door behind her. Quickly she threw the heavy bolt and leaned against the stout door, her hands to her cheeks. Oh, God, he didn't, he couldn't. It was all a lie, a trick. A dirty, sneaky Mongol trick. Fool! her mind shrieked. Stupid, foolish Cossack woman! She had believed all his lies. "I knew I should never have trusted his damn slanted eyes," she moaned as she slid to the floor, her back never leaving the door. She sat huddled there for what seemed like hours.

Some time later, a knock sounded on the door. Katerina's eyes flew open but she said nothing, her body stiff and rigid.

"Katerina! It's not what you think. Open the door so I can talk to you. I can't leave you thinking what you're thinking. I love you," Banyen said harshly.

"Liar!" Katerina whispered.

"It's not what you think. I'll not apologize for something I didn't do," he called through the door in an agonized voice.

"Bastard!" Katerina hissed between clenched teeth.

"I'm asking you to let me in so that we can talk. We must clear this up before I leave. I won't ask you again."

"Dirty, sneaky Mongol, I should have known better than to believe your lies. All men lie," she muttered to herself, the tears streaming down her cheeks. "I believed you and you lied to me," she whimpered as she crawled to a warm place near the fire. "It was the horses, it was always the Cosars. I saw the way you looked at the princess and I . . . I still thought, I still believed that you could love me. Liar!"

Banyen, standing outside, refused to believe the silence that roared in his ears.

"Katerina, I meant every word I said to you. I love you, I'll love you for the rest of my life. You didn't see me do anything except comfort the princess. Ask her yourself. It's you that I love. Let me prove it to you."

"You would lie to it and the princess would swear to it," Katerina whispered. "Oh yes, you can try to prove it, come into this room and rape me again. Oh no, Mongol, this is the last time you make a fool out of me. I believed you, I loved you!" she cried.

"If you loved me, you would open this door!" Banyen shouted gruffly.

"Well, I don't love you any more. Go! Take the stallions, I no longer care. You know where they are. Take them. All of them," she shrieked, long and loud. "That's all you ever wanted. You lied to me. You tricked me. Take the stallions, that's what you wanted all the time. They're my gift to you on leaving!" She continued to shriek.

Stunned, Banyen could only stare at the door. His shoulders slumped as he lashed out with his booted foot to kick at the door. Damnable woman, if she thought he was going to stand here and beg her, she had another thought coming! He rubbed at his temples as a film swept over his eyes. He shook his dark head and was jolted from his angry thoughts by the sound of Katerina's heartrending sobs. They tore at him, ate at him, as he walked away, his head lowered, his shoulders shaking. He knew he would never see her again.

When all the sound ceased outside the door, Katerina jumped to her feet and threw back the bolt. He was gone! A few moments of pleading and he was gone! That was all the time he could allot her, a few seconds. He would leave and she would never see him again. What did it matter if he took the stallions? Her life was over. In a few hours he would be gone and she would never see him again.

Throughout the endless night Katerina sat like a sick animal and licked her wounds. Her mood alternated between searing anger and devastating despair. It was over, there was no point now to anything. All her magnificent plans to regain the Cosars would never come to fruition. It always came back to the horses. She told herself she was a fool. A foolish, lovesick woman who couldn't see what was in front of her eyes. Banyen must be beside himself with glee, she thought bitterly. Another conquest to add to his credit. Fool! Fool! her mind shrieked.

An hour before dawn she stood up to ease her cramped legs, and was about to crawl into bed when she heard banging.

"Katerina, I have to speak with you," Mikhailo called through the thick door.

"Go away. There is nothing to talk about," Katerina answered.

"Open the door, there is much to be said. We have to talk."

"It's over, finished. There is nothing to discuss. Go away."

"I stand here alone, no one is with me."

"I don't believe you. The Mongol put you up to this. I wouldn't open the door to him, and now he thinks he'll use you to get to me. I thought you were my friend, Mikhailo. From the first you liked him, all he has to do is ask you to intervene and you do it. Go away."

"Have I ever lied to you? You know I haven't," he continued to plead. "Open the door, and you can lock it again as soon as I am inside. I tell you, I'm alone."

"If you're lying to me, I swear I'll kill you, Mikhailo. I'm in no mood for tricks. Swear to me on the icon."

"I swear to you on the icon. Now open the door."

Katerina slid the bolt and quickly looked right and left. Mikhailo was alone. Her mouth tightened into a grim line as she stood aside for him to enter. Damn sneaky Mongol, he couldn't even have Mikhailo plead his cause, she thought unreasonably.

Mikhailo was shocked at Katerina's appearance. Her eyes seemed as cold and dead as the ashes that lay in the grate. The deep purplish smudges on her tawny cheeks frightened him. Quickly he threw logs on the fire and poked at the ashes with tongs, his mind racing with the words he wanted to say. He had never thought he would live to see the day when she could be cowed like a cornered animal. Where was her spirit, the sense of fairness that she was known for? Females were stubborn, he knew, but he had never thought stubbornness was one of Katerina's traits.

"What is it? What did you want to talk about? Whatever it is, I'm not interested in hearing it. I only allowed you in this room to show you that I care for you."

"The Mongols are preparing to leave. If you look outside the window you'll see them. Banyen is leaving," he said distinctly, making sure she heard him. "He was in the kitchen talking to Kostya for a few moments before he left to see to his men. Kostya, in case you're interested, is no better. I haven't been able to make the fever abate. He's been in a delirium since midnight. Once or twice he has had lucid moments, but then he lapses into his ramblings again. I am concerned, and I tell you this because I know you are worried about him."

"Was worried. I'm no longer worried," Katerina said in a flat voice. "I've changed my mind since last night. When he recovers, if he recovers, they can leave. You'll take them to Volin and give them the gold I promised. I don't care what they do, I don't care where they go. Harness the stallions together and give them to the Mongol. All of them, even Whitefire. I never want to see those animals again. Tell him . . . tell him they are . . . Just give them to him," she said bitterly. "Leave me now, Mikhailo, and no tricks. The stallions are mine to do with as I see fit, and I

want that bastard to have them. Every day for the
rest of his life I want him to remember where he got
them and why. Do it, Mikhailo, and no questions."

The Cossack stood, dismay covering his face. She
couldn't be serious. Not the stallions! His mouth
worked convulsively as he waited for her to throw the
bolt on the door so he could leave.

"No tricks, Mikhailo. I'll watch from the window
to be sure the horses are outside. If you harness and
ready them, they'll not kick up a fuss. They'll follow
him docilely. Do it!"

The ring of iron in her voice startled him, but he
said nothing. What could he do? He was an old man.

Banyen's face wore a look of controlled anger when
he entered the kitchen. Kostya looked up from his
cocoon near the fire, and Banyen was relieved to see
that though his face was heated and his hands trembled, his mind was clear. Banyen dropped to one knee
and spoke in a hushed tone so that Halya wouldn't
hear him.

Kostya frowned, but listened intently to the prince.
Weakly he nodded his head, agreeing to look after
Katerina during Banyen's absence, and tried to wipe at
the perspiration on his brow.

Banyen placed a hand on Kostya's shoulder. "Each
of us must do what he must do; I know that you understand this and hold no animosity toward me. That is
the only reason I'm here now. You have many qualities that I admire, and I wish you well. Perhaps we'll
meet again someday. If not, this is our last farewell."
He was saddened as he watched Kostya's eyes cloud.
He was no longer lucid but mumbling strange, inco-
herent words that Banyen didn't understand.

Even though Halya's green eyes were fearful, her
tone was light and confident. "I know he will recover.
I pray constantly that it is not his time to join his
Maker. Surely God will answer my prayers. Good-bye,

Prince Banyen. I wish you a safe journey back to your camp. One day our paths may cross again."

Banyen nodded farewell and strode from the room.

Outside, in the damp, cold corridor, he hesitated a moment. Should he try to see Katerina one more time? His heart thundered in his chest. What did she want from him? To crawl on his knees, to beg her to believe him? Why was it that you could lie to a woman and she would believe you, but if you told her the truth it was suspect? It made no sense. Real men didn't beg; men didn't grovel. He had spoken the truth to her. He had pleaded with her to open the door so that he could explain that she didn't see what she thought she saw. Women! Rage whipped through him at the injustice of his position as he stomped from the corridor to take his place with his followers.

Busy with the wagons and his men, he didn't see the stallions at first. When he looked to the end of the small caravan, he almost lost his footing. Holy Mother of God, she meant what she said! The four stallions were harnessed together and standing docilely, waiting for the order to move. Panic gripped him, a feeling he had never experienced before. Even in the face of death he had never weakened. If he wanted to he could step out and touch the horses and . . . The scar on his cheek began to ache as he walked over to the waiting animals. A month ago he would have asked no questions; he would have taken the animals and been ecstatic. Now he hated them for their sleek beauty, and he hated the fact that they stood in front of him, waiting for him to take them wherever he wanted to go. There was no question in his mind as he loosened the harness and led the animals back into the fortress. They weren't his. They didn't belong to anyone except Katerina, the beautiful woman with the amazing eyes. The stallions could never be his. They could never belong to anyone but her.

Mikhailo's mouth dropped open when Banyen led the snorting Cosars to the oak doors.

"Tell Katerina that I have no need for so priceless

a gift. These stallions belong to her for now, forever more, just as I thought she belonged to me. Tell her that for me, will you, Mikhailo?"

"I'll tell her, but she won't listen. I tried to talk with her this morning, and while she heard my words, they made no impression. She's like a wounded animal —not responsible for her actions. A person does what he has to do to survive or he dies. It is as simple as that," the old Cossack said quietly.

Banyen touched the old man's shoulder and then abruptly moved away. He mounted his horse and spurred it forward. He didn't look back as he led his soldiers from the House of the Kat. Banyen was going home to the Khan, the only home he had ever truly known. Returning without the breeding secrets of the Cosars, and leaving behind four white stallions and the only love he had ever known.

From her window Katerina watched as Banyen led the stallions out of sight. She frowned and tried to see what was going on below. She saw him return to his horse and ride away. He didn't look back, but rode straight ahead. She blinked her eyes to clear her vision. Whitefire and the others weren't with the caravan. He wasn't taking them! What did it mean? A clever trick, that's what it meant, she told herself.

For five days Katerina remained in her room, almost hoping as each hour dragged by that Banyen would return. At the end of the fifth day she emerged from her room, her face gaunt, dark smudges ringing her vacant doe eyes. She made her way to the kitchen and stood impatiently waiting for the princess or Mikhailo to notice her. It was Halya who walked over to her and tried to take her in her arms. Katerina brought up her arm and swung out, striking her full across the face. "Send the falcon to Kusma," she directed Mikhailo. "Saddle a horse for her, she leaves within the hour. Have one of the men take her as far as Volin, and from there Kusma can see to her well-being, whatever it is."

Tears welled in Halya's eyes. "You can't send me

away. Kostya has not recovered. Mikhailo says that by morning he thinks his fever will break. I want him to see me when he awakes. Please," she pleaded, "you can't be so cruel."

"Think again," Katerina snarled. "Within the hour, Mikhailo. If you have to, tie her to the horse."

Halya's eyes were bitter. "You're wrong. I'm ashamed to call you a woman. You act like a thoughtless child. There was nothing between your prince and myself. He comforted me. He belongs to you, no one could ever take him from you. Are you so foolish that you didn't know that? If you truly loved him, there would have been no doubt in your mind. Yes, you have the right to send me from this fortress. And, yes, I'll go. I have no other choice. But you can never separate me from Kostya. I love him and he loves me. I've seen cruel, heartless men, many of them, but never have I seen one as cold and as unforgiving as you, and that's what makes you a disgrace to all women. It's no wonder men have a low opinion of women."

Katerina reached up and gave her a second resounding slap on the side of her head.

Halya took the blow full force, her head reeling. "He'll never come back here for you. Is this how you acted with my brother, my brother that you killed? He's well rid of you even if he had to die to do it. If it will pleasure you, strike me again, it doesn't matter. I'll leave, and I wish you misery for every hour, every minute that you breathe for the rest of your life."

Katerina hated her, hated the words that spewed from her mouth. Her own lips trembled at what she was hearing and at the look on the princess's face. Was it possible that she spoke the truth? No, Mikhailo was right, the slant-eyed Mongol was a son-of-a-bitch.

"Save your breath and do not concern yourself with my well-being. If I live, I live; if I die, I die. It is no concern of yours. I allowed you in my house and I confided in you and you betrayed me."

"You betrayed yourself," Halya said softly. "You played a game and lost. Now you have nothing. Live with that for the rest of your life," Halya said bitterly as she gathered up her silver-fox cloak. "I'll fetch my belongings and be gone from your sight."

Katerina's eyes shot sparks as Mikhailo watched her, speechless at her tirade. She defied him to say a word, anything to chastise her. The old man resumed bathing Kostya's flushed face, his heart heavy in his chest.

"I thought I told you to loose the falcon!"

Mikhailo didn't bother to look up. "I have a sick man that needs my attention. I want no deaths on my conscience. Since you're as perfect as Almighty God, do it yourself."

"And just exactly what is that supposed to mean?"

"It means whatever you want it to mean," Mikhailo said, just as harshly. "Leave me, I can't bear to look upon your face. I never thought I would live to see the day that I would hate the sight of your beautiful face, but that day has come. Go, send your falcon to Kusma."

Katerina was stunned at the old man's words. How could he talk to her thus? Who did he think he was? He had never spoken to her before with anything except kindness and understanding.

"You were the one who said no Mongol was to be trusted. Tell me now you didn't say that."

"Yes, I said that, and at the time I meant it. Foolish words from a foolish old man. Your prince is not like that, nor are his soldiers. They're all men to be proud of, and I am truly sorry I ever uttered those words. The princess's words were just words also. You hurt her and she retaliated in the only way she knew how. You yourself are guilty of the same thing. You've just left girlhood behind and become a woman, a difficult transition."

He looks rather like a fat, precocious squirrel, Katerina thought as she saw him tilt his head to the side as if his own speech surprised him.

"You still don't know what you've done, do you?"

Katerina frowned, not sure she knew of what he was speaking.

"You are guilty of the very thing your father was guilty of. How does it feel, my dear? You assumed, you judged, and you found the prince guilty just as Katlof found you guilty. Now tell me, how will you live with that? Your father is dead and you're alive."

"Oh my God, you're right!" she exclaimed, a stunned look on her face. "Banyen!"

"He tried to explain to you that you were mistaken, and you wouldn't listen. You didn't even give him the chance to defend himself. Your father at least gave you that chance before the council. True, they found you guilty, but you had your say. Which is more than you allowed Banyen. He *loved* you. I don't know what he feels for you now. Possibly disgust, probably hatred. You ridiculed him, denied him the chance to defend himself. It would be a rare man who could still care after all of that."

"He never loved me, all he wanted was the horses," Katerina spat, stunned at the Cossack's words.

"Then why didn't he take the stallions with him? He told me to give you a message."

A spark lit up Katerina's large eyes as she waited for his words.

"He said the stallions belonged to you for now, for forever more, just as he thought you belonged to him."

"He said that?" Katerina whispered. "If you're lying to me, Mikhailo, I'll cut your tongue from your throat."

"I'll say no more. You must be the one to decide what is true and what is false. And," he said snidely, "you still have the falcon to turn loose. Or have you changed your mind?" Where am I finding all these words? he wondered as he again dipped the cloth into the pan of water to sponge Kostya's feverish face.

"Did Banyen really say that?" she asked huskily. "Tell me, Mikhailo," she pleaded with moist eyes.

"Where would an old man like myself hear such fancy words? Only men in love say things like that. I never heard such words before he uttered them," he snapped, a crafty look on his face.

"You can be a sly fox when you want to be." Katerina grinned. "I'll apologize to the princess and send her down the mountain. It's time for her to leave anyway. Kostya will recover."

Halya strode into the kitchen, her belongings tied up in a canvas sack. "There's no need for you to apologize to me. I understand, for I love Kostya the way you love the prince. One day you'll make amends, I know you will. When Kostya recovers, tell him that I'll be waiting for him in Moldavia. I could never hold bitterness for you in my heart, for if it wasn't for you, I would never have found Kostya."

Katerina floundered for words. "I'm sorry that I lashed out at you. I have never, in all my life, felt so hurt. I had to hurt something, and unfortunately it was you that I hurt. Forgive me."

"It's not my forgiveness you need, it's Banyen's."

"Yes, I know. One day perhaps he'll forgive me, if I can find him," Katerina said sadly, "and if it isn't too late."

"It's never too late," Halya said, clasping Katerina to her breast. "Remember that. Take care of Kostya for me, will you? I wish you well, and I wish you success in finding your Cosars. Just send Kostya to me when it's over. Promise me that and I can leave here with a light heart."

"You have my vow. Come, I must release the falcon and see that you have an escort down the mountain."

Mikhailo smiled to himself as he rocked back on his heels. Love! Women! Foolish men with their fancy words! Bah!

True to Mikhailo's word, Kostya's fever abated by dawn of the following morning. He was weak and shaky, but managed a few spoonfuls of broth from time to time. He apologized for his illness, saying he knew it delayed her descent down the mountain.

"A few days longer makes no difference. Another three days and you'll be fit as Stepan's fiddle," Katerina said. "The Mongols left a week ago, and Halya yesterday. She waits for you in Moldavia. She made me promise that I would return you to her safely. I told you that many times, but you were feverish, and I want to be sure that you understand what I'm saying."

"Then our plan is still the same, nothing has changed?"

Katerina grinned. "If you had asked me that a week ago, my answer might have surprised you. Nothing has changed—myself possibly, but that is all."

Kostya lay back exhausted, his mind wandering. Something teased at his mind, but he couldn't grasp it. Did he forget something, was he supposed to do something? What was it Banyen had asked? He sighed. He needed sleep. Later he would remember whatever it was that nagged at him.

Each day found Kostya's strength returning twofold. He was like the stallions, champing at the bit to move, to get it over with so he could begin what he said was the rest of his life.

Ten days from the time Kostya's illness broke, the Cossacks assembled outside the great fortress known as the House of the Kat and waited for Katerina's signal to move.

Astride Whitefire, she leaned over to speak to Mikhailo. "Another week and you can see to the burial of Grandfather and Valerian. Say the same words over the Mongol that you say for my zedda. After that, go to Volin with the others and see to the rebuilding. The process is slow with so few men. Leave this fortress unmanned. There is nothing for us here now. It's possible that I may never return—you understand that, don't you, Mikhailo?"

Tears burned in the old Cossack's eyes at her words. He knew what she meant. "You must let me know if the wild flowers have sprouted when you get to the Dnieper. If you don't return, I'll never know. Take your new Cossacks and go. I'll wait for you in Volin."

Kostya mounted Darkfire, while Rokal leaped onto Snowfire's sleek back. "We leave you Wildfire to ride to Volin," Katerina said softly. "Take care of him." With a jaunty salute, she dug her heels into Whitefire's flanks, and the stallion burst from the enclosed compound, clumps of sod and bits of snow flying in his wake.

Mikhailo shielded his eyes from the glare and thought he had never seen such a magnificent sight. They were Cossacks, and she had done the very thing she had promised she would do. There was not one among the lot of them who had betrayed her or tried to undo the bargain she made with them. This new breed of Cossack will serve her well, he thought smugly. He had known all along she could do it. Not once did he have a moment's doubt. His conscience pricked him slightly at the thought. Perhaps a dozen or so times, he consoled himself, but no more than that. The only thing that mattered was that she was successful. He knew she would return. But when she did return, would the Mongol be with her or would she be alone?

Chapter Twenty-one

❧ ❧ ❧

BANYEN AND HIS MEN made the journey to the Khanate with few utterances. Banyen trotted ahead of the others, his thoughts on Katerina and their time in the House of the Kat. On the long ride he alternated between fits of rage and melancholy at his circumstances. She's just another woman, he told himself over and over. At night his empty arms proved the thought a lie. She was part of him, a part of him he needed to live. Without trust, what would happen to their love and the life he planned for them? He told himself that women were foolish in the ways of love and men were strong and forceful.

Would he ever see her again? His recurring nightmare of her lying broken and battered in some raid swam before his tired eyes. All for those damnable horses. Why couldn't she be like other women, who thought only of lovemaking and babies? He admitted to himself that if she were like that he wouldn't want her. Katerina was like no other. She was his. When all his affairs were in order he would go back for her and try to make her understand. Women liked men to say sweet words and hold them close. There were worse things in life, he told himself. But he wouldn't beg; he would never beg.

His mood lightened somewhat as he let his gaze take in his surroundings. An hour more and he would be at the Khanate. He would soon be home. Home meant Afstar and telling him he didn't have the secret and that he had given back the stallions. No more lies or half truths.

Banyen rode his mount fast and hard, and brought him to a skidding halt outside Afstar's yurt.

"My ears are delicate, Banyen. A little respect, please," Afstar said smoothly, his eyes taking in Banyen's appearance and dark look. He didn't fail to see the deep scar pulsating and twitching. Something was wrong. "Come, I've missed you. Join me in some wine and some real food. I'm most anxious to hear all about the winter. And tell me, did you beat the snows?" he questioned affably, holding the flap of the yurt aside for Banyen to enter.

His hand to his cheek, Banyen strode through the yurt, remembering another time he had entered it, when a burnished-haired girl sat on a pile of cushions inside it. "No, I didn't beat the snows, and yes, we had problems, your detestable wagons for one. That girl is smarter than both of us put together. The long months worked their magic, and I fell in love with her. I'm returning to you without the breeding secret, and I rejected her offer of the four white stallions. We had a misunderstanding, rather your niece misunderstood something she saw, and I left with hatred between us. One day I'll go back for her and explain fully, if that's possible. That, Afstar, is the beginning and the end of it," he said, bringing the wine to his lips and drinking greedily. "Your men are as good as any Cossack. They'll serve you well. There will be no complaints."

The Khan was outraged. "Is this how you repay my generosity? I send you on a mission and you return and dare to tell me you had the stallions in your grasp and gave them up for love of my niece! I never expected Katerina to keep her promise, but I did expect more of you.

"You failed me, but you won't a second time. I have another mission for you, Banyen. You will go to Moscow and seek out those who can aid us when we attack. All the necessary preparations must be made. I will not and cannot tolerate failure this time."

The Khan's anger cooled. "You failed, and that is the end of the matter. Tell me, did my niece say she was withdrawing her offer of the filly and the colt?"

"Not withdrawing it," Banyen said, coldly, "not fulfilling it. We both know she had no intention of ever giving you the animals. She would lie through her teeth for those animals, and that's exactly what she did. They're hers and no one else's. They belong to her, not you and not me," he said, bringing the goatskin to his mouth a second time.

The Khan sighed. "I hoped," he said pathetically. "It wasn't too much to ask, one little colt and one little filly."

"It was too much. If you had asked her for her life, she would have given it to you. She'll never part with those horses."

"And I thought you were the man that could turn the trick," Afstar said sourly. He shook his head and leaned back in his comfortable nest of cushions. "Is there more?"

"No," Banyen said curtly. "Arrange for a bath and a woman in my yurt. Any woman will do as long as she has two arms and two legs," he said, emptying the wineskin and reaching for another.

"I never thought of it in quite those terms." Afstar grinned. "I myself require a few other . . . It makes no mind. Go, you're smelling up my yurt with your unclean body. Your request will be taken care of. We'll talk tomorrow."

Banyen staggered from the tentlike dwelling and entered his own, his head reeling from alcohol. So what if he was drunk? Who was there to care, and what difference did it make? He would live each day as it came. What more could he do?

Banyen stripped off his clothing, muttering to himself as he drank yet more wine. Even in this condition, he had seen the new men at the end of the camp. Things looked different. Afstar must be rebuilding slowly. Well, the hell with him.

The moment the sun rose in the east, a resplendent Tatar chief rode into the Khanate, his men trailing respectfully behind.

Khan Afstar stood outside his yurt, his dark eyes speculative and wary. He motioned with his pudgy hand for the chief to dismount, and stood aside for him to enter his yurt. They seated themselves on the colorful cushions and watched the brazier as the coals flicked to life, neither of them saying a word. It was understood that they waited for one other confidant, Prince Banyen.

The Tatar chief looked around the dwelling and nodded his round head appreciatively. He pursed his mouth as he caressed the sable carpet that rested at his feet. While he preferred bear rugs himself, he acknowledged that each man had his own tastes. The slanted eyes moved slightly as the flap parted and a tall man stood outlined in the bright sun. Now it would be business.

Batu, the Tatar, motioned for Banyen to sit and join the discussion. Crossing his arms over his massive chest, he looked at Afstar and Banyen, then spoke carefully, his voice deep and guttural. "Word reached me at the beginning of the new year that you search for, and are in the process of buying, an army. I have such a force, and my warriors number two hundred thousand. I know that it has been your dearest wish for many years to avenge Kazan and Astrakhan. With my soldiers and the army you're building we can accomplish that which you desire. You'll help me and I'll help you," he said matter-of-factly.

Banyen regarded Afstar and Batu with amusement. You pat my back and I'll pat yours, he thought.

"My plan is to attack Moscow at the onset of winter, if you feel that your fighters will be ready. By my figures your army should number one hundred thousand. With this amount of men we can't fail."

"What is it that you want?" Banyen asked coolly. "I haven't heard why you seek out this Khanate. The Khan and I know why we're preparing to go into battle. I wish to hear your reasons."

Batu twirled the ends of his long, drooping mustache as he stared at Banyen. "I need women for my slave trade."

Afstar, seeing the look of stunned surprise on Banyen's face, quickly spoke. "Your business is your own, but I want it understood that I do not approve. In no way will we help you in this endeavor. My army will join strength with yours, but it will be every man for himself. Let us understand each other, Batu."

The chief nodded his bulbous head slowly. "It is understood. We will rendezvous on the outskirts of Smolensk. Agreed?"

Afstar nodded and stood up. The meeting was ended.

Banyen followed the Tatar chief outside. With one

long, steady look in Afstar's direction, he headed for the military compound, where his men waited for him. Now it would be drill and prepare, prepare and drill, until a messenger arrived from Batu.

Chapter Twenty-two

❧ ❧ ❧

KATERINA RODE the Cossacks fast and hard down the mountainous terrain. Whitefire was in his element, racing across and pounding the earth as though the devils of hell rode his heels. The other horses, trained to perfection, followed quickly behind.

They stopped once to feed the animals and for a quick meal themselves, then remounted, the earth spewing behind them like a giant swell of water from the sea.

When they arrived at Volin, Katerina dismounted and looked around the village that had been her home for so many years. She sought out several of the elder Cossacks who were already busy rebuilding the village. Rapidly she told them that Mikhailo and the rest of the men from the fortress would arrive within days to help with the new construction.

"We camp here for the night and then we ride north. A light meal and a good night's sleep, and we'll depart at dawn."

Katerina and her followers left with the first sun and began their trek across the steppe in their search of the Cosars. No village went unnoticed. As was their plan, Kostya rode ahead with a two-man patrol. Each settlement was inspected, and long, lengthy discussions with the Cossacks who inhabited the towns ensued.

One month followed the other, the Cossacks unsuccessful in their attempts to learn the whereabouts of the famed horse herd. One evening, weary to the point of exhaustion, Katerina sat near the campfire and complained bitterly to Rokal and Kostya. "One would think by now that somebody, somewhere, would have seen or heard something. Especially the Don Cossacks, my own people."

"Is it possible that your people are lying to you?" Kostya asked cautiously. "You told me they branded you a traitor, and that you are in disgrace."

"I, too, thought that in the beginning, but no, I don't think that now. These are my people. They understand what I'm doing, and for that reason they wouldn't lie. What belongs to a Cossack belongs to a Cossack. We kill to regain what belongs to us. I am no different from any other Don."

"Another month and summer will be at an end," Rokal said, stirring the fire with a long stick.

"Yes, I know. And we still have a two-week ride till we reach the Terek territory. It'll be another month before we can cover all their camps on the grasslands. By that time the snows will have started and God alone will be able to help us. I can tell you now that the Terek is a bloodthirsty Cossack. They kill for sport. A life to them means nothing. When we ride into their camps they will tell us nothing. One Terek will lie and another will swear that he speaks the truth. We have to be prepared to search, and we must have eyes in the back of our heads. I want you to add more men to your patrol, Kostya. My gut tells me that our search is almost at an end. I can think of no one who would have the manpower to have raided Volin, save them. The Don would never steal from their own. But a long time ago I learned that you don't trust your instincts one hundred percent, and that is why we rode through every Don village. I'm tired and I need to think. Give me the map of the steppe, Kostya, I want to look it over one more time before we leave tomorrow."

True to her word, the next weeks found the Tereks

hostile and closemouthed. Katerina knew instinctively that each and every village they rode through was bringing them closer and closer to the Cosars.

It was Kostya's idea to free the horses from their pens in each town they rode through. "We need no advance warning of our coming," he said shortly to Katerina as a herd of horses galloped across the plains. "It will take the men weeks to gather them together. We have the advantage now, and I want to keep it that way. Every day becomes more important to us.

"In the last village before Khortitsa a mealy-mouthed Terek said he knew where the white horses were being kept. Then he laughed and said it was a joke, the Cosars have been in Moscow for many months. He boasted that it was his brother Gregory Bohacky who was responsible. His brother is now a hero and a saint to his people. A rich hero and saint," he amended. "No amount of persuading could make him change his story."

Katerina nodded to Kostya and watched as the horses ran free.

Gregory Bohacky! Could it be the same Gregory who came to Volin with Yuri? Was it possible that that was what Yuri was trying to tell her? It was the Tereks who killed him, and not the Dons! If that was true, then it was they who raided the village. Her mind raced. Bohacky, he's the man responsible for my father's death!

The days were never-ending so far as Banyen was concerned. Spring passed into summer as he drilled and trained the new men who came in droves to the Khanate. Day after weary day passed with him doing nothing more than working out with the latest arrivals, eating, and sleeping. Summer was fast ending when the Khan called him into his yurt and told Banyen it was time for them to make their move. The agate eyes narrowed and Banyen nodded curtly when the Khan informed him that a messenger would ride at dusk with a message for Katerina, advising her of his plans.

The Mongol courier had been riding for days, following the trail of Katerina and her Cossacks. Finally his perseverance was rewarded as he caught sight of the band leaving a village on the outskirts of Azov. Carefully he followed them and watched until they camped for the night. As the skies blackened he approached the campsite, making as much noise as possible. Immediately he was stopped by a Cossack guard posted in the tall grass a hundred feet from the main camp. The Mongol identified himself to the guard as one of the men who had trained in the Carpathians with the Kat, and spoke of Prince Banyen and the Khan of Sibir. Reassured, the guard felt it was safe to deliver the messenger to Katerina. When her tired amber eyes looked upon the face of the young man, Katerina recognized him immediately as one of Banyen's soldiers.

"Come, Igor, sit by the fire and tell me what brings you this far from Sibir. Join us in a drink and a bite to eat."

He took a long swallow of vodka, chewed on a piece of bread, and said, "Your uncle sent me to find you and tell you that he and the Crimean Tatars have joined forces. Their plan is to attack Moscow."

"Why are they doing this?" she asked Igor before he could go on.

"You know your uncle and Banyen wish to avenge Ivan's raids on the Khanates of Kazan and Astrakhan, where family and friends were killed. When Afstar heard that the Crimean Tatars numbered two hundred thousand strong and were making plans to attack Moscow, he and Banyen set out to meet with them. The Tatars are seeking women for their thriving slave business. Certainly the Tatars don't need your uncle's men, but after listening to your uncle's story of avenging his people, along with Prince Banyen's tale, the Tatars agreed to unite. Khan Afstar's army has grown somewhat larger since your visit. Many men have come, and his riches have brought him many more horses. He feels confident now that Moscow can be taken. The Mongols and Tatars stand thousands strong. Now he awaits word from you if you wish to join him. He also asked me to find out if you have found the Cosars."

"And what of Prince Banyen?" she asked coolly. "Has he whipped the Khan's men into a fighting unit with the help of the boys I shaped?"

"The prince is still very hard at work with the newer men. He puts them through a rough training, similar to yours. When he is finished, they can compete with any man and be proud of how they handle themselves."

"That's good news," she went on, hoping he might mention a word from Banyen for her. When it didn't come, she continued. "We haven't found the Cosars yet, but we have one village left to raid. I saved it until last, until my Cossacks had proven themselves. I'm proud of them; they fight as if they were born to the saber. We have lost only two men in all our raids, and that was in one village where the people fought us. Most of the towns we pillaged were small, and the people harmless. We didn't fight with them; in fact, in most of them we rode in and asked if they heard or saw anything of the Cosars. After a search convinced us the horses weren't there, we left peacefully. The larger villages, where people resisted, we fought. We haven't raided the smaller Don Cossack villages because I know they are our friends and wouldn't steal from us. We have one place left to visit, and that is the Tereks, across the river on the Island of Khortitsa. The Cosars are there or have disappeared, I'm sure of it. Tomorrow before dawn will be our true test, when we commence our raid on the island. These Tereks are known to be the most savage of the Cossack tribes. They will work for anyone or do anything for gold. If we win a victory tomorrow, my men will truly be men of stature. They'll be able to hold their heads high and proud, for they will have beaten their toughest enemy.

Then they'll be known as the Cossacks to be feared. If you wish to ride with us you may, but if you want to wait for us, do so. Tomorrow, after our visit with the Tereks, you will have my answer for my uncle. Will you join us?"

The man shook his head. "No, Katerina, I can't. I'm too weary. I've been traveling for days searching for you. I'll wait in a safe place where I'll be able to watch you and your men, and I'll meet you afterward. In the meantime I'll rest, for as soon as you give me your answer I must leave and return to Sibir."

"You're right, you must stay alive to bring Uncle Afstar his answer. Let's all get some sleep now, for in a few hours we'll move toward the Tereks' village."

In the tall grass on the east bank of the Dnieper River, after the guards were posted, Katerina and her men bedded down under the stars on the sweeping steppe.

Across the river, on the west bank, was the Island of Khortitsa, the outskirts of the Terek village. One by one, on foot, several of her men would cross the water and scatter, seeking out the guards and killing them. Quickly and without a sound, horses and men would then also cross and storm Khortitsa.

Katerina was still awake, her mind not allowing her to sleep. The Cosars had to be there; they had searched everywhere else. She knew her men would find them. Her men—she liked the phrase. They *were* hers, for she no longer worried about them killing her in her sleep or deserting her. They were all one now: the Cossacks of Volin. Volin . . . By now Mikhailo and some of the elders from the fortress would be rebuilding the village. She had told Mikhailo that she at least wanted an enclosure put up, so that if they found the horses they would have a place to quarter them, if all was done before the winter came. Knowing Mikhailo, Katerina was sure he was busy chopping trees. Once more her mind insisted that the horses have to be in the Terek village. Secure in the knowledge that her plan would work, she closed her tired eyes and slept.

She heard her name called, and she thought she was dreaming. Then she heard it again, and someone was shaking her shoulder. She opened her eyes to find Kostya kneeling beside her.

"It's time."

Katerina leaped to her feet and ordered the group of Cossacks to seek out the Terek guards. Within the hour, one man returned, announcing the sentries were no longer a problem.

Katerina mounted Whitefire and signaled her men to cross the river quickly and quietly. When they reached the west bank they rode silently to the gateway of the village. With a forward motion of her arm, Katerina gave the signal to attack. The raid was on.

Whitefire needed no second urging. He snorted loudly and galloped down the road, Darkfire and Snowfire in his wake. At the end of the settlement Katerina reined in the stallion and, with a quick look right and left, saw that the entire encampment was surrounded by her Cossacks. Her voice was shrill in the quiet night.

"Send Gregory to me or every man in this village will die! On the count of three, bring him to me."

Silence met her ears as doors opened and a few old women walked out to the road and stood huddled together.

"He was here at sundown, but I have not set eyes on him since then," one woman said in a reedy voice.

Rokal dismounted and dragged a protesting man to the middle of the road. "Count, Katerina." He laughed loudly. "On three I'll slice his ugly head from his neck!"

"One! Two! . . ."

Rokal brought up his saber with a quick slicing motion, his hand steady, a grin on his face.

"Three!" Katerina shouted.

"In the barn, in the barn!" the Terek squealed in a high, thin voice.

It was Kostya who sprinted to the building, just as the door opened and a giant of a man walked out. Two Cossacks pinned him by the arms, and Kostya dragged him to stand before Katerina as he fought his captors with all his strength.

"Are you the one they call Gregory?" she asked him hatefully, recognizing him instantly. "You! You're the buyer who came to Volin with Yuri Zhuk. Now I understand. You weren't there to purchase horses. You came to spy on us and steal the Cosars, you bastard!"

Gregory was belligerent, a sneer on his mouth. His eyes widened at the sight of the white stallions.

Katerina noticed the surprised look and laughed. "A mare is a mare, right, Terek? Without the stallions a mare is just another horse." She leaned over and whispered, so that Gregory had to strain to hear her words. "Where are they?"

Gregory shrugged. "What are you talking about?" he blustered.

Katerina remained silent atop Whitefire. The Cossacks closed in, forming a circle around the sweating Terek.

"Since the beginning of spring I've been searching for the mares and haven't found them anywhere. I know they're not in any other Cossack village. Where are they? I won't ask you again! For now, all I seek is the horses, but later you'll pay for what you did to my father and the people of my village. You can't escape me."

The hackles rose on Gregory's neck, and his stomach turned over at what he knew she meant to do. His mind shrieked for him to lie. Lie to her and she'll let you go. He had a long, rich life ahead of him, with more gold than he could ever spend. "They were stolen from me when the village was asleep."

"That's very amusing. It's almost as sad a tale as the night Volin was plundered. I don't believe a word of it." She laughed, the only sound in the quiet night, with the exception of the horses' deep breathing. "Do

I have to count again? How much were you paid for the Cosars? Who did you sell them to?"

A sharp jab with Rokal's saber and the man lurched closer to Katerina, who was leaning over, her position relaxed and nonchalant. "Whatever you were paid, you were cheated. I'll kill you if you don't answer me. I want those animals back in their rightful pens by the time the first winds of winter come. Either you tell me now or I'll slice your tongue from your mouth. Then I'll castrate you in front of everyone, and I'll laugh while I'm doing it. The same thing will happen to every man in this village. Your death will be slow and painful, and the road will turn to a river of blood. Now where are my horses?"

She was bluffing, she was a woman, she wouldn't cut out his tongue or . . .

Free of the imprisoning hands, Gregory backed off a step and licked at his dry lips. Faster than the blink of the eye, he had Rokal's saber free of its sheath and in his hand. "Now tell me what you're going to do if I don't answer you," he sneered. "Yes, I stole your horses and I raided your village. Yuri and I were under orders from Ivan. Crazy Czar Ivan is the buyer. But now I have a weapon, and it makes us evenly matched. I can take a woman in my stride seven days out of the week. I'll fight you, but I want none of your men to interfere."

Katerina nodded and stepped closer to the sweating Gregory. "I find it strange that you should say what you just did. Every Cossack stands and fights alone. My soldiers will not interfere."

The men's eyes were glued to Katerina as she advanced a step and then stopped before the fearful Terek. Before Gregory knew what she was about, she had brought up her saber and flexed her knees simultaneously. She slashed out at his weapon, jarring his arm, causing it to jolt backward with the force of her blow. Gregory, stunned for a second, retaliated quickly and thrust his saber at Katerina's midsection. Nimbly, like a dancer, she sidestepped him as her weapon again struck out, this time whacking his shoulder. The sound of his shattering bone was loud in the quiet night.

Katerina laughed at the look of pain on Gregory's face. "With little effort I can do the same to your other shoulder. Tell me where the Cosars are! I can smell your fear from where I stand."

Gregory spat for an answer, bringing his weapon up clumsily to strike out at the woman in front of him.

"So you pay no heed to my words. Then you shall suffer, and if you die, then it will be your own fault." She laughed as she feinted to the left, the saber finding its mark across the man's other shoulder.

The crack of the splintering bone brought shouts of approval from the Cossacks. Before Gregory could recover, Katerina danced out of the way and then crouched low in a sprint, lashing out at the Terek's leg. Blood splattered in the dusty road. Gregory looked with disbelieving eyes at his injured leg. The saber dropped from his numb hand.

"Now tell me, where are my Cosars? If you don't speak, then your tongue will lie in the dirt with your blood."

Gregory reeled uncontrollably, falling in a puddle of his own blood. He fell face down, the blood and dust settling over his face, making a hideous mask.

Kostya stretched out his foot and forced the Terek to roll over. "Answer the lady when she speaks to you."

"In Moscow. The Czar has the Cosars," Gregory gasped. "You're too late. By now they're scattered all over Russia. You'll never get them back," he said shrilly.

"I'll get them back, no thanks to you. If I could find you, I'll find the Cosars. Where is the gold you were paid for the animals? Make fast work of your answer."

"He can't hear you," Kostya said. "He's out of his mind with pain. Ask one of these other . . . puppets."

Katerina lifted her saber and looked around. She waited, saying nothing.

"In the barn," came a babble of voices. "In the chests beneath the saddles."

"Take it all," Katerina ordered Rokal. "It's yours to divide among the men. When we get to Moscow you can thank Ivan for his generosity personally."

"What do we do with these . . . this scum?" Kostya questioned.

"Put them in their own stockade. Shackle them together and move the poles in the way the Mongols do."

"They'll die," Kostya said softly. "Is that what you want? Do you want men's deaths on your conscience for horses? If so, you'll have to find someone else to obey this particular order. The stockade, yes, but no shackles, and the poles stay where they are."

"You're right. I'm sorry, I wasn't thinking. For a moment I was blinded by my own hatred. Place them in the stockade, and when the men are finished in the barn we ride out."

Katerina and a patrol of five men made camp for the night in Kharkov on the outskirts of Smolensk. Patiently she waited for the rest of her force, traveling in small groups so as not to draw attention to themselves. She was exhausted, more so than she ever remembered being, and now she was faced with a week's wait until it was time for her rendezvous with the Tatars and her uncle, Afstar.

As the men trickled in she was not surprised that those whose loyalty she had once doubted were now steadfast and committed to her cause. She wondered if the loot from Gregory's barn had anything to do with their decision to stay with her. All were now as determined as she to regain the Cosars.

Never one to remain idle, Katerina found the endless days a living torture. As always when she had nothing to do, thoughts of Banyen filtered through her mind. Where was he; what was he doing? Did he think of her? Would he forgive her? When the amber eyes filled with tears, she would get up and have the men practice. When she tired of watching their expertise with their weapons, she had them brush and groom the animals. At sundown they ate their evening meal and sat around the fire, their voices pitched low in serious conversation.

Shortly before sunrise on the sixth day the Khan cantered into her camp. Briskly he ordered his men to dismount and set up tents. Katerina's eyes widened at the sight of the thousands of men who rode with him. All seemed fit and hearty. Banyen did well, she thought.

"You look well, my child," the Khan said, dismounting. "Tell me, have you any news for me?"

"Everything is well, Uncle, but this waiting is beginning to play on my nerves. How many more days?" Unable to contain herself, she blurted, "Where is Banyen?"

"In Moscow," Afstar said, watching Katerina carefully.

"Moscow! Why? But I thought . . . I expected . . ."

"He arrives tomorrow," Afstar said, sparing her the need to ask further questions. "He's been in Moscow for a week. The Tatars are also due to arrive tomorrow, sometime after dusk. Our plan is to camp for one day and go over our plans. However, in order to do that we must wait for Banyen and the information he is bringing us. Our plan is to attack at night, and it was left to Banyen to arrange our entry for us. Does that answer all your questions? The one-day delay is necessary, but any longer would only harm us. By now the peoples of the steppe are no doubt wondering where this massive army is heading. There is bound to be one among them that has sent word to Ivan by now."

"Are you telling me that Banyen is spying in Moscow?" Katerina asked, her eyes reflecting fright. "It can't be safe, and his life could be in danger."

"He is the only man who has allies there, and that is why the decision to send him was made. He agreed,"

Afstar said gruffly. "No harm will come to Prince Banyen. I'm tired, my young niece, and I wish to bed down for the night," he said, walking over to join his men, leaving Katerina staring at his retreating back.

As the sky darkened, the multitude of bonfires glowed like fireflies on the edge of the grasslands. Guards were posted as the Mongols and Cossacks ate and then bedded down for the night.

Settling herself beneath the stars, Katerina anxiously waited for sleep to overcome her. Please, she prayed, let nothing happen to him, keep him safe.

Chapter Twenty-three

WITH A SHARP TUG on the reins, Banyen brought his black Arabian to a halt. Moscow stood before him, a little less than a mile off. Never having been in this metropolis before, he wanted to observe it from a distance. Prior to this visit, all his dealings with the boyars had been on a prearranged no-man's-land or by messenger. Now he needed to know the city and its secrets. A week in Moscow, shown around by the boyars, and he should be able to lead the attack through it without any problems. He knew he had to be careful, because as much as the boyars hated Ivan and constantly undermined him, they were a lot not to be trusted by anyone. What was it the boyar had said? Banyen ran it through his mind again: "Take the main road into Moscow, through the Wooden City, then travel the White City, which will bring you into Kitai Gorod. You will know Kitai Gorod from the other cities by the fence built around it. Once in Kitai Gorod you'll see an inn, a large log building, and you'll recognize it by the wine pitcher which hangs over the entrance. We'll meet at the inn after dark, but before you enter Moscow you must dress yourself in the clothes of a rich merchant."

Banyen, dressed in the appropriate attire, spurred the horse in the flanks and headed for the way into Moscow.

He rode his stallion slowly through the Wooden City, choked with log houses and a maze of streets lined with poor artisans and laborers. Weavers, gardeners, sheep skinners, and coach drivers were busy working at their trades. He trotted on into the White City, where he noticed a difference in the buildings, many made of ivory-colored stone. The filth and wooden buildings in the Wooden City were here, too, but here also stood ornate stone churches and palatial homes. Pungent markets along the main roadway, selling foodstuffs and objects of all descriptions, dotted the sides of the street. He was amazed at the unfamiliar sights and the number of people who milled and thronged the crowded, narrow roads. He knew that the masses of people would pose no problem when it came to the actual attack. To his discerning eye, the streets revealed only women, children, and merchants. Seeing no sentries to alarm him, he rode on, his eyes constantly on the alert.

Momentarily wrapped up in his thoughts, he almost lost sight of the wall that stood before him as the sun, blotted out by the cover of the archway he passed under, awakened him to the fact that he was now in Kitai Gorod, or Basket Town. As his agate eyes raked the city he knew the boyar had spoken the truth, for in front of him were the kitais filled with earth, piled one on top of the other, reaching as high as the top of the wall. Banyen smiled to himself. The dirt-filled baskets would not deter the attack, only add fuel to the fire when the time came to burn the city. His eyes darkened and were sharp and alert for anything that looked the least suspicious as he continued toward the meeting place.

Noticing a busy crossroads ahead, he approached, seeing a log building to his right. As his Arabian minced his way closer, he saw the wine pitcher hanging in front of the building. Nudging his horse to the side of the inn, he dismounted. Unsure as to what he should do with the animal, he tied it to a projecting log near the back of the building. Once he had spoken with the boyars and knew his way around, he would stable the animal.

Entering the inn, Banyen was amazed to see the interior was large and bare. Except for the massive wooden tables and benches scattered about, a counter where the food and drinks were served, and a huge fireplace, nothing else was in the room. The starkness took Banyen by surprise, for Mongols always had drapings, rugs, pillows, and clutter around them. He walked to a simple table and sat down. He leaned back on his rickety chair and knew that he would draw no attention in his gray caftan.

Banyen eyed a Russian serving girl and motioned for her to take his order. The oblique eyes narrowed as he watched her approach, her long chestnut hair billowing out behind her, her heavy breasts bobbing. Her bright, green eyes were bold and speculative as she leaned over to take his order, her breasts touching his shoulder. When she made no effort to change her position, Banyen reached out his hand and gently stroked the outside of her thigh. Still she didn't move. "Soup, meat, and bread," he said coolly as he continued to touch her leg. The girl smiled as she straightened and reached down to remove his hand. He matched her bold look and nodded slightly. Later he would investigate her charms. For now, he was impatient, knowing that darkness was fast approaching. And soon the boyars would arrive. He cautioned himself to watch for men who wore gold medallions around their necks. He knew that the attire of the boyars was to be tall black sheepskin hats, black caftans, and black robelike capes decorated with golden tassels.

When the girl brought his food, he ate heartily. The soup was so thick it was almost a stew; the roast lamb was succulent; the black bread was warm and tasty. Again he motioned to her, ordering a tall glass of kvass. A smile tugged at the corners of Banyen's mouth as the girl pressed herself to him again, this time more heavily. When she reached over to pick up the kopecks, her gown fell away, revealing large, creamy orbs. Banyen drew in his breath, wanting to reach out and fondle them. He grinned as he watched her eye him languorously. His loins began to ache as he watched her sway back to the kitchen regions. Later, he told himself, there's always later. For now, he would sip at the kvass and wait for the boyars.

He was finishing his third glass when the inn became crowded with the supper patrons as twilight gave way to total darkness. Still Banyen waited, enjoying the bold glances the serving girl was bestowing on him. His own gaze became sleepy as he watched her swaying buttocks when she walked around the inn, serving the patrons. The moment the ache in his nether regions became a pain, two men walked through the door, dressed exactly as the boyar had described them. Banyen recognized one of them.

Banyen watched them closely as their eyes scanned the room, coming to rest on him. Bright gold medallions hung around their necks. The men fingered the medals and slowly maneuvered their way to his side of the crowded room. As they approached the table where he sat, Banyen stood and spoke.

"I beg your pardon, my boyars, might I have a quiet word with you?"

Both pairs of eyes took in Banyen's merchant attire and the oblique eyes. They nodded. "Of course, how can we be of assistance?" they asked, seating themselves at the table.

Holding up his hand, Banyen ordered kvass for his guests.

The older of the two boyars spoke first. "This inn is not the place to discuss details. Tomorrow, during the day, we must do the Czar's bidding, but in the evening we'll meet in my home in the White City. When we finish our kvass we'll ride through Moscow so you can become familiar with the sights and the names of the places of which we speak. As we ride, I'll tell you of the many details you'll need to know. We'll also ride past my home so you'll know where to meet me tomorrow evening. Might I say, Prince Banyen, you look well. It has been many years since I last saw you. Fortune has been good to you. Soon you'll be able to avenge your family." His voice was sad and solemn as he stared into Banyen's eyes. "How long ago it was that we played together as children. I'm happy that I can now be of some help to you."

Banyen nodded, saying nothing.

"I suggest you take a room here at the inn, as it would be the obvious thing for a stranger to do. Most newcomers to Moscow stay at this particular inn. It would be best if you booked your room now. We'll wait here for your return. Where did you secure your animal?"

"I tied him to a log at the side of the inn. Is there some place I can stable the animal?" Banyen inquired with concern.

"There's a stable in back of the inn. When you secure your lodging tell them you wish your horse to be taken care of, and they will tend to the rest. Just pray your horse is still where you left him, for it isn't uncommon for horses to be stolen."

Alarmed that his black stallion could be missing, Banyen first checked his steed. He was relieved when he found the animal still tied. Rushing back into the inn, he took a room and asked that his horse be tended to. The owner called out, and a moment later a stable boy appeared, listened, nodded his head, and was off in the direction of Banyen's horse.

"What name did you give?"

"Ivan Toborschev."

"That's good. What did you say for business?"

"I said that I was a merchant from Kiev."

"Good."

Growing impatient with all the chatter, the elder boyar suggested they finish their drinks and leave for their ride around Moscow.

"How did you gain entry to the city?"

"Exactly as you instructed me. I came in on the main road through the Wooden City to Kitai Gorod."

The two nobles looked at each other, frowns on their faces. "Perhaps we should take him farther on and show him Red Square and the Kremlin. This will give him a working knowledge of the city and the way the roads are laid out."

"A commendable idea," the other agreed as they walked toward the stable and his waiting coach.

The men boarded and drove through Red Square and the Kremlin. The two boyars pointed out the palace and surrounding buildings, which were heavily guarded and closed to the public. As the coach turned and headed back to Kitai Gorod, the driver was ordered to go through the other cities.

"Even in the darkness you'll be able to see parts of the cities you did not see on your ride in. Tomorrow, during the day, become familiar with as much as you can. If necessary, ride through more than once, and pay attention to the things you think will be important to you. Tomorrow evening, when we make our plans, sites we speak of may be recognizable to you." Their drive at an end, the two men bade Banyen good night and were off, their coach lumbering down the road.

Exhausted, Banyen laid down on the soft bed, mulling over the activities of the day. His thoughts turned to the plans for the attack due to take place in less than a week. Satisfied that he hadn't overlooked anything, he let his thoughts drift, and he remembered the wanton smile and the firm, hard breasts that had pressed against his shoulder. A warm glow swept over him, and Katerina's face swam before him. He ached for her touch. Warmed by his memories, he fell into a deep sleep.

Refreshed and rested, Banyen dressed and descended the stairs for breakfast. He was relieved to note that the Russian girl was not in evidence. He knew that if she continued to flaunt herself, desire would take hold of him, and he would bed her like an animal. The girl's absence and the work at hand drove passion to the back of his mind. He finished his meal and left the inn. Done saddling his horse, he began his ride through the streets of Moscow. As he trotted he made mental notes concerning the various roads, bridges, rivers, and sights which he felt might be of importance to him. At the end of the day he made his way back to the inn, had his supper, freshened up, then walked to the house of the elder boyar.

The finery of the home impressed Banyen to a degree. The wealth of the noble and his trappings were different from those of a Mongol. The overstuffed chairs with their beautiful carvings and the small highly carved tables which sat around the large rooms, holding ornate lamps and art objects, drew his attention, but seemed utterly useless. A Mongol liked the best of things, but they were things that had a practical purpose, not merely for display. He complimented the boyar on his home, however, as they made their way to his private business chamber, where the others waited.

Quickly the boyar closed the doors behind him. "These are some of the other men who will aid us. They too would like to see Ivan fall from power. We have been together for many years, and I give you my word that they can be trusted."

The nobles and Banyen sat around a big table in a corner of the room as the elder boyar unfolded a map of Moscow and placed it in the center of the group. "Banyen, study this map carefully and pay special attention to the places that are marked in red. The marks represent the weak spots in the chain of Ivan's defense. There are many entrances into the cities through the main roadways, but when you reach Kitai Gorod, Red Square, and the Kremlin you will see they are surrounded by walls, the highest of which is

around the Kremlin. The plan is for you to have your
people surround all of Moscow. You will not have any
trouble with the Wooden City or the White City, as
they are open to raid. Have your main thrust come
through the main roads of each city. Push straight on
until you see the walls of Kitai Gorod. In the meantime you can have the rest of your army surround the
entire outside walls of the Kremlin, Red Square, and
Kitai Gorod. My men will be stationed at the un-
guarded places to open the gates to your men. As your
army storms through the main road of Basket Town
and keeps Ivan's soldiers at bay, the rest of your men
can pour through the gates. Moscow will be yours! We
must now set the exact time of attack, and it must
happen at exactly that moment, as seconds may spell
the death of my comrades at Ivan's mad hands!"

"Understood," acknowledged Banyen. "The supper
hour will be the time. The moment the church bell
chimes."

"Yes, an excellent idea. It should be dark by then,
when most people eat, including the Czar and the soldiers. It will take them at least an hour to get back to
the garrison where the main bulk of the weapons and
ammunition is kept. Are you all in agreement with
the plan and time for the attack?"

"We agree," said one voice, representing all.

"Banyen, you will spend three more days in Moscow with my men, a different one each night, showing
you the exact gates which will be opened to you. On
the fourth night the attack will take place. Are your
armies ready and together, waiting for you?"

"It has been planned. When I ride out on the fourth
day, all will be ready," Banyen said, choosing his
words carefully. As much as he trusted these men, he
had no intention of giving them the exact location of
the rendezvous point of the Mongol army. He did not
regret his decision not to divulge exactly how large the
force was, or that it would be joined with Crimean
Tatars numbering in the hundreds of thousands.

Motioning to one of the nobles, the boyar spoke,

"Tomorrow you'll go with this man and be shown the locations where my men will be stationed. Do this in the evening. I suggest you make yourself unavailable during the day. This way you will not draw attention to your actions. The hour is late, so let us leave one by one, quickly and quietly, so as not to arouse suspicion. Banyen, if I don't see you again before you leave, good fortune."

"What do you gain by helping me? Is overthrowing Ivan enough? I offered you and your men gold for your help, but you refused. I don't understand."

"If Ivan is overthrown or killed, we can place a man of our own in power and be the guiding force behind him, perhaps even one of our boyars. We'll have control of the Russian people and want for nothing. If we lose, then it will be all over for us. What good would the money you offered do us then?"

Banyen held out his hand. "I hope we both succeed. Good fortune to you too, old friend."

Following the boyar's instructions, Banyen rode along the walls of Moscow for the next two nights. During the day he kept to his room except for his meals, which he took in the dining hall. At the end of the second day he waited for the serving girl to lean over him, her smile wanton and her breasts pressing against him each time she served him. Each time he thought of the Russian girl, Katerina would intrude into his mind, forcing the smiling, chestnut-haired girl into the background.

The third and last day of his stay in Moscow began. Normally he did not stay in bed past dawn, but this day he made himself remain beneath the covers and rest. The forced inactivity drove him into a near frenzy as he dressed and went downstairs for his breakfast. His meal finished, he headed for the stables to make sure his stallion was properly fed and watered. The animal had to take him to Smolensk and back to Moscow, and he prayed the stable boy had followed his instructions.

Banyen nodded to the young boy tending the animals and praised his care.

Carefully, his eyes alert, he walked around Kitai Gorod. A vague feeling of unease seemed to be settling over him. Several times he glanced over his shoulder and thought he saw someone following him. Each time, the street was empty. Still, the feeling persisted as he walked back to the inn. Bolting the door of his room, he lay down on the coarse bedding to think. As always, his thoughts drifted to Katerina and their time in the mountains. Each day was bringing him closer to when he would see her again. Somehow he would make it right with her, convince her he had done nothing wrong, that it was she he loved for all eternity. Tomorrow he would ride to Smolensk, and even that ride would bring him nearer to Katerina.

He shook his head to clear the thoughts of Katerina from his mind. He had to think of other things. The Russian servant girl—there was something about her that bothered him. Each time she stared at him, her eyes would drift to the kitchen, as if she were working with someone. He admitted that he wanted her, desired her flesh next to his, but not at the expense of his life. Tonight he would take her and see if his theory was right.

Seating himself at a table in the dining room, he watched through slitted eyes as the girl walked languorously toward him to take his order. As before, she leaned over him, her breasts pressing against his shoulders. She gazed at him with the same bold scrutiny, saying nothing, almost daring him with her sleepy gaze. This time Banyen let his hand trail up the inside of her tunic. She shivered slightly, but made no move to stir from his side. "Come to my room after you finish work tonight." She nodded, and Banyen was not surprised that she didn't bother to ask him which room was his. His mouth tightened when he saw her eyes go furtively to the kitchen, where a figure stood outlined in the doorway.

Banyen ate leisurely, knowing the girl had a full

hour of work ahead of her. When he left the table to go to his room he could feel her eyes boring into his back.

She walked back into the kitchen and held out her hand to the man slouched against the door. "Pay me now!"

"I'll pay you half now and the other half when the merchant you claim is a spy proves to be so. As an Oprichnik I can't afford a mistake."

"My cousin, the cook in the boyar's house, listened outside the doors and overheard the merchant called Ivan Toborschev from Kiev and the others making plans to attack Moscow. Pay me the full sum we agreed on."

"I followed him on several occasions. With what you just told me and his furtive attitude, I'm convinced. He can only mean trouble for the Czar." The Oprichnik placed a small pouch of gold in her outstretched hand. "The hour grows late, make fast work of your seduction."

Banyen waited, and the door opened slowly. He motioned for her to enter, neither saying a word. When he made a move to throw the bolt on the door, the girl threw her arms around his neck, kissing him soundly. He let his hand drop, then cradled her head in his hands, kissing her passionately. All desire left him as he felt her lick at his ear, her hand moving down the side of his body. He forced himself to play her game, and again he kissed her, his hand busy removing her shirt and slipping the peasant skirt down over her hips. When she stood naked before him, her eyes full of lust, he sent her reeling against a chest in the corner of the room.

"If you make so much as a sound, I'll slit your throat," Banyen said quietly. "This way you have a chance to live, unless the man who is coming here kills you. Not a sound, do you understand?" he said, bending over the cowering girl.

He waited, his eyes going from the fearful girl to the door.

Suddenly the door was flung open with such force that it crashed against the wall and came to rest drunkenly against the door frame. "Where is he, you had enough time?" bellowed a voice. "The man is a spy and is to be taken to the Czar!"

Banyen stepped from behind the armoire and grinned. "You're wrong, my friend, she did not have enough time to play your game with me. Did you think I would fall for such an age-old trick?"

Banyen's eyes quickly took in the size of the man charging into the room. He was built like an ox and obviously was just as strong, if his bellow was any indication. Banyen would need his wits about him to deal with the burly man, who had hands the size of a newborn colt's head.

The girl remained mute as the husky peasant charged across the room, the floor shaking beneath his weight. The moment he was abreast of the armoire, Banyen sent it crashing down upon him. A roar of rage filled the room, but Banyen was up and racing out into the corridor, taking the plank steps two at a time in his wild descent.

Outside he ran in the crisp, cold air, skirting the buildings and staying in the shadows and hoping and praying he had enough time to get to his horse before the man called the guards.

Staying in the shadows, he cautiously made his way to the stable and stallion. He saw that a guard was posted at the wide double doors. Banyen circled, came up behind the sentry, and flung his arm around the man's neck. The guard jerked free, yanking out his saber and slicing at the air, missing Banyen. Again the guard lunged and missed. Desperate, Banyen knew he needed a weapon. Somehow he had to get into the stable, where he could grasp something, anything, to defend himself. He couldn't be caught now, not after all he had gone through.

"Dance as if you have eggs on your head." Katerina's words roared in his ears. He laughed, never taking his eyes from the advancing guard. Nimbly, as good as any dancer, Banyen leaped and cavorted and backed himself into the barn. The guard, his eyes wide and full of shock at the insane man in front of him cavorting and laughing, blinked and momentarily lost his advantage in the darkness. As Banyen continued to leap and twist, his hands struck out at the wall, trying to reach for something that would help him defend himself. In one of his jumps he fell backward into a pile of straw. Flinging out his arms to break his fall, his hands found an upended pitchfork that rested in the dry stalks. His hands reached for it as he got to his feet, the fork thrust in front of him. The sentry thrust outward and upward, slicing the handle of the fork in two as he drove Banyen back against the wall. Banyen held on to the fork end, and as the guard lunged at him a second time, Banyen leaped into the air, coming down gracefully as the guard raised his eyes to take in his spectacular jump. Banyen struck out, the tines of the fork finding their mark in the center of the guard's chest.

Quickly Banyen picked up the saber and tossed it across the length of the stable. He saddled his horse, keeping a sharp eye on the door for any further intrusion.

In the cold, bracing air, his mind clear, he realized he couldn't go to the boyar for help; the Oprichniks would be watching, and he couldn't expose his friend to danger. He was alone.

Through the rest of the night he and his horse, who walked behind him, moved under the cover of darkness from one place to another. He watched for a shadow, a move or a noise indicating the soldiers were still on his trail. He felt them, smelled them around him, and although he couldn't see them, he knew they were there. Slowly he made his way toward a doorway in the wall so he could be near an exit. Crouching low, his ears alert, he waited.

As the first rays of dawn lightened the area, exposing the hidden crevices and flushing out all that hid in the night, Banyen made his move and tried the handle of the door nearest him. Slowly he turned the knob and pushed the door with his foot. There before him stood four of Ivan's soldiers. Quickly he slammed the portal and turned to run, grabbing for the reins of the stallion. As he did so, two oprichniks seized the animal and led him away. Taking a deep breath at his narrow escape, Banyen raced for cover.

The morning hours passed quickly as Banyen and the Oprichniks played a cat-and-mouse game. He had to be free and ready to ride by the noon hour; he had to do something, and he had to do it now. Slowly he inched his way between some barrels, and was surprised by the four soldiers once again. As they lunged for the kill, one by one, Katerina's training rose to the fore. He parried a thrust, a lunge. Steel met steel as he leaped and nimbly danced his way among the startled oprichniks. His face grim, he looked down at the dead bodies and felt no remorse.

Seeing his stallion being led from the city, he climbed onto the wall and slithered along the top on his belly, praying no one would notice his movements. He lay still as two soldiers reached the gateway, leading his horse. Banyen jumped from the wall, his arms outstretched, knocking the Oprichniks to the ground. Like a streak of lightning, he leaped onto the stallion and headed toward the main road, leaving Red Square, Kitai Gorod, and the White City behind him.

Two hours outside of Moscow, he dismounted and concealed himself in some dense brush, watching to see if he was being followed. He saw and heard nothing to alarm him, so he mounted the Arabian with relief. He sighed wearily as he spurred the horse, urging him to a full canter. The closer he rode to the rendezvous, the more erratically he rode the stallion. He knew he couldn't travel straight toward the waiting armies, for word was out that an attack was imminent. At the last moment he deliberately rode through Smolensk. When he was sure he was not being followed, he continued on to the meeting point. Silently he prayed that the armies were still waiting.

Katerina was beside herself with anger and concern. "Uncle, where is he?" she snapped. "We stand ready to ride and can't make a move without him." Suddenly her anger gave way to concern. "Uncle, what if something happened to him? What if he never arrives?"

"Banyen will be here. Where is your faith, your courage? You can't allow your men to see you in a fit of tears. He will be here," he said firmly. "Any man who wants to taste Ivan's blood as badly as he does will not let us down. Compose yourself. Check your men and see if all is in readiness."

"I've checked them five times. I can't stand this endless waiting. We've been waiting for five days and now we must wait again. I don't know how those Tatars can sit so placidly. Nothing seems to bother them."

"When you number in the hundreds of thousands, why would you worry? They can overrun anything in their path. I'm happy they're on our side." The Khan grinned. "Their leader rides toward us. Perhaps he, too, is becoming concerned."

A tall, yellow-skinned man rode majestically on a sleek brown horse, the animal strutting its pedigree. The deep, slanted eyes of the rider bored into the Khan. His body looked immense in the quilted vest which covered him to his elbows, knees, and up the back of his neck to the bottom of his hat. The heavy padding would stop the blow of a saber, Katerina knew, just as the heavy sheepskin vests and coats protected her men and herself.

"Where is the man we wait for? Time is growing short, and we have a four-hour ride to the city of Moscow," his deep voice boomed.

"He will arrive within the hour," the Khan said reassuringly to the chief.

The Tatar leader was impatient and in no mood for further delays. "My men are ready to ride now. Our slave trade works on arrangements also, and promises have been made to deliver girls to ships that wait on the Black Sea. You see the baskets my men have

placed on each side of their horses? Those baskets
will each hold a young girl. When we attack Moscow,
we steal the girls, and then we ride back to our village
by the sea, where the ships wait. It will take us three
days of hard riding to get back to Crimea, but my
men will ride straight through, stopping only to rest
their horses. My arrangements with the captains of
the vessels and other slave traders were for the arrival
of the girls three days from now. If your man doesn't
arrive within the hour, we'll ride ahead and storm
Moscow alone." Angrily he jerked the reins of the
horse, turned his back on the Khan, and rode to wait
at the head of his army.

The Khan's eyes were furious. Why hadn't Banyen
arrived? Something must have happened to him.

Suddenly a guard shouted from a distance, "Prince
Banyen is coming! That cloud of dust you see in the
distance is the prince!"

Katerina's heart raced madly, her anger forgotten.
Thank God he was safe! Once again she would see her
love. Her eyes never left the speck of dust. She
watched, her heart pounding, as the speck grew larger
and larger, until Banyen and his black stallion stood
before them.

Time was crucial. There wasn't a moment for anything but the discussion of the plan. Banyen drew a
map in the dirt, representing the wall around Kitai
Gorod and the Kremlin, as the Khan, the Tatar chief
and Katerina watched and listened. He explained that
the boyars would be stationed at the points he circled,
ready to open the gates at the first chime of the bells
at sunset. He explained about dividing up the army to
surround the walled cities and the charge down the
main road through the Wooden and White Cities.
When he finished, he looked up and smiled at Katerina. With that smile, all was right between them once
more. There was no need for words. The Khan and
the Tatar chief decided on the disposition of the men
who would surround the walls and those who would
lead the charge down the main road. Katerina asked if

she and her men could join those who would ride through on the main road. The Khan and the Tatar agreed. It was decided that Banyen and a division of the Khan's men would make up part of the same contingent.

Plans finished, each leader aware of his part, they assumed their places at the head of their armies. All was in readiness. The signal was given, and the earth shook under the thousands of hooves that pounded it, carrying death and destruction toward Moscow, just as the first snowfall of winter began.

The soldier trembled as he reported to Ivan the news of a spy in the city. He waited, a feeling of dread settling over him, hoping, wishing the Czar would dismiss him. Instead, Ivan's face closed in rage.

"Spy? Spy? Possible attack? What are you talking about? You must be mad! No one can spy on me! No one can attack me! My Oprichniks see to my safety." He wrung his hands, and his eyes rolled wildly in his head as saliva with bits of chewed food dribbled from his mouth. "Spy! Be gone, soldier, before I have you beheaded before me for such a stupid story. Take him out of here. Get him out!" the Czar shouted insanely. Ivan pounded his gold staff on the floor in a frenzy as the soldier ran for his life.

The boyars and nobles whispered among themselves with the news. Could it be so? Tales of a spy in Moscow were an everyday happening. What could one man do? Their bellies full of breakfast, and in a rush to escape from Ivan, they paid their homage to the Czar and left the room, deciding Moscow and the Kremlin were not in any peril.

Several boyars among them smiled knowingly to themselves as they left the room and continued with their affairs of court.

Chapter Twenty-four

❀ ❀ ❀

THE POPULATION OF MOSCOW'S FIVE CITIES were relaxing around their evening meal as the sun set in the west. Without warning, thousands of men on horseback stormed through the City of Wood. Everything and anything that stood in the path of this well-honed machine of destruction was slaughtered. The city became a tinderbox blazing across the night skies as the Mongols, Tatars, and Cossacks rode into the White City. Within an hour, it too was leveled, all killed and the buildings set aflame. While the city crumpled, the second segment of the massive army reached Kitai Gorod. The boyars, at their appointed spots, opened the gates for the thousands of Tatars and Mongols who poured into the Kremlin and Red Square. The battle raged as they fought on the streets, on the walls, and in the palace.

The citizenry died by the thousands in a vain effort to flee the horde. Many sought safety near the Kremlin, hoping to take refuge behind the gates, not knowing they had been opened to the enemy.

As the battle waned, the Tatars began their search for slaves. Moscow burned like a torch in the night. The Moscow River became so choked with the bodies of people that the course of the river was diverted, the waters crimson for miles downstream.

Katerina worked her way through the city, searching for Banyen and Khan Afstar. She galloped in the direction of Red Square, still without any sight of the two men. As she approached St. Basil's, she looked up. There, for all to see, was her uncle on the execution block where Ivan performed his mass murders and tortures, his body sliced and cut to pieces. She turned away, fighting back the tears, hoping with all her heart that she would find Banyen alive. She rode Whitefire into the Kremlin, looking, searching, weaving the animal between broken, lifeless bodies. She found Banyen sprawled on the steps of the Terem Palace. When she saw how motionless he was, she panicked and screamed. "Banyen!" tore from her mouth, from her heart, as she slid from the horse and ran to him. "Let him live! He can't be dead!" she cried out.

Bending over the still body, she turned him over, searching for a wound. There was a deep gash across the left side of his head, oozing blood. She put her head to his chest and listened. He was alive but unconscious. Quickly she removed her outer garments and ripped off a sleeve from her shirt. Wrapping it around his head, she covered the wound. She donned her outer garments once again as the snow began to cover the bloodstained streets. Before it got too cold, she knew, she would have to move Banyen. Slipping one arm beneath his back, she lifted him to a sitting position. The weight of his body proved too much for her. Gently she lowered him to the steps and called for help.

A low moan escaped Banyen as he tried to move his head, his eyes glazed and full of pain.

"You're injured, Banyen, you must lie still. You must remain quiet until help comes. I'm with you now. It's over, Banyen, it's finished."

"What happened? Ivan, where is he? I must keep my promise and put my saber through his heart," he said, trying to struggle to his feet. "Katerina, where is Ivan, you must tell me, it can't all have been for nothing. Where is he? Is he alive?"

"If you lie still, I'll tell you. You're still weak from your head wound, and the gash on your leg needs tending. You must forget the Czar."

Before she could utter another word, Banyen

shouted, "Katerina, where is Ivan? Will you tell me or must I seek him out myself?"

"He's gone, Banyen."

"Gone! What do you mean, gone? Gone where?" he demanded harshly.

"When we captured the Terem Palace, the boyars and nobles were trapped inside. They were the ones that told us Ivan and his family escaped with the Kremlin treasury. The boyars informed us that the Czar headed toward the north of Russia. Your saber will not draw Ivan's blood this day, Banyen. The Czar is a tormented, insane man. What pleasure would you gain in killing a madman? Tell me I'm right, Banyen. There would be no revenge in killing a diseased dog, so why persist in your desire? There has been enough death. The Khan . . . he's . . . he's dead."

Banyen's eyes closed. What she said was true. It was over.

"As usual, you're right," Banyen said, trying to force a smile. "It no longer seems important to me. If I set out after him, I would be as insane as he is. One day he will reap his just rewards. Tell me of Afstar."

"My uncle . . . the Khan . . . your friend . . . The Russians strung him up on Ivan's torture rack in Red Square. I couldn't take him down. I had to look for you."

"Katerina, where is my stallion?"

"I haven't seen him."

"My black is never far from me." He whistled two short bursts, and the stallion appeared. Banyen grinned. "See, he's never far from his master. Horses, horses, I almost forgot—have you found the Cosars?"

"No, not yet. My men have been searching, but when I could no longer see you or my uncle after the battle, I came looking for you both."

"Let us go to Red Square so the men can take Afstar back to Sibir and give him a chief's burial. Then I'll help you find the herd."

"Are you sure you're all right?" Katerina asked, not convinced he was ready to ride.

"My head throbs and I'm a little weak, not just from the cut but from last night's escape, this morning's battle, and the ride from Moscow and back again. I need rest and food, but first the Cosars. Katerina," he whispered huskily, "there is so much I want to say."

"Later, later we'll talk," she said, kissing him lightly on the mouth.

Together they rode into Red Square to the rack where her uncle was tied. They cut the ropes and gently lifted his battered body. Banyen tied the lifeless Khan to his horse and mounted behind Afstar.

"Now for the Cosars, Katerina."

Their progress was slow, as the streets were strewn with the bodies of men, women, and children. "It's a sad sight to see, but innocent people are always the victims of war," Banyen said sadly. As they proceeded around the cities, soldiers and Mongols still skirmished here and there. A Russian, hidden away, would try to make his escape and chase would be given.

"I think we'll find the horses somewhere around the palace. We'll ride in that direction," Banyen said with assurance.

They rode toward Terem Palace, inside the Kremlin. Searching on foot and on horseback, they found nothing. Kostya, with a small patrol, also reported no success in finding the Cosars.

Angry and frustrated, Katerina lashed out. "The raid on the Tereks placed the horses in Moscow. Gregory sold them to Ivan. What did he do with them? Did he sell them off before we stormed Moscow?" She turned to Banyen. "Do you think the Czar sold them to someone else?"

"No. If Ivan bought them, he wanted them for himself and his bodyguards, the Oprichniks. Ivan would never sell something that was one of a kind. Has anyone checked outside the wall behind the palace?"

Kostya's men looked at each other and shook their heads.

"It's possible Ivan had them taken out of the city when he heard it was being attacked. If he fled with the Kremlin's treasury, he wouldn't waste time on the Cosars. They must be somewhere outside the walls of the city." Calling two of the Mongols to him, he ordered them to remove the Khan's body from the stallion. "Secure a litter to the back of a horse with a stout rope and pull his body home," he ordered gruffly.

Beyond the Kremlin walls, a quarter mile away, a hill rose up out of the flatness. Narrowing his oblique gaze, Banyen was aware that the attack now came from the west. The outlying section was remote, and he was sure no man was near. As they rode closer, noises could be heard coming from behind the hill. When they reached the top, there stood the mighty herd of Cosars, in the middle of snow-covered brush and dense fir trees. Katerina was beside herself with happiness. She leaped from Whitefire, and was about to run into the herd of horses when Banyen shouted for her to stop.

"Why should I?"

Without warning, a small band of the Oprichniks emerged from within the herd. They had hidden themselves among the horses, hoping to escape with a Cosar or two. As they charged toward Katerina, Banyen, Kostya, and the patrol swooped down, killing them in the first rush.

"The next time wait until your men are sure there aren't any Russians lurking about," Banyen said harshly.

"Yes, my master." Katerina grinned as she ran into the herd and seemingly smothered herself in them. Now, she had everything. Now, she had avenged her village, its people, and her father. She had fulfilled the promise she made to herself and Mikhailo: the Cosars once again, and forever this time, belonged to the Don Cossacks. The secret and the horses were still theirs. At last she could rest. It was finished.

The Mongols avenged the raids on Kazan and Astrakhan, but had lost their leader. But now Prince

Banyen could lead them, and he would have a Khanate to rule. She had her Cosars, and the old men would soon have a hut or two ready in Volin. By now there would be a compound fenced in for the horses which she would bring back. Lastly, the Tatars had their baskets filled with young women for their slave trade. Everyone had been successful, save Banyen. He would have to settle for victory without the blood of Ivan on his sword. But his people and the village of Kazan were avenged, so it should be enough. Katerina prayed it would be enough.

Banyen sat atop his black Arabian, his bloody sword in his hand, watching Katerina running through the horses in the white snow. He knew he loved her deeply.

"It's time to take your Cosars where they belong."

Katerina ran to Whitefire, who whinnied in delight at the scent of the mares. She leaped onto his back and laughed aloud. "Kostya, we ride for home. Inform your men. The Mongols will drive the herd to Volin.

"Banyen, can you make the ride, or should we prepare a litter for you?" she asked, her face full of concern.

"There's no cause for worry, Katerina. The wound on my leg is a mere scratch. The bleeding has stopped, and my head is clear. We have much to say to each other," he said huskily. "Many decisions have to be made. And," he said softly, "you must be the one to make them."

Slowly the animals followed the Mongols and the Cossacks to the road that would lead them to Volin. Katerina's eyes were misty as she saw Kostya raise his hand, the Cossacks shouting in victory as they thundered down the snow-covered road.

They rode in silence, intent on their own thoughts, the Cossacks and Kostya long gone from their sight. The moment Whitefire's hooves set down on the plain, he threw back his head and snorted, rearing up on his hind legs and almost unseating Katerina. She laughed as she gave him his head, and the white stallion pounded his way across the familiar ground. He galloped like the wind, the girl on his back laughing and shrieking in delight. Once she turned her head and saw Banyen hard pressed to keep pace with Whitefire. She knew he would catch her, and what better place than here, on the steppe where it all began? Only this time, atop Whitefire, she knew she could elude him if she wanted to. Now the dream was behind her and she welcomed the reality. "Easy boy, he has to catch us."

Imperceptibly, the stallion slowed, and Banyen gained on the racing woman. The moment he was abreast of her, he reached out and pulled her from the animal's back onto his own racing mount. Katerina giggled in delight as her legs flailed the air, her arms clutching Banyen, whose own seat was unsteady on the racing, snorting steed. Suddenly he, too, laughed, and they both slid from the horse into the deep snow. In their tumble, Banyen's pack slid from the horse's rump and came to rest at their feet.

"All the comforts of the mountains," Banyen said, reaching for the sable carpet.

"Love me," Katerina whispered throatily.

"Forever," Banyen said huskily, his mouth finding hers. "For now, forever more."

"Banyen, where will we go, what will we do?"

"It has to be your decision, Katerina."

"While I waited in Smolensk for you and the others, I made my decision. My plan is to give Kostya and Princess Halya a filly and a colt, and, of course, some of the other Cosars. I can't take a chance of this ever happening again. I would never feel secure if I and I alone kept the secret. I'll set aside certain conditions, but he will be in charge of his own breeding in Moldavia. I can either go back to Volin with my horses or I can go with you to the Khanate that is yours now to rule. I want you to help me make the right choice. When I am with you, my judgment is faulty. Where will you be happy?" she asked, gently tracing the outline around his oblique eyes.

Banyen laughed. "The day you make a faulty decision will be the day I'll take to my bed, never to stand on my legs again. You could never be happy separated from the Cosars. I have no desire to rule the Khanate; there are others far better suited than I. I vote to go with you to Volin, where we will work with the Cosars together. Has it been decided that Kostya's men will stay in Volin?"

"I offered them their freedom and they chose to stay." Katerina smiled. "Tell me, are they Cossacks or not? I left none dead in Moscow, and only two men carry flesh wounds. They're Cossacks, and what better place for them to live than Volin, the Don village? One day there will be none left that remembers they were not Cossacks by birth.

"Love me, Banyen."

"Always, for all eternity," he said huskily as he crushed her lips to his.

About the Author

Shortly after high school, IRIS SUMMERS was employed by a toy manufacturer and became a reporter for their monthly house organ. Later, a position as a laboratory technician led her on to quality control in a pharmaceutical house. There she started a monthly newsletter, working as editor, reporter, and layout artist.

Iris managed to squeeze in a marriage and five children, four boys and a girl. Her home displays various ventures into handicrafts: a stained-glass lamp, paintings, fabric flowers, and crocheted items. Music plays all day long on the stereo, and when the urge strikes, she sits down and plays—admittedly badly—on a small organ. A parakeet and a cock-a-poo named Muffin that the children wanted and quickly abandoned are hers for the care and feeding.

Iris Summers has been scribbling short stories since the age of thirteen. Encouragement from members of her writers' association and a pesty neighbor who is a successful author combined to motivate Iris to write *Whitefire,* a novel set in the Ukraine, her own ancestral background.

THE OUTSTANDING #1 BESTSELLER BY

John Cheever

Falconer

"CHEEVER'S TRIUMPH...A GREAT AMERICAN NOVEL!"
—Newsweek

27300 $2.25

Also Available from Ballantine Books

BULLET PARK

27301 $2.25

LG-1

journey, or in shooting at marksmanship or exercise
with their weapons, she had their brush and groom the
animals. At sundown they ate their evening meal and
sat around the fire, their voices pitched low in serious